Evil Omen . . .

A flock of birds appeared in the sky, flying from the east. Adred tilted his head to watch them. It was a huge flock: hundreds and hundreds of birds swarming in a dotted pattern in the gray-blue sky, aiming away from the mainland. They could not be on migration; it was not the season, and besides, birds in this part of the world didn't migrate west. There was nothing to the west but ocean.

"Odd," muttered the scholar.

Adred nodded and glanced at him, returned to the birds. They were not plovers or terns or ship-followers. They appeared to be ignoring the merchanter entirely.

As Adred and the scholar watched, the birds circled in a huge wheel in the sky, forming a dark, spotted ring. Then the ring broke and formed a line as the birds flew straight down to the ocean.

Within moments the birds had plunged into the ocean, all of them, the straight line of them shortening and shortening and disappearing just upon the remotest edge of the horizon, and not rising up again.

THE FALL of the FIRST WORLD

The Master of Evil

David C. Smith

PINNACLE BOOKS   NEW YORK

The verse by Michael Fantina appears in this book through permission of its author.

This is a work of fiction. All the characters and events portrayed in this book are fictional, and any resemblance to real people or incidents is purely coincidental.

THE FALL OF THE FIRST WORLD BOOK I:
THE MASTER OF EVIL

Copyright © 1983 by David C. Smith

An original Pinnacle Books edition, published for the first time anywhere.

First printing, January 1983

ISBN: 0-523-41783-1

Cover Illustration by Carl Lundgren

Printed in the United States of America

PINNACLE BOOKS, INC.
1430 Broadway
New York, New York 10018

With love,
for
MY PARENTS,
who gave me values

Major Characters in *The Master of Evil*

The Athadian Ruling Family, in Athad, Capital of the Empire:

Queen YTA, widow of King Evarris I
Prince ELAD, her eldest son
Prince General CYRODIAN of the Imperial Army, her second son
Prince DURSORIS, her third son
Lady ORAIN, wife of Cyrodian
Prince GALVUS, son of Cyrodian and Orain

Others:

Count ADRED, a young Athadian aristocrat
Lord ABGARTHIS, elder Councilor and Court Adviser
Lord UMOTHET, a Councilor
Captain UVARS, of the Imperial Army
Count MANTHO, an aristocrat of Kendia
Captain THYTAGORAS, commander of troops in
    Athadian Erusabad
RHIA, a rebel in Bessara
Lord SOLOK, a liberal sympathizer in Bessara

In Emaria:

King NUTATHARIS, of Emaria
EROMEDEUS, adviser to Nutatharis
General KUSTOS, of the Emarian Army
Sir JORS, adviser to Nutatharis

In Gaegosh:

OGODIS, the Imbur of Gaegosh
Lady SALIA, his daughter

The Salukadian Ruling Family, in Ilbukar:

HUAGRIM *ko-Ghen*, Chief of Salukadia
AGORS, his elder son
NIHIM, his younger son

Others in the East:

THAMERON, a young priest in the Holy City of Erusabad
HAPAD, friend to Thameron
MUTHULIS, Chief Priest of the Temple of Bithitu in Erusabad
ANDOPARAS, Metropolitan of the Temple of Bithitu in Erusabad
ASSIA, a prostitute
TYRUS, her father
IBRO, a taverner and whoremaster
GUBURUS, a sorcerer

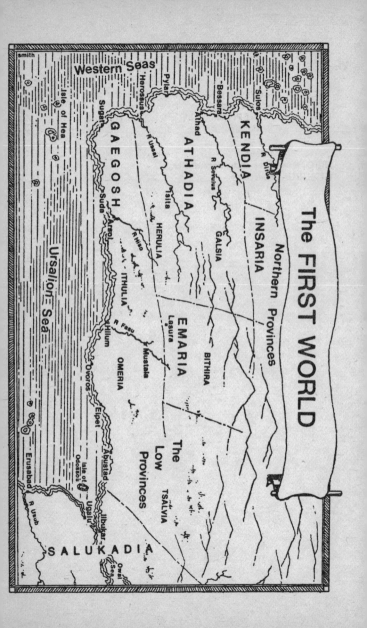

Es Atu

When earth was first sundered from heaven,
When God first rejoiced in the skies,
When evil announced its intention
With death to imprison all life:
    Then man was born from the clouds and rain,
    Man was born for limitless pain,
    Man was born for tears and lies,
    And made to wonder all his days,
    And made to wonder all the days.

—Opening chorus of Sossian's *Of the Lost Earth*

There once was a world very much like our world. It was destroyed, its nations and its peoples shattered and blown by the tides and reduced to a new beginning. A world very much like ours, with people very much like us—the first world. And when it died, it gave birth to memories, which grew to become legends and myths.

These are the memories. . . .

PROLOGUE

The Prince of Eternity

The tavern had reminded him of autumn. An isolated tavern in southern Emaria; animal skins drying on racks outside, horses shivering and coughing in the stables behind. The noises from within: Laughter; yells; songs; more laughter. Twilight always seemed like autumn to him, and night ever a winter.

Jokes ceased in mid-sentence when he entered the room. Women looked askance when he passed by, and their men trembled for no reason. Animals did not love him; not for the tastiest scrap of meat would any dog approach him. Horses nickered when he came too close to them. Birds flew farther away from him than from other men.

Was it simply that visitors here, outlanders, were uncommon? He had crossed the half-filled room, approached the counter, and spoken with the proprietor. May I have a cup of cold brew? Would it be an imposition if I did a few magic tricks by which to pay for my lodgings? Yes, yes, I'll wait until the singer has finished. I'd like to rest a moment, anyway.

He had taken a table in a corner and stared at the floor, allowing the other patrons to get used to him.

The singer, a young blond boy with a lute, finished and retrieved the few coins that had been tossed to him. He sat down in a corner to examine them and bite them. A fat woman with greasy brown hair approached the boy to ask if he wanted supper now; the great rolls of fat on her upper arms shivered and there was perspiration dewing the mustache on her lips.

The intruder finished his brew and stepped to the center of the tavern, placed his bag on a chair and withdrew objects

2

from it, placed them on a table. A few faces looked away. Impatient jokes passed, and laughter erupted. Finally the stranger faced his audience.

"I am an illusionist," he announced humbly. "Allow me a few moments to charm and entertain you."

He stood proudly, regarding his audience through narrowed eyes. A tall man, nobly made, perhaps in his late forties or early fifties, the gray entering his hair and beard, but the eyes still bright and brilliant, and with no hint or betrayal of age or disease or weakness in his frame. Surely, thought some in the tavern, this man has been brought low. Surely this is extremely degrading for him, for surely he must have known a better life sometime in his past.

There were soldiers in the tavern, a few young women, and men with the pallor of crime upon them. The intruder looked upon them and knew them all. The wonder of it had ceased long ago. Was it that souls migrated to new bodies after death? Or was it simply that this man here was related to the father or grandfather or more ancient sire for whom he had done these same tricks generations ago?

"My name," he announced, "is Eromedeus. My games, while very ancient, always seem new. Watch, and I will astonish you."

Look at them, he told himself. Look at that soldier, so far from home and farther yet from the dreams he once held for himself. Wouldn't he love to *embody* the immortal fame he wishes for?

Look at that dog. A thief or robber or murderer? Wouldn't he love to outlive his enemies, and outlive their sons and their sons' sons, so that his crimes would become more forgotten than the first breath of life? What better refuge could he hope for?

And look at that young woman. Is she ill? She is dying. She's trying to earn money any way she can, but she must hurry; there isn't much time left for her. Time? Dear young woman, I would gladly trade you this ancient soul for your decaying body. But you would refuse. At the first hint, the first intimation, you'd cower in fear, and you'd clutch your dying body and hold it with all the fervor of a fish on a bank working its gills, dying the faster as it tries to live. You'd no more trade souls with me than you'd trade your past life for

3

all the gold of all kings. Because it's yours. Your life. And you're a fool. You're all fools. I'm a fool.

"My first attempt, then, at trying your patience . . ." Eromedeus showed his audience two empty halves of a walnut, turned them this way and that so that all could be certain. Then he cupped them between his palms and shook his hands, pulled them apart to reveal a whole fresh walnut.

Grunts and faint smiles.

Eromedeus begged their indulgence. He cupped the whole walnut between his hands once more, shook, then released three walnuts upon the stained tabletop.

Voices called for beer or spread gossip.

Eromedeus took up a pink silk cloth, bunched it in his right hand, and tapped his fist with his left hand. When he opened his fingers, the silk cloth stood upright, balanced in his palm, and twined like a rope, as sturdy as wood.

Now some honest smiles—but no coins.

He bunched the silk again, tapped his fist. Opening his hand this time, he revealed, not a stalk of silk twine, but a flaming pink pillar—a short rope of flame, burning and flashing, erect in his naked palm.

That won them over. There was great applause for him, and three coppers.

Eromedeus carefully brought his cupped left hand down upon the right, enclosing the flame, squashing it until it was trapped, glowing between his long fingers. A word, and he opened his hand instantly—to let a butterfly flutter free.

More applause. More coppers.

Eromedeus bowed thankfully.

A rogue in the back, dressed in an Emarian cavalry uniform, drew a knife from his belt and without warning threw it toward Eromedeus. It bit accurately into the wooden table before him. There was a hush; but Eromedeus did not assume this to be a threat.

"Show us what you can do with that knife!" came the brawny, drunken challenge.

Eromedeus smiled. He reached into his bag, withdrew his hands, and showed them empty. Then he began to move his hands softly at first but then more rapidly, until the flesh tones created a blur around the hilt and blade. With a word, Eromedeus stepped back and pointed to the knife. It was no longer a knife. It had been transformed, somehow, into a miniature pear tree with four ripe fruits upon it. Eromedeus plucked the pears, all four of them, and threw them to his audience. The ill young woman bit into one and pronounced it a perfectly fine, fresh pear.

The rogue who had thrown the knife stood up, glowering. "Are you a sorcerer?" he cried.

The word brought a nervous tension upon the house. But Eromedeus shook his head sagely and showed the crowd his open palms. No scars; no marks; no brands.

"I am no sorcerer. Have I done evil?" he asked, playing with the words. "I am no charlatan, but I am no mighty wizard whom you should fear. My tricks are feats of the imagination."

That seemed to reassure them, though it was a lie.

"Would you like your knife returned?" he asked the cavalryman.

"If you please!" roared the response.

Eromedeus repeated the blurring motion with his hands, and the miniature pear tree once more became the knife—with part of the hilt missing.

"My apologies," Eromedeus called to the soldier, holding up the weapon by its blade. "I gave away the pears, so your knife is no longer whole." He flipped it across the room; heads ducked as it spun through the air and dug itself into the wall beside the soldier's face.

The rogue drew it out and examined it, shook his head suspiciously, returned it to his belt. He had to take it out again to show his companions and others seated nearby.

One of those companions was a fat, jovial man who now reared up and waved to Eromedeus. "Come over here!" he bellowed. "I'd like to buy you dinner!"

Eromedeus bowed his head, pushed his magical objects into his bag, and collected his coppers—and gold—and crossed the room.

"Sit down, sit down," urged the fat man amiably. He pulled an empty chair from an adjoining table, and his comrades shuffled to make room for the newcomer.

"I am Sir Jors," the obese man introduced himself, slapping Eromedeus on the back. "Your tricks are wonderful."

"I thank you." Eromedeus did not miss the double stars sewn onto the man's shoulder patches.

"Ilma!" called Sir Jors. "Bring him a dinner! Will you have dinner?"

"Certainly."

"Bring him a dinner! And more beer!"

Eromedeus studied the five faces around him, all soldiers of the Emarian army, and found scant trust in them. But the knife had been returned to its belt.

"Yes, those are excellent tricks," enthused Sir Jors. "Are you certain you're not a sorcerer? No, no—I mean no offense! Have you been long in Emaria?"

A thousand years, thought Eromedeus. "Not long," he answered in a friendly tone. "I've traveled far and wide, but seldom this far north."

"You must come with us to the capital."

A few of his companions gave Sir Jors sharp looks, but he was obviously in charge. "Yes, yes," he insisted. "Have you ever met King Nutatharis?"

"I have never had that honor, no."

"He loves wise men and tricksters and entertainers of all sorts. I'm sure he'll reward you generously for your little feats—perhaps make a home for you in his court."

"He'll probably torture him to find out his secrets," muttered the man with the ruined knife.

Sir Jors made a throaty sound. "Nonsense! Such ill will because his brother was a traitor! Won't you come to see our king? He'd love your display. And it won't hurt me to get in his good graces by introducing you."

Eromedeus gave the proposal some thought. Ilma, the overweight woman with the damp mustache, pushed her way to them and set a plate of beef and vegetables and two gourds of beer on the table.

"Eat up!" Sir Jors commanded. "We're riding back to Lasura tonight. King Nutatharis will be glad to receive you."

Eromedeus nodded and began eating his food. *Nutatharis,* he thought. *He was but a young boy when I was last in Emaria. I remember him. . . . Scar on his left cheek; thrown from the saddle as a boy. Now he is king. And a temperamental despot, no doubt. Dangerous man. His great-great-grandfather was that pimp for the Nusarian army. His grandfather tried to kill me, once, on the wharves of Elpet. Became angry when I turned his sword into a chestnut tree. . . .*

6

PART I

A Throne of Blood

1.

Two days out from Sulos, and Count Adred could not sleep. He sat up in his bunk. The roll and sway of the galley on the ocean could not lull him to slumber; he was too plagued by thunder and worry and images of doubt.

Then you had best return to the capital, yes, Mantho had told him. *It will be expected of you. Give Queen Yta my love, won't you? And her sons. This is such a sad day. King Evarris was a wise man, a strong monarch. After twenty-nine years of rule it has become habitual to think of him ruling forever.* . . .

Sighing, Adred pulled his bedpan from under the bunk, knelt and urinated, and carried his bedpan to the port window. Unlatching the window, he emptied his pan; then he stood for a moment, setting aside the pan, to watch the sea and open sky at dawn. The sea had ever held him. In a way, it was surprising that he had never gone to sea for his livelihood. But he was a son of the aristocracy.

Fully awake now, Adred left his window open and crossed the floor to his washstand, where he cleaned himself as best he could. He dressed quickly. He was as openly careless about his dress as he was cautious and deliberate in his thoughts. After lacing his boots, he stood back and examined himself in the mirror behind his door. Thirty-one years old— but he looked far younger. Self-conscious, Adred stroked the beginnings of the beard. It was the fashion among the students and intellectuals and the liberal gentry in Sulos to sport their beards, in emulation of the working men whom, theoretically, they championed for the reformist cause. Adred, on a dare from Mantho over a lost game of *usto*, had agreed to grow his beard during his return to the capital. Studying

8

himself now, Adred decided that the beard wouldn't look bad at all, once it was full-grown and trimmed. He decided he rather liked it. But his posture was sagging, he could see that. He was definitely in need of a good bath and some exercise once he got back to Athad.

Athad. There to extend his sympathies to the family of the dead king. Evarris's death portended much. It was a swift end and not a dissolution. Adred did not trust it.

But there was time enough to worry over that. He left his cabin quietly and made his way down the gallery of the *Delios*, to the middeck. Seamen were busy at lines on the poopdeck and forward decks. He walked toward the starboard rail, inhaling the strength of sea air and water. There was a mist on the waves; the sunlight played in bars through it, like angled pillars of brilliant nonsubstance, striking the moving, restless waves with glimmering dewdrops of light, a myriad of them, flashing and glinting and disappearing upon the rolling surface to reappear elsewhere, a moment away, in an endless mesmeric dance of dreamery.

". . . so this poor fellow dies, you see?" spoke an elderly nobleman to Adred's right, gesturing to a companion who, like the speaker, was dressed in fine silk, an embroidered vest, and fashionable boots. "He enters the Silver Portals and is greeted by a minor god and is promised an eternity of goodness. Which is all fine enough, but it seems rather dull. So the beggar looks down from the stars and sees a rich nobleman in one of the hells. Flames are erupting and there is gas and smoke, but the rich man's bouncing a beautiful young woman on his lap—yes! right!—and he's holding a wine jug in his free hand."

"Yes, yes, go on," urged Fashionable Boots, his lips working in anticipation of an explosion of laughter.

"So—so the beggar says to the god, he says, 'I don't understand. I spent my whole life humbly, doing good work, and I remember that nobleman being a coward and a liar and a hypocrite. You sent him to Hell, but look at him! He's having a splendid time. He has a girl on his knee and a wine jug. What did he ever do to deserve such a reward as that?' And the little god says, 'All things work according to divine plan. Do you see that wine jug?' 'Yes, I see it.' 'It has a hole in the bottom of it. Now, do you see that girl?' 'Yes, I see her.' 'Well, she doesn't.' "

9

An uncertain smile erupted into a guffaw of laughter. Fashionable Boots slapped the joke-teller on the shoulder and stomped the deck with great delight. "The wine jug does and the girl doesn't!" he repeated, laughing uproariously. "The jug does, and she doesn't!" He coughed, wiping tears from his cheeks. "Oh, oh—that's a good story, Semma! I'll tell that one in Bessara!"

Adred smiled thinly, out of politeness because he had overheard, and turned to walk farther down the middeck. Behind him, Semma the joke-teller began a new one.

The knot of sailors was a short distance away, but now there was a woman with them, an ill-dressed young woman holding a baby in her arms. The child was perhaps nine months old; the mother held onto it protectively, bouncing it once in a while, as she talked with the sailors.

"It's a fine son you have there, lady."

"Thank you."

"And will he grow up to be a sailor?"—grinning.

"I imagine so. His father was a sailor. He'd've liked him to."

"A sailor? Out of what port, if we can ask?"

"Herossus. Our home was in the south, and he usually sailed from Herossus."

"Is he sailing now? If I met him in some port I'll tell him you're well and that he has a fine—"

"He's dead. He was killed in a storm six months past."

"Very sorry. . . . Did he—never see his son?"

"No."

"Very—sorry."

The young mother turned away, memories welling up within her, although she couldn't blame the sailors, although she had come to terms with her loss long ago. As she crossed the middeck she passed by Adred, who could not help overhearing. The baby boy in her arms cooed and giggled and reached out a small pink hand, attracted by an amulet Adred wore about his neck. The mother paused and eyed Adred carefully over the gulf between two separate and distinct houses.

Adred smiled, held out the amulet on its chain so that it twinkled in the sunlight and amused the baby. "It fascinates him."

The child grabbed hold of the amulet and tugged it, pulling Adred close. He tried to pull the amulet into his mouth.

"Here, here, Jaso, leave the nice man's pretties alone."

"Oh, it won't hurt him."

The mother pried the baby's fingers loose, and an enormous frown filled the child's face, the eyes and nose and mouth wrinkling with shock and resentment.

Adred reached his hands behind his neck and unclasped the chain, handed the amulet to the baby. "Here you go. Play to your heart's content."

It took a moment for the young mother to understand. "Oh, my lord, we can't let you—"

"Oh, go ahead, take it. It's nothing."

The amulet was worth perhaps thirty-five or forty in long gold. It was enough to keep her alive for a year. It had been given to Adred by a lady friend in Sulos, but it had no sentimental value for him. He fully expected that the young mother would sell it at her first opportunity, the moment the *Delios* landed. And Adred wanted her to do so.

"We really can't—"

"Oh, go on, now. See? He really likes it!"

The baby held the amulet to his mouth with small, pudgy hands and turned wide brown eyes up at Adred.

The mother was extremely nervous. "Thank you, then. Thank you—"

"Have a good voyage."

The woman stammered and moved away. Adred watched her go, his smile fading. It was not charity that had moved him to do what he had done; charity is the deprived helping the deprived. This was rectification, balancing. When he turned again toward the rail, he noticed one of the sailors, the one who had conversed earlier with the woman, watching him. Aristocrats were notorious for buying the favors of unfortunate women. The two pairs of eyes held for a moment, and then the brown-faced sailor made a gesture to Adred, quick and familiar: thumbs up.

Adred nodded to him. The sailor looked away. It was done.

An old man in the white and gold robes of a scholar joined Adred at the rail, keeping a respectful social distance. Adred thought to say something, make some greeting or comment, but he refrained. And his companion seemed content, likewise, simply to watch the lightening landscape.

11

A flock of birds appeared in the sky, flying from the east behind them. Strange. Adred tilted his head to watch them. It was a huge flock: hundreds and hundreds of birds swarming in a dotted pattern in the gray-blue sky, aiming away from the mainland. They could not be on migration; it was not the season, and besides, birds in this part of the world didn't migrate west. There was nothing to the west but ocean.

"Odd," muttered the scholar.

Adred nodded and glanced at him, returned to the birds. They were not plovers or terns or ship-followers. They appeared to be ignoring the merchanter entirely. But why?

As Adred and the scholar watched, the birds circled in a huge wheel in the sky, forming a dark, spotted ring. Then the ring broke and formed a line as the birds flew straight down to the ocean.

"What are they doing?" Adred asked aloud.

A number of sailors and passengers had by this time noticed the flock's strange behavior and were lining up at the rails too.

Within moments the birds had plunged into the ocean, all of them, the straight line of them shortening and shortening and disappearing just upon the remotest edge of the horizon, and not rising up again.

"They've dived into the sea!" exclaimed someone.

Adred continued to stare at the far waves, supposing that the birds had only dived out of sight and would soon reappear.

But they did not.

"They've dived into the sea!" the same voice repeated. "Isn't that the strangest thing you've ever seen?"

Adred's brow wrinkled; he couldn't understand it.

But the scholar to his left let out a deep breath and glanced at Count Adred and shook his head. "This portends something," he muttered strongly. "This is a bad omen."

"What do you mean?" Adred asked him. He was reminded immediately of King Evarris's untimely death.

"When do animals ever behave so radically?" the old man rejoined, shaking his head once more. "This is unheard of. Surely this is a bad omen."

He walked off, crossing the middeck and going down into the hold. Adred watched the sea. The flock did not reappear. Truly, the birds had committed suicide in the water. It was beyond belief. He glanced at the others there, but already they had forgotten the wonder and were sauntering about, discussing breakfast or political events or fashions.

Adred slouched down against the rail, his chin on his crossed arms, staring at the sea and sky that were no longer, for him this morning, bright and promiseful and good. . . .

2.

The bier was a framework of gold and silver and iron; atop it, glistening in the rain, sat the long cedarwood box containing the purified body of King Evarris of the Athadian empire.

Queen Yta stood with her family and royal entourage directly before the funeral bier. Around her swelled the respectfully hushed multitude. From the towering white-walled city resounded the loud braying of oliphants and the endless rumble of bronze gongs.

Yta, tall, gray-haired, stately, as became the queen of the realm, stared upon the ocean of people with lidded eyes. Hypocrites and sycophants she knew them to be—pompous and false, politicians and liars, gathered in the rainy mist of Death.

Death . . .

She had not even been there when Evarris had succumbed, when his heart, suffocating, had screamed in his chest, ripping him with pain, stealing him from—

"My lady," whispered Abgarthis beside her. Lightly he touched her shoulder.

Abgarthis: old when Yta had first come to the palace as a happy-mad young bride.

"My lady . . ."

"I am strong, Abgarthis. Listen to the priest."

She did not care to do so—even priests lie, and some with great skill—but Yta turned her ears toward the High Master of the Temple of Bithitu, who stood upon a platform before the bier and lifted his arms for the call to worship.

The ocean of people bowed their heads in waves.

"Divine watchers! Bithitu, Messenger and Prophet of the Eternal Ones! Look down now and lend your charity to us! O

14

ye gods of Heaven, O Bithitu, who sits in judgment and knowledge, guide us. . . ."

Yta let her gaze travel to those close by her, her sons. There—Elad, her eldest, too much like Evarris in his weak ways. Yta, with a mother's ability and a queen's insight, saw the usurper beneath the patient son, and marveled at Elad's skill in seeming penitent while a serpent coiled in his heart.

And Cyrodian, beside him. Could he really be her son? Or had some incubus possessed her one night? Was he some changeling? His life was the army and the battlefield, even as Elad's was the court and ceremony. Yet Cyrodian outdid his elder brother in cunning and in cruelty. Yta had heard from good sources that Cyrodian made new recruits to his squadron of retainers drink a bowl of blood before admitting them to his trust. The queen could believe such a thing of her second son. . . .

"Guidance!" called the High master. "*Essa te porru ke anta bei usus*! Guidance to our weeping empire! Guidance to the King of Athadia in his journey through the Valley of Shadows!"

"Guidance!" responded the chorus of thousands. "Guidance through the Valley of Shadows and safety in his journey across the Sea of Spirits!"

"Guidance . . ." whispered Yta.

Dursoris, her third-born, lowered his head in prayer. Surely Dursoris was one of the few truly bitten, today, by the bitter serpent of sadness.

Standing not far from Dursoris was Orain, Cyrodian's wife. What mockery that this beautiful, love-hearted woman should be married to the changeling son. A test of the gods? Yta, even at this moment of public grief, could not dissuade her heart from dwelling on her sons, for they must eventually inherit the empire, even as she must inherit the corpse of that empire's monarch. . . .

"*Itsusu!*" cried the High Master. "Grant peace! Grant strength! Grant guidance! *Elmethu! Essusu!*"

"*Itsusu* . . ." whispered Yta. "Peace . . ."

Or was it as folklore contended—that the firstborn is ambition, the second is anger, the third hope?

"*Essusu!* Grant guidance to him who gave guidance to his children of field and tribe and town, the children of the endless empire!"

Itbosi di anta bei rarum. Children of the endless empire . . .

15

Trumpets blew, unnerving Yta for a moment, followed by the mad, ugly braying of the oliphants and the resonant ache of temple gongs. Too much noise, too many prayers. Yta could not read the harmony or the honesty in any of it.

She saw that Orain, overcome, had begun to weep volubly. Galvus, Orain's son, gripped one of her hands. Far across from them Cyrodian, husband and father, paid no attention.

Yta looked upon Galvus. He was tall, like his mother, and handsome. Fifteen, and perilously close to manhood. He and Evarris had shared a simple, direct love, the pure affection, unalloyed, that can come between the very young and the very old. Between grandfather and grandson, wisdom and eagerness.

"Itsusu!" cried the priest, unstoppering an ornate wine jug and pouring a libation upon the cedarwood box.

"Peace," whispered Yta, fearful of soul, afraid to look beyond the Master to the naked raining skies with their promise of eternal sunlessness. For the gods were there, surely, staring down at her with her own eyes, seeing into her bruised soul, knowing her anguish, knowing her fear.

Not fear of death. Fear of life.

Not fear for Evarris; he was safe. But fear of his sons.

Not fear of Bithitu or his god, but fear of a far older prophecy.

The High Master motioned to the ring of Khamars, the palace guard, who circled the bier. Each one held a flaming torch, and, at the priest's gesture, the Khamars turned and dropped their torches into the kindling at the base of the bier.

The fire caught quickly and flames leapt high, rising eagerly up the metal framework to the wine-soaked cedar casket. Yta looked, looked away. Gusts of damp wind whipped the inferno, making fast, slapping sounds that boomed across the plain. Thick billows of scented black and gray smoke lifted to touch the clouds, the seat of the gods.

"Sia bu sulula!" chanted the Master. "Mercy upon all things!"

"Mercy upon all things!" answered the crowd of congregants, as one.

"Mercy . . ." whispered Queen Yta to herself.

Not fear of Bithitu or his god, but fear of a far older prophecy, fear as old as flame and wine, as old as guilt . . .

16

3.

Five days out from Sulos, the *Delios* made port at Bessara, a
cosmopolitan port. Not as large in area or population as
Athad, it was nevertheless looked upon by the capital as a
sister city. Bessara boasted great schools of learning and
important businesses. But like Athad and other cities in the
empire, it teemed with multitudes of the poor. As Adred
walked the cobbled streets, he saw richly caparisoned mounts
wend through the crowds as mendicants lifted cups to high-
seated lords, begging coin. He saw formations of troops,
soldiers of the city guard, pass down the lanes and avenues on
patrol, sullenly eying the crowds that lined every wall.

The wealth of the empire, Adred thought. War veterans,
asleep in the sun, resting on their crutches, with flies buzzing
around their amputations. Fourteen-year-old mothers with babies on their hips, short-tempered and snapping at young men
in the streets. Blind old women with eyes puffed and seeping,
trying to dodge the thrown stones of street urchins.

In Miru Square, as Adred noticed when he entered it, a
troupe of acrobats were performing gymnastic exercises. He
watched them for a moment, joining a crowd, enjoying the
display of physical prowess. A tall young man balanced two
lissome girls on his shoulders; the girls called for attention
and, as all eyes watched, they somersaulted into the air,
holding hands, and landed on the cobblestones, fingers still
clasped. The motley audience of paupers and children and
low-level city bureaucrats applauded them and tossed coins,
which the father of the group—a thin, balding man with
tattoos on his chest and back—collected into an old oil lamp
slung about his waist.

Adred went on until he came to the public baths at the end

17

of the square, directly across from the Temple of Bithitu. The huge statue of Bithitu the Prophet raised its arms to heaven and cast its shadow across the square. Below Bithitu, supporting columns which flanked the main entranceway, were statues of two creatures that were holdovers from an earlier era of pantheism, and they were still popular with the people as characters in bedtime stories and in some dramatic plays and comedies: Sirimu, a beautiful woman with six fingers on each hand; and Atetos, a strong, handsome man holding a scale of justice in his right hand and a two-bladed sword in his left.

Adred was about to enter the bathhouse when his attention was drawn to an orator who stood just beneath the statue of Atetos. She was a very pretty young woman, red-haired and dressed scantily in rags. Adred wondered seriously if this were her everyday dress or if she wore rags to get attention (she had beautiful legs).

"There are nobles in the streets wearing clothes so luxurious that the money they spend would feed most families for a month! Enough money is wasted by our government every day to feed the poor of Bessara for an entire month! Who wastes this money? Is it the people? I myself have seen old men and old women in this city picking food from the alleys that even dogs wouldn't eat! Why are they living this way? Why are they eating everyone else's garbage? Have you seen how the holy priests of this temple dress? And they take vows of poverty! I'd rather have their kind of poverty than the kind I see in this avenue right now! Have you seen how the politicians help the people? Have you seen how the city troops attack ordinary citizens and break into their homes? Have you seen how the guilds turn away people who want to do honest work? Do you know why?"

On and on she railed to a stream of passers-by, fiercely eying anyone in the square who smacked of wealth or influence, yelling for the poor to join her in her cries for justice, and defiantly glaring at the city patrols, who did not arrest her. Nor would they arrest her; there would be no point in chaining her and making her a martyr. She argued against hypocrisy in government and the unfairness of religion and the ineptitude of the bureaucracy and the blindness of the wealthy: an erosion of values and principles, the erosion of dignity and justice, which seemed to have been going on forever, like the prearranged descent of a wheel in a track.

18

Everyone in the square knew that these things existed and had always existed, so what was the good of it? As long as this young woman swore and spoke and yelled in public, and did not take a knife to a city official, she was a diversion for the masses and an outlet for frustration, and any money she collected she could do with as she pleased.

"Thank you! Thank you!" she called to those who tossed her coins. "This money is not for myself. This money goes for food and medicine for the people in this city who really need it. Thank you, citizens! Thank you!"

Perhaps, as an aristocrat in a crowd of paupers, Adred simply felt self-conscious, but it seemed to him that the socially deprived gathered there stepped away from him or kept a wide distance, as though contact with his good robes or jewelry might transmit a deformity or an illness. Giving in to an impulse, he took out his purse and looked at his money. He had rather a large sum on him, though no more than he was prone to carry when he traveled. More money awaited him in Athad. One gold coin would certainly cover all his immediate expenses.

Replacing that gold coin in his purse, he stepped ahead and motioned with a closed fist to the young woman. She paused to give him a cold stare.

Adred opened his hand. In his palm rested two silver *udas*, three large gold *ieds*, four small *mises*, and sixteen copper *douds*. Enough to buy, perhaps, a dozen books or a serviceable pony. Or food staples for the entire crowd in this avenue. Adred tipped his hand and spilled the coins, and the young woman had to move quickly to catch them all.

"What's this?" she asked, uncertain, counting quickly. "Have I touched some guilty nerve in you, aristocrat?"

Adred smiled into her cold eyes. "I agree with you."

"You? You agree with me?"

"Yes."

"You must be touched by the moon!" There were, of course, liberal aristocratic sympathizers in Bessara and elsewhere in the empire, but none like this man, who dumped a handful of wealth into a street crier's open palms.

"Not touched by the moon," Adred assured her. "But I agree with you. Take the money and do what you can for the people. But I ask you this: What good will it do?"

"What do you mean?"

19

"You can help these people for a little while, but you can't change a society that's existed like this for hundreds of years, can you?"

She stared into his eyes, looked at him and into him, and replied to his challenge in a quiet voice. "Yes, we can. We can change it. We are changing it."

Behind her a strong youth growled, "Take the money, Rhia! It's good money."

Several in the crowd laughed.

Adred glanced at the youth, again at the young woman, then turned and walked off, while the crowd muttered in the square. He was no longer in the mood for a bath.

When the merchanter left port, Adred was in his cabin, reading through a small notebook in which he had kept, ever since his father's death, the man's private letters and diaries. He had argued the same things with his father—an aristocrat and a bureaucrat, well rewarded by his government, yet secretly appalled at the injustices, the crimes. Though they had drifted apart during the older man's last years, as time continued to pass, Adred felt himself becoming more and more like his father—becoming, perhaps, his father in more than just a symbolic way. He had died, this good man, a victim of government negligence, poisoned by many years' service in the Galsian mines and left to suffer by a bureaucracy that refused to acknowledge its responsibility.

4.

"I cannot allow Elad to have the throne."

Abgarthis turned. She had not moved, and she had spoken so low that for a moment he thought to ask her to repeat what she had said. He approached her. "My Queen?"

"How can I?" Still she did not move; her hands were folded in a religious posture, a habit she had brought with her to the throne twenty-eight years earlier: the fingers locked together, the hands resting upon her belly—the joining of two equal halves, the right female and the left male, over the womb. Her eyes studied some far shadow of the room. "He will rip this Athadia apart with his ambitions. He and Cyrodian—"

Her words floundered. Abgarthis marveled at the strength of her.

"I cannot decide," Yta whispered. "I cannot decide, O adviser."

Abgarthis swallowed thickly. He set down his cup. "Shall I call in astrologers?" he suggested. "Seers? Wine-readers?"

"I am trapped upon the rock, between the serpent and the sword, Abgarthis."

"I do not understand."

"When I left the Holy Order of Hea, in my young womanhood, to marry that dead King, that was my counsel: 'Upon the death of this man you will find yourself pinned on a rock between a serpent and a sword.' Those are my sons, Abgarthis."

Abgarthis studied his Queen, noticed her paleness, and sensed, now, the frailty her strength sought to defend. He moved to light an oil lamp.

"No light, please, Abgarthis."

"But night comes."

"Please . . ."

He moved away, feeling the cramped closeness of shadows.

"I carry a curse, Abgarthis. Do you know how deep my love was for the King? You understand, though you never took a wife. Do you know how I trembled with joy when I left Hea Isle to come to the continent? How I trembled with joy to become wife and Queen to the young King?"

Abgarthis did not speak.

"How, when I heard from my mother's sister at court that Evarris had loved me since boyhood and had suffered when I left for the Order—do you know how I thrilled at the idea of renouncing my vows? I was a young woman, fiercely independent. Hea has cursed me for that one wild, happy moment."

"I know that you loved Evarris."

"I always wanted him to die first, adviser. I never wanted him to suffer this grief over my passing. But with our first child, and the second, then the third . . . How," she asked, "can a woman give birth to living sons, raise them and guide them, instill her love and patience and hopes in them, and see them become men who have nothing to do with the things she saw in them as boys?"

Abgarthis felt compelled to speak. "Men are not boys, Queen Yta. They forget their boyhoods. Boyhood is the molting skin they leave behind."

Yta drew in a slow breath. "A serpent, and a sword, and a rock," she said. "I must go to the Oracle, Abgarthis."

"Queen Yta—"

"Council can delay itself for a day or two. I must speak with the Oracle at Teplis. I must go to her. And I will follow her words. Whatever they may be, I want . . ."

Abgarthis listened carefully.

". . . I want to return to Hea, Abgarthis. With all my strength, I do. I want to return to Hea Isle to die. But I want to remain Queen as well. I have never been a good Queen. I was a good wife, a fair mother, a poor Queen. Now I want to be a good Queen, and I want to die. I want to escape and I want to achieve, in the same moment. What could come of that? What does that mean?"

"Only that you are human. A woman. On the funeral day of your husband."

22

"The world looks at me—I can feel their eyes now. I want to hide from their eyes."

"Perhaps you should rest," Abgarthis suggested, abandoning the hope that Yta might come to a decision tonight. And he rankled inside—rankled that he, an official, should have to put such pressure on her in her hour of grief, rankled that it was necessary.

He softly crossed the room, thinking it best to leave; as he put his thin hand to the door latch, he looked back to his Queen.

"Good night, my Queen."

Yta moved. Turned her head. Her features, white clay, seemed surprised at him, as if she had just noticed his presence. And Abgarthis was distressed and astounded to see in Yta's eyes an emotion he had never before known her to exhibit.

Carefully she turned her face away. "Yes, yes—good night."

Fear.

5.

Cyrodian, the second prince of the empire, was indeed a man to inspire fear. Huge—taller by a head than the tallest soldier in the Khamar palace guard—he was broad-shouldered, buffalo-chested, with arms and legs the size of oaks. His beard and mustache were coarse, and he wore his hair in a modified soldier's cut: far back from the forehead, unkempt at the shoulders. In aspect he was a human bear; in temperament, as wayward and explosive as a demon; in intellect, intelligent though roughly schooled, preferring muscle to argument. Truly might Yta, in comparing her second to her first and third sons, wonder if Cyrodian were some strange changeling.

Yet he was not evil. He was a brute, a braggart, an ill-tempered mammoth, a man of unswerving and unservile opinions. "Hrux," some of his men called him, borrowing a name from religious parable—for Hrux had supposedly been the wild ox made human for a year, which, when returned to its animal state, bewailed the fact constantly. Hence the ox's constant low bellow, sounding as of pain or torment.

Hrux, he was called by his men. The youngest general in the army of the Athadian empire. Cyrodian: a man of strength, sword, anger.

Tonight, while Khamars guarded his late father's ashes out on the plain, while Yta sat speechless and immobile in her chambers with Abgarthis, while the temple gongs and bells tolled death and anguish to the heavens, Cyrodian sat in his elder brother's lavish rooms in the east wing of the palace and played with his daggers—six of them, the edges keen, their points undulled. He was in a large wooden chair, feet up on a hassock, watching Elad as Elad paced back and forth before the fire in the wall.

24

"Sit down, brother."

"I am nervous, Cyrodian."

"Sit down. You're making me ill with your old woman's games."

Elad paused, threw his hands behind his back, regarded his brother. "Old woman, eh?"

"Let Yta cry over the passing of the King. You and I must talk. Sit and drink your wine."

"I am not thirsty."

Cyrodian barked a laugh. "Not for wine, anyway."

A slight tapping at the outer door. Elad called, and a servant entered with a tray of fresh wine and hard brown bread and meats.

"Put it over there," Elad instructed.

The servant set down the tray, placed the decanter on the table, and the plate of bread and meats, took up the half-empty, warm jug.

"Where is the Queen?" Elad asked him.

"In her chambers, my lord, resting."

"And Abgarthis?"

"In his own room, I believe."

"Drafting the Queen's formal abdication, I trust?" Cyrodian said.

Elad shot him a hard glance.

"I—I know not," stuttered the servant.

Cyrodian aimed a knife and let it fly. It chunked into the wooden jamb; the servant, astonished, cried out, jumped, and dropped his tray and wine decanter on the floor. Cyrodian howled with laughter.

Elad spat at him. "So very humorous, isn't it? Fool!"

Cyrodian made an expression of mock intimidation. The servant, sweating, bent to the floor, placed the empty jug on his tray, and sought to soak up the spill with his apron.

"Just let it go," Elad ordered him impatiently.

"My lord?"

"Clean it up later!"

"Y-yes . . . yes . . . ." Hastily he got to his feet and scrambled out.

Elad scowled at Cyrodian. "You make enemies of all the small people. A fine monarch you'd be."

Cyrodian quickly aimed his other knives and hurled them.

All five struck close to the first in the doorjamb, their blades not farther apart than a finger width.

"You have to keep them on their toes," Cyrodian explained, reaching for the new wine after his display of targetry. "Make them dance to your song, my weak-stomached brother, or you'll dance to theirs."

"You learn that in the army?"

"I taught that to the army."

"I have more than the army to worry about. I have the Council and cities and merchandisers, ten thousand aristocrats, a hundred thousand bureaucrats—"

"Not yet, you don't," Cyrodian reminded him. "Now pour yourself some wine and sit down." He swallowed a long draft as Elad at last followed his suggestion.

"Our mother is not our problem, Elad. At least, not our paramount problem. We can outflank her. Drive for the center—hard, fast. Cut off the poisonous part of the snake first; the rest you chop up at your leisure."

Elad seated himself in a cushioned chair, rolled his goblet between the palms of his hands. "Meaning—Dursoris."

"Meaning Dursoris. You have the Council—let's be frank, if you made your bid tonight, two-thirds of them are with you, if only because they think you're not man enough to be King and so the more easily manipulated—and I have the army."

Elad scowled, set aside his cup, slumped in his chair.

"In a civilized society," Cyrodian continued, "you have two ways to get and hold power—legally or illegally. Short of causing another civil war, I think our best chance for now is to bring Dursoris around to our way of thinking. Yta has just enough faith in you to give you the throne; she doesn't want succession, yours or hers, to drag on to the detriment of the empire. Which is just what could happen if we decide to throw it before the Council, even on the most transparent of motives. Are you listening, brother?"

"We've discussed this so many times I know it by heart. We've recited it like a ballad. 'We must win Dursoris, we must win Dursoris.' But if Dursoris doesn't wish to be won? What then? 'Another civil war'?"

"Of course not; that leaves us far too unprotected." Cyrodian finished his wine and wiped his sprinkled beard. "He meets with an accident. As simple as that. Happens in the army all

26

the time. Happens often enough in court, too; you know that. Happens all the time." To Elad's look of dismay: "The right of the nation is stronger than the right of blood. To sacrifice one life for the empire is far better than sacrificing the entire empire because of one dissenting voice. The common good, Elad." He laughed mellowly. "But I don't relish killing my own brother, and I don't think I'll have to. Dursoris knows how we feel, and I'm certain that at this very moment he knows where his loyalty lies."

6.

At that very moment, however, Dursoris's loyalty to his brothers was not his chief concern.

Orain murmured and nestled herself more securely in his arms, and Dursoris pressed his lips to her hair, inhaled the good perfume of her. "Happy?" he whispered.

She smiled at him.

The cushions rustled as he rolled onto his back, threw a hand behind his head, and stared lazily at the ceiling.

Orain grunted in her throat, moved and laid her cheek on Dursoris's chest, blew softly on his belly. The dark hairs around his navel fluttered like black wheat in a windy field. She tickled Dursoris's navel with her thumb, then reached below; she held his damp penis in her fingers and stroked it.

"Don't. Please, Orain."

She dropped her hand to his thigh, asked in a disappointed tone, "What's the matter with you? We haven't seen each other in two weeks." Resentful, she kissed his chest, lifted her head and tongued one of his nipples.

Dursoris sighed heavily.

"You don't expect Cyrodian to come through the door, do you? I haven't seen the sharp side of his sword in over seven years."

"It's not proper," Dursoris admitted in a low voice. "Not at a time like this."

"That's not it, either."

"Tomorrow," he said dully, "Elad will make his bid for the throne. You realize that, don't you?"

Orain looked away. "But it's already decided. It was decided months ago. Even if Yta fights him, the Council can overrule. It's no secret that, unless Yta deliberately calls for a Vote of Reprimand, Elad can win the Council's approval.''

"Yes, and Cyrodian controls the army, and the Council is afraid of what the army might do. I'm the only remaining question mark, aren't I?"

"You're not serious! You mean you're going to fight him?"

"Mine is the only sensible voice remaining."

"Dursoris!"

"Keep your voice down, you'll—"

"*You'll* destroy us!" Orain exclaimed. She sat up, flushed, pushing back the loose hair that had fallen in her face. Then a slow smile fought the quivering of her lips. "I know what you're going to do," she guessed. "You're going to goad Elad just enough, just to remind him that—"

"I'm going to fight him to the death, if that's what it takes."

Orain couldn't speak. Frightened, anxious, uncertain, she looked away, shivered, then faced him fully and entreated him. "You can't"—in a terrified, hushed whisper.

"It is the law. Am I the only one who remembers what law is?"

"He will get the throne anyway!"

"If Yta abdicates, yes. If she decides to continue her rule, the law states that attempt at succession by partisan force is punishable by death. It doesn't exclude firstborn princes any more than it does anyone else. I intend to enforce the law, no matter how fully Elad has stuffed some of the purses around here."

Orain got hold of herself. "But that means it's academic. Yta doesn't want the throne."

"We don't know what Yta wants. But if Elad makes a motion in Council tomorrow to protest her continuation as monarch, then I am bound by the Code to call him down."

"And he will fight back! He and Cyrodian both will!"

Dursoris put a hand to her shoulder. "Orain . . ."

"Your hand is cold."

He removed his hand, letting the fingertips linger on her soft shoulder. "Orain, the right of the nation is stronger than the right of blood. You know that. If I were to sacrifice all that civilization—this civilization—stands for, merely on the grounds that Elad as eldest prince would get the throne anyway, I would be betraying not only myself, not only my

29

nation, but everything mankind has fought to preserve. We're not savages, Orain. Whether or not Elad and Cyrodian believe that the right to rule belongs to the man with the strongest sword, those days are done. We have laws that are older than they are. We have laws, and laws are history, and history is justice of one sort or another. Don't you understand?"

She waited a long time before answering. Dursoris watched the tapers as they glowed in the thick darkness of the chamber. He watched the back of Orain's head, marveling at the silken texture of her golden hair, and sought to look inside her skull, inside her brain, to see the mechanism of her mind—stared at her lovely hair and sought by some power of will to influence the working of the mind underneath.

"It grows late. We had both best be gone."

"Orain, heart—don't you understand?"

"I made one great mistake in my life," Orain admitted to him, "and that was marrying your brother. I've rectified that by trying to raise Galvus into everything his father isn't. Now I've made another mistake: I've fallen in love with you. And if you stand up in Council tomorrow and fight Elad, I'll still love you. More than ever, probably. And when Cyrodian's assassins hunt you down some dark night in some alley somewhere, ten years from now, and cut your throat, I'll still love you—more than ever. And I'll think how great a fool you were, and I'll love you for that, too. And I'll wonder for the rest of my life whether I was a wise woman or a fool myself, to love a man who loves ideals so much, justice so much, that he couldn't even feel any satisfaction in finding a moment's happiness for *himself!*"

Dursoris stood up. "Orain, please! That's not fair, it's not!"

"Evarris's ashes are still warm, and the jackals fight for his seat! Athadia is a bed of serpents! Evarris has left a legacy of—of hate! Can't you see it? Don't you smell it? Who will they kill for? Yes, kill! Tell me! Elad? My husband? You, Dursoris? Yta? Why don't you fight it out here?

"Oh, damn them all!" she spat, not crying now, infused with rage and hopelessness. "Damn them all! Damn this nation of pride and *justice!*"

She got up from the bed, stood, and began to dress. Dursoris watched her, pain mixed with utter affection. The fall of her hair, the trembling of her small breasts, the outline of her slim body against the lamplight, the soul of all of her . . .

Sobbing, she yanked her boots onto her feet and ran across the chamber and went out.

Dursoris cursed softly and sat down on the bed.

7.

"You've heard?"

"Yes." Elad did not pause with his knife.

"Then what are we to do?"

"First of all"—sipping his tea, then wiping his lips and chin—"I think we'd better face some facts. Sit, brother. Eat some food."

"I am not hungry."

"As you please. But—sit." Elad gestured.

Cyrodian dropped awkwardly into a chair, sprawling his legs. He poured himself a goblet of wine, stamped his feet impatiently on the tiles.

"At the rate her train will make"—Elad spoke in a low, careful tone—"it will take Mother at least till dawn tomorrow to reach Teplis."

"And? So?"

"We can take another trail and reach the Oracle first. Hear her wisdom, make our own decision. It's the only choice we have, brother, short of waiting here for Yta to return in two days."

Cyrodian flexed his fists. "The Oracle will tell her to keep the throne."

"Very likely she will, yes."

Cyrodian scowled, studied his brother's placid face. Something was peculiar about his reaction to things this morning. "Then we must ride at once."

"There is time for breakfast."

Cyrodian got to his feet. "No. We must ride at once."

Elad pushed himself from the table, pressed his stomach, and emitted a controlled burp. "Dursoris as well," he suggested.

Cyrodian stared at him.

"I don't want him here by himself while we're away from court. No telling what kind of trouble he might cause."

"He won't come willingly. Not with us."

"Certainly he will. Our threat weighs heavily upon him. He'll think that during the ride he can convince us with logic and law. Maybe he will, Cyrodian. What do you think?"

Cyrodian absently lifted his left hand to his sword.

Elad shook his head strictly at him. "None of that. I want to be King—I will be King—but—" He stopped short, looked out across the low stone wall of his veranda. "If we're lucky, the weather may lift yet. It will be a pleasant journey."

Cyrodian mumbled something.

"Call the servants," Elad told him. "Rouse Dursoris. I don't want to waste any more time."

8.

The *Delios* made port at Athad that afternoon, tying up at the northern docks. Adred disembarked and entered the majestic pandemonium of the capital: grand, wide, crafted of endless tall towers and walls, huge fountains, escarpments of temples and public and government administration buildings. He had been away for over four months, hoping in his absence to live down the two disappointments that had seen him leave: his father's death early in the year, and a silly-serious love affair with a nobleman's daughter.

It was raining. Despite that, Adred found his spirits rising, anticipating seeing Dursoris and Orain and the mothering Queen Yta. He stopped at a public bathhouse, (as he had promised himself he would), and then took rooms in the Indura, a few blocks from the palace. He visited his banking house and was greeted there by old friends of his father; while withdrawing forty in long gold, Adred told how things were with Count Mantho in Kendia. (Old-timers still referred to Kendia as the "uplands," although the province and its immediate surroundings had been annexed to the empire in the second year of Evarris's reign.)

The rain was a downpour by the time Adred reached the palace. He waited for a moment beneath the propylon set before the east wall's pedestrian gate, then dashed on through and across the brick patio to the small inner courtyard. Roofed walkways edged the gardens there, and Adred followed one, sidestepping puddles as best he could. As he jogged up the steps to the wide front portico, thunder boomed from high beyond the Bithitu Temple, and Adred glanced back, expecting to see the last of the lightning. Under the portico roof he shook the rain from his hair, then took the last few steps to

34

the entrance doors; at the top he paused to scrape the mud from the bottom of his boots, adding wedges of drying muck alongside those of others who had entered this morning.

A servant in the reception area greeted Count Adred and requested that he wait for a moment while Princess Orain was informed of his arrival. The palace seemed uncommonly quiet—due, no doubt, to the King's death. When the servant returned to conduct Adred upstairs, the young nobleman inquired about Evarris's funeral and was disappointed to learn that he had arrived too late.

Directed, on the third floor, toward Orain's apartment, Adred moved down the corridor, reaching inside his shoulder cape to take out a package he had brought for young Galvus. A gift from Kendia: a book of the humanistic philosophy of Radulis. He had no doubts what Prince Cyrodian would do with such "anti-militarist, anti-expansionist, socialist trash," should he find his son reading it.

Orain was standing in the center of her receiving chamber, waiting nervously, as Adred entered. He closed the door behind him and, coughing slightly, stood there, feeling rather awkward in the gray, dark room. "Orain?"

She ran to him abruptly, naked feet slapping on the stone. Adred, surprised, held out his arms, and Orain hurried into them, embraced him strongly.

"Oh, Adred, thank the gods you're here!"

"Orain, what—"

She began to sob. Adred held her close for a moment, self-consciously dropping the Radulis on the chair beside his cape. He took Orain's shoulders in his hands and held her back a pace. Looking her in the eyes: "What's happened? Orain, what's wrong?"

She sought to control herself. "All I've been doing is crying and crying," she confessed, turning away. "Can't eat, can't sleep. . . . Gods!" She faced him. "Adred, they're going to cause a civil war!"

"Who? Who is?"

"The princes! Elad and Cyrodian—Dursoris! They're going to be at each other's throats!"

"Tell me what's happened. Where are they now?"

"They've ridden off to the Oracle at Teplis. Yta's gone there too. She left this morning; they followed. Oh, Adred!

35

They all want the throne; they were *waiting* for Evarris to die!''

"Come here. Orain, come here. Sit down. Have some wine.''

"I can't drink any wine.''

"Did you have any breakfast? Any lunch?''

"I can't eat.''

"Here. Sit down. There. . . . Now, drink some wine; it'll calm you down. Go on.''

He called for a servant and had Orain's plate brought in, made her eat some lunch and insisted on her drinking a goblet of wine. She told him, clearly and succinctly, all that had happened within the past few days.

Adred was chilled. What had he returned to?

Galvus entered his mother's room and said a bold hello to his Uncle Adred. Bold, because now he was the man of the palace, for a day or two, and had some very real knowledge of what was occurring.

Adred gave him the Radulis, and Galvus was ecstatic.

"But keep it to yourself," Adred warned him. "If anyone around here finds you with it, they'll probably have my head.''

"Do you know how long I've wanted a copy of this?" Galvus asked. "Did you find it in Kendia?''

Adred nodded. "Just read it with patience, Galvus. The world won't change overnight. Radulis gets carried away with himself sometimes, but neither the Prophet nor the gods are coming down from the heavens to make a new world.''

Orain spoke. "Galvus, would you leave us now, please?''

"Yes, mother.'' He seemed to go along with his mother's attitude that he was somewhat ignorant of events. "Thank you, Adred, for the book. Thank you very much.''

"You're more than welcome. We'll talk later.''

When he had gone, Orain asked, "What do you think of all this, Adred?''

He stared into her face for a long time. He listened to the rain. He thought then of the Dursoris he had known, the princes he had known, the Yta he had known. He was drinking wine, Orain's wine, on an empty stomach, and he was becoming light-headed.

"What, Adred?''

Her face, cold and gray as the rain-dampened shadows.

Warm and close and tearful as memories that are good memories.

Perhaps because of the wine, perhaps because Orain was close and near, perhaps because Galvus was the only man of blood in the palace, Adred remembered himself and the white-robed scholar on the *Delios,* that morning when the birds had wheeled in the sky, arced down, dipped into the sea, and died.

"Surely this is a bad omen. . . ."

"Adred?"

"A bad omen, isn't it, Orain?" he said. "What else can the Oracle say? It's surely a bad omen."

Athad, the capital, which had seemed to him large and colorful and full of every vitality, every memory, able to manifest everything to him, suddenly shrank to the gray sound of rain within the perimeters of Orain's chamber.

9.

The day had been damp and drizzly, the ride long. Dursoris had whistled and hummed songs. Cyrodian had never passed up an opportunity to make a snide comment or a crude jest. Elad, becoming more agitated as the day wore on, at times moved his horse ahead of his brothers', hoping to relieve the congestion in his soul by putting distance between them.

But strange forebodings gripped him. Memories, fears, and adumbrations. Their road passed across field and by riverbank, through woodlands and forests. Late in the afternoon, as the three followed a dark forest path to the base of Mount Teplis, Elad found himself thinking of Bithitu, the Prophet. A story. How Bithitu had met Archas, the demon-king, in a forest two thousand years ago, and had tricked Archas into picking up two pine needles for every one he dropped—thus distracting the demon from causing trouble in the world. For a time, at least.

Elad glanced at his brothers and wiped the rain from his slick face.

The Temple of the Oracle was situated upon an outcropping of Mount Teplis. Flat stone stairs, cracked and lined by fallen pillars, led to the entranceway. There was no door; the Temple itself was no more than a cave decorated with tapestries and old statuary. There was a well-worn brick walkway leading inside the Temple; it stopped short where a fissure in the earth, perhaps an arm-length wide, divided the front of the cave from the Oracle's dais deeper within.

Tall braziers of smoking incense ringed the dais. Oil lamps and wax candles cast the only light. The Oracle herself—a nameless entity, supposedly immortal, but surely replaced upon death every few years by priests from her diminishing

38

cult in the capital—sat in the cross-legged *umhis* position, slim hands folded upon her lap. She wore a heavy white robe. Neither her face nor her hair was distinct; the Oracle wore a large bronze mask, one side cast and decorated in a male aspect, the other in a female aspect. Fumes from the burning incenses played about her, swirling in a dry mist. Flames of candle and oil lamp shone foggily through the smoke, played in colors upon the strange bronze visage.

Elad stood at the fore, Cyrodian behind him, Dursoris to one side. The first prince of Athadia had never before visited the Oracle, nor did he know many who had, save his mother. Should one offer a prayer? Money? Should one bless oneself or damn oneself? Was the fissure a test? Should he leap it to prove that he was worthy of approaching the Oracle?

"Stand," said a metallic voice that resonated through the misty confusion of Elad's uncertainty. "Stand where you stand, Prince Elad. I know who you are; I know why you have come."

Elad glanced back at his brothers; wary, he clenched his hands together. They were warm and damp in their gloves.

"You wish the throne," said the Oracle.

Elad moved forward one step.

"Speak." Clearly a woman's voice, yes, though hollow, echoing.

"*Will* . . . I gain the throne?"

The Oracle moved. The brothers could hear the intake of her breath. Fumes swirled at her command. She lifted her arms, the white sleeves of her robe dropped down her forearms, and all three princes saw the amulets and ornamental pieces she wore.

"The throne means wealth more than gold, Prince Elad! But spiritual gold weighs far more heavily than temples built of earthly gold. As each human being has three selves, so do you have three enemies. Your first is a mirror, your second a blade, your third a foreign countenance. Mirrors betray depth while having no depth. Blades have two sides, two edges, and one point. Countenances are masks for the minds beneath. The foolish man accepts all three as they present themselves, not as they truly are."

Elad was perplexed. Neither Cyrodian nor Dursoris said anything. Elad passed from wonder and tension to annoyance and doubt. "I don't understand what you mean, Oracle. Explain yourself."

"I speak for the gods; the gods do not explain. You must explain for yourself. All is not what it seems; what things seem is not all. It is not the mirror's reflection that is real, but what it reflects. It is not the sword that slays, but the man behind it. It is not the wall that weakens, but those behind who do not repair it. The tree that stands in the forest reaches for the sunlight but cannot live without its roots. Temper your sword, Prince Elad. Nourish your roots. See beneath your mirror."

Elad grew angry. "Speak true words!" he cried. The mask, the flames, the mists . . . words, and words, and words . . . the resonant voice, metallic, hollow . . . pine needles . . . "Tell me what I came to know!" he yelled, stepping ahead, toes now at the edge of the fissure. "I didn't come here for lessons in poetry!"

"You came to learn if you will have the throne."

"Tell me, witch!"

"You came to learn if Queen Yta's heart is too great a price to pay for her throne."

"Tell me what I want to know, damn you!" He was perspiring; his skin itched from the fumes; his hair was damp and matted to his head, and sweat was dripping like a wash down his face.

"Shall I tell you that the future holds only truth, Prince Elad? Shall I tell you that already blood grows on your hands? Shall I tell you that four shall become three, and three two, and two one, and the one—"

"Tell me what I wish to know!"

Now Dursoris stepped forward. "Calm yourself, brother. This is of the gods."

But Cyrodian slapped Dursoris on the shoulder and chortled, "Of the gods, hell! It's no different from priests hiding in hollow idols. Yta owns her, Elad. She's playing with you. You gave her the dice, and now she's weighed them to her own—"

Elad grunted and drew his sword, teetered on the edge. The flames . . . the fumes . . . the voice . . . He waved his blade behind him, gesturing Cyrodian to silence, and stared into the Oracle's bronze mask. "Tell me!"

"Already the future takes hold of you, Prince Elad," came the low, unstartled voice. "You do not know yourself; how then can I tell you things which otherwise you may wish to know?"

"Speak to me of the truth, damn you, damn you!"

"The mother raises the child," spoke the Oracle woman, spoke the misted, flame-reflecting, fume-sheltered mask, "but the child is not the mother, and the mother is not the child. When animals breed they bear animals of a kind; when man and woman breed they bear animals of all kind. Each man and woman has many animals in his and her soul."

"I want the *truth*!" Elad screamed. "No more poetry! No more—"

"I speak the truth, Prince Elad. Listen with more than your ears."

"You are telling me nothing! Nothing!"

"There is no throne you may not have, if mother's blood is the price you are willing—"

Elad shrieked. Reckless, guilty before the crime and with the shadows of forest in his brain, he leapt the narrow fissure, jumped the steps of the dais, and in a sweeping, even movement brought up his sword, placed the keen point beneath the chin of the Oracle's mask.

"There is a throat here," he growled. "You are mortal. You speak of blood—"

"*Elad*!" Dursoris howled. "This is outrageous! You cannot—"

Cyrodian grabbed his younger brother by the arm, held him in a strong grip.

"*Tell me*!" Elad grimaced, the sweat pouring down his face, pain and anger shriveling inside him, his head aching. He stared into the Oracle's mask, saw the old gray eyes beneath the bronze slits, heard the nervous respiration from the labored breast. "You are not a *goddess*. You are a *woman*, an old woman drunk on fumes and smoke! If you have any truth in you, old woman—if you read the future truly—then, for the sake of your own future, tell me mine and let it be the truth. Or your future ends here."

His arms tingled. The blade shivered in his grasp. It was almost as though he had become an entirely different person, or as though some other Elad within him, long held in check, now came free with the strength of vengeance. *You do not know yourself.* . . .

"Tell me, now," Elad whispered, feeling the trembling of the throat beneath his swordpoint, seeing the old gray eyes within the mask water with emotion.

"You"—in a whisper, in a whisper for Elad's ears alone—

41

"you will take the throne, and none other after you, and you will rule to see everything precious destroyed, every hope ruined, every man and woman wailing in torment. You will rule Athadia and see the world die in anguish."

He waited one heartbeat; he held long enough to see tears in the gray eyes beneath the mask. Then the fumes worked on him, and the horror, and the future—and Elad leaned into his sword; the point met no resistance in the soft throat; the Oracle coughed. Screaming wildly, Elad ripped savagely with his blade. Blood flew in an intricate pattern, and the bronze head fell to one side, lolled, hung, then slipped free altogether and crashed to the earth. Blood poured down the simple white gown in a wavering purple cascade as the gushing neck made frantic sucking noises. The body slumped forward in the *umhis* position, rocking still, rocking still.

"Gods!" Dursoris shrieked. "Gods! Gods! What have you—"

"Silence!" yelled Cryodian, holding Dursoris all the more strongly.

Horrified, Elad backed away, blood dripping from his sword.

"The hole!" Cyrodian called out to him.

He remembered, pivoted on the edge, almost fell in, reacted and jumped, landed on the brick path.

"What have you done?" Dursoris shrieked. "What have you done? Gods, gods, what have you—"

Elad dropped his sword, rose to his feet, stared at the bloody trail.

"Outside!" Cyrodian grunted. "We must begone!"

Dursoris broke from him and staggered on weak legs, staring at the bloody corpse on the dais. "What . . . ? What . . . ?"

"Elad, pick up your sword and let us begone!"

Elad sank to his knees again, reached for the crimson blade.

"Pick it up!" Cyrodian bellowed. "Damn you, pick it up and let us—"

"What have you done?" Dursoris shrieked. *"What have you done? Gods! Gods!* You have damned yourself!"

Dawn was breaking as they returned through the forest. The horses' hoofs crushed pine needles; their saddles creaked; birds chirruped, and small burrowing animals scampering undercover, left trails of noise in the low carpet of morning mist.

Elad's hands, red, were still shaking. His sword, in its scabbard, was still bloodied; dried blood encrusted the scabbard where the wet blade had been thrust. Blood on his sword. Elad, the virgin murderer.

As the three fled the forest in the gray of dawn, Dursoris looked upon the muted greens and browns of wide-flung farmlands and said, "This must be reported to Council."

Creak of saddle. Look of horror. "What the hell are you talking about?" Elad demanded in a dry, raspy voice.

Dursoris turned his head slowly, giving Elad every benefit to study the seams of pain in his face. "I mean what I say, brother. Such a crime cannot go unpunished. When Yta arrives at the Oracle's cave and sees what has been done, she'll know one of us did it. Either you or Cyrodian. The murder of anyone connected to religious office carries a heavy penalty. It is a High Moral Crime, as Code Seventeen—"

"*What the hell are you talking about?*" Elad repeated, astonished, very loudly now. Beyond Dursoris, he saw Cyrodian grimacing darkly, working his teeth together.

Dursoris reined his horse still; his brothers did the same. Facing Elad, his back to Cyrodian, Dursoris explained himself. "The fact that I'm against your taking the throne doesn't enter into this, Elad. That will have to come later. For the present, you have committed an inexcusable crime—murder—an unspeakable crime. It will have to be reported, and you—"

"*Nothing* will be reported!" Elad yelled at him, a grin of fear stamped on his face.

Without warning, Cyrodian moved. Elad saw him and instinctively jerked back, pulling his horse so taut it reared. Arms thrown wide, Cyrodian hurled himself from his mount. Dursoris half-turned in his saddle; then his horse bucked as the giant crashed into him. Wrapping his arms tightly around his brother, Cyrodian held on as they both toppled free and crashed to the ground. They landed heavily, Dursoris pinned, and he groaned numbly, the wind knocked out of him.

Elad quieted his horse and dismounted, fell, got to his feet, and ran. "Cyrodian!"

Wordless, fierce eyes blazing, Cyrodian pulled free his side-knife and struck Dursoris across the side of the head with the heavy handle. The younger man moaned and fell flat.

Cyrodian didn't look up at Elad. "Build a fire."

"What?"—breathless.

"Build a fire, damn it!" Sweating, growling, he turned his knife in his hand and, bending over Dursoris, forced open his brother's mouth, reached in with thick fingers, and pulled up on the slippery tongue.

"No, Cyrodian! *No!*"

Swiftly, showing the mastery of a craft that had silenced many traitors and informants, Cyrodian slipped the slim, sharp point of the knife into the mouth, sliced. Blood runneled out. Cyrodian stood up and pulled the unconscious Dursoris over onto his belly, so that he wouldn't choke to death.

"Gods!" Elad whispered, backing away.

Cyrodian roared at him, "Are you going to build a fire? Or are you going to let him bleed to death?" Wiping his side-knife on the grass, Cyrodian sheathed it, then pulled out his sword. Holding Dursoris's left arm to the ground, he set the edge of his blade a little below the wrist, pushed down, and yanked back. Huge biceps rippled beneath his tunic; bones crunched toughly; the silver blade cut clear down into the muddy earth.

Elad turned away, beginning to vomit.

Cyrodian shook his shaggy head, pinned down the right arm, cut off the hand.

Elad stumbled to a tree and embraced it, pressed his wet cheek against the bark, stared at the world through hot, teary eyes as his stomach folded up.

Cyrodian got to his feet, bent to wipe clean his sword, then gathered together some twigs and scrub and put flint and steel to them. "I'm a man of my word, Elad," he said darkly, fanning the sparking fire. "If he can't tell what happened, he can't take it to court. You're going to be king, and *no one* is going to stop that! I haven't put in a lifetime of planning to have you back down now. You're going to be *king,* damn your woman's stomach!"

A short time later, far down in the river valleys, farmers awakening to their chores heard anguished screams ring down from the mountain—awful, tongueless, bellowing screams that pierced the misty dawn with echoes of unending, unnamable agony. . . .

10.

Approaching Mount Teplis from the southeast, Yta and her train did not meet the three princes. At dawn, when gurgling screams rent the quiet of the morning, Yta froze in her palanquin and ordered her bearers to a halt. The screams continued—piercing, eloquent, so full of anguish as to defy tolerance.

One of the courtiers with the queen made the sign of the gods before his face and spoke humbly to his mistress. "Perhaps it is some farmer—some farmer trapped in his grinding wheel."

"No," Yta replied, listening to the echoes that hung in the air.

No. She knew the scream. How could she not know?

How could she not know the screams as the first of many— the screams of a dying empire? . . .

The blood was still fresh on the dais steps, still gummy on the cloth of the white robe. Yta herself, helped across the fissure by servants, examined the blood.

The servants were fearful—murder of a voice of the gods was a crime unthinkable—but some of them were moved more toward immense sorrow. "How could this have happened? Oh, Queen Yta! How could this have happened? Who could have done such a thing?"

Not averting her eyes from the corpse, not shielding her eyes against the glare of the bloody bronze mask, Yta inhaled the stench of death and the fumes of incense. "Bury the body," she whispered. Facing one of them: "Bury the body, Osutu. Bury the head. Both in one grave. Here." She walked across the floor of the cave, tapped her foot on the soft soil.

45

Uncertain, but using their swords as spades, the armed guards of the train bent to the task and within a short while had dug an adequate trench.

Yta, standing all the while in a dark corner of the temple, now strode forward, removed her brilliant gold and crimson cape. "Lay the body in this," she instructed. And when her servants had done so: "Place the head upon the breast. Yes. Now move the arms so that they embrace the head."

The arms were not yet stiffened; it was done.

"Cover her with the cape. Lay her to rest."

Yta returned to her place in the shadows and watched, unchanging, as the fresh earth was returned to the grave and tamped down with boots.

"Osutu, bring me wine from your saddle. And the rest of you—remove yourselves now, please. Wait outside in the sunlight for me."

They backed out, and Osutu returned with the wine. "Leave me now," Yta told the man. "The Oracle will yet speak with me. I will be but a short while."

When the last of her people had gone, Yta, standing above the freshly turned earth, unstoppered the wineskin and poured a slow libation. As she did so, she whispered an old prayer, one she had memorized in her girlhood on Hea Isle, one she had not spoken aloud since the day her feet left that place. She pronounced it now, summoning old spirits and old guidances, as the wine ran out. Then Yta lay down upon the damp new earth, stretched out on her back, clasped her hands upon her belly, closed her eyes to sleep.

She had been awake for a long time, full of tension, and she was exhausted. The darkness of the temple, and its incenses, filled her body and lulled her mind to quiescence. When she had fallen to slumber, Yta allowed her mind to repeat the same prayer she had pronounced with the libation.

She did not stir when the ghost of the Oracle came to her. Flowing white, in Yta's dream, with gray eyes shining beneath the mask of bronze, the Oracle spoke truths which Yta recited after her, as the spirit crossed the gulf between old life and new death.

"You have committed no sins willingly, and your life has been good, your sins forgiven. Hea herself forgives you.

"Your thread is nearly run, your tapestry nearly complete. Life yet remains to you, however. You are no more responsible for the children you have brought into the world than are the gods for their bringing evil into the world. Fate runs its course.

"You will live, Queen Yta, in your purity and goodness, without sin, one with the goddess, when you return to the capital and renounce your throne. Abdicate forever to your eldest, for he will have the throne by blood or not.

"When you have abdicated, leave Athadia and the empire for Hea Isle. Your work is done. The goddess awaits you with warm breast and spread arms.

"Crimes have been done; they are not yet completed. My body was slain by Elad, your eldest. Your youngest, Dursoris, was slain by Cyrodian. When you return to court, inquire; these truths will bare themselves. Yet give Elad the throne.

"Know this in the name of the gods, and in the name of Hea, and in the name of all gods as one god: you are purged, Yta of Athadia.

"Fearless as you have been in life, a strong woman, honest with yourself and honest with others, a monarch, you will yet live, but not in pain. You will not live to suffer the end entire. For know, Yta, that this world has nearly run its thread. New gods wait, new worlds aspire, and new lives groan, waiting to be born. All this you will be spared; the end and the new beginning. Upon your death, Hea will welcome you across the river. You are purged.

"You are purged, Yta of Athadia."

When she awoke, she left the temple, entered her palanquin, and ordered her servants to return her to the capital.

The words of the Oracle's spirit lingered, and Yta repeated them to herself. The screams that had swept down the mountain no longer pierced the morning and no longer pierced the mother's heart.

11.

The temple bells on the near side of town clearly rang out the first hour of dusk, then night. Adred had just finished eating alone in his chamber; he paced the floor and nervously tugged at what was becoming a fairly strong beard. Opening a window, he restlessly tapped his fingers along the sill. He leaned out, looking for any sign of the three princes; but his view gave upon one of the palace gardens and he could not even see the street or the eastern courtyard. The myriad lights of the city, glowing brightly from every building, created a halo that shone against the falling nighttime like a crowd of candles in a darkened room.

Sighing, he closed his shutters, and just then a commotion came from somewhere in the palace. He hurried to his door and pulled it open. Down the corridor, where wide stairs led to the second-story landing, a crowd of servants had gathered, and Adred saw Cyrodian's large golden helmet bobbing through the busy cloaks and rustling robes.

"Call Sotos!" came Prince Elad's voice. "Quickly! One of you run to Sotos the physician!"

Adred hurried down the hall. Behind him, farther down the corridor, he heard Orain's door open; he turned and saw her.

"What's happened? Adred?" She hastened toward him.

Adred looked back at the stairs. Cyrodian, pushing his way through the servants, carried the head and shoulders of a man in his arms, while Elad struggled with the feet.

Orain's sandals slapped on the polished marble. "What's happened?" she nearly screamed.

"Out of the way!" Cyrodian called out, warning those in the corridor.

"Prepare his chamber!" Elad ordered the servants. "Go on! Prepare his—"

The crowd was moving down the hall. Orain, reaching Adred, clutched his arm as her husband and Prince Elad came past, carrying the bloody figure slung between them.

Orain gasped.

Adred took hold of her, reached to move her face away, even while he himself stared in utter shock.

"*It is Dursoris!*" Orain screamed, digging her nails into Adred's arm.

"Get . . . *Sotos!*" grunted Elad, as he and Cyrodian shambled past her. "Get some water and clean cloths! Hurry, damn it!"

"Oh, gods, no, no," Orain whispered. "No . . . no . . . *no . . . !*"

Adred held her. Orain struggled weakly, stared numbly. . . .

Dursoris. A ruin. Blood caked upon his mouth and cheeks and throat. Blackened stumps of wrists—charred flesh and hacked bone—dangling limply from his sides. Body swaying like some broken buck's between his brothers as they carried him.

"*What happened?*" Orain shrieked, turning, yelling at them.

"Bandits!" Cyrodian called back, glimpsing for a moment the burning intensity of his wife's stare. "Bandits!"

"Gods, I—" She fought to go, but Adred's grip was tight.

"Wait," he told her in an awed, low voice. "Wait. Let Sotos look at—"

"But it's *Dursoris!*" Orain cried, straining now, with her arms pulled behind her, to run after him.

"Orain! Or—"

"Gods, gods, it is *Dursoris!*"

Halfway down the corridor, as hovering servants held back, Elad and Cyrodian hauled the body into a chamber from which the orange glow of torches seeped. Sotos, the court physician, bald and overweight, dressed in his blue and gold robe, came huffing up the stairs; he hurried past Adred and Orain, not saying a word.

Orain, shivering, stood.

Adred felt the tension in his arms weakening. He released his hold on Orain, touched her shoulders, turned her around.

She faced him silently with her wet, damp face, golden hair in disarray. . . .

And such a look of personal horror in her eyes . . .

The chamber door closed.

"Wait," Adred whispered, watching where the orange glow had vanished from the floor.

Such a look of horror in her eyes . . .

Now Galvus came up the stairs, confused, brow creased. "What's happened? Mother? Adred? What is it?" Boots shuffling, robes whisking. "What—" at the stare of his mother's eyes.

Beneath the covers of his bed in the center of the chamber, he lay, white and damp, flesh waxy in a ring of candle flames. Orain was standing at his side, staring at his mouth, his nostrils, his closed eyes. The stumps hidden beneath the covers. The mouth, cleansed, partially open and gasping in air.

Sotos had gone. Four Khamars, armored, guarded the closed door. Elad was gone—to his own chamber. Cyrodian still stood in a dark corner of the room, watching Orain as she watched her silent, dying lover.

Adred, with Galvus, stood in the opposite corner, in the shadows away from the half-circle of bright candles above Dursoris's bed.

A servant girl knelt, wiping Dursoris's wet brow with a damp cloth. Periodically, the only sound in the room was the tinkle of water in the bowl as the girl dipped the cloth, rinsed it, wrung it, applied it again to Dursoris's hot forehead and cheeks.

Orain looked up. Adred was behind her; he could not see her eyes. But her golden hair, caught in the candlelight, glowed with a nimbus, and her robe, pale pink, bound with a silver cord, rippled with movement.

Orain was staring at Cyrodian, whose eyes burned in the gloom. "You slew him."

The servant girl's hand stopped its wiping. The Khamars looked up, alert.

Cyrodian's armor, bronze and leather, creaked in the corner. "What?"

Voice of shadows, voice of candles. "You slew him."

Adred's stomach began to knot.

"You slew him"—in the same unchanged tone, flat, hollow, true—"because you knew we were lovers."

A moment of eternity. A gust of cosmic cold. A blazing of inner suns.

Adred felt himself beginning to step forward.

Cyrodian's voice boomed across the room so that the taper flames bent beneath the unleashed breeze of his anger. "What are you saying?"

"You slew him because you knew we were lovers."

Huge footsteps, crushing the stone. Huge arms, reaching out as if to burst from the clothes. Terrible eyes, white with rage. Cyrodian hulked to the bedside, stared across at his wife. "*What* are you saying?"

"You are not my husband. You never were my husband—not in your heart. You slew Dursoris because you knew we were lovers—we loved one another, you knew it. The Oracle was only a pretext because—Elad must have known it too—" The words, tumbling.

Cyrodian's breath came in gusts of wind. He said, "Bandits" —then shook his head. "I never—" He seemed to lean back, and his hands, hairy paws, lifted on the air. One candle fizzled. "Lovers?"—in a wholly perplexed, disbelieving voice.

Orain shuddered. Her knees caved in; she dropped to the floor and threw her arms upon Dursoris's breast. "Why didn't you just kill him?" she shrieked at Cyrodian. "Why didn't you just kill him? Do you hate me that much? Did you have to *mutilate* him? Did you have to *torture* him? Why did you—"

"What are you—"

"Did you have to torture him?"

Swaying on his feet, Cyrodian drew in a great breath, let out a massive roar. "Lovers!" he bellowed berserkly. *"Lovers? You and—lovers? You—"*

"Stop him!" Adred yelled to the Khamars. "Name of the gods, he'll—*Stop him!*"

Cyrodian was around the bed in one lunge. Orain, arms across Dursoris, head bent, cackled with lost laughter. Cyrodian's hands settled on her head; with a powerful wrench he forced her face up.

Adred winced, expecting to hear the sound of bursting bones.

"Lovers?"

Sorrowful, half-mad cackle of laughter.

Adred flung out a hand, holding back Galvus.

51

The Khamars came on, hands on swords. "Prince Cyrodian—"

"*Lovers!*" And to her sobbing groans: "Whore! Whore! *Whore*!"

"Prince *Cyrodian*!"

He twisted her head; Orain gurgled and fell back. Cyrodian grabbed for her hair. She shrieked. The giant lifted his arms, made fists; his biceps bulged beneath the cotton of his tunic.

A sword ripped from its sheath, and a Khamar stepped between.

"Run!" Adred urged Galvus. "Gods, *run*! Get Elad! Hurry!"

Roaring, Cyrodian turned to face the Khamar, ignoring the dangerous blade. "Whore!" he yelled into the guard's face.

The other three surrounded him.

Galvus threw open the door, raced down the hall with quick, receding footsteps.

Each Khamar drew his sword, held it out at Cyrodian. "You will not touch her, Lord Prince. No law permits—"

Orain was cackling with laughter again. Sobbing. Sucking in mouthfuls of air. Cackling. Sobbing.

"Whore! Whore! Whore!"

"Stand away!" yelled the first Khamar. "Prince Cyrodian! Stand back imme—"

But Cyrodian, wrathful, more than a head taller and twice the soldier's bulk, swung his fists and caught the guard on the side of his head. The man was thrown back, grunting dully. His steel skipped on the stone floor as he landed on his back, armor clattering.

The remaining three moved in, aiming for the prince's chest.

"Get her!" one of them called.

Adred reacted. Numbed, as though suffering a dream, incredulous, as if witnessing his actions through some outside observer, he instinctively bent low and scuttled to Orain, grabbed her by the arms, and pulled her away. Stood her up. Leaned her against a table.

She drew in a long breath, eyes wide, staring at Cyrodian. "Whore! Stand away from me, I'll kill you all!"

Adred held onto her, pressed her face to his shoulder. He stared, frightened, at the immense Cyrodian, at the rage—boundless and jealous—huger than the rage of gods.

"I told you to—"

Noise, and a shadow in the doorway. Adred looked. Cyrodian, growling, turned his head, expecting more guards.

"Brother . . . Cyrodian . . ." And drunken laughter.

Galvus held behind, moving only when Elad advanced on unsure legs, a wine jug swinging in his right hand.

Cyrodian watched him with hot eyes, gurgling low in his throat.

But Elad ignored him, and instead crossed the room to Dursoris's bed and stared down. He hiccupped, smiled, swayed.

Still Adred held Orain's face to him; her body trembled against his like a thing mechanical suddenly released from pressure.

"What?" Elad asked Cyrodian, looking up with a flushed face colored by the candlelight. "Have they named you, brother? Did they discover the blood on your sword?"

"Liar!" Cyrodian roared.

"Hold him!" Elad cried out to the Khamars. "I want a thousand swords on him! A thousand guards!"

"Coward! You dog, you—"

But already more Khamars were rushing down the outside corridor; as the thunder of their boots dimmed, they appeared in the doorway, a blotting crowd of shadows, watching. Some drew weapons.

Elad's head dropped low. He hiccupped again, sniffled, whispered to himself, stared up. Faced Cyrodian's mad anger. "Murderer," he whispered in a slow, quiet voice, irrevocable.

Orain sobbed.

Cyrodian growled, an animal in chains. The Khamars' swords wavered, ready to plunge into him at an outburst.

"Murderer," Elad whispered again. "Oh, gods, brother, what crimes have we done—what crimes have we done?"

One of the Khamars glanced at him.

"Take him," Elad ordered. "He drew the knife. He attacked—He—Take him! Bind him with chains! Remove him to the prison!"

"Liar!" Cyrodian howled. "Traitor! Liar! *Liar!*"

His arms shot out; one Khamar, surprised, was caught in the throat by a heavy fist and fell, gasping and sprawling.

Those in the doorway rushed in, swords up. In a moment more than a dozen were crowded around Cyrodian, their blades aimed at his face, throat, heart, belly.

"Liar! Traitor! *Whore!* Both of you, *whores! I gave you the throne, traitor!*"

Chains—brought by the Khamars summoned by Elad. Chains—looped over Cyrodian's head, wrapped tightly to pin his monster arms. Chains, binding his wrists and chest, though he struggled and, struggling, moved into three sword points; though he bellowed of liars and bandits and whores and traitors.

Chained, and driven from the room, spurred with swords.

"Liar! *Liar! Murderer! Whores!*"

Screaming, bellowing, he was moved down the corridor. Screaming from the steps that led down and down and down, into the stone prison beneath the palace of Athadia, to be housed with the sewer rats and the decaying urns of dust and silent ghosts that populated the cells of political revolt.

The whisper of candles.

The sobs of Orain.

Adred, shaking, held her.

Elad fell to his knees, crouching, dropping the wine jug to the floor so that it spilled. Elad, sobbing—mouth agape, tears running down his face—moaned. "I did not want this!" His hands clawed the blankets of Dursoris's bed. "Brother—live! Live! I did not want this! I do not want this throne!" Gasping, sobbing in a man's naked voice: "Brother, live! The ghosts are here! I did not touch you! I did not touch you! Gods, *live*! Dursoris, live! Come awake and live! Let me touch your—your hands! Oh, *gods*, I do not *want* this! Liiiiive! *I do not want this throne!*"

Dawn, gray at the window.

Tapers burned low, some extinguished.

The servant girl crouched above the bed, still applying the damp cloth to Dursoris's brow.

Sotos, alone with her in the stillness, watching.

Watching.

Listening . . .

Placing hand to forehead, neck, breast, mouth.

Sotos, tired, pushed away the servant's hand. "No more. He is past all that."

Dawn, gray at the window.

Tapers burned low, some extinguished, smoking.

12.

Queen Yta arrived with her train late in the morning, and learned from Abgarthis and Sotos, from Elad and Adred and Orain, from dozens of servants and Khamars, what had happened—confirming the Oracle's words to her.

She ordered that a special High Council be convened.

Early in the afternoon, Yta, robed, crowned, sceptered, sat upon the mighty throne of Athadia and faced her son, brought in chains before her, guarded by twenty guards. And faced her son, her first son, dressed in the crimson and gold and blue. Faced her wings of Council, nobility to her right, public administration to her left.

"For the plotted crime of fratricide, and for the plotted crime of sedition against this throne of Athadia, Cyrodian dos Evarro edos Yta, second-born prince of this empire, holder of the title of General Rank Crescented in the Imperial Army of this state, is hereby ordered executed, his head to be severed from his body, his head to be exhibited on the west wall of the city, his body to be buried in an unnamed location, on the fifth morning following the immolation of his brother, the murdered Prince Dursoris, third-born son of this empire.

"For the plotted crime of sedition against this throne of Athadia, for the murder of a religious oracle—which is a state offense of the first list—and for the crime by association of murder of his brother Dursoris, Elad dos Evarro edos Yta, first-born son of this empire, is hereby ordered to assume the kingship of this state and empire, effective immediately upon my own renunciation of the throne, crown, and scepter of imperial Athadia. No greater punishment can I offer than for Prince Elad to rule this throne of blood for which he has shown such unseemly desire. And may the high gods have greater mercy upon him, in his days of trial, than they have bestowed upon me.

"I, Queen Yta of Athadia, widow of the late crowned King of the empire, Evarris dos Othmathis ak Athadia, do hereby renounce this throne, abdicate my rule, and grant this crown and scepter to the new monarch of state, Elad, King of Athadia. Prosper and grow wise. Rule forever, imperial son, in the name of all the gods."

She removed the crown and stood up.

She dropped the crown to the seat of the throne.

She leaned her scepter against the arm of the throne and stepped down.

At the bottom of the dais stairs, Yta approached Elad, who was unable to control his sobs, and embraced him, kissed him thrice, knelt low on one knee before him, and spread out her arms.

"Prosper and grow wise. Rule forever, imperial son, in the name of all the gods."

The High Council stood as one, in total amazement, and repeated the call of succession.

Yta walked out of the throne room.

Cyrodian, grim and silent, was escorted away by the Khamars.

The Councilors all stood, silent, for the entire afternoon, as Elad stood, silent, at the base of the throne before deciding, at twilight, to ascend and sit, crown himself, and take up his heavy imperial scepter.

PART II

A Lamp in a Storm

1.

Erusabad, on the other side of the world, across the wide Ursalion Sea, far from Athad, where West becomes East.

A great city, Erusabad, with its history etched in every brick. A crossroads, a port and a wharf, a city of paths, of businesses, of merchants; city of men and animals; city of windows and lights, city of taverns and halls, of prayers and curses; city of moneylending and purse-thieving; city of sailing ships at rest; and city of a thousand crowds, of voices, of clothes and robes and sandals and rings and jewelry, of perfumes; city of faces, hands and feet; city of arts; city of crimes; city of loneliness amidst plenty: a drug and an aphrodisiac, an overflowing vessel, a crossroads of a thousand thousand souls and a thousand thousand dreams, a city of wine and dust, the city of cities. Erusabad. City, metropolis, home, port, pathway . . . With accents and beliefs, with people and peoples, ships and commerce, temples and rooms and inns and libraries. Holy City—elusive and real. City of many cities—cities within one great Erusabad city. City piled to the edge of the waves, city pushed into the fields and land. Foundation. Maker of turbulence, owner of souls, dealer in lives. City between two empires, sharing both, clashing with both, groaning beneath the weight of both. City of east and west, city of west and east. Holy City—uncertain . . . savior, judge, orphan-child, warrior-man, harlot-whore. . . . City on the edge—song of the docks, song of the temples—city of a two-edged sword, city of no repose, city of destiny: aye, of empire, and a destiny. . . .

When Erusabad, the Holy City, the foundation of Bithitu's religion, came to be regarded as a city holy to the eastern peoples as well as the western, the throne in Athadia did not see any reason to drive off the infidels who—with their money, their goods, their businesses—did not (incidentally) happen to worship the Lamp and the Ring. Salukadians, were the eastern peoples, named after a desert somewhere at the end of the world, members of an ethnically diverse race as myriad and strong and populous and human as the ethnically diverse peoples of Athadia. And if the eastern peoples in Erusabad worshiped nine gods instead of many-in-one, if they had no Prophet but only a king, if they looked upon Erusabad as a sanctified city because their religion taught them that "the world began in the west"—then so be it. Athadia would not go to war with a people whose money was stamped with an animal's head rather than a god's.

When, five hundred years before Evarris, the eastern peoples began to intrude upon an Erusabad which had become westernized, there was dissension, there were antagonisms, street fights, conflicts, racial problems. Fair sons and dark daughters did not woo; east and west clashed; merchants stole goods from one another; and riots took place on ships docked in the harbors. But as the city grew—as its commerce grew— it became evident that some form of order must result from the anarchy. Resident advisers from Athad held council in the same building, at the same tables, as ministers from the eastern world. They began to rule together, setting up codes and laws and byways for interaction; and it was decreed that the River Usub would divide northern, Athadian Erusabad from southern, Salukadian Erusabad.

City of many cities—cities within one great Erusabad city. City piled to the edge of the waves, city pushed into the fields and land. Maker of turbulence, owner of souls, dealer in lives. City between two empires, sharing both, clashing with both. Holy City—uncertain—city of a two-edged sword, city of no repose. . . .

In the Temple of Bithitu on the far north side—a temple many times changed since its original inception two thousand years earlier—priests and high priests looked back upon a glorious history and wondered of the future when they watched out their windows and saw visitors from across the bridges: dark-haired, olive-skinned, blackeyed women dressed in pearls and rose sandals and transparent gowns, walking the same streets the Prophet had once walked, and believing in nine gods instead of one.

2.

As a young priest, one just admitted to elevated service in the Church of Bithitu, Thameron had much time to himself; for regulations held that young ministers just enfolded should have time for contemplation and thought, time to walk the world in their robes and sandals and rings, to listen and communicate with the people of the world, and time later to discuss these things of the world with Church elders, and be indoctrinated into the Church's position.

As a young man, barely eighteen summers old, zealous and strong, filled with the light of the Lamp, Thameron was somewhat overwhelmed with his new white robes and blue sandals and golden rings, his persona of priest. Six years of study and discipline had brought him to this door. An orphan, left to the world when his father had died, Thameron had become a ward of the state and, through the draw of the state lottery, had been removed to the Church, just as other homeless children had been removed to schools or businesses or military service. He had not loved the Church then, when he'd first entered it. Young manhood was upon him; he had yearned for a free life. But stern discipline and thoughtful communion had brought him around; he had journeyed through fear and uncertainty to at last realize that the Church was good, that Bithitu was the Prophet of the Light, and that he himself—Thameron, an outcast, lost and unloved—could do much good for the world. Six years of diligent occupation at lessons, with no tolerance for play or frivolity, had earned him at last his white robes, while it had taken others seven, eight, or more years to accomplish the same.

The Prophet Bithitu shows the way and the path. He is the way and the path to the eternal favor of all the gods.

Thameron followed a strict schedule, which he had drawn up for himself. He arose at dawn, with his brethren in the dormitory behind the Temple. An hour of fasting and prayer followed, and then morning devotions: a single-file march past Muthulis, the Chief Priest of the Temple, while each young man bowed and whispered purities before taking breakfast. Breakfast, as always, was meager, with prayers and silent offerings as heavy as sauces. But following the meal young priests were left on their own until midday. Most took to walking the grounds of the Temple, where a large park had not yet been taken over by the city for new apartments; others retreated into the silent world of the vast Temple library. Some, in pairs or groups, went into the streets to spread the light of faith in all directions. And some few held jobs, employment in businesses or in the homes of the advantaged, by which they earned money to bring to the coffers of the Prophet.

Thameron habitually spent his mornings alone, in the streets, in the poorest sections of northern Erusabad. Bithitu himself had gone to the poor, the aged, the whorish and gambling, the diseased and lost of humanity, to administer first to them, to teach them of the light within themselves. Thameron himself, lost and orphaned, had been saved by Bithitu; now he would save others, by the aid of Bithitu.

The sum total of all humanity that ever was, is, or ever will be cannot equal and cannot comprehend the goodness and love of Bithitu our Prophet.

As he walked down the streets, happy and jaunty, Thameron smiled at everyone he passed and wished them morning graces. Many of the wealthy or the poor, the guilty or the most devout, would stop him and reach into their purses. Offerings. One of the ways the Church judged the success of the young priests' ministries was by how much money each brought to the coffers at evening.

Today Thameron visited the tenements and taverns down by the docks. These were the poorest sections of the city, but when Thameron looked upon the dirty streets, the shabby people, the refuse and the contamination, the hunger and the meanness, he saw only the work of Bithitu to be done.

There was an apartment house on the corner of Dock and Miet Avenues where pimps, and thieves and other criminals resided, and Thameron came here once a week, unafraid of being robbed or harmed. The thieves and other criminals looked forward to his visits. For Thameron did not speak in platitudes; he did not live alone in some high room of the Temple and look down from a balcony a few times a year during festivities. He came into the streets, into the gutters and dirty alleys, to talk, listen, advise, chastise, purify, demand, and encourage. He did not apply the Prophet's teachings here as he would a hammer on an anvil, for the Prophet was very far away for these men and women. Thameron brought only himself and the silent knowledge that Bithitu was within him, and that in time—at the right time—Bithitu would reveal himself to each of these men and women. To force Bithitu or any philosophy or dream upon them could only do harm; to let them accept naturally, a little at a time, from the single light deep within themselves, was the way of patience and guidance.

"This man is ill," Thameron commented to some others in one room of the apartment house. He laid his hands on the forehead of an old, haggard pickpocket. "Where is the nearest physician?"

"There aren't no blood-takers around here, priest."

"Then you must take him to one."

"Let him die, Thameron. His time's come."

Thameron faced the speaker, a fat, weathered man. "I don't believe that. Where there is life, there is hope. If he can be saved, he will reawaken and perhaps see things with new eyes. Are you just waiting for him to die so you can pick his pockets?"

A few of them laughed.

"Are you?"

"He'd do it to us, Thameron. This isn't no church down here. We have to live down here, remember? If we could sell his body for some long gold, we'd do it. His time's come. Our time'll come. You can't scare us."

"I'm not trying to scare you." He reached into his purse, withdrew some of the silver given him by the devout and the guilty. "This money is cursed if you steal it from me," he remarked to one of the men. It was a common superstition. "But if you accept it, you must do with it as I tell you."

A tentative brown hand reached out.

"Take it, and do with it as I say, or demons will follow you and you'll suffer an accident. Take this man, your brother, to the nearest physician. Do it in good faith. Whatever is left from what the doctor asks as a fee is yours. Drink, gamble, find your pleasure, and know that Bithitu watches; but first take this man to a physician. Do you understand?''

Someone chortled. ''Why don't you just light candles and pray for him?''

''This time I'm praying for him with silver. Do you understand?''

They understood. His calm reasoning, his unprovoked sympathy, his goodness, his tolerance, his honesty, won them where proud priests and city guards and court downcallings had ever failed. Two of the men took up their friend and, with Thameron's silver in their fists, carried him off, down the stairs and out into the street, to get him proper attention.

''I am a lamp in a storm,'' said Bithitu; ''I guide the lost with unwavering light.''

And always, when he was in this pocket of town, Thameron made it a point to visit Assia. Sometimes he wondered if (had life gone differently) Assia might somehow have been the sister he'd never had. As it was, he cared for her, sought to nurture her and awaken her. Something in his spirit one time, sometime, had sensed something in Assia's spirit, and both had felt it; since then, Thameron had felt a compulsion toward the young woman, and he grieved that her dangerous life must someday shadow her inner light unless she could get away from here.

He entered the tavern on Sirruk Street, nodded to the burly man behind the counter, ignored the chortles of some of the patrons at tables. He went to the rear and took the creaking stairs up to the second floor, walked halfway down the landing till he came to Assia's door. It was a while before noon yet, but Thameron felt she must be awake. As he knocked on her door a tired face poked out from another room farther down.

''Thameron.''

''Morning graces, sister.''

''I thought it might be you.''

He smiled and made the Sign: a circle in the air and the line of the flame. The prostitute smiled back at him, withdrew, and closed her door.

From within Assia's room: ''Ibro?''

''No. Thameron.''

63

Quick footsteps, and the door was opened. Assia's crisp black eyes, her flowing blue-black hair, her smile. "Oh, come on in. Come in."

He entered, quietly closing the door behind him. Assia, half nude, had not yet finished dressing. He realized that she probably spent half her life undressed, so he did not take her casualness as an affront. He was glad, however, that he could appreciate Assia's beauty—although her inner beauty counted for much more than her outer. Her face, oval and dark; her eyes, deep as pools; her slim arms, slim legs. Foamy, cascading hair. Her heavy breasts, far too large for a woman of so slight a build. Her dainty feet.

Assia sat in a chair and pulled on her skirt, stood up and wriggled to get it over her hips. Thameron smiled tolerantly. She crossed the room; her hair floated, her breasts swayed; retrieving a short cotton vest from her bed, she pulled it on but left it unlaced in the front. Then she perched on the end of her bed, took up her comb, and began to do her hair.

Strong sunlight fell through the window; by it, Thameron noticed how pale Assia had become. He crossed to her, took up a chair, sat in it facing her.

"How have you been?"

"Well enough. I have to hurry—"

"What happened to your eye, Assia?"

She ceased combing so diligently, glanced at Thameron apprehensively. "Some character last night."

"I'm sorry."

She shrugged.

"Why are you hurrying?"

"Ibro . . . is angry with me again."

"Why?"

"Junis. She told him some things."

"Money?"

Assia nodded. "My father needed—I didn't give everything to Ibro. I think this"—she pointed to her eye—"was planned. He could've hurt me a lot more. Now Ibro wants me to go visit some nobleman. Lots of gold there. I have to go."

Thameron reached into his purse. "If this money goes to the Church, they'll only waste it on themselves. It belongs to the people. Here—how much would you have made?"

Assia stared at the money in his hand. "I—can't . . ."

Thameron poured all the gold into her palm. "That much?"

64

"Gods, at least!"

"Take it. Give it to Ibro. Any left over, use for yourself. Hold some back for yourself, now. Assia, please, go see a physician."

"I'm all right, Thameron."

"No, you're not. You look weak, pale. Are you eating properly?"

She laughed shortly, as though he had told an obscene joke.

"Don't, Assia. . . . Please, now, just—"

"Thameron, really—I'm all right."

"Take the money. At least buy yourself some decent food, not the slop they make here. Take care of yourself—and, Assia, don't gamble it. Do you hear me?"

She frowned, set the money on the bed. She held onto Thameron's hands, searched his eyes, softened. "He'll know if I don't visit that nobleman."

"Tell him you found a better prospect on the way."

Assia laughed merrily. "Tell him I found a priest?"

Thameron didn't smile.

She sighed. "Why are you a *priest,* Thameron?"

This—all over again. The feel of Assia near him. The strange sense of a shifting balance within him. "There is much good to be done in the world."

"It can be accomplished without a priest's robes."

"But Bithitu is the Light. He protects, he guides—"

"Those priests at the Temple protect and guide no one but themselves; they're as corrupt as anyone. Anyone except you, Thameron."

"Yes, I know. But even they can be saved. They have strayed—we all stray. I stray, in my heart."

Assia loved this Thameron, and in a way more profound than the way in which he loved her, or the way in which he loved the Prophet. She did not love an enigma, an idol, a lesson or a spiritual challenge; she loved a young man, this young man, and she loved his spirit. Sometimes she idly wondered if the same mischance that had made her a prostitute had also made Thameron a priest. She wondered, too, at the frailty of emotions and the fleetness of time, and how difficult it was to manage truth when often truth was very obvious and ordinary.

And she knew she desired Thameron; but she wondered,

with all her truth, if the desire was actually for Thameron, or simply for Thameron the priest. . . .

"Noon," he announced abruptly, standing up. "I must return to the Temple."

It was for Thameron, although she could not tell him, though she could not show him, though he suspected it but acted as if he didn't, though the love and concern she felt for him were equal to the love and concern he felt for her.

"Thank you, Thameron. . . ."

"We can leave together. Here. Ibro will think you're going to that nobleman. Just spend some of that getting a good meal, will you?"

"I'll try."

"Don't gamble it, and see a physician, Assia! I mean it."

"I'll see."

"Come on. Are you finished?"

"Yes." She tied her vest in the front, very loosely, then glanced at herself in her cheap copper mirror. "Do you like my hair this way? I could always—"

"It's very pretty. You've very pretty, Assia."

"Are priests allowed to compliment women?"

Thameron grinned ruefully. "This priest, I'm afraid, does a lot of things most priests aren't supposed to do."

Yes, it was for Thameron, although she could not tell him. . . .

"I am the Heart and the Hand and the Eye," said the Prophet Bithitu; "feel with me, touch my hand, see with my eyes."

On his return to the Temple, Thameron managed to collect additional gold and silver; he was used to turning in sparse purses at the end of the day. He felt good only when he had been able to give more than he had received—in gold, in heart, in replenishment.

If only his masters at the Temple could understand these things as he understood them. . . .

3.

That evening Thameron was absent. He had not deliberately left the Temple to provoke his masters but—on business of the spirit—he had returned to Ibro's tavern to make certain that Assia had done as he had insisted. To his disappointment she admitted to him that she had stopped to see her father, a retired seaman, while on her way to a physician; and her father, learning that she had money, had taken half the gold Thameron had given her. That left her without enough to take care of herself, for Ibro expected to be paid.

Upset with her, Thameron found it hard to contain his anger. But before he'd been able to talk further with Assia, Ibro himself had intruded and demanded that the priest either pay him for the woman's time or get on his way. A rude jest. Thameron, promising to visit Assia again, left to walk the night streets with a heavy heart.

The day that had begun with such promise ended with severe frustrations. Thameron was reprimanded when he returned to the Temple. Hapad, the brother who slept on the cot next to his, a young man whom Thameron considered a friend, whispered to him in the darkness, "They are disappointed in you."

"They are always disappointed in me."

"I'm serious, Thameron. I heard talk at supper tonight. Muthulis knows your name, and he's losing patience. He may confine you for a week."

Thameron didn't answer, but the threat found a home in his heart. He wondered why it was so difficult for him to do good, when all he wished was to do good. He lay awake in the darkness.

* * *

Muthulis, Chief Priest of the Temple of Bithitu in Erusabad and Head of the Synod of Masters and Priests, was an officious man who believed that human error—especially error stemming from enthusiasm—was more a matter of self-awareness than it was an act of outright defiance. He was, by nature, a sympathetic but cautious man. Forty-five years of service in the political backways of the Temple had taught him that strong convictions are sometimes difficult animals to leash. Thameron erred; Thameron was young and headstrong. It was splendid to have strong personalities in the Church, so long as they used their strengths in the right direction. Muthulis remembered himself as a young man. . . .

Thameron was ushered into the Chief Priest's private office and left there, standing before this stern, grandfatherly man who, from behind his desk, fixed Thameron with steely gray eyes.

Thameron stood still in the silence of Muthulis's grand, lavishly decorated office.

The long moments passed.

Muthulis's eyes did not waver.

At last, when Thameron had begun to perspire and his imagination was beginning to run rampant within him, Muthulis lowered his hands from his chin, spread them upon his desk, and asked in a grave tone, "Do you know why you have been brought here?"

Thameron cleared his throat audibly. "I—I think so, my lord."

"You *think* so?" The tone reduced Thameron to the status of a dullard. Quietly Muthulis rose and stood behind his desk. "Why, then, do you *think* you have been brought here, Thameron?"

They are disappointed in you. They are always disappointed in me. But before the stern and grave Muthulis, he was able only to mutter, "I know that I—I returned late last night."

Muthulis's brow furrowed.

"And—some other times, too. I returned late."

Muthulis sighed heavily. "We run this Temple on a schedule," he told Thameron, "and we appreciate it when our young priests are respectful enough to do as we ask of them. Our regulations are quite lenient toward our recruits, as I think you know. But don't you think it rather odd that I would require your presence here, simply because you were late in returning to your cot for a few evenings?"

Thameron felt himself coloring.

Muthulis walked around to the front of his desk, clasped his hands before him. "Let us be honest with one another, Thameron. You know as well as I that you deliberately do things which are outside the recommendations we set for our young priests. You have been reminded of this; you have been reprimanded. Now you have been brought before me. What would you have me do with you?"

Thameron was confused. "Sir, I don't quite understand." When he saw Muthulis's reaction to his comment, however, he blurted, "Do you mean—that I spend my time in the city?"

"Thameron, you spend your time in the city with the waste of humanity."

The words bit into him like an ice knife. "The—? Sir, the *waste* of humanity?"

"Why do you do it?"

"My lord, to *help* them!"

"Our doors are open to them. Must you spend all your time with them?"

"My lord Muthulis—with all due respect—I have yet to see many beggars and prostitutes enter our Temple to stand in prayer beside our businessmen and our aristocrats! Our Prophet Bithitu, in his day, sought himself to win such souls to the true Light. In point of fact, he expressly phrased many of his lessons in words to reach such people. It is not my intention to—"

"Thameron."

"Sir?"

"You are not Bithitu. And the world has changed greatly since the days of Bithitu, hasn't it?"

Thameron was startled anew. "Lord Muthulis, I don't pretend to *be* Bithitu! I merely follow the method he himself used when he brought the Word of the Light to his fellow men."

Muthulis raised a hand. "I understand what you're saying, Thameron. I truly do. You have eagerness in you, and I appreciate that. You see some come to worship with us and you see others who do not. You wish to educate those who do not, and they are usually the lesser of society."

69

"Lord Muthulis, that is exactly what I wish to do."

"I understand this. But when I tell you that the Church has ordained certain ways to accomplish this, and that you are ignoring these methods by serving the Church in your own way, you bring yourself into conflict with some basic proscriptions. I·don't think you wish to do that, do you?"

"My lord, all I wish to do—"

"Is serve your Prophet. This I know. But you must realize that the Prophet is served by his Church. I am his Church, and you are his Church. Those who fall outside our Church, either through ignorance or blasphemy or apostasy, will be dealt with—their souls gained, or their souls punished—according to the words of the Prophet and the scriptures of this Church. You are a priest. Do you not wish to be a priest?"

Terror struck him. *It can be accomplished without a priest's robes.* He felt two different voices exploding within him at once.

"Thameron, do you not wish to—"

"I *am* a priest!" he nearly shouted. "My lord—sir—I *am* a priest, you conferred that honor upon me, my status—"

"Then do honor to your robes, if you are a priest. Follow the rules and guidelines we have set down, Thameron, if you are a priest."

Prolonged silence. Thameron was thoroughly confused. "My lord. May I ask a question?"

"Certainly, Thameron."

"If—Lord Muthulis, if the words of Bithitu say one thing, but if the laws of the Church say another thing, if both set down principles—"

"Thameron—"

"—which we are to follow, then which am I to follow?"

"Thameron." Now there was an edge to Muthulis's voice. "You are a priest of this Church. You are to behave according to the regulations set down for priests of this Church."

"But if there is an apparent hypocrisy—"

"That is enough! *You* do not decide what is policy and what is not policy for this Church! You entered into an agreement with this Church when you took your vows and received your robes and rings. Did you not do that?"

"Yes, my lord, I did so."

"Then meet those obligations! Do not presume to be Bithitu!

Do not presume to know the ways of the Church when you are not even familiar with the ways of a priest! Am I understood?"

"My Lord Muthulis—"

"Am I understood, Thameron?"

"Yes."

"You are being placed on probation, and you will be monitored. You are not to spend any more time with the rabble of the city. We have set up commissions and prayer groups to help the indigent and the disadvantaged of Erusabad. Join one of them! But do *not* go into the city yourself to take money from the wealthy to give to cutthroats! Do *not* go into the city to spend your time with prostitutes! And do *not* stray from this Temple without first reporting to one of your masters your business for leaving! Is *that* understood?"

"Yes—yes, Lord Muthulis."

"Then you may go. Now. And hereafter, Thameron, as you wear your priest's garments, see yourself as a priest and believe yourself to be a priest of this Church! Is *that* understood?"

Thameron stared at him. Stared in mute astonishment.

"Is it? *Is that understood?*"

"Do you realize what he said to me?" Thameron asked Hapad. They were sitting on one of the benches that lined a wide avenue not far from the Temple.

Hapad's reply was a careful one. "I tried to warn you, Thameron. You must—"

"Hapad, he is a hypocrite! The Church is built on *men*, not on the Word of Light!"

His friend chuckled. "For someone so intelligent," he commented, "sometimes you're very naive, Thameron. Look you." He pointed.

Across the street a trio of mendicants sat on the ground, their backs to the wall of a building. From time to time they listlessly lifted their hands, holding out empty palms to passers-by.

"You are a priest," Hapad reminded Thameron. "You're not a beggar. You have a cot to sleep on, you have food when you want it, you have friends, you have—"

"I have a knot in my soul, Hapad. Don't you understand that those beggars, whatever condition they're in, may be

71

closer to Bithitu in their poverty than Muthulis is, with all his wealth?''

"I understand what you're saying, yes. Thameron, if you look for perfection, you'll always be disappointed. At least on earth. The Word of Bithitu must be spread. The Church is the best method for that. Perhaps some things are wrong with the Church—it is only an organization of men, after all—but those things can be changed.''

"I'm not so sure.''

"Even if they can't be changed, then isn't more good being done than harm? Don't the important things the Church does far outweigh the imperfections?''

Thameron shook his head. "He told me—Muthulis as much as said that if I did not follow the Church, then I did not follow Bithitu. Bithitu came before the Church.''

"Perhaps he was becoming upset. Knowing your personality, you drove him to it.'' Hapad smiled.

"I am not wrong,'' Thameron insisted.

"Nor is the Church, my friend. But you are not completely right, either.''

Thameron lifted a fisted hand to his chin, settled into a brooding posture.

"Thameron, do you see the dome of the Temple?''

"Yes.''

He did not look to see it, but that wasn't necessary. The dome was the tallest in Erusabad; it towered far above them and, with its gold facing, glowed all day long, every day, in the brilliant sunlight, with eye-hurting intensity.

"The Temple,'' Hapad argued, "is bigger than we are and can see farther than we can, and more clearly. I think of the Church in that way. Perhaps it can't see everything—only Bithitu can do that—but it's stronger than we are, taller than we are, it has survived longer than we will, and it can see—''

"There is a way,'' Thameron interrupted him.

"What?''

"There is a way.''

"A way for what? To do what?''

"Muthulis told me to join one of the city groups of priests if it was so important to me to serve there. Hapad, it won't work! I've spent months in the city; the people there trust me, they know me. If I become like other priests, all the work is lost and the people won't listen any longer.''

72

"What do you mean, there is a way?"

"A special dispensation. The Church grants—"

"Oh, Thameron!"

"The Church grants them. You know they do! If a priest can draft a proposal and show just cause—"

"Thameron, they'll never allow you to do that!"

"They must hear me!" he shot back, volatile and strong-willed. "If I request a hearing for a special dispensation, the Metropolitan must hear me!"

Hapad let out a heavy breath. "That's true, but—"

"I'll draft the proposal, and Andoparas will hear me. They cannot refuse! I shall build an argument that will make sense even to Muthulis's closed mind. And when they see the sense of what I'm doing, they *will* allow me to do what is best!"

What is best, my friend, or only what it is you want to do? Hapad shook his head forlornly and stared at the high golden dome of the all-seeing Temple.

4.

Every morning, following services, Thameron went to the library in the southern wing of the Temple. Every afternoon and every evening he returned to the library. He studied the scriptures of Bithitu and the important commentaries and epistles. He borrowed arguments from as many sources as he could, all orthodox in doctrine. He paraphrased Omu-thates, sanctified as the first High Priest and Commentator of the Light. He borrowed from Gheini of Soramand and Thos-othos of Benadbar, both profound Church scholastics. He took words from the scriptures of Bithitu himself.

And if you see the heart of a child, listen to that heart and listen to its voice: for the child is not afraid but full of wonder, and the heart of the child is eager to learn, to share and know. Be as the child.

When at last he had composed a rough version of his proposal, Thameron turned to one of his learning masters for help in presenting his paper in accepted form. His master was bound to aid him, for that was the way of the Church; but at every opportunity he adjured Thameron not to pursue the matter.

"They cannot refuse me," Thameron reminded him.

"But you will make enemies."

When we reason to illumine the Good, we worship at the altar of On, the all-in-one; but when we dissemble and make argument to confound the Truth of the Light, we dwell in Shadow and serve the actions of men.

It was such a small thing, really, but small and simple as grand designs and great actions are essentially small and simple. The truth of it, the sense of it, seemed to him

74

tremendously compelling. It even occurred to Thameron, as he pored over the old texts, as he imaginatively relived the early days of the Church, brought to life for him from old scrolls, that perhaps he was creating a new dimension in the affairs of the Church. Perhaps he was broadening its attitude, reawakening it to fundamentally powerful things; perhaps he was at the forefront of some new direction for the Prophet's Church. For the Church could not continue as it always had; it could not remain stolid and old while the world quickened around it. Bithitu himself had observed that all things are change; the Church must change, grow, become fresh and vital, become new again.

When at last he was finished, and satisfied with what he had done, he read his finished proposal to his master, and later to Hapad. Both agreed that they felt Thameron was making too great an issue of an unimportant matter. They did not agree with him that he was breaking new ground in Church direction: all he wanted, in essence, was the freedom to work with the poor and wicked of the earth on his own terms. Neither thought that his argument would alter the opinion of the Council.

Thameron refused to let their pessimism disenhearten him. Boiling with enthusiasm, he requested an audience with Muthulis and was admitted into the Priest's office the following afternoon. There, with all deference and protocol, Thameron submitted his argument, stated his case, and asked to be interviewed by the Holy Council once his proposal had been deliberated upon.

Muthulis accepted the small scroll. He regarded the youth sadly and asked him, "Have you learned nothing? Is this the result of what we have taught you? Why do you persist?"

"I wish to have my argument submitted, and I wish to have it reviewed and decided upon by the Council."

"And so it shall be done, Thameron. But I ask you again: Is this truly what you wish to do with all that we've taught you?"

What does it mean to a man to hold the wealth of coffers, if his heart is cold to his neighbor's heart? Truly I say to you, there is more bounty in one soul of a man than there is in all the gold in all the coffers of all the world.

He learned two days later that his proposal had been accepted for review by the Holy Council, and that his interview would take place in three days. Thameron was ecstatic. He wished to celebrate in some way, but he knew—even without Hapad telling him—that for his own sake it would be best not to go into the city. Thameron wished to; he was in high spirits and he wanted to share that enthusiasm, and he hadn't been to visit the people in the streets for well over a week. But he felt certain that, once his decision was delivered, he would not only be given the freedom to preach the scriptures to the unfortunate of the earth, but encouraged to do so by the Church itself.

Satisfied of this, he became a model priest during those three intervening days. He rose early and stayed wide awake during matinal services; he spent his days on the Church grounds, helping his elders or entering into the discussions of doctrine and policy that were held spontaneously in the gardens and the classrooms. His change of manner was noticed by his masters and was reported to Muthulis, who reacted with some doubt as to the validity of Thameron's change of heart and commented that the child is always on its best behavior when it expects to be rewarded for a good performance.

On the morning of his interview, Thameron awoke in good spirits, cleaned his robe before donning it, ate a hearty breakfast. Following the morning devotions he was escorted into the chamber of the Holy Council. Thameron had been here only once before, when as a novice he had been given a tour of the Temple. Unfamiliar with the chamber and unaware of what exactly he should do, he took a seat, changed it, then changed it again when informed where he should position himself. He had assumed that his interview would be the first matter on the agenda, and as soon as Andoparas, the Metropolitan, and Muthulis and three other elders seated themselves behind their table on the high dais, Thameron rose to his feet. One of the wards standing nearby whispered to him to be seated and remain seated until called upon to advance.

Thameron watched as a long, slow parade of men were called forth one by one, as they advanced before the judgment seat and heard their complaints settled or their suggestions vetoed. One priest was petitioning for a change of quarters, another asking for an allowance to perform some deed or service, a third demanding that action be taken with the city patrol to control the loitering of certain beggars and other

76

undesirables on the western steps of the Temple. One by one they advanced; one by one they heard their proposals read back to them and listened to the verdicts as set down by Andoparas. A change of quarters was impossible at present, for there were no free cells; but the man would be given any materials necessary to effect needed repairs in his current quarters. Money requested for such-and-such a service was denied at this time, but the proposal would be placed on file with further action to be determined upon at a later date. As for the loitering of the beggars and others . . .

The wait became interminable. Thameron's mind wandered, he thought of Assia and—

"Thameron, Priest of the Third Rank of the Temple of Bithitu of Erusabad, step you forward!"

His stomach jumped, his heart danced as he jerked up from his bench and moved ahead, stepping on the toes of those seated by him, to reach the aisle. Advancing toward the judgement dais, Thameron became painfully aware of his poor posture and his awkward gait. He seemed to walk forever beneath the stern gaze of the five elders, and when at last he reached the first step of the dais he almost collapsed from agitation before managing to kneel obediently. Rising up again, he stared into their faces. Five of them: all old men, dressed in their colored albs of station, perspiring in the stifling heat of the closed chamber, looking down at him with blank or bored expressions.

While scribes copied his words on parchment rolls, Muthulis stood and read Thameron's proposal. When he was finished, the Chief Priest handed the scroll to Andoparas, at his left, and resumed his seat.

Thameron, trembling with anticipation, stared up at the Metropolitan of the Temple, the most powerful man in the Church.

Andoparas glanced at the scroll. "There is good thought here," he admitted. "Unfortunately, it is misguided thought. This issue has been raised several times. The matter was settled satisfactorily four generations ago by Andosaras the Second, who guided the creation of secular work-groups to help bring the Light to the unfortunate. We suggest that Priest Thameron, whose aptitude for research seems considerable, busy himself more properly by placing his sentiments with the labors of these work-groups. It is not advantageous for the

Church—in fact, it is obviously self-defeating for this Church—to encourage individual interpretation of doctrine by members of our caste, and certainly so by members this young and inexperienced. Proposal denied.''

Thameron was stunned. He could not speak; he was stunned. But he raised a hand to attempt something in his own defense; this was, after all, ideally an interview—

Muthulis leaned toward Andoparas, whispered something in the Metropolitan's ear. Andoparas regarded Thameron critically.

"My—my lord," Thameron protested, "if you please—"

"Furthermore," announced Andoparas, a coldness apparent in his tone, "we think it pertinent to add that any appeals on this matter, or any further attempts by Priest Thameron to pursue this course of action independently, will be met with the strictest of probationary punishment; and continued violations of the common regulations dealing with our secular brethren will be met with by dishonorable expulsion from the ranks of the priesthood and the order of this Church."

It seemed unbelievable. Head swimming, Thameron stared at Andoparas; and in that moment nothing existed in the world for him save that elder's cold eyes, broad forehead, tight mouth, cynical expression. A growl, a reaction, flame boiled in his throat; his heart pulsed; he stared at Muthulis and fought down an impulse to leap, run, jump at the man—as hatred, disgust, anger possessed him—

"My lord! If you would—"

Andoparas slapped his hand loudly on the table. "The verdict has been passed. Make way for the next petitioner. That is all!"

5.

Thameron was as astonished by his reaction to the Council's verdict as he was by the verdict itself.

Never before had he felt such things. Rage. Hatred. Impotence. Desire for vengeance. He had been lied to; he had been made a toy in some elaborate game; he saw himself as a fool. It was as though all around him made a mockery of him and made a mockery of the ideals, the belief he had always thought made him one with the world. Whatever tenuous, half-visualized image he had held of Bithitu, the Church, and its masters was now dashed. Whatever hopes he had seen for himself, whatever goals he had hoped to accomplish, were now brought to an end. He was a fool, he had been a fool, he had been regarded as a fool all along.

He had hurried from the Council chamber and raced through the Temple, his mind a cloudy red furnace. Voices called out, but Thameron had not even looked up in response. Only peripherally aware of what he was doing or where he was going, he fled with quick, angry steps from the Temple grounds into the street.

He began to walk, to clear his mind, to order his universe, and to try to fathom the depths of raging emotion within him, to make sense of all the lies he had been told today, last week, all those long years.

"Priest!"

The voice was unknown to him. Thameron paused and looked up, flushed and trembling. It was an aristocrat, pressing two gold coins into his hand.

"For the Church," the aristocrat told him solemnly and passed on.

Thameron stood looking at the gold in his hand. For the

Church? For the *Church*? Was he a fool? His first impulse was to throw the coins to the ground or hurl them across the avenue. Better to cast them into a fire, have them melted and turned into some pornographic object of art—

Thameron looked around him. He realized that in his impassioned anger he had hurried halfway across the city. Around the next corner was Ibro's tavern.

Assia would be there.

Heart pounding, head aching, Thameron shoved the gold coins into a pocket of his robe and continued down the street, around the corner.

Early dusk was filling the overcast sky as he entered Ibro's tavern.

He took a chair at a table hidden in a corner, sat silently, and stared at the few patrons in the place. Behind the counter Ibro and an overweight, unattractive woman were taking orders for drinks and meals. A man at the counter asked for another gourd of ale. A thin red-haired woman came down the stairs at the rear of the tavern in the company of a porcine man. She looked depressed; he looked depressed. He crossed the room and went out by a side door, while she asked for something to drink, then returned upstairs with it.

Ibro, glancing at Thameron, whispered to the fat woman. Irritably, she walked to his table and asked him what he wanted.

"What did you say?"

"Do you want anything? To eat? To drink?"

He shrugged. He wasn't hungry, and he had never—"A cup of wine."

The fat woman arched one eyebrow.

Thameron reached into his pocket, drew out one of the gold coins, and handed it to her.

She took it. Murderers, thieves, pimps, sailors, soldiers, aristocrats—now a priest buying wine in a tavern. Well, why not? The world no longer made any sense; we might as well offer the priest a jump at one of the girls, too. Back at the counter, she poured a cup of wine. "For the priest," she told Ibro.

He chuckled and made some obscene comment, told her that the priest was a regular visitor, made change for the gold piece. The fat woman returned to Thameron, placed his wine and change on the table, and stared at him for a long moment.

Thameron met her look. Finally she shook her head and turned on her heel, huffed away.

And he watched her as she walked away. There had been a time—years ago? but yesterday?—when he would have looked upon this woman's obese body as yet another aspect of the marvelous design of the immortal On, the all-in-one. But now he was repelled by her, saw only her ugliness, overloaded with flesh and wrinkles.

He sipped his wine.

The old man at the counter finished his brew, turned and looked at Thameron, advanced on unsure legs toward him.

"Brother, I am a criminal in the eyes of our Prophet."

Thameron regarded him darkly. "So am I, friend."

"Please, brother. I'm drunk, but I need help, I need—My boy died yesterday. He was a good boy, he was; he—"

Impatiently Thameron asked him: "What do you want me to tell you? That he was saved?"

"Please, brother . . ." Tears threatened at the rims of the man's puffed eyes. "My boy is dead. I don't know why. It was an accident, it never should have— My wife—I think she blames me because I only—"

"Listen to me," Thameron rasped at him. "I'm not a priest. I'm not a real priest. I'm an actor. I'm only wearing these robes because I'm an actor."

The drunken man went ashy-faced, despondent and ashamed; he dropped a loud hand on Thameron's table to support himself as he swayed. "I—I thought—"

"I'm a false priest," Thameron admitted to him. "I can give you no comfort."

"I—I only wished to—" The old man turned away, looked back at the counter, wove an uncertain path across the floor to the door. He paused there, stared back at Thameron, shook his head, and went out.

Thameron swallowed more of his wine.

I'm a false priest. . . .

Sandals first, then slim white legs appeared on the stairs across the shadowed room. An arm and a hand on the railing, a slim waist revealing an open-fronted embroidered vest . . .

Assia.

Suddenly he was shocked by her appearance.

"Thameron?"

Ibro, behind the counter, laughed harshly. "He's drinking,

81

too!'' he grunted. "I knew there was a human being under them robes! Priest! He wasn't coming here to be no priest!''

Assia glowered at him and hurried across the floor. "Thameron! What's the matter? Why are you—''

"Look at that fat pig!'' Thameron growled angrily, staring at Ibro with mad fire in his eyes.

Assia was frightened; she'd never seen him like this. "Thameron! What is this? Something's wrong, what's happened?''

Tilting unsurely in his chair, he faced her and slurred, "They're liars.''

"What are you saying?''

"They're liars. Liars! All of them! Muthulis, Hapad, the Church, the Prophet—all of them, they lie! They lied to me! They wanted to see me crawl; they have no vision; they resent my vision; they wanted to trap me; they wanted—''

"Oh, Thameron, what's *happened?* Tell me.''

He threw a hand to his face and began to sob.

Assia sat down beside him, put her arms around him, held him to comfort him.

They went upstairs to her room. Assia made him lie down on her bed so that he could rest. He insisted that he wanted wine. To calm him, Assia went downstairs and took a jug of wine from the back room, telling Ibro to mark it on her bill. As she returned upstairs, Ibro followed her into her room.

"I don't care why you're here,'' he announced to Thameron, who was still on the bed, "but she's one of my girls, and anybody who spends time with her pays for it.''

Thameron's eyes lit up hotly; throwing himself forward, he reached into his pocket, pulled out his second gold piece. "Here!'' he snarled, throwing it directly at Ibro's massive belly.

Ibro caught it with a deft movement.

"How much is that good for? The hour? The night? The week? What kind of price do you get for her? Or does it depend on how much she does without complaining?''

Ibro laughed at him. "Assia's worth one in long gold for the night. But do you know what to do with her, priest?''

"Get out of here!'' Thameron snarled at him.

"You're in my house now, priest. I'm not in yours! Be polite, or I'll dump you down the stairs!'' Ibro unleashed a string of laughter as he went out, closing the door behind him.

"Dog!" Assia spat.

Thameron groaned and fell back on the cushions. "Give me a cup of wine."

No, she didn't love the robe or the office; she loved a young man, and she loved the young man's spirit. And she knew she desired Thameron—not the priest in him, but the man in him, Thameron himself.

"They lied to me," he complained to her again, his voice losing none of its bitterness.

"The world always lies to us," she whispered. "You must realize that, Thameron. But don't let it—"

"I'm no fool, but—I've been a fool all my life, believing—"

"Please, no. Don't let them do this to you! Thameron—Thameron, now you're free. You're free of all of it! Don't let them do this to you. You're not a priest; you never were a priest; you're much more than a priest! I—I can see that in you."

"It's all that I know. All that I am, Assia."

"No, no," she disagreed. "You're much more than that. I've always felt it. *You* must understand that, too. Thameron—look at me."

His senses were fogged with wine, but he was alert, awake. Still on the bed, he turned his face to her; Assia was sitting on a chair.

"What am I, Thameron?"

"You are—Assia, a woman."

"No, no—*what* am I, Thameron?"

He didn't understand. "You're a—woman," he repeated.

"I'm a prostitute, Thameron. A whore."

It hurt him to hear her refer to herself that way. "Assia, what have I always told you? That's only a name, and a name means nothing by itself. You're Assia, a woman. If you choose—if it has been chosen for you—"

"Are you a priest, then, Thameron? Is that what you are? That name? Or are you a man, first?"

He was startled. The obviousness of it. The truth of it. Everything he had believed, everything he had habitually looked at with such clarity, turned around. He began to weep.

Assia set down the wine jug, leaned forward. Thameron sobbed quietly while she, with a warm hand, stroked his hair.

"I love you," she told him.

The room was very still, lighted only with the glow of two oil lamps. They were alone. The wine had taken its effect on Thameron, as had emotional exhaustion.

"I love you, Thameron," she told him quietly.

"Do you?" he whispered.

"I always have. I fought it, at first. It seemed ludicrous. But it's true. I love you. I know, too, that you love me."

He groaned. "What can I do? What can we do?" And he rolled over, turning his back to her.

"Look at me, Thameron."

Slowly, cautiously, he rolled over, stared into her deep eyes.

She removed her vest, dropped it to the floor. Her flesh glowed in the warm lamplight.

"Kiss me, Thameron."

He was a man. He kissed her, pressing his lips to hers. Assia opened her mouth, forced her tongue into Thameron's mouth, and they shared wet, frantic kisses.

Gently, then, she urged him down, because she loved him. He was a man; he was not a priest but a man, and all that she recognized in him was true, true for her, when he kissed her, when she urged him down and he kissed her arms and her breasts.

He was frightened, excited, ashamed—all at once. He felt the shadows in him vanish before a new light, a new glow.

"Kiss my breasts, Thameron."

He was surprised at the weight of her breasts; he marveled at them, marveled at their texture. He stroked them with his fingers, thumbed their nipples, and smiled childishly as Assia's nipples grew hard and thick beneath his touch. Smiled because he was responsible for that, and responsible for the moans of pleasure that came from Assia's throat.

She stood up and removed her skirt, bent to unfasten her sandals. She told Thameron to take off his robe, and he did. He removed his under-robes as well, and his sandals, then lay back on the bed. For the first time in his life he was naked with a woman. Assia lay down beside him and ran her hands lightly along his body. Thameron shivered.

Assia smiled at him, kissed his mouth, then moved her head to his chest and licked his nipples. Thameron told her not to do that, but Assia ignored him. She stroked his penis with her hand, gripping it firmly, moving her hand up and down. Thameron felt a hot thickness gathering in his bowels, felt a heaviness possess him.

"Assia . . ."

She kissed his belly, moved her kisses down to his thighs, then took him in her mouth. Up and down, her eyes still looking up at him with familiar friendship. Thameron's hands curled tightly on the bed; his fingers knotted on the cushions. He moaned. His body was glossy with sweat. He felt the hugeness in him building, growing thicker, aching . . .

Thameron felt the hot hugeness exploding from deep within him. He gasped and groaned. Assia reached up with her free hand to stroke his chest; Thameron looked down and saw her sparkling eyes, saw her grin at him.

She did not explain why she was doing this, and Thameron, worried, was not certain that he wished her to explain.

Assia stretched out alongside him, her body aglow in the lamplight, her flesh damp with perspiration, her long legs shimmering, her belly soft, the hair between her legs like one of the warm, dark shadows of the room.

"Kiss me, Thameron," she urged him softly. "Kiss me wherever you please."

He began to weep.

"Oh, I love you," she promised him.

He wept for joy.

Alive with the sense of his own body, aware of himself as he never had been before, he crouched beside her, feeling awkward but proud, and kissed Assia's face, kissed her pulsing throat, trailed his gasping kisses down her breasts and belly and legs. He moved his face between her thighs and explored, with tongue and lips, with teeth and fingers, the pungent secrets of her, his doubts and questions, tentative, answered by Assia's gasps of pleasure. Excited, because he was exciting her, he was amazed and delighted with the taste of her; he discovered fine wonders in the thickness of her damp lips, in the aroma of her. He licked, kissed Assia's folds of wet flesh and her sensitive little bud (she called it) as she moaned and rolled her thighs, hunched her hips, moved her fingers in his hair, scratched his shoulders, and laughed, moaned, sighed. . . .

*   *   *

85

When he awoke, he thought it was to the light of dawn. But the room was still dark, and the light was the glow of the oil lamps.

Assia, awake beside him, kissed him, rubbed her hands on his body, tickled him and licked his face, sucked on his ears.

"I love you, Thameron."

Who was he? Where was he? And what . . . ? Was he . . .?

A man, some deep resonance in him promised, reminded, urged.

He moved atop her. Assia guided him into her, and Thameron grunted at still another intense sensation. Was this his body? Where had this body been? Was this his body, the same body that was attached to his mind, his thoughts and worries and arguments and emotions?

They moved with one another, hips rocking, grinding together, Thameron at one moment imagining himself as an animal coupling in some primitive, secret fashion, and in the next feeling himself soaring to incredible heights of transfigured glory.

The room tilted. The lamplight glowed in his eyes, dazzled his brain. Drops of sweat broke from his forehead and splashed on Assia's face. She clutched him. He bent into her, felt her muscles guiding him, pulling on him, felt his own body more aware of what it was accomplishing than his mind was. He grunted, moaned, spasmed in quick little bursts of wet life, while Assia dug her fingers into him and pushed, shrieked, pushed, twisted. . . .

He awoke to the dull light of a gray dawn at her window. The oil lamps had burned out. Half asleep, feeling like a phantom consciousness roused to some uncertain life, he was aware of Assia's sticky body next to his, aware of the weight in his arms and the warmth of the naked flesh. Aware, too, of her quiet sobs. Not happy sobs, now, but sad ones. She was crying. Her back was to him; he held her in his arms, and he could hear her muffled sobs.

But he was not entirely awake, and though in his mind he wanted to sit up, speak with her, share a thousand more things with her, kisses and words and thoughts and promises, he was too exhausted; and he fell asleep once more, listening to her broken moans, feeling her body in his naked arms. . . .

6.

Late that morning, Thameron made his way up the wide steps of the main entrance doors, walked slowly down the central nave, and followed the bending hallways to the rear of the Temple, where the sleeping chambers were. He felt the eyes upon him.

But he no longer cared.

He heard voices whisper as he passed by, but he did not care.

In his room, he lay down on his cot, threw his hands behind his head, thought of and rethought all that had happened to him since the Council interview of yesterday.

"When you have cleaned yourself and made yourself presentable, you will report to my office, Thameron." It was one of his masters, regarding him with a look of painful disquietude.

Thameron stared at him.

"Do you hear me?"

With no deference in his tone: "Yes. I hear you."

"Clean yourself. You look like an animal."

His master turned and, with a grunt of complete disgust, left him.

He lay where he was for a long time, thinking. . . .

He heard the bells sound the noon meal and sat up as several young priests returned, some to change clothes, others to urinate in the pots in the corners, or to retrieve personal objects they had forgotten. Hapad was among them.

"Thameron!" He was shocked; he hurried to his friend, sat on the cot and stared, wide-eyed. "Where have you been? What's happened to you?"

"I left."

87

"They are furious with you!"

"Are they?"

"Why did you do it?" Hapad asked him with grief. "My friend, my friend—why are you doing this? Don't you know they'll punish you?"

"Let them punish me," was Thameron's cold reply. "My eyes have been opened to truths far greater than Muthulis or Andoparas know."

"Don't speak that way!"

Thameron grinned at him. "Everything has turned around, Hapad! You can't imagine what visions have opened to me!"

"Thameron, don't speak this way. You're a priest—my brother, you must—"

But Thameron waved an impatient hand at him, quickly glanced around the room to see if he would be overheard. The others had already left for lunch.

"It is *life*, Hapad!" Thameron announced, chuckling.

"Thameron, what—"

"They are *fools*!" he declared. "They lie to us every day! They are dogs! Hapad, Hapad—I left yesterday, I was furious, I went into the city—"

"Oh, Thameron—"

"I went into the city, my friend. I got drunk. I did! I visited a woman I know—"

"Thameron, no!"

"I did, I *did*!"

Hapad stood up quickly, terror on his face, and anger, disappointment. "You wore the robes of a *priest*!" he shouted. "How could you do such things in the robes of a *priest*?"

Thameron did not feel in the least humiliated. "They drug us!" was his hot reply. "They play us for fools, Hapad! They connive, they lie, they twist us and turn us until—"

"*Silence*!" came a loud voice from the door.

Both turned their heads, looked upon the dormitory's archimandrite—and the gray visage of Muthulis.

"You!" Muthulis pointed a finger at Thameron. "Go with your master. You"—to Hapa—"come with me!"

It came swiftly.

Weeping, Hapad betrayed his friend, falling to his knees before the Chief Priest and praying for forgiveness. "I am confused!" he sobbed. "Where is my loyalty? To my friend or to our Prophet?"

Muthulis did not hesitate to remind Hapad that his loyalty unquestionably belonged to Bithitu and Bithitu's Church. For the guilt of being friend to someone so lost and insolent as Thameron, Hapad was sentenced to a week in a solitary cell. Muthulis passed that verdict upon him; but when the heartbroken youth screamed out in total agony at such a punishment, Muthulis suspended it and reduced Hapad's reprimand to a week of probation, as long as he kept to the Temple grounds.

Thameron was ushered into Muthulis's office by the archimandrite, even as the crying Hapad left. Standing before the Chief Priest, Thameron was defiant, his stance bold, his eyes red with wrath.

Muthulis's verdict was swift and cruel; in two sentences he accused Thameron of his crimes, denounced him, stripped him of his caste and rank, excommunicated him from his Prophet, and banished him from the Temple.

"And if there were any greater penalty I could heap upon you or exact from you," Muthulis proclaimed, "I would not hesitate to do it. You have soiled your faith."

Thameron sneered at him.

"You may go now," Muthulis told him. "If you wish to wait for us to draw up the final Orders of Expulsion, you may appear in Holy Council tomorrow morning and have your reply to this sentence read into the Codex. I would prefer that you go now, as quickly as possible, so that you will no longer defame this Temple with your presence."

Thameron answered him, "You are a fool, and I have only one answer to give you, and Andoparas and your whole hypocritical Temple, your whole hypocritical religion. You will be destroyed!"

You will be destroyed, [Bithitu had said to his judges] by a love greater than the hatred which compels you.

"Begone!" Muthulis yelled at him, getting to his feet and waving a trembling hand at him. "Begone! You have defiled us—defiled us!"

How should we deal with the guilty? Let us treat them as though they were innocent. Let the criminal be taken in by the family he has harmed; let the thief work for the merchant from whom he has stolen; let the murderer repay his wicked-

ness by selling his life to the family of the murdered. I say to you, let those who have strayed learn that they have strayed in ignorance, and that wisdom, through love, joins them to their brothers, where ignorance, through hatred, casts them from their own brothers.

"I am sorry!" Hapad exclaimed mournfully. "I am sorry, so sorry, my friend!"

"You have no reason to feel guilty for telling them anything, Hapad. You did what you believed to be the right thing. But, my friend, I'm more sorry for you than you are for me. You still believe their lies. You are good, Hapad. I am good. But it is not good to be in the service of liars."

Hapad fell upon his cot, weeping.

Thameron removed his priest's robes and pulled on what street clothes he had been able to find—a pair of breeches, a shirt and vest, and a long leather coat. Into an old purse he deposited the remainder of the money given him by the aristocrat the day before.

"I go now," he told Hapad. "But I will see you again, my friend—someday. Trust to that."

"Oh, Thameron . . ." Hapad sat up, stared worriedly at his friend, then, impulsively, plucked from his finger the golden ring that he wore. Thameron had removed his own, but Hapad offered him his as a reminder of their friendship. "Know that there was good here," he told Thameron. "Please. The world is wide. I am afraid for you. Wherever you travel, my friend, please keep this with you, to remind you—"

"I will, my brother. And I thank you for it." Thameron took him in his arms, hugged him, and looked him in the eyes. "On be with you, my brother. I know not what path I will take, but—I am not evil, Hapad, and I do not wish to hate. On be with you!"

"And with you, Thameron. And with you. I am very afraid for you. . . ."

The afternoon was cool and cloudy, and a strong wind, harbinger of storm, scatted litter down the streets as Thameron made his way to Ibro's tavern.

Assia was astonished to see him dressed in old clothes; she had never seen him without his priest's robes.

"They have expelled me," he admitted to her. "I am no more a priest."

"Oh, gods! Thameron!"

He told her that it was far better this way. New things had blossomed in his spirit. He declared to Assia that he felt he had to go away—make a voyage. It would clear his mind, prepare him for a new life. And he wanted her to go with him.

"Take what money you have," Thameron urged Assia. "We'll go together. Board a ship, sail to—"

"I can't!" she cried, amazed and puzzled by his sudden change. "I cannot, Thameron! My father—he needs me—"

"He brutalizes you!"

"But he needs me, Thameron! And *I* need to—"

"*I* need you, Assia!"

"I—I cannot." She began to cry. She coughed.

The realization of her illness struck him afresh. He calmed and told Assia to go see a physician. He would help pay.

"You go away, Thameron," she urged him. "You sail away. Come back to me in a month, in two months. I'll save some money. . . . I'll run away from Ibro when you get back; then we can go. Find us a city, Thameron—find us somewhere to live, and I'll go with you. I will!"

"Do you mean that?"

"I do, Thameron! I do!"

He threw his arms about her; she lavished kisses upon him. He wanted to stay; he wanted to go; he was a stranger to himself. . . .

"I love you, Assia."

"Then come back for me, Thameron."

He touched her hair, looked into her eyes, embraced her. Outside her window the day was gray, cloudy. Raindrops began to fall. Holding onto each other, in a room above a tavern, they were alone, and young, and frightened.

PART III

End without Mercy

1.

The season of grief, speechless, the hour of mourning, forever.

On the seventeenth day of the month of Elru the Lion, in the Year of the Lion—five days after the death of King Evarris of the empire—Dursoris dos Evarro edos Yta was placed in a cedarwood box on the wide, white plain of warm ashes and, beneath a summer sun, immolated and returned to the memories of the gods. Wine was poured. Gongs were struck. Prayers were lifted; breasts were beaten. Against the curved azure sky flecked with white clouds, Sim the Moon yet glowed and birds wheeled and floated—perpetrators.

O fears profound, cauterizing memories! O pain boundless, shrinking full life to a whisper of shadows! O death of king, death of prince, death of empire! O torments waiting, tears unflowing, flames unlit, passions unspent! O clay, O clay, O journey of sins! O Children of Empire, misbegotten of the gods, gratuitous—you have sown vengeance's crimes, you shall reap long trails of ashes watered with tears, nurtured with agonies! O uncounted years, travails are upon you! The serpent has suckled at the lamb, the sword has cleaved the dove, the wine is bitter with blood! O gods, die with us, do not survive us!

Yta—alone on the plain, long after dusk. Alone with the torches on poles—alone with the long parade of sorrows, the tired procession of crimes. No debasement, no humiliation, no confusion enough to purge the endless, unending end.

O gods, die with us, do not survive us!
O crimes, where are your promises?
O mother's sins, find the door in the fallen ruins!

*　　*　　*

Deep, where unending pain causes an end to pain—low, where the ceaseless cries reduce themselves to whispers—soft, where torment finds knowledge . . .

In the Hall of Darkness, where there is no light, no light, no light . . .

. . . a light will grow . . .

. . . to make the darkness darker still. . . .

Uncoil, serpent!
Rise, furrowed seeds!
Carry back in echoes, all sounds raised!
Return, life, to the womb your grave, cradle of fears!
Come, death, with laughter, no shouts.
Come, death, with the friendly sorrow.
Come, death, with no blood, no ache of years.
Come, death, laughing, wrap up my soul, cleanse my eyes, caress me with the lover's touch, last Friend. . . .

Yta, alone on the plain of warm ashes, visited by Death, as the cold closes in, as the night revolves down in promise:

"You have known me all your life, and though my guises are many, my masks myriad, my purposes are uniform. Touch my fingers of bone—yes—breathe the ashes of my mouth, come into my closet and reproach no one, gaze upon the stars—you are immortal. Time waits here, with me—and no crimes exist. . . ."

Yta, escorted by slow, silent guards, sentinels grim as heartbreaks, led the somber procession back into the city, to the palace. Yta, the uncomforted. Yta, prepared at last, resolved at last, to return herself to Mother Hea's mercy.

And may the gods reduce the golden crown to golden ashes. . . .

2.

Late in the evening, with the fresh smoke of funeral still in the air, untouched cups of wine before them, and the silence, heavy as clouds, all around them, Adred and Galvus sat in Adred's chambers.

"Why?" Galvus wanted to know. "Why?"

Adred shook his head.

"I feel as though I've been transformed, turned into another person, turned into . . . rock—steel. My body doesn't feel the same to me."

Adred understood. "Cry, if you want to, Galvus. It's good to cry."

"Do you think I'm still a boy? That I should cry because—"

"Men cry."

"I don't feel like crying. There are knives and poisons in me, Adred. Everything's a lie. Everything is a lie."

"Galvus, if anything were to happen to Elad now, you're next in line to inherit the throne."

"I don't want the throne."

"Listen, now. I don't care to talk about this, but you must understand. Elad has committed great crimes. What if this . . . whirlpool of blood isn't over yet? Elad might be assassinated—poisoned—he might die by accident. But there's fear in the air. Tonight, tomorrow, twenty years from now—revenge may come. Like in a play, Galvus. Unless your uncle marries and has a child, you are next for the throne."

Galvus wanted no part of it. "Let the throne fall then, when Elad dies. Let the throne die. Let jackals fight over it, let the people rule themselves. I want no court life! I don't want men like my father surrounding me, men like Elad,

96

killing their own brothers, betraying their own mothers, to gain the throne! Is that why we're here?''

Adred admired the young man: everything a good king should be. "It—doesn't have to be that way, Galvus. You know that. The throne is as good and strong as the man or woman who sits upon it—or as evil and weak.''

"But suppose, Adred, all this is planned by the gods? Suppose grandfather wasn't the great King we think he was, from the gods' perspective? Suppose, for the history of the world, he was actually a poor King? Suppose that Elad, for all this, become a great King? Suppose all this was necessary for him to become a great King?''

Adred smiled strangely. "I appreciate the thought, Galvus; but to suppose is to stray from the facts. You've been reading Radulis, but you've been misreading parts of him, too. You don't believe any of what you just said. I don't believe it. It isn't true, any of it. I, for one, would lose faith in everything if Evarris weren't the good King we all know he was.''

"But suppose—''

"Suppose," Adred interrupted him, "that it's just as it is? Suppose Evarris was a great King? Suppose his day is done? Suppose your father murdered your uncle, Dursoris? Suppose your father is executed? Suppose Elad takes the throne and is not a good King? Suppose it's all exactly as it seems to be?''

"I did not want this. Not this life—not this pain. There is a limit to what humanity can endure.''

"You'd think there must be.''

"We lived in good times; I was raised by a good mother in a great nation. Can that end overnight? Can the world end overnight? Could the gods be dying, and slaying the world, or causing us all to go insane as they die?''

Adred looked away from him; this came too close to feelings of profound, fearful truth. Hollow, he watched the dance of a candle flame and thought of religious parables. Small comfort, now.

Soon, in the dimness beside him, he heard Galvus—a man—beginning to cry. . . .

"Is it my fault?" Orain murmured, wondering aloud.

Quiet, in white robes, Yta, haggard and undone, sat with her.

"Perhaps I was the cause of it, somehow, when I left Cyrodian, when I turned to Dursoris."

"Hush," Yta solaced her. "Shhh. . . . It's not your fault. Yours is not the blame."

Orain began to weep. "Oh, Mother. . . ."

"Orain, I leave tomorrow to do my penance, but you must keep your heart in trust to strong things. Orain, believe me. . . ."

Orain with a child's face, child's eyes, child's heart in a woman's body, woman of guilt and wants, lady of long, sad shadows, stared at her in shock.

"Remember this always, though it may be small comfort. If the pain continues, if the tempest increases, if our world should end—daughter, this is all the truth that remains: The gods are not in the temples, and they are not with the priests. I have worshiped Hea all my years, though I have not been to her temple. But Hea is not in her temple only, Orain; she is everywhere. Hea, the gods—the one god—they are within us. Remember this: The gods are within us. We are the gods; we are our crimes, we are our sins, we are our destiny, and the cause and end of all our dreams and ambitions."

Orain sobbed, strengthless, not wanting to listen. Too tired. . .

"I love you, daughter not born of my flesh. You have done no crimes; the crimes have been done to you. Orain, how can I face the goddess, when to face her is to look into my own mirror? These pains have come, so awesome, because we have refused our deep secret, and we cannot share or understand what we refuse.

"Orain, live with this—I go with this—the gods are within us. We are the gods. We are their masters, and we are very poor masters, poor masters indeed, of our gods and ourselves. . . ."

Orain sobbed. Yta watched the candle flame and saw a funeral pyre, saw the fire grow, grow—grow to devour the world. . . .

3.

On the quay Abgarthis, white-haired, stood with Galvus to bid farewell to Yta. Along with them had come Adred. Elad had confined himself to a chamber of his palace—as had Lady Orain, for quite different reasons.

Yta was dressed in a pale scarlet robe and was devoid of jewelry other than the wedding band she wore upon her right hand. She was silent as she watched the last of her belongings taken aboard the merchant bireme, which rested far out on pale waves. There were no tears in her eyes, no expression on her lips. O torments waiting, tears unflowing, flames unlit. . .

One son dead, another a murderer in chains, the third upon the throne of empire. And a week ago—a mere few days ago—she and her husband had sat upon their patio and shared remembrances of days past, and had made plans for their future.

"My Queen." Abgarthis addressed her solemnly, refusing to acknowledge her at this moment as other than she had always been. "Do not return to the goddess with old griefs in your heart. Whatever becomes of us, be glad of Evarris's reign, be glad for yourself."

"Do not flatter the past, wise adviser," she answered him. She studied him deeply—the lines of his face, the sorrow in his eyes, the trembling of his lips—and Yta told him then, quietly peering into Abgarthis's spirit, "Guard, as well as you can, the best of the empire." She glanced briefly at Galvus, and the old courtier understood.

"By all that I am able, my Queen."

She turned to her grandson. "You are a man now, Galvus."

"Yes, my lady."

"Keep your heart clean. Strive, please, to believe in great things—things greater, even, than the throne."

"With all my heart, Grandmother, I do."

"Then act on them, Galvus. And, for me—for yourself—protect your mother. She is my daughter, and I have always loved her. Guard her with all your love."

"I—I'll try." He began to weep.

Yta turned, looked out to sea where her ship waited. The skiff was waiting at the quay, ready to row her out. She looked back upon her city and then noticed Count Adred, standing a short distance away.

"You will be staying in the capital, Count Adred?"

"For a time, yes, my lady."

"I am sorry we did not have time to talk. Events—I remember you well, Adred. I remember your father. Even your mother—yes, though she died when you were but a babe."

"Thank you, my lady."

"You and Dursoris—you were good friends when you were boys."

"I hold those days dear to me, Queen Yta. I'm only sorry that I had to return—now."

"Surely it is for a purpose."

"I would trust so, my lady."

"Adred, I see your heart. Do not mourn. Do not look behind. May I entrust you with a philosophy?" she asked him.

He was touched. "I would be honored, Queen Yta."

"Strive. Aspire. Never look behind, save for lessons. We enter—" She paused reflectively, then spoke the words in her mind. "We enter a dark age, friend of Dursoris. I have seen the future, and it is dark, but there is a light. Will you aspire toward it?"

"I—I will try. Queen Yta."

Yta wanted to trust him—but there was a vast gulf between them, a gulf of time and opportunity, and she had now to leave her life behind her. Sighing, she faced Abgarthis once more, lent him her hand. "Guard the empire with your love, all your strength," she commended him.

Abgarthis bowed, understanding his trust: the empire, not specifically the throne. "To the end of my strength," he vowed.

Yta turned to the Khamars, who stood awaiting her in the

skiff, and lifted a hand to them. The guard in command pulled free his sword and aimed it in the air, called out. Yta turned her back on her loyal hearts, turned away from her city, her empire, and her throne, and stepped down the quay with the regal majesty and feminine grace of a true ruler. The Khamars helped her settle herself in the skiff as the rowers pulled the boat from the dock.

It was early morning. The mists had lifted from the sea; the sun was bright and the sea shining brilliantly.

They stood, the three of them, in the company of councilors and court elders, surrounded by palace guards, and watched silently, heavy emotions binding them, as the skiff reached the ship. With distant, tiny flutters of movement was Queen Yta brought aboard, and the skiff lifted to the gunwales by leadlines. Then small voices cried out, sails were loosed, gulls flapped free of the masts. Blowing winds swelled the gold and scarlet and blue sails into huge bellies, and the bireme was steered out, oars splashing lazily, to begin its slow beginning toward the islands south of Athadia, beyond the horizon.

Its journey to Hea Isle.

It struck Adred that, with every wind and every wave, Yta was taking a journey into the past. Perhaps it was best for her that way. To him then came the memory of certain lines by the poet Leakhim, verse written to honor the Oracle in the pack of cards fortune-tellers used:

Behold the pentacle, dark diviner;
To you the opulence of love and life,
Or discord and the potent seeds of strife,
Sable succubus or bright entwiner.
Upon your tawny neck your head inclines;
You see within the golden pentacle
All opposites unite, prophetical;
To you alone are known the gods' designs.

* * *

Elad was not entirely drunk, but already this morning he had finished a bottle of dark Samesian wine, and the members of his Council recognized it in him.

But there were matters of state to attend to. The hurricane of events which had swept, tidal, over the capital had numbed the High Council—especially those men who, via gossip, had

101

been privy to certain late-night speculations. That, within the period of a few short days, the death of the monarch should lead to the butchery of fratricide and the abdication of the only stable voice remaining was looked upon with fear and foreboding by many members of Council. Half of them were aged and had begun their employ in the palace during the first years of Evarris's rule. Most of the others were middle-aged. None were women; all, to some degree, had aristocratic backgrounds, and all were moneyed, either because of their social rank, business acumen, or fortunate nativities.

Elad, thrust so suddenly upon the royal scarlet and gold, was far from prepared to deal adequately with the many emotional intricacies, the privileges of protocol, the deceptions of stance that figured importantly in the Council chamber. For the Athadian High Council, while not ruling the empire with anything approaching direct control, nonetheless exercised a profound influence upon affairs of national scope. To some degree they were shadow-kings, and their prejudices, their favors, and their own webs of influence made their collective motives sometimes suspiciously sinister, at other times merely blatantly self-aggrandizing. Power corrupts the way pleasant poisons linger: with a sweet aftertaste. If Elad had taken his crown and scepter in the best of times, it would have cost him long months of prudence to unravel and fully appreciate—and turn to his advantage—the inner workings of the High Council. As it was now, many of the forty-two there looked upon him as a criminal, a boy, and a mock-excuse for a king. They intended to pressure him, use him, manipulate him. A power struggle within the throneroom—far less transparent and potentially much more volatile than the heart attack or the knife wounds that had brought the empire to its current awkward position.

The half-drunken Elad, however, had ideas of his own.

Abgarthis opened the session and, following preliminaries, addressed his fellow councilors with bold words and sincere sentiments. All eyes fell on him, and Elad watched him carefully. "I ask for a truce between those warring emotions which, I know, many of us contend with. This chamber is not the place to work out those grievances. We are men of law. We are men of duty. We have served, many of us for long years, in this chamber, upon the supposition that whatever else may make life, we make our lives and we fashion the life

102

of the empire for the furtherance of, and guidance of, that throne. It is that throne—it is Athadia—which I urge you gentlemen to keep uppermost in your hearts now, and in your minds. And I think, at this moment, that every one of us ought to take to our feet right now, face our throne, and make due obeisance to our King."

It was the charge entrusted to him by Yta, and it was a challenge flung in the face of every high-minded yet immoral man in the room.

"We grant you the justice of the gods, and devoutly swear our love and allegiance to the King of Athadia, and to none other. May the gods guide and protect." Some mumbled it bitterly, under their breaths. Some coughed or scratched or looked away as they said the words; but they said them, and the words were duly copied down by scribes into the record.

Elad, at least ostensibly, had his Council; the fact sobered him. He had issued the announcement for their convening this afternoon with no real plan, no actual intent in mind, save one daring assumption. *You know how I won the skirmishes in the islands?* Cyrodian had asked him. He had wavered—one moment deciding to act arrogantly, the next considering doubtful or uncertain behavior. *You drive for the center—hard, fast—and demoralize, immobilize.* In the end, the wine had calmed him, and he had entered the Council chamber a few moments late, had looked upon the ungracious stares and had met them, seated himself—and waited for the pieces to begin moving into place. *You cut off the poisonous part of the snake first; the rest you chop up at your leisure.*

Abgarthis, familiar with the temperaments in that chamber, had done that which Evarris had always praised him for doing: put events in perspective. Now the elder seated himself and nodded to his lord monarch.

Elad, with only a slight fluttering in his stomach, turned to face his Council. He tried to age himself, in one moment, ten years; he began seriously to play the role of king.

"My ears are open," he announced in a solid voice, "to any pertinent issues."

There was a moment of silence in the room; it was as though he had issued a dare. Then one of the councilors—a thin skeleton of a man with warm coals for eyes—took to his feet and asked straightforwardly, "Lady Yta set down one condition for your ascension to the throne, my lord—that

103

being the death of Prince Cyrodian. I ask you, do you intend to follow through with that edict?''

Without hesitation: ''I do.''

The man remained standing.

''Is there more,'' Elad queried, ''to be said upon the matter?''

The skeletal man coughed and answered, ''Council believes the matter ought to be debated.''

''Does Council? Why?''

''My lord, it would cause repercussions.''

''Without a doubt it would cause repercussions.''

''Grave repercussions, my lord,'' the man persisted. It almost sounded like a threat.

''Lord Bumathis''—Elad leaned forward and fixed the man with a stare—''we in this chamber should be most knowledgeable when it comes to recognizing and dealing with . . . repercussions. Don't you think?''

The man did not answer; after a moment Elad moved his eyes from him and scanned all others for reactions. He noticed Abgarthis's expression and wondered about it. Did it reflect respect? Surprise?

A councilor two seats down pounded on the table, wishing his chance to speak. Bumathis, watching his King guardedly, made no sign that he wished to debate the man, and so he reluctantly dropped into his seat, and Lord Umothet arose.

''My lord. The arrest of Prince Cyrodian, in spite of the heinous charge leveled against him, has incensed the army.''

''I'm not surprised at that. Do you expect them to protest the edict? Protest, perhaps, with more than words?''

''I think we can expect,'' Umothet replied slowly, ''that the worst we can anticipate, my lord, has a better chance of occurring than the best.''

''That, Lord Umothet, is a constant in life. I believe you are right. Let me pose a question to my collected Council: Do you gentlemen think it better for a king to anticipate matters and move on them before he is certain of them? Or do you think he causes those matters to occur actually, when he moves in his anticipation?''

None there answered him. All remained silent. They had not expected this from the mock-king.

''Well, perhaps,'' Elad allowed, ''it's a little of both. Let me present you with another question. Do you think a king

104

should make a policy? Or should he react to policies that, generally, already make themselves apparent?"

Uncertain of what he was going for, none answered but only watched him.

"Lord Councilor Abgarthis," Elad allowed, "wished our talk today to concern only those matters which seem most pertinent at the present moment. I think we have a matter as grave as that of my brother's punishment present with us in this chamber. I think it has to do with the present state of our economic affairs. I think our economy is in need of repair. And I think we should debate this problem as fervently as we would like to debate the arrest and proposed execution of my brother.

"You men each have many interests at heart; this is the nature of man. And this chamber is the arena to air and resolve them—your interests, your opinions. But I would contradict myself if I told you that I had many interests in my heart, all equal, all wishing to be resolved simultaneously. They resolve themselves, gentlemen, into one large interest: this, my throne. Men may be impolitic, men may be greedy, men may be headstrong; perhaps some are obliged to overrepresent certain interests, in this room, and let others go wanting; then again, some may be selfless and true. Some may be all of these things. I am but one thing." He surveyed his Council, settled his eyes upon Lord Bumathis. "I am your King."

King.

He looked upon them from his throne, fully aware of what he had done, of what he was doing, of what he had commenced: a lifelong game of *usto* with these men, a game of bluff, a game of chance, a game of intimidation, a game of skill and of hidden knowledge. Squares, and gaming pieces, and dice, and a secret pattern of movement revealed slowly, with only one piece at a time to maneuver.

Appearing as king, Elad knew that he was not yet a king. Strong of word, he had as yet taken no actions. To all apparently decisive, inside he burned with indecision.

He looked upon his Council, looked upon Abgarthis—old man, still with the aura of Yta and Evarris about him—and he thought, did King Elad, not of the words of Bumathis or of Umothet, but of the Oracle of Teplis, words that had not yet begun to haunt him.

105

You will rule Athadia and see the world die in anguish.

He did not believe those words, and he did not know how to interpret them.

But he was King.

The cells for those guilty of crimes against the empire were situated deep underground, accessible only by a corridor which led from beneath the palace proper to the subterranean prison beneath the Khamar barracks and guardhouse. Visitors to these cells were few.

But with the arrest of Prince Cyrodian, the lone guard seated at the entrance to the cell hall was kept busier with visitors than he had been for many years. Officials, councilors, and army personnel came and went with increasing regularity. And now, inevitably, the wife and son. The guard nodded solemnly but said nothing to Orain and Galvus, opened the door for them and stood at attention as they passed through and down the corridor to the prince's cell.

Cyrodian was well accommodated in his bondage. His corridor held six cells, all of them vacant save for his. And his cell was far from barren; the stinking, rotted straw had been cleared out, and the cold stone bench replaced with an army cot. There were numerous candles and oil lamps, tables, writing instruments, scrolls of law, ample plates of fruit and jugs of wine—all that he might desire, were he in his own chamber high upstairs, save the freedom to leave of his own volition and access to his weapons.

Orain recognized him, when she saw him in his cell, as though remembering some stranger lost to her for years. This was her husband; yes: caged like some rare, well-protected beast. She faced him through the bars of his prison, her hands working nervously before her, afraid of him, afraid of the emotions that filled her. Afraid of the decision she had come to.

Galvus stood beside her, tall, proud, not in the least intimidated by his caged beast of a father.

Cyrodian stared at Orain with burning eyes. "I don't want you here. Why did you come?"

She looked at him, full of agony. "You are my husband. You have been ordered—executed. It is a wife's privilege to—to die with her husband, if he so wills it."

Cyrodian stared at her in disbelief.

106

"I *will* die with you, husband, if you order it."

Galvus was stunned. "Mother, you can't—"

But he was cut short by Cyrodian's brutal guffaw. "Die with me!" he shouted, wholly insensitive to what burned inside her. "No, no, my wife. You don't need to *die* with me!"

"But I will," Orain moaned, "I will, if you—"

"Why?" he grunted. "Because Dursoris is dead? That's the only reason you want—"

Orain sobbed loudly; great tears poured down her face, and she brought up her hands, nearly fell to the floor.

Galvus moved to hold her and shot a look of wrath at his father. "Why don't you kill yourself?" he yelled at him. "Isn't that what soldiers are supposed to do?"

"True, son of my lust. But I think I'll forgo giving you that pleasure, since I believe the empire needs me. One fool is dead already—but another sits on the throne. I'm needed more than ever."

"Dog!" Galvus spat.

Orain sobbed afresh.

"Whose son are you?" Cyrodian asked him angrily. "You can't be mine. Have you lifted a sword yet? Or are you getting humpbacked from carrying books?"

"Books are more powerful than any sword, Father. I like seeing you in prison! You can't slap me around now, can you? You can't beat me now, can you? You can't beat your wife, all you can do is—"

"Son of a whore, shut your mouth, *shut up!*"

Anguished, Orain released a series of heaving sobs and dropped to her knees.

"Witch!" Cyrodian howled at her. "Is this what you gave birth to? A weakling? A boy without—"

"Silence, *silence!*" Orain groaned.

Quiet reigned for a moment. Galvus and Cyrodian, both breathing hard, stared at one another.

Then Galvus, in a calmer voice: "The world is changing, Father. Your kind will all perish." He was thinking of Radulis, of philosophy, of dreams he held for a new empire, days of glory without bloodshed, violence. . . .

"I should have struck you harder," Cyrodian told him curtly. "I should have strangled you in your crib."

"Strangle a hundred of me," was the young man's answer. "I am a man of ideas, and men of ideas will always—"

"*Ideas!*" Cyrodian roared, as furious as if Galvus had touched him with hot iron. "Ideas! Ideas! There are *too many ideas*! Ideas have killed the throne! Now another man with *ideas* sits on the throne, and he will idea this empire to death! Grow steel, boy! Cowards always hide behind *ideas*! Learn to be a man!"

Heart-torn, Orain, shivering and weeping, got to her feet. "Take me from him," she whispered to Galvus.

"A *man!*" Cyrodian roared.

They turned from him, hurried down the corridor.

"Be a *man!*" Cyrodian howled, gripping the iron bars savagely. "Be *strong*, born of my lust!" He began to laugh like a maniac.

Galvus opened the door; Orain hurried through, and Galvus followed, not looking back.

Fool, he thought, damning his father to nine hells as a traitor and a monster.

"Fools!" Cyrodian cried after them, damning them for their weaknesses.

Not long after, the prince received another visitor to his cell—this time an individual with sentiments Cyrodian could understand and work with.

Lord Umothet came down the corridor and stepped directly before the bars of the cell. He was wearing a long talar that reached to his ankles, and from beneath the folds of it he produced a small rolled parchment.

Cyrodian watched the man carefully.

Without a word, Umothet handed him the scroll, passing it through the bars.

Cyrodian nodded approvingly as he scanned the brief text of it. "And you have the men ready?"

"A squad of them," Umothet assured him, "eager to move at your word, my lord. But affix your name and sign to this, and they will sail with the evening flood."

"Done, then." Cyrodian moved to his desk and there signed his name and, dripping fatty wax from a burning taper onto the parchment, stamped it with the seal ring he wore on his right hand: a lion, a crown, and a sun—mark of the Imperial House of Evarris. He blew on the wax to cool it

quickly, then rolled up the document and handed it to Umothet.
"Take it to them. Have them sail on the hour."
"My lord, it is done."

By my order, dispatch those loyal to my name to assassinate the Lady Yta of Athadia, as a traitor to the true empire. Kale Athadis im Porvo.
                              CYRODIAN SXo.

4.

When the second Council session of his reign disbanded late in the afternoon, Elad remained seated on his throne, alone in the chamber. Moody, he allowed rapid, contradictory thoughts to storm and blow through his mind. An hour passed, and two hours. A servant appeared and in a very docile voice inquired if the king were having his supper delivered to his upper chambers. Elad replied that he was unsure when he would have his supper, but for the moment he would be very happy to drink a cask of wine. The servant quickly fetched him two jugs.

He drank. Evening darkened. Silent, the king privately chastised himself for errors he had made. Probably they were trivial errors; but gone, this afternoon, had been his self-control of the previous day. He had been able to lead the regiment of aristocratic old men into a speculative discussion of the economy, and they had argued about that until the word had come of the army in revolt. And that had caused Elad to lose all patience and protocol, and he had reverted to the kind of man his brother could have easily baited into a trap. With the sounds of unrest growing in the streets during the afternoon, Elad had spoken hastily and angrily to the very men upon whom he was, presently, complexly dependent in a political way.

When at last the Council had adjourned, it was with trepidation and uncertainty as to whether or not their new king was a master of the gaming or a poor and desperate amateur trying to bluff and parrot.

And now, as Elad sat silent, the sounds of growing tumult in his capital's streets lifted to his ears. Elad rose from his throne and stumbled to the gong at the opposite side of the dais and struck it.

Even as the last echoes reverberated hollowly, Abgarthis opened a far door of the chamber and entered.

"Lord King?"

"The army. What of the army?"

Abgarthis's voice reflected his displeasure at the sudden turn of events. "They do as they have been doing all afternoon, Elad. Troops of them gallop up and down the Fountain Square. They are drunk, they are displaying their arms, but as yet—"

Abgarthis turned, and he and Elad witnessed the succinct climax of their afternoon-long suspense: the noisy arrival of a small band of state army officers making their way into the council chamber. They pushed ahead of them, like leaves before the storm, half a dozen palace servants, who, squeaking and whining, demanded that the officers respect protocol.

"Announce us, then, damn you!" boomed the foremost, a stout man in the bronze armor and clean badges of a grade second captain of infantry. "Announce us, and quickly! We have words for the King!"

Elad, walking haltingly, resumed his throne and stared murderously at the offensive trespassers as they crowded into the chamber. Abgarthis quickly moved aside and strode halfway to the throne dais. The grade second captain, stepping forward while the dozen other officers behind him quietened and held still, faced Elad arrogantly.

"I've been chosen as the spokesman, King Elad."

"Spokesman for what, Captain—?"

"My name isn't important, but what I have to say is. We stand here in formal defiance, lord King, of the imprisonment of our fellow officer Lord General Cyrodian, and to tell you that—that we formally protest the verdict that has been placed on his head."

"The order for his execution, Captain?"

"We don't want him killed, King Elad, and we're asking you for pardon."

"*Asking* me?" Elad laughed scornfully, and his harshness betrayed the liquor in him. "Upstart! Do you realize what you're saying? My brother is responsible for killing Prince Dursoris. He is a criminal."

The officer's eyes shone brightly. "We all know about

111

that!'' he replied with sinister intelligence. ''We know all about criminals and kings, Lord Elad! I'll put the matter to you simply. The army is in a mood to revolt, lord King, unless you spare Prince Cyrodian's life.''

''Who put you up to this?'' Elad demanded, hunching forward in his seat. ''Is this some conspiracy against me by Cyrodian? Is it? What you demand is against every law of the—''

''We don't care what it is. He's one of us; he's an officer. We respect him. You can issue all the orders you want, King Elad. But you've got seven squadrons of Athadian soldiers out there, and they're angry, and they know Cyrodian is going to be beheaded unless they do something about it.''

''You are speaking to your king!'' Elad reminded him hotly, half-rising to his feet and shaking with wrath. The man wouldn't dare act this way unless Cyrodian . . . ''You—''

''My lord—'' began Abgarthis, attempting to intervene.

''You, lord King, are talking to a cityful of soldiers who demand—''

''*I* demand that the cityful of soldiers—''

''*My King!*'' barked Abgarthis.

Elad stared at him, caught the stern look of warning in his adviser's eyes. Calming himself, Elad sat back in his throne and stared squarely at the malefactors.

In a quieter tone: ''Council held session this afternoon to debate just this issue.'' The surflike sounds of grumbling came from the collected officers. ''We have every intention of holding another session tomorrow, and I advised that certain leaders of the military be invited. I am well aware of the . . . respect my brother elicits from certain men of the sword.''

The man refused to be intimidated. ''King Elad, you can't stop a raging fire by talking to it, and what you have outside is a raging fire. I was elected spokesman by a drawing of the lot; I'm only telling you what anyone else here would have told you if they'd drawn the colored straw. Unless these men are given something better than a death-order for General Cyrodian, I can't promise you what will happen. I can't control them; there isn't one officer in this city to control them. They're angry. They understand Cyrodian, and they know him—and they don't know you. You'd better give them something, and soon. It's a time for politics, King Elad—not

112

for issuing orders. Like I said, you can't issue orders to a raging fire."

Elad's attitude had calmed somewhat, his nervousness or anxiety, perhaps, having passed or worked itself out. He read that clearly. Paramount, was his concern for keeping the strongest by him, and the strongest certainly included the army. He judged that while any spontaneous revolt by the army would burn itself out quickly, much damage would occur in the meantime; and he decided that while in the long run the army would return to the office which issued its pay, its sentiments for the time being would play havoc with any loyalty other than to one of their own. Without doubt Cyrodian was engineering this staged revolt by the army; and, just so, the wisest course open to Elad, as neophyte ruler and untested monarch, would be to appear to yield for the short run and turn events to his advantage in the long run.

He leaned forward once more, a light in his eyes. "Go out there," he instructed the nameless officer, "and tell those squadrons to restrain themselves. Tell them you have spoken to me and I have completely understood your ultimatum. Tell them . . ."

He read the eagerness in their faces, the anxiousness in their postures.

". . . that you will have my decision at dawn. But in the meantime . . ."

Low dissatisfied groans, until the officer-spokesman urged them to quiet.

". . . in the meantime, I want no harm coming to the populace and absolutely no damage done to this city. Tell those men to rein their horses and return to their barracks and await my edict. You will have it at dawn."

Silence. The spokesman turned to the others; all of them shared eyes and nodded slowly.

"So be it, King Elad. At dawn." The captain saluted his monarch and led the way out of the Council chamber. To the thunder of retreating boots, Elad sipped another goblet of wine.

Abgarthis, soundless as a spider, approached the throne dais and climbed the steps until he was standing beside Elad.

The King set aside his cup. "I must speak with Cyrodian."

"It would seem appropriate. King Elad—"

"What is it?"

113

"Today . . . when you faced the Council . . . and re-minded them of a king anticipating events or reacting to them—"

"Yes, Abgarthis?"

"Do you believe what you said?"

A hardness entered the young monarch's eyes. "I do."

"And that, in anticipating events, a king may cause that to happen which might not otherwise have happened?"

"What of it, Abgarthis?" *A mirror reflects depth while having no depth itself . . . a sword has two edges, it may cut the one who wields it as well as his enemy . . . is the wall weak, or those behind it . . . ?*

"You have good people in your house, my lord. I don't mean the politicians and the aristocrats. Lady Orain, this afternoon—she visited Cyrodian." Elad raised his brows. "She promised to take her own life, as is a wife's privilege, if Cyrodian were executed."

Elad blanched. "This is true?"

Abgarthis nodded solemnly. "There is—an old image your father liked to use when he and I spoke in private. I hope you will consider it. It has to do with repercussions. Your father used to compare the actions of a king to the stone that is dropped in a pool of water. Concentric waves speed out from all around the dropped stone—from the king—with inevitable ramifications that hurry on despite—"

"I understand the metaphor, Abgarthis." Elad cut him short. He pondered for a moment; then: "Come with me down to the prison."

The jailer was half asleep when King Elad and Councilor Abgarthis, carrying an oil lamp, hastened down the last steps into the corridor that contained Cyrodian's cell. The man quickly roused himself and apologized profusely for his conduct; but Elad ignored him and simply ordered him to unlock the corridor door quickly.

Prince Cyrodian was awake and lying on his bunk, hands behind his head, when his brother walked up to his cell. The prisoner laughed cruelly at the sight. "Celebrated prisoners," he opined harshly, "certainly invite the world to turn its values upside down! Welcome to where maggots feed, my King!"

"You are foul, brother."

114

Cyrodian stepped up to the bars. "I disagree. I believe you are the foul one. And from where I stand now, it could easily be you behind these iron poles, and I the free one. But you screamed the louder, didn't you, brother?"

Elad stood with feet apart in a solid stance, hands behind his back. "Cyrodian, I'd be pleased if you'd keep quiet while I tell you what I have to say."

A humorous expression lit the giant's face. "Speak, then."

"Pressure is being put upon me to overrule Yta's judgment in regard to your verdict."

"Pressure, hey? Welcome to the world of real politics, Elad."

"Specifically, the army has threatened violence if I have you beheaded."

"Well, the army is something to fear, that's certain."

"So is the throne. I know you're behind these events, Cyrodian; but keep in mind that it does neither you nor I any good to have the army and the throne at odds."

"I'm only a criminal! What does it matter to me what passes for judgment up there?" He glanced toward the ceiling of his cell.

"I will make a bargain with you, Cyrodian." The King's voice was as steadfast as his poise.

Cyrodian smiled and glanced at Abgarthis. "He's learning, isn't he?"

"I intend to tell the army, in the morning, that I will exile you from the borders of the empire. You will remain alive, but you will be banished. What do you say to this, brother?"

"I get my life, but you still keep your throne and the empire, hey?" Cyrodian smiled hugely, leaned forward against the bars; he twisted his massive hands around them, as if hoping that he could snap them with his human strength. "You're frightened, aren't you, King brother? And well you should be. You see? Any man should be frightened when he seeks power over any but himself. Kings sleep in a bed of asps, not cockroaches. And where will the serpents strike next?"

Elad maintained his composure. "I ask you again: Do you agree to this bargain?"

His brother moved away from the bars, sat down on his cot, stared hard at Elad and thought heavily. Many images . . . many visitors . . . many ripples in the pool. . . .

115

"Well?"

"I agree."

Elad nodded curtly to him. "Then I will release you in the morning. You will be chained, and an escort of my choosing will lead you from the capital."

"Where am I going?"

"Where?" Elad did not smile. "Far away from me, dear brother. Far away from me."

Count Adred could not sleep. The noise of the soldiers in the streets had dwindled somewhat, but the squadrons had not—despite King Elad's request—disbanded entirely. With news coming from the palace in the morning, half the army remained in the Fountain Square, eager to hear the decision.

Adred read for a few hours, until his eyes began to burn. Then he got out of bed, pulled on his breeches and a loose tunic, and left his chamber. Intending to look in the Audience Hall for Elad, he changed his mind when he noticed Abgarthis seated on a marble bench just outside the closed portals of the Council chamber.

"You cannot sleep?" the old man asked him as Adred stepped near.

"Impossible. What are they celebrating out there?"

"The army." Abgarthis sighed. "They're not celebrating. They've demanded that Cyrodian not be executed. Elad has promised them an answer in the morning."

"Yes," Adred said, "of course. . . . The coals heat quickly, don't they?"

"I'm afraid so."

"Is Elad with his ministers, or—"

"No. He's inside." Abgarthis nodded. "Drinking."

Adred frowned.

Abgarthis smiled faintly, a touch of wisdom in his tired, aged features. "He is in there, King Elad, drinking wine and casting small colored bones, to see the future."

"Is that so wrong? He only looks for solace."

"But he already knows the future, Adred," Abgarthis told him. "Why can't he put away the bones, and stop staring in his mirror? He already knows what he will do, no matter what the bones say."

5.

At dawn, King Elad was asleep upon the throne of empire, stretched out and dozing in an awkward posture. Abgarthis, in the company of several other councilors (those who had spent the sleepless night in palace apartments), intruded upon his monarch and awakened him. Elad was brought a washing bowl, a change of clothes, and a breakfast plate of bread, soup, and tea. And as early morning filled the misty streets of the capital with its first full light, Elad ordered the spokesman of yesterday brought before him for the decision.

Scribes in attendance dutifully copied down the exact words.

"In regard to the matter of the execution of Prince General Cyrodian of Athadia, an order based upon partial testimony brought before Queen Yta, let it be decreed that the previous command is hereby ratified and amended; the verdict of death is overruled, and Prince Cyrodian is to be on this day . . ."

The morning was lost to madness. Merchants found it impossible to open their stalls for business, shopkeepers were unable to travel in safety to their doors, and the daily routine of tens of thousands was wholly disrupted as seven squadrons galloped madly through the boulevards and city squares, shouting and drinking and blaring their trumpets. Elad took no action against them; rather, the King reviewed with Abgarthis the list of army officials who might best be entrusted with the dangerous task of transporting Prince Cyrodian to his exile. Cyrodian was far too popular and—as the confrontation yesterday proved—far too influential to allow any but the most trusted to fulfill the crown's command.

Adred busied himself with writing a letter.

*　　*　　*

My Dear Good Friend:

The gods embrace you and guard you and grant you peace and long life and all true rewards. Kale Athadis im Porvo.

Mantho, you would be, I am sure, as alarmed as I at the events I have witnessed here since my arrival in the capital a few days ago. We have been stricken with an outbreak of madness unmatched, I am sure, since the high crimes of the days of the Civil Wars. Be sure that I am truthful when I tell you that, since my arrival, I have witnessed the death of one prince at the hand of another, the arrest of the guilty son, the abdication of Queen Yta, and a new monarch upon the throne of our land. And more lightning, I fear, yet lingers in this storm. . . .

There was an obvious attitude of relief among the councilors that morning when Elad assured them that his decision to banish Prince Cyrodian was final and irrevocable. The King insisted to his Council that this in no way reflected a leniency of the throne toward criminals, nor did it mean that hereinafter justice could be bought or sold by threats, importunities, or verdict-bargainings; Elad emphasized that, because many viewed the events of the past week as a prelude to crisis or disaster, he had taken his action solely to keep the ship of state on a straight course. A spontaneous round of applause, led by the effusive Lord Umothet, greeted the proclamation. And then the Council settled down to business.

Umothet was the first to raise the question of who would mastermind the banishment of Cyrodian; security was uppermost in his mind, he claimed. Elad replied that measures had been taken to insure that Cyrodian's escort to the border of the kingdom (in which direction, he did not say) would be handled secretly and strictly by a squadron of men hand-picked by himself. This statement naturally segued into a discussion of the many insincere persons who, it was known, dallied daily in the halls of the palace. These ministers of misfortune, Umothet opined, sought to sow seeds of discord even as Elad struggled to lay the foundation for his new government.

"My lord," the conniver offered, holding out a scroll he had brought with him. "I have taken the liberty of drawing up a list of names for your benefit. I think—"

118

A chorus of enraged voices erupted, and Abgarthis shot a frightened look at Elad.

Elad leaned forward. "Do you think this wise, Umothet?"

"My lord?"

"If it is your honest intention to help me weed my garden, this is fine. But I think you seek to make me a lackey to your own ambitions. Those names are—"

"Not so, King Elad!" the Councilor protested self-righteously. "I would never do such a thing! If I gain favor from you for performing a service—well, this is my duty, is it not? But these names I culled from a memory of long experience in the affairs of this court!"

"Long experience?"

"I have served seven years in this chamber."

Subdued laughter from some seats; there were men in that room who had held their positions since before Umothet's birth.

"I believe you attempt to do me, and members of my royal staff, a disservice, Umothet. A disservice and an injustice," Elad reprimanded him.

"I did not mean to." Lord Umothet sounded truly hurt. Abgarthis, staring at him, went white with repressed wrath. "My King, believe me when I say—" But Umothet cut himself short then and, in a dramatic gesture, applied one end of his scroll to an oil lamp that was burning near him on the table. The flames quickly ate at the paper, but Umothet held onto it, as if daring the fire to bite him, displaying his discipline to all in the chamber. Finally someone grunted in alarm, and only then did Umothet cast the scroll of flame from him. He dropped it onto the stone floor, where the last of it burned into charred black fragments.

"Do you believe me now?" he demanded of Elad. "I curry no favor that anyone else would not, and I have not forced this list upon you. But let his be enough to indicate how dire I feel the emergency is, that you . . . weed your garden of backstabbers and sycophants."

Elad was not unimpressed, although he felt sure that this little show was nothing more than that, and that Umothet's paramount concern was to turn things to his own advantage. Still, this was the time for every man here, openly or obliquely, to jostle for recognition and prestige before the new throne.

119

King Elad opened the discussion upon exactly this point. "We need not read Lord Umothet's list to know, gentlemen, that there are indeed many in this palace and in its offices who seek to take advantage of the current crisis. Gentlemen, I have no wish to be unfair. I want facts, not speculation; I mean to do no one any personal injury. But if we have a bureaucrat in our family who is wasteful, frivolous, or damaging to the ultimate concerns of this court—name him! We will remove him from the capital and set him up in office elsewhere. We will demote him, or send him on a vacation. We will take a man from the treasury and put him with the army. We will, in short, clean the board and pluck our weeds."

Another surprise from the new King; another ambitious move to create a strong impression—for the sake of impression?

Elad smiled coldly and studied the faces of his Council. Then, one by one, pointing up and down the long tables on both sides of him, he called for the names from his ministers, called for the names to be debated, and swiftly ordered the names entered onto the scribe's list, along with the new positions of those names. In this way Elad efficiently rearranged the bloated hierarchy of his court, and began a long period of misunderstandings, ill will, and jeopardized sentiments. . . .

That evening the Councilors retired from their chamber and returned to their homes or apartments in the city. There had never been a purge of this magnitude within the government. For a monarch to disrupt the flow of the bureaucracy by wholly reorganizing its personnel and perhaps dismissing a vast number of its members—such a thing was unprecedented and dangerous.

Very dangerous.

Fear that King Elad would continue on this course of action weighted mightily on his Councilors. Silently and secretly, each of them determined to obstruct the new young king in this new, volatile program. There was too great a chance for it to rock out of control.

Abgarthis was of the same mind, and he said as much to Elad later that evening, as the King took his supper alone in his chambers—alone save for one indignant, tenuous voice of reason.

120

"You are banishing them!" Abgarthis fairly yelled at him. "You are destroying the faith of everyone, from your Councilors to the smallest employee in the most forgotten office! You will anger them, turn them against you!"

"I am," Elad reminded him, "doing what is my privilege and right as King."

"Where is your sense?" the elder demanded of him. "You'll make enemies all—"

"I'll make them aware, Abgarthis, that I am the King, and the law, and the final word in any decision."

Abgarthis refrained then from voicing whatever he meant to say next. Eying Elad coolly as the King ate his meal: "You are treading dangerous land if you have begun this policy merely as a show of your own power."

"I have the power, don't I?"

"Too much power is as hazardous as too little, for a king."

"Power," Elad replied, in just as distant a tone, "is only as forceful as the direction behind it."

"And what direction do you take?" Abgarthis retorted. "Do you move everything all at once—your infantry, cavalry, and lieutenants of the cooking oil? Guard your rear and your flanks, King Elad." And then: "I know that you're probably a frightened man these days, but, in the name of the gods, be an *intelligent* frightened man!"

Elad set down his fork, looked up at him—and smiled.

"What does it mean?" Orain wondered aloud when she heard of what had happened in the Council chamber.

She was with Adred in the eastern gardens outside the palace. It was early in the evening, and Orain was not hungry, so she had decided to stroll among the blossoms and the trees. Adred, relaxing after his own early supper, had found her there.

His attitude was as grim and perplexed as hers. "It means," he conjectured, "that Elad is desperate. Afraid that every eye that looks upon him thinks him a criminal and no true king. He's performing a show with his power; he's posturing to make certain everyone knows who is in command."

"But there's no reason to do that," Orain suggested. "He'll only anger many people and cause problems where there are none."

"I know that, I know it," Adred replied. "I had hoped—" He paused.

She looked at him. "What, Adred?" She went silent, saying nothing more to him, obviously feeling awkward.

Adred changed the subject. "Orain—I'm going back to Sulos. To see Mantho, my friend. To clear my mind, put things in perspective."

"That would be a good thing, yes."

"I wish you'd come with me."

She was surprised at his offer.

"You and Galvus," he urged her. "We can stay a month at Mantho's villa—spend two months, if we want to. Just for the change. When things have settled themselves here, we'll return. It might help us."

"And my husband still lives," Orain continued, staring at the brick walkway. "I saw him today. They took him—chained to his horse—to banish him. . . ."

Adred said nothing.

"And I'm still married to him, aren't I?"

"Only if you believe so. Otherwise, none think that."

She considered it. "You may be right." She reflected on it in the falling dusk. "Adred!" She almost laughed, then. "Do you know what you've done?"

"No, what?"

"You're exactly right! I've had this picture of myself moping around here, just walking around, feeling useless, all— But you're right. It would be good. I haven't been to the uplands in years—"

"It'd be good for Galvus, too."

"Yes, yes." She stood up briskly, looked down at him, still holding his hand. "You're a good friend, Adred," she whispered.

He smiled.

"Give me another few days—all right?" Orain suggested. "To arrange some things—just to get ready."

"Of course."

"No wonder"—she gripped his hand strongly—"no wonder Dursoris thought so highly of you."

"Did he?"

"Absolutely. He missed you—missed all the good times you two had had together, before he started studying the law and you began traipsing around the world."

122

"Traipsing around?" The image amused him.

"Maybe he was jealous." Orain grinned at Adred. "He used to say that you had some sweet young blossom in every port from Sulos to Pylar."

Adred acted shocked. "Not true! Besides"—looking at Orain in the last golden light of the day—"I can't imagine Dursoris being jealous of me."

He said it, and then realized what he'd said as he did so. It embarrassed Orain slightly, and she let her hand slip from his. "Anyway," she mumbled. "In a few days . . ."

"Yes. In a few days. . . ."

A few days . . .

The assassination galley had traveled fleet upon the waters, lent speed by its slim design and its limited numbers—a crew of a few dozen seamen and a squad of hired murderers, soldiers loyal to one badge and one officer: Prince General Cyrodian. Hrux.

As the sun died, melting like a boiling core of hot metal upon the distant rim of the world, the killers' ship sighted Lady Yta's bireme just ahead of them, flying the golden pennant of the lion and the crown. The galley closed in, making no pretense about its intention to overhaul the merchanter and draw close to it. As night finally covered the ocean with a starlight-dappled blanket of wet shadows, the death ship came close enough for voices to exchange.

"Name yourself!" called the commander of the Khamars on board Yta's sails.

"News from the capital!" came the reply. "News from King Elad, concerning Prince Cyrodian! Word for Lady Yta!"

The Khamars were suspicious, but Yta herself ordered them to furl their sails and pull about into boarding position.

The death galley lifted oars and rolled close.

It drew up beside Lady Yta's bireme; grappling lines were thrown out and launches lowered. The pilot of the killer ship held his wheel solid as the vengeful soldiers crossed the black waves to the merchanter and clambered up its sides.

"What word?" asked the chief of the Khamars, disgruntled to see such a sizable company of swords intruding upon his decks.

They lined up, two deep, on the boards, against the gunwales. Their leader announced to Yta and the gathered guard, "Word from the capital for our lady."

Yta nodded to him. "What word, Commander?"

He produced from beneath his short cape a long scroll. "Word of Prince Cyrodian, Lady Yta."

Her brows furrowed. In the moonlight, her eyes betrayed deep worry. "Word . . . of death?" she asked doubtfully.

"Aye," answered the soldier. "Of death."

Suddenly he lunged forward with the scroll, plunging one end of it into Yta's bosom. The parchment tore free, revealing the silver blade of a sword. Yta gasped, stumbled back, grasped at her heart.

The Khamars howled furiously and reached for their weapons, but Cyrodian's killers were upon them before many could move in their own defense. The guards found themselves outnumbered, and the crew of the bireme were unarmed—a precaution ordered by Yta herself, in view of her destination.

She dropped to the deck, and a dozen pieces of sharp steel sank into her. Screams and cries of anguish lifted into the night, and blood flowed—more blood. . . .

6.

Elad's fourth day as King.

Following a morning of continued rearrangement of officials and bureaucrats in the government hierarchy, the collected Council that afternoon argued unanimously that the reappraisals had gone far enough. Over a hundred men had been reviewed, but from the least to the highest there were a hundred thousand workers in the bureaucracy—aristocrats and menial scriveners, lodged in every city, port, and town of the empire. Did King Elad intend to spend the first several years of his reign reviewing these persons and determining their qualifications for maintaining their positions?

Elad smiled generously at that comment. And he agreed with the motion that this restructuring, reorganizing, and weeding could better be handled by the chiefs and heads of the hundreds of scattered departments that made up the throne's web of rule all across the empire. Ripples in a pool . . . But Elad had already gained what he wanted—a show of strength for himself, a display of the suddenly unmasked personalities of his Councilors.

"Abgarthis," he said that evening, "you have spent all your years in service to kings and aristocrats and landed lords. Yet you have never to me seemed eager for power. You have never sought to usurp even control of a kitchen, let alone a throneroom. It astounds me. It gladdens me—I can trust you for that—but I wonder why."

"Do you, truly?"

"Yes, certainly."

"It is because, King Elad, I have seen what power does. I have seen the two sharp edges to every sword. I have seen how power controls men and how it attains its ends as if it

125

had a life of its own. And it struck me long ago that what comes from the use or misuse of power would have come just as well from any other means or by another method, and would have come by those ways better. But because the world is made as it is, and men as they are, there is indeed power, and there are pretenders to the seats of power. You are the outward symbol of power, my King, and all men recognize you for it; yet I ask you this: Do you think I am unpowerful? Why should I rule the kitchen when I have access to it every day, whether I rule it or not? I am still a man in the kitchen, and more easily able to digest my food, it seems to me, when I can enter the kitchen without being lord of it.''

Elad pondered and within a heartbeat countered with the only argument to this that had ever haunted Abgarthis. ''But what if, Councilor, your access to the kitchen were taken from you?''

Abgarthis nodded carefully. ''That,'' he said, ''is why we have law.''

''That, my friend, is why I want to have and maintain power. Let us look at this in another way, Abgarthis. What is a country without its king?''

But now Abgarthis was on firmer ground. Lifting his head proudly: ''It is still a country, Lord Elad. But I ask you this: What is a king without his country? Is he still a king, and a power?''

Elad pondered the words. And later in the evening, as others in the palace settled down to listen to music, or went to worship at the temples, or began to bet money on cards or games of *usto*, or cajoled servant girls into side rooms for quick moments of passion—as life, then, went on in the palace—Elad retired to a divan in an antechamber of his sleeping room, poured himself a full cup of wine, and began to read.

And continued to read for long hours into the night, from bound volumes he had taken from his murdered brother Dursoris's chamber.

''But what if, Councilor, your access to the kitchen were taken from you?''

''That is why we have law.''

But that is why, Elad thought, *I am lord of the kitchen.*

Yet it would no doubt have astonished Abgarthis (a man

126

for whom astonishment seemed as ancient as memories of the crib) to discover that King Elad was spending every night private to himself with the notebooks his earnest brother Dursoris had kept while serving for seven years on the Law Council.

Elad, criminal, young King, bitter in his heart, feeling it needful and somehow wise to posture, incite, or intimidate—Elad, trying hard, every night, to master the good law codes of the throne, even as he tried to master himself . . .

Umothet, restless, sat on the outer patio of his apartment in the capital. The bells from the temple nearby proclaimed midnight. Promptly upon the striking of the hour, there sounded a knock on one wall of the breezeway leading to the patio.

Lord Umothet stood up. He reached to his belt—merely a gesture, but it placed his fingers nearer his decorated dagger, if such expediency proved necessary.

"Speak your name," he hissed toward the breezeway.

"I am a shadow."

Umothet breathed faintly. "Come forward."

Into his garden stepped a tall, thin man, his visage unclear beneath the tattered hat he wore. He made a sign to Umothet as he drew close.

"What word of the riders?" the Councilor asked him.

"Late this evening, my lord, they reached a small village this side of the Sevulus. They head eastward."

"Indeed. And left by the southern gate. Elad is not so crafty. . . . How does Prince Cyrodian fare?"

"My lord, the prince is the butt of jokes, but he is a soldier. He is well; they feed him—he is well."

Umothet nodded appreciatively at this word. "And our man is still with them?"

"With them and unknown to the others. This information came from him."

Lord Umothet moved his hand—away from his knife, toward an inner pocket of his light tunic. He withdrew a heavy, full pouch and passed it to the intruder. "Cyrodian's gold."

The messenger nodded succinctly.

"Now get from here. Buy passage on a ship to the south, and do not return to this city for six months."

"My lord, I am gone, and I do not know your name."

To the easy sound of the man's vanishing footsteps, Umothet

127

returned to his bench on the patio and relaxed. He felt inspired. Elad was a fool, Cyrodian by far the stronger of the two, and the true king—the king in exile. Events moved forward as though predetermined. Soon enough the time would come—with Cyrodian alive, with enemies inside the palace removed—for the true king to return to the capital and take the crown of sun from the bloody head of the imposter who wore it now.

In the morning word came to Elad that a number of aristocrats and others close by the palace were preparing to leave the city, at least for a short while. The end of summer was near, habitually a time for the gentry to retire for two or three weeks from the city and relax in their country villas. Elad was concerned, however, that there might be more to it. Abgarthis was the first to remind him that his forceful commandeering of the throne halls and Council chamber had disturbed many courtiers, and now would be the ideal time for the King better to review what he had done and what course he intended to follow in the near future.

Still, Elad became even more concerned when Orain and Adred spoke with him later that morning. "You, too?" he asked them. "Abandoning me?" He tried to appear whimsical.

Orain was quick to allay his mistrust. "Not abandoning you!" she exclaimed. "Elad, my brother, I wish you, too, could retire somewhere away from here."

"Not quite possible. Where will you be?" he asked her. "Are you taking Galvus with you?"

"With us, yes. We're staying with a friend of Adred's."

"You might know of him," Adred told Elad. "Count Mantho. He lives in Kendia."·

"I've heard the name, I think. Ensutus's son?"

"Yes, that's him. He served here for a time, years ago."

"Yes, yes—I know Mantho. You'll be leaving in the morning?" Elad asked Orain.

She nodded. "It'll take us three or four days to reach Sulos."

"I hope you don't mind if it's an extended visit," Adred commented. "A month at least—maybe longer."

"Yes," Elad responded quietly, his mind drifting. "Yes. Of course." He looked away, then looked back; his eyes settled, not unsuspiciously, on Adred.

128

The King wondered if Adred, whom he did not know very well, were attracted to Orain. Or if Orain were attracted to him.

And he wondered if, because of this, they might be potential threats to his throne. Intruders in his kitchen . . .

Later that afternoon a second messenger came to Lord Umothet to report that Cyrodian was nearing the far eastern borderlands of the empire and by that morning must have been heading into the Province of Galsia. Umothet paid him with gold and a warning—Cyrodian's gold and the order to head south on a ship for Port Sugat.

And as early evening descended, a certain galley tied up at the southern docks of Athad, a squadron of troops disembarked, and their leader—after renting a room in a tavern and washing up—sent word to Lord Umothet that Lady Yta of the empire was dead, the guards who had escorted her slain to the last man, and the bireme on which they had been traveling had been fired and sunk to the depths of the ocean.

Lord Umothet returned a coded invitation, by the same messenger, for the leader of the expedition and several of his retainers to meet with a select number of highly placed officials at his apartment on the following night. A celebration feast was in order.

Abgarthis saw them off. He went with them as far as the boarding dock, there to wish them well and warn them, once they had enjoyed their stay in Sulos, to return with fresh anticipation of King Elad.

"We have spoken, he and I," Abgarthis confided to Adred, Orain, and Galvus as they stood in the morning sun. "I think he is righting himself. It is difficult—"

He was interrupted by a wild confusion behind them: cries and howls, galloping hoofs and screams erupting from a small avenue half hidden by flanking warehouses.

They turned and watched, as did others in the crowds on the dock. To their amazement, half a dozen mounted city guards in full armor rode bucking horses into a wide path just outside the alley, reined their mounts, and jumped to the ground, swords out. Immediately the massed people on the wharf pushed forward, and the soldiers yelled for them to stay back.

"What is it?" Galvus asked, craning his neck to look. "I can't—"

Loud barks and yelps carried to them then, and screams from the packed onlookers.

"Get back!" shouted the guards. "Get back, stay away from—"

"By the gods!" Abgarthis breathed in amazement. "It is a pack of dogs—wild dogs, attacking in the streets!"

An ache struck Adred, and he released a groan. The crowd ahead of him, ordered back by the soldiers and shoving now to stay away from the mad animals, parted to give him a view of what was occurring. He saw the pack of dogs—domestic animals, large and small—all of them snarling, slobbering, barking, and yelling, heads pulled to one side, crawling stealthily forward toward the guards. Adred was horrified. The dogs of the capital, though often roaming free, had never behaved in such a way. A stray once in a while became angry, that was true; but this . . .

One of the soldiers cried out in pain as three of the dogs in unison leaped for him. Swords flashed in the sun; the man went down as the mad dogs growled and howled, writhing. Blood flew into the air, and onlookers gasped. There was a disorganized scuffle. The short capes of the city guards billowed and flapped, armor flashed, steel blurred, and naked arms twisted and turned; patches of fur and snarling white fangs bobbed and swirled in the confusion.

It was over shortly. A second city guard went down and, bleeding from the belly, tried to haul himself to safety. But as the crowd pulled back, Adred and Abgarthis, Orain and Galvus saw lying upon the stones a sickening array of smashed, mutilated dogs—bodies torn, carcasses bleeding, split organs still pumping. Blood everywhere. And the two wounded soldiers, groaning and wiping their slick red hands on the stones, trying to pull themselves up; they slipped, rolled, moaned in torment.

Thunder, as another mounted patrol galloped down the main avenue to help their comrades. Several of them circled around to keep the crowds back and watch for other animals; others dismounted to tend to the wounded.

Behind Adred a sailor, shivering beneath a heavy bale but unmindful of it, swore. "Damn me to the gods, isn't that the cursedest thing you ever, *ever* saw?"

Adred tensed. It was not, for him, the strangest thing he had ever seen. He had seen something even stranger, and only a few days earlier: he had seen birds dive into the ocean and kill themselves. Then he had seen a throne topple, a prince murdered, a queen exiled. . . . And now, as if they were all pieces of some complex puzzle, he had seen a pack of wild dogs attack horses and soldiers in the streets of Athad.

"Odd," whispered Abgarthis, sounding reluctant to admit it. "Odd, very odd."

"It's more than that," Adred whispered, staring at the bleeding animals. But he said it to himself, and no one there overheard him.

Lord Umothet's secret council that night was composed of only a handful of men—men sworn to utter secrecy, men disposed toward belief in Cyrodian and committed to seeing him returned to Athad as king, devoted to seeing the weak, criminal Elad deposed and beheaded. Umothet, traitor and manipulator, proudly boasted to his cohorts how successful he had been so far in gaining the trust of his King; Elad was persuaded by him, Umothet reported, and this would make it simple for their secret loyalty to Cyrodian to gain its foothold on the throne dais. Others at the meeting reported that sentiments still ran high for Cyrodian in many sectors of the army barracks and the dockside bunkhouses, in the taverns and in the gymnasiums.

It was important, all agreed, that these passions be taken advantage of swiftly. The longer Elad held the throne, the more secure it became for him, the more familiar he would become to the public at large, and the more tolerant they would be of him. Umothet was aware of this; he acknowledged the danger but insisted that their cause could best be served by biding their time a little longer and continuing to spread gossip and innuendos against Elad. Everyone was eager to listen to foul gossip, and a secret campaign could be begun easily in the shadows of taverns and in the lazy city squares; Elad could be slandered and Cyrodian vaunted as the true king in exile. People always preferred to believe the sensational wonder rather than the sensible truth; and when their fears were played upon or baited, the masses could be led like cattle down any avenue chosen by their leaders.

Cyrodian was still alive; Yta was dead. Elad's decision to

purge much of his bureaucracy had led to tension and misgivings. The time was ripe to espouse Cyrodian's superiority.

And as for a plot against Elad's life, Umothet was of the opinion (and all there agreed with him) that unless untoward events provoked some rash and premature use of force, it would be best to have Cyrodian return a free man, with public opinion behind him, so that the exiled prince himself could judge the King.

The conspirators congratulated themselves; all lifted cups to Lord Umothet. The gods, they decided, were with them. They drank, pledged loyalties to one another, told jokes, and spun visions of some splendid future when Cyrodian, the killer-prince, would inherit the throne and command the empire with the strict, heavy hand that it so desperately cried out for.

When the plotters parted, it was late at night. They returned to their villas and city apartments on horseback and in palanquin and litter. Some of them were so drunk that, unable to walk steadily or speak coherently, they had their servants escort them through some of the narrower alleys and darker byways of the capital.

And one of these, full of wine and garrulous of tongue, let slip certain secret things as he stumbled to his bed. His manservant, a gossip, overheard and listened for more. Tending to his master, he reappeared several times during the night to awaken him and feed him water and bread—so that, said the servant, the lord would not suffer in the morning.

This man heard much as he listened to his master's babbling, sleepy chatter, his rambling, sonorous reenactments of scenes at Umothet's table, his drunken toasts to Prince Cyrodian and effusive calls for King Elad's death.

The servant was no fool. Like many selfish, shortsighted individuals of means, the nobleman had often mistreated the servant and all his home-tenders. If there was here an opportunity to discredit or bring low such a man, the prying servant was not adverse to having his chance at revenge.

Those same accidents of fortune which seem sometimes to lift one man to unwarranted heights of acclaim or possession can just as often disrupt or ruin the man of position or esteem—and who is to say that one man's drunkenness in the middle of the night is not part of some mystery of the gods? Shortly before dawn the servant left the kitchen, his usual

132

station, and hurried down the street to the temple where he usually worshiped. There he waited until his favorite priest had concluded the morning devotions, then presented to the cleric what he knew. The priest was very upset; he questioned the manservant closely to make sure that he was being truthful before Bithitu's presence, in the Prophet's house. The servant swore that he was being honest in his report and, further, being himself illiterate, he wished the priest to do a favor for him—anonymously, of course.

The priest searched his heart; wanting the best for his empire, he at last did as requested.

An hour later, when the servant was in the city square doing his morning shopping, he made certain to loiter near a certain stall where he knew the seneschal of the palace kitchens made his daily selection of wines and cheeses. When the seneschal appeared, the servant—taking advantage of the growing crowd—passed by him, slipped a note into his hand, and hurried on.

Elad's seneschal looked up quickly but saw around him only a throng of brown tunics and white robes. He was an educated man (requisite for his position on the palace staff), and he knew how to read; glancing at the note forced into his hand, he saw that it was addressed to the High Lord Councilor Abgarthis, For His Eyes Alone, in the Name of Our Prophet Bithitu.

The seneschal was much disturbed.

Cutting short his visit to the market, he hastened back to the palace, greeted Abgarthis at the minister's morning meal, told him the circumstances of the event in the square, and handed him the note.

Abgarthis opened it, read it—and went white. Immediately he hurried to King Elad's chamber.

An hour later, Lord Umothet was enjoying breakfast in his apartment and making suggestive comments to the bare-breasted Siralian girl who served him, when a pounding at his door drew his attention. Momently a servant came to him to announce that a coterie of city guards requested his presence. Anxious, Umothet hurried through his house, wondering what this could possibly portend. Was Elad calling another special meeting of the Council at this time of the morning? The fool was apt enough at games to make that a distinct—

"Lord Umothet of Athadia, High Councilor of the empire?"

133

"You know who I am," he retorted impatiently. "What's the meaning of this?" He glanced warily at the officer as four other soldiers stepped boldly into the foyer and, surrounding him, lifted their hands to their weapons.

"Lord Umothet, you are hereby requested to come peacefully with us and present yourself instantly to King Elad of Athadia, to face charges of high treason against the empire."

A century earlier, Athadia had drawn an arbitrary border between itself and the province of Bithira. Bithira was a land of mountains and fields, its people farmers and shepherds. It had no industry to speak of, and no access to important waterways. Situated north of Emaria, it was a quiet, isolated land, a hodgepodge of principalities and small towns which had remained unchanged for virtually a thousand years.

The mounted squadron which had escorted Prince Cyrodian to the border between Athadia and Bithira ceased its advance within sight of the most eastward fort of the empire, a small command post manned by less than a hundred men, who suffered more from boredom and bad food than from conditions truly perilous. It was on a hill overlooked by this fort that Captain Uvars of the Athadian imperial army trotted his horse to Cyrodian's and unfastened the gyves that had chafed the prince's wrists for nearly ten wearisome days.

As Cyrodian listened impatiently, returning the stares of the baleful eyes that lowered upon him, Captain Uvars loudly read the formal proclamation of crime and verdict and sentence, and ordered Prince Cyrodian to begone forevermore from the boundaries of Athadia, never to return, on pain of immediate death.

Cyrodian laughed in his face. His horse nickered. A cold wind blew down from the steely gray skies, high clouds swarmed like living things far above the mountains to the north, and a few distant birds wheeled and arced in the high haze. Cyrodian fastened his wrathful eyes to Uvar's and was prompted to reply.

"Traitor," Uvars asked him, "have you anything to say before we release you to your fate?"

Cyrodian opened his mouth and drew in a breath. He craned his neck, spat high in the air, aiming the trail of phlegm toward the border. "Anything to say?" he repeated. "Tell Elad, tell my brother . . ."

134

The wind blew, the horses whinnied, leather creaked and armor rattled, voices coughed.

". . . tell my brother that if I am a traitor, then he rules a nation of traitors. Tell him that he's outnumbered. Tell him—tell him he has not seen the last of the blood, that the blood is only beginning, that he will drown in blood." Cyrodian grimaced and chortled thickly. "Will you tell him that, Captain Uvars?"

The commander did not answer; he lifted his hand in a signal, trumpets blared behind him, and hundreds of horses' hoofs pranced about, aiming their riders back toward the west. Uvars made another signal and, with his retainers, galloped to the head of his troop.

Cyrodian sat on his mount and stared for a long hour, watching—silent—watching as the imperial squadron slowly disappeared westward, returning to Athadia, returning to Athad—returning to an empire ruled by a criminal, a dog, and a liar. His brother.

His brother, who would—who must—drown in an ocean of blood. . . .

PART IV

The Dispossessed

1.

He had sailed from Erusabad to Ugalu and wandered the streets there for three days, and as he did, his ecstatic vision of himself and the world rapidly deteriorated. In Ugalu, Thameron spent the last of his money—two coppers—on a loaf of bread; he was unable to wash down this meager meal with anything other than water cajoled from a horsetender he pestered down by the docks. By that evening he was hungry again and unable to buy any more food, let alone pay for lodging. He tried to stay awake by walking the avenues all night long. Shortly after midnight he noticed a wealthy-looking man come out of a tavern near the center of the city; Thameron considered approaching him to beg money, but before he could do so the aristocrat was attacked by a street bandit. Though drunk, the rich man tried to defend himself. As Thameron watched, the attacker knocked his victim to the ground and began to punch him in the head. The aristocrat called for help. Thameron was frightened, undecided what to do, but at that moment he spotted a city guard turning a corner farther up the street. Thameron cried out to him for assistance and, emboldened by the rapid approach of the soldier, crossed the street to aid the aristocrat. He threw himself on the bandit and forced him to the ground, and for his effort received several hard blows across the face. But the city guard arrived and, drawing his sword, forced the robber to return the purse he had stolen, then roped his arms securely and began leading him away. The bandit, protesting and screaming loudly, yelled back to Thameron, "I don't know who you are, but I'll find you, I'll find you and kill you for this!"

Thameron was bleeding from the punches he had received. He didn't give the attacker's threats much thought, however, as the wealthy man proceeded to thank him profusely for his interference. Thameron instantly felt a thrill; surely he would be rewarded with money for having been so heroic.

But that didn't happen. The drunken aristocrat, after thanking Thameron, began cursing about the unsafe streets and walked on. Thameron stood in the moonlight, staring after him, desperately wanting the man to turn around and apologize for his forgetfulness and press a gold piece into his palm. But the man did not turn around; he took a corner, leaving Thameron alone with bleeding face, bruised hands, and pockets as empty as ever.

He felt betrayed. And as he stood there, he felt frightened. Ugalu was not safe. His life was in danger here.

He wandered on through the city, found a lamplit doorway in an alley, and sat down. He was cold and tired; he rested his head against the doorjamb and, wondering what would happen to himself, fell asleep.

When he awoke in the morning, it occurred to him that he had better look for employment. But he knew no trade, had no skills; he was refused at door after door, office after office. An ironsmith told him that he could perhaps find some money laboring at the docks. Thameron hurried to that side of town and approached several warehouses; he was referred to the port authority and shipping offices. In one of them he was asked if he intended to stay in Ugalu of if he was willing to travel.

"I'll do whatever I have to," was Thameron's reply. "I'm hungry. I need to earn some money."

He was told to report within the hour to a merchant galley called the *Wave Rider*; the master needed men for ordinary labor on board during a passage from Ugalu to Hilum in Omeria.

Thameron got the job, although the ship master complained that he looked too scrawny to be a good worker. They set sail that evening; Thameron worked like a beast until night when, almost fainting, he made his way to the common table in the hold and devoured the food set before him (a stew which resembled someone's mischievous regurgitation). He managed to rebut several crude comments from the other sailors on board and fell into a exhausted sleep in his hammock.

As the days passed on the *Rider*, Thameron felt himself becoming annealed by the rigors of his duties; the work seemed to improve both his body and his outlook. He told no one that for all his life he had been a priest—Bithitu only knew with what derision that would have been met. But to explain his boyish naiveté about many of the basic things of life, he made up a story concerning his past as a servant in a rich man's house. He had had to do nothing all his days—(he claimed)—except wait on tables and clean floors; he had educated himself with the help of a friendly priest and one of the wealthy man's daughters. But the man's businesses had failed, and Thameron had been let go. He had been out in the world only a month, and was still wet behind the ears.

The *Rider* made port at Abustad to take on supplies, stopped at Elpet to make a partial exchange of crew, and reached Hilum a week later. As was usual, the crew members were paid half their earnings and allowed a night ashore. Thameron, in the company of half a dozen other sailors, visited many dockside taverns, nearly involved himself in three fistfights, drank wine as he never had in his life and became very drunk, and awoke, half insane with a pounding headache, in a strange room, late at night, with a fat, middle-aged woman who informed him that he had been the finest lover she had ever experienced and that he owed her two in short gold for her amorous services.

Thameron, appalled, refused to pay, so the fat woman began to scream and rave. Frightened, the young man ran from the room—tying his belt as he did so—and escaped down a hallway as thunderous bootsteps resounded behind him. Running through a back door, he discovered an alley and hurried down it and continued to race through a maze of back streets and alleyways until he came near the docks. But greater misfortune awaited him there.

He was young, slim, and not unhandsome. Two large ruffians, dockhands, spotted him wandering half drunk along the quays, to all appearances homeless and nameless. For sport they accosted him, striking Thameron brutally and partially ripping away his trousers. Thameron screamed, thrashed like a maniac, and worked his way free to escape back up the street. He hid in an alley. There, nursing his wounds, he fell asleep.

When he awoke it was to the bright light of late morning. Aware that he was due back at the *Rider* in time for its morning sail, he raced through the crowded streets, afraid that

140

the ship's master would beat him or curtail some of his payment for his tardiness. But he received a rude shock when he reached the quay and spotted the *Rider* nowhere in sight. Frantic, Thameron searched up and down the long rows of anchored ships and finally asked where the merchanter was moored. Told to inquire at a shipping office, he learned to his dismay that the *Rider* had set sail on the morning flood, as scheduled, without him aboard.

Life, he discovered, was—for the inexperienced and the unaware—a thing of cruelly, a confusion, a series of pits and mazes, bluffs and beatings, a fight for survival.

He wandered throughout Hilum, seeking work, gradually using up the limited money that remained from his half-pay as a sailor. For three days he lived in near-desperation, sleeping in alleys, buying only the meagerest amounts of food, even begging in an attempt to save what money he still had. There was a Temple of Bithitu in Hilum, but Thameron did not visit it—a matter of pride. In unguarded moments, when he reflected upon his life in the Temple in Erusabad, it was with disgust and loathing, and he refused to admit that his present life was less rewarding materially than had been his spiritual life in the Holy City. But when he remembered Assia it was with utter regret, for he had left her on a whim, full of naive ambitions and woeful ignorance, and he had been brought low as a lesson. The night of love they had spent together brought an ache to his bowels; her promises that indeed she did love him reduced Thameron to despair. They were very far apart, and he wanted her near him, he wanted her, he wanted Assia.

At last he found work in Hilum with a merchant's caravan that was traveling inland to trade with small villages and towns. When he returned to Hilum two weeks later, it was with money in his purse and a heart more reconciled than ever to the vagaries and discrepancies of life.

Following another period of aimlessly casting about in the city, Thameron secured another job on board a ship, doing the common labor he had done before. It was not a mercantile galley, however, but a pleasure barge, one of many that made a slow passage across the Ursalion Sea to the port of Erphat far to the south. Only the wealthiest bought passage on this ship, and they made the journey for but one purpose: to spend languorous days and incensed nights in the company of prostitutes and other seductive traders of vices, who were used like so many pleasure-giving devices during the voyage. Wealthy aristocrats bought the services of whole companies of boys and girls for long afternoons and evenings. Deformed prostitutes commanded and earned high prices. Rich dowagers were serviced, often in the galleries or out in the open air, by gigantic men of all races. One old man, addicted to the splendors of the narghile, relaxed in fumy dreams as nude courtesans performed tongue-dances up and down his body. An old woman particularly inexhaustible in her need for pretty young girls would savagely bite and scratch the children while in the midst of orgasmic throes, hour after hour. Two notorious businessmen often shared the delicacies of a handsomely painted crippled boy, day after day after rose-colored day. Lesbians performed secret tricks with pearls and oddly-shaped instruments of ivory and glass. Narcophiles shrieked into the night as the lovers atop them transformed into giant laughing beetles or creatures from the depths of the sea.

Thameron quickly became disgusted with all of them, but—as he had been warned by his employer—he did not interfere with either the patrons on board or the prostitutes. Daily he hauled lines, washed decks, and cleaned out the cabins, meanwhile overhearing the choruses of moans, screams, and yelps of pain and pleasure that constantly filled the atmosphere of the barge. He came to regard this ship as a swamp or a hell, and its passengers as inhabitants of some especially loathsome, transported pit.

The slow days passed, misty with incense and aromatic excesses, and Thameron found himself watching one particular young prostitute on the ship. After a time he noticed that she returned his glances. She reminded him somewhat (or so he told himself) of Assia. Her body was similar to Assia's—the girl was short but slim, with slender legs and large breasts. She had a head of foamy dark hair. Her face was something like Assia's, too, with heavy dark eyes and generous, full lips—and when, one afternoon, the young woman made a comment in passing to Thameron, he told himself that her voice, while not as musical or as deep as Assia's, nevertheless contained a quality that seemed to—

He wanted her.

He wanted Assia, but he wanted this girl.

Thameron fought nightly with himself against this madness; he tried vainly to pull back memories of his life before he had left Erusabad. Masturbating frequently every night, he invoked remembrances of Assia's kisses as though performing a magical ceremony. But everything that had seemed golden or splendid to him—small moments, laughters and insights and wise teachings—now seemed to him lies or mistakes. Even the ring Hapad had given him (which he twisted continually around his finger, in what had become a nervous habit) seemed to him symbolic only of things forever lost.

When the pleasure barge docked at Erphat and the voyagers disembarked for a season of continued play, Thameron worked up the courage to talk to the young prostitute. He found her vapid and dull-witted and interested only in what money he could provide her with or what strange new sensations he could introduce her to. Yet, still, he desired her. When night came down they both sneaked off the ship; they passed the evening in Erphat with talk and lovemaking. Thameron discovered that there was more to appreciate in the young woman than he had previously thought; she, for her part, decided that she liked Thameron's eyes and the shape of his buttocks and the way he talked (so different from the coarse men she knew), and his somewhat savage, somewhat boyish manner of making love. In the morning Thameron decided not to make the return crossing on the pleasure ship; he told the girl that he would move on and with his money perhaps travel overland. The young woman asked him if he would like a companion.

The weeks passed as they journeyed throughout the southlands, gradually making their way north. Quickly Thameron lost interest in the girl, but because he didn't want to simply abandon her, he kept her with him. Meanwhile, she began to complain. One night they had an intensely vicious argument; Thameron had been drinking and, outraged at some of the things the girl said to him, struck her. She laughed at him. He struck her again and began to beat her, and as he did, flashing visions of his old life erupted through his mind: the Temple, Muthulis, Andoparas, rich men, rich women—all moved like fleet phantoms alive in his brain, goading him on to strike the girl more brutally. At last, awakening from this, he stopped

143

and stared at her, stared at what he had done: her bloody face, the wet red that drooled from her nose and mouth. Aghast, Thameron dropped to the floor and groveled at the young woman's feet; she pulled him up and kissed him passionately, smearing her blood on his mouth and face. They made love, violent love, on the floor of their rented room, and as they made love the girl shrieked with delight and laughed and begged Thameron to slap her, to continue slapping her as he ravished her. . . .

They continued north. It became habitual for the young woman to steal away from Thameron for an afternoon or an evening, always returning with the soiled smell of other lovers about her and gold in her purse. She shared the gold with Thameron, and sometimes (thinking it would excite him) told him about the things her lovers did to her. Her stories only depressed him.

One afternoon when she was gone, Thameron wandered into the city of Odema and passed beneath the shadow of a holy place. It was not one of Bithitu's temples, but the effect was as though it had been. Thameron suddenly felt a second self erupt from inside him; in the middle of the street he began screaming like a madman, foam flew from his lips, and astonished passers-by jumped from his path. A priest hurried from the church to aid him, but Thameron ran away. Without waiting for the young woman to return, he left the city. He bought a donkey for half the money he had in his purse and went north; in two days he reached Karshesht. Karshesht, he knew, was the first large city one came to when sailing south from Erusabad. So he had, in his travels, almost come completely in a circle, and he was close, very close, to the Holy City. Yet he was not sure if he wanted to continue to Erusabad, so he sold his donkey, rented a room above a tavern, and proceeded to squander his money for the next three days, drinking wine at a table in the serving room.

It was late at night, there was a chill breeze in the air, and Thameron was in a stupor. He was sitting at his table, paying no attention to anyone—patrons or singers or prostitutes—when the door of the tavern opened and a pale, medium-sized man entered. Voices hushed as he came in; people stared, then looked away. Thameron, dully aware of the commotion, looked up. He was intrigued.

144

The stranger was dressed in the robes of a scholar. He carried, also, a tall walking stick of hardwood carved with a strange variety of sigils and cartouches. He was the most profoundly disturbing person Thameron had ever looked upon; there was a sense of repulsion, of foulness—but also of mighty strength—emanating from him.

He walked straight across the floor to the counter and demanded a jug of wine. It was delivered hastily, and the stranger paid with a gold piece. Even from where Thameron sat he could see that it was no ordinary gold piece: it seemed larger, and thicker, than coins currently in circulation. The stranger took his wine, the tavern-keeper made no remark about his coin, and the man quickly turned on his heel and passed again across the room. Ignoring the eyes upon him, he left.

Immediately a babble broke out. Thameron overheard whispers of conversation near him. Turning to a soldier seated at the next table, he asked him—and the gangly red-haired girl he bounced in his lap—if he knew who the stranger might be.

"*I* know!" the girl replied with an air of exaggerated mystery.

"Who is he, then?"

"His name is—"

"Oh, shut up, wench!" the soldier warned her nervously and slapped her head.

"His *name*," she told Thameron insistently, "is Garbaros, and he's a—"

"All right!"

"—a wizard, that's what he is!"

Thameron's eyes went wide. "*What* is he?"

"He's a—"

"Shut up!" exclaimed the soldier, grabbing her hair and pulling it back so that her head jerked. "And you"—to Thameron—"you shut up, too!"

Thameron stared at him for a long moment. Then impulsively, drunk, he threw himself from his chair, ran across the tavern floor, pulled open the door, and hurried outside.

The night was cold. Thameron, sweating, full of wine, instantly felt himself becoming ill from the blast of chill wind which struck him. He ran down the path to the dirt road out front, looked up and down it for sign of Garbaros. He saw no one, so he began to run, calling out the strange name. He ran on wobbly legs, on numb feet he barely felt.

"Fool! What do you want?"

He yelped, astonished, and almost fell on his face as he skidded to a halt. Just before him, standing under a tree, stood the man in the scholar's robes. "Are—are—"

"Idiot! You're drunk. Go back to the women and the dice."

"I—I want to—" Thameron stared into the man's eyes; they were singular eyes, deep-set but almost luminous in the night. "I want to—talk with you—"

"I have nothing to say to drunken idiots."

"Please, please. I want to know—"

The sorcerer stared at him; Thameron felt a wave of power strike him, almost as palpable as a slap in the face. He wondered if it were his imagination, or the wine.

"Is . . . your name Garbaros?" he slurred.

The man seemed to smile in a sinister way. "No," he replied.

"But—but they said—"

"My name is Guburus. And they said I am a sorcerer, didn't they?"

"Yes. Yes, they did."

"Don't you have enough sense to be frightened of sorcerers? Or are you too drunk?"

There was an uneasy pause as Thameron cleared his throat and tried to plan what he should say. He felt as uncomfortable as he had that day he'd faced his masters during his interview before the Holy Council. He flustered, coughed, finally managed: "I—My name is Thameron. I want you to—"

"To what, boy named Thameron?"

"I want to know if you'll let me . . . travel with you. Be your—your servant. I want to study with you."

"But I don't want you to study with me. I don't want a servant."

"Listen to me, please." His senses were clearing; the night was chill, and this man's eyes were inhumanly bright and magnetic. "I—I was once a priest. I studied—I was thrown out of my temple—" Unable to find words, he lifted his hand and showed Guburus his right hand; upon one finger of it was Hapad's ring.

The sorcerer's brows knit. "You were a priest to Bithitu?"

146

"Yes. Yes."

"You jest. From whom did you steal that ring?"

"I did not steal it, Gobor—Guburus. I was a zealous priest. Now I have wandered, I have seen the world, I have smelled its stench—"

"A victim of life. You wish to escape it, or you wish to learn if there is more."

"I know there is more."

"You want power. You want revenge upon someone. Or you think that by becoming a dark mystic you can regain what you lost as a priest."

"I don't want to be a priest. But I am better than other men, I know I am. Yet I am trapped with them. I have searched—All that happens to me—I fall into the mud, I am mocked, humiliated—"

"Yet you sincerely feel that you are better than other men, that you are gifted?"

"Yes," Thameron proclaimed, his voice gathering strength. "Yes, I do."

Guburus regarded him. "Are you willing to trade years of isolation, a lonely existence, for knowledge beyond what taverns and streets can teach?"

"I have known solitude," Thameron answered, voice dropping. "I have been alone in crowds of men, and I have been alone by myself. I know that humanity is weak, and yet I am strong. I have wondered about the rain, and the sunlight." He faced Guburus intently. "I know that there is some mystery which joins all things to some purpose, some great design. But I dwell only among the fragments, the pieces that do not join."

"Thameron," the sorcerer asked him in a deep voice, "do you feel a light within you?"

"Guburus, I do. Yet it shows me no path."

The sorcerer grinned. "The path will find you, if you truly have the light." He reached out with a robed arm, passed an open hand over Thameron's face. "You," he whispered "—aye, you have the light within you."

"Guburus, please. I will be your servant, I want to study with you, if indeed you can teach me, if indeed you are a sorcerer."

"Oh, I am indeed a sorcerer, and a strong one. So you

have heard that betimes sorcerers and wizards take young men into their tutelage, to pass on their knowing?''

"Yes. . . ."

Guburus stared for a long time, a long moment, at the young man before him. His eyes burned more brightly, for a heartbeat, in the night darkness; he glanced back toward the tavern, then again at Thameron. Finally he handed the young man his wine jug.

"Here. Your first task, as servant, will be to carry my parcels and baggage." He turned on his heel and strode down the dark path.

After a moment Thameron, perplexed but relieved, followed him.

2.

Finally, Ibro had had enough. His patience had reached its end. The girl was doing him no good; she couldn't even support herself any longer, and when that time came for anyone it was better to cast them out.

As he made his way up the creaking stairs to the second floor of his tavern, he could hear her loud coughs and wheezings, and they made him even angrier than he was already. Ibro knocked loudly on her door only once, then pushed his way in.

"No more!" he shouted. "You're not bringing in any customers—you're driving customers away! No one wants anything to do with a woman who's sick all the time. Get your things and get out!"

On the bed, Assia lay still, shuddering. This latest attack had been worse than the others, yet she knew that if Ibro would allow her to rest for another day or two—

"Did you hear me?" he growled. He stepped toward her bed.

Weakly she turned her head on her pillow. "Please . . . just let me rest. . . ."

"You're as sick as a sewer rat!" the taverner complained. "I can't let that bed go to waste. I'm not the government—I can't pay anyone to sit around all day and do nothing! I run a business. I've given you more chances than I'd give anyone, just because I like you. But now your luck's run out. Do you hear me, Assia?"

"Please . . . p-please . . . ." she moaned.

Grunting an obscenity, Ibro stalked to her bed, bent, and grabbed one of her arms. Assia winced.

"Stand up!" he yelled at her.

149

Behind him, at the open door, some of the other women peered into the room and drew away, shaking their heads.

"Stand up, damn you!"

He yanked her from the bed. Assia, nude, barely found the energy to stay on her feet. Ibro grabbed her shoulders, forced her chin up so she could look at him.

"Damn!" he growled fiercely. "I've been good to you! I run a clean house! You're sick as a sewer rat! There's no meat left on you!" He slapped her hips with a heavy hand, grabbed one of her breasts and pushed it up so that the nipple stared at her like a strange eye. "Men pay good money for these, but not when they belong to a walking cough! Get your things!"

"Oh, please, Ibro . . ." She began to cry and sank back on the bed; as the tears rolled down her cheeks she inevitably began to cough, more loudly than before.

"Come on, I've had just about en—"

She lay back, stretched her body full out on the bed so that she resembled a pale shadow, a totally abject victim. "I can't!" she whined. "I can't go anyplace. I don't know anyone!"

"Be friendly to them," Ibro suggested. "Be friendly to them! You'll find someplace to stay. Just get your butt out of here before noon, when paying people come around. You understand me?"

She sobbed and tried to roll over.

Ibro smacked her brutally hard on the belly. "I said, did you hear me?"

Assia, coughing, doubled up and rolled over on the bed. "I heard, I heard!" she moaned, burying her face in the pillows.

Ibro marched to the open door. "By noon, Assia! Or I'll throw you naked into the street. I'll have you arrested." And he thundered down the landing, down the steps into his tavern.

Assia cried and cried. Gingerly, double-checking to make sure that Ibro wasn't returning, three of the girls crept into her room, knelt on the floor beside her bed.

"The son of a bitch!" one of them swore.

"We ought to just knife him!" exclaimed another.

"He's a monster, he's sick!" the third added, pouting.

"Listen, Assia, listen to us," the first pleaded. "We'll get you some money. We haven't got much, but we can give you a little—enough to get you a doctor. Assia?"

She groaned and sobbed, curled her legs up and bit her hand, coughed, coughed.

"Assia? Please. We don't want him to hurt you. Will you take some money? Will you go see a doctor? Assia?"

Tyrus, in his early fifties and in reasonably good health, shared a room with three other sailors. He was a cranky old dog, used to giving way to no man. His face was pitted by an early bout with disease, and scars on his cheeks and arms attested to numerous fights he'd taken part in, on ships and in taverns. Temperamental, irritable, by turns dour or robust and possessed of a crude sense of humor, Tyrus was happy to see his daughter only when she brought him extra money from her earnings on the street. So he did not exude overly affectionate paternal warmth at Assia's return to him this morning.

"Why can't you learn to take care of yourself?" was his first remark to her. "Didn't I teach you how to take care of yourself? What's the matter with you? Now you're coughing and spitting up all over the place. No, don't sit on my bed. Sit down over there. In the chair."

They were not alone. As Assia, weak and exhausted, collapsed into the shaking wooden chair set at the single table, Tyrus shot a look at the two other men in the room—his companions, roommates. The same age as he (and older than the useless rascal who, armless, occupied the fourth corner of their quarters), both men had, on more than one occasion, sampled Assia's wares. They regretted seeing her in this condition; there was little sentimentality involved, but they liked the girl as they might have enjoyed a trained puppy, and few can take joy at the idea of a sick puppy.

"Didn't bring much with her today," one of them commented.

"Won't be bringing much tomorrow," opined the other.

Tyrus, standing beside the table and frowning at his ill daughter, was well aware of this. Here was his gambling money; here was his drinking money. Gruffly he asked her, "Will he take you back?"

"He told me—" Assia coughed at length. "He told me to . . . see a doctor."

Tyrus worked his mouth, scratched his stubbly chin with bony fingers. He glanced at the other two, who were lying

151

abed and watching Assia as she slumped in her chair. Her skirt, loose and slipping over her hips, had partially revealed her buttocks, and they were entertained by that. Tyrus walked over to them. "You"—he pointed—"owe me two in silver. And you—it comes to three in short gold."

They looked at him with surprise.

"She needs a doctor, doesn't she?"

They stared at him, mute.

"I know where you hide your purses," Tyrus reminded them. Casually he reached his hand behind his back—as if to finger the knife sheathed in his belt there, although he did no more than scratch an itch.

The two men looked at one another.

"Eh," admitted one finally. "Aye . . . she needs a doctor. . . ."

Sodulus the physician kept them waiting all afternoon. The reason was simple: Tyrus and his daughter were Sabhites. It was not that Sodulus himself was a strongly prejudiced person; he was, however, a man of common sense. And common sense dictated that, in the Athadian sections of Erusabad, westerners were shown preference over easterners. The opposite held true on the other side of the river. For Sodulus to have practiced otherwise would have meant for him to lose business; and while he had served patients for over thirty-five years in the Holy City and had striven to apportion his talents equally to all, regardless of racial or tribal background, still—barriers existed, he could never change them, and so he had adapted to them.

Tyrus and Assia waited impatiently, the old seaman voicing all kinds of complaints but never going so far as to make threats—never going so far, in fact, as to raise his voice very loudly. He, too, knew that barriers existed, and he, too, had adapted. That he lived in the Athadian section of Erusabad was his good fortune; that he was half-eastern by birth was no great calamity in such a metropolis; that he had earned his livelihood with the crewmen of western ships was due to his perseverance and will. And so if he occasionally had to wait a long time in line, or if once in a while he had taken a barbed comment about his "dark meat" too much to heart—well, such was life.

It was, in any event, Assia's coughing that affected his

temper more than the wait outside the physician's door. It irritated him. The presence of his ill daughter portended too many things, loss of extra money paramount among them, but also a loss of self-esteem (no parent should live long enough to see his own child sicken to death); and also—also—Assia's sickness brought back memories of her dying mother.

She, too, had been a prostitute. And even more beautiful than her daughter. And subjected to the murderous life on the docks by circumstance, although Tyrus, when he'd married her, had vowed to improve their conditions. He had failed. Away at sea, he never witnessed his wife's debauches with others; and though she had sworn to him that Assia was truly born of his own seed, Tyrus had never been certain, could never be certain. . . .

"Come in now," Sodulus called to them from the opened door.

Tyrus helped the hobbling Assia within. She sat in a chair in the center of the physician's small examining chamber. Everywhere was the stench of many combined medicines, oils, plants, and herbs and powders.

Sodulus did not apologize for having kept them waiting. But he did not delay in seeing after Assia. He had her remove her vest and shirt and he listened to her heart, then listened to her lungs by placing a hollow reed between her breasts and pressing his ear to the opposite end. He tapped her chest, felt beneath her breasts, pressed her belly, and fingered her throat and behind her ears.

Tyrus watched the physician's expression for any sign that might give away his thoughts. But Sodulus was saturnine.

At last he told Assia to put her clothes back on, and he turned to Tyrus. "You are her father?"

"Yes."

"Your daughter is quite ill."

Assia moaned as she buttoned her vest.

Tyrus became afraid. Had she contracted a disease from someone? If so, then . . . "What's the matter with her?" he asked.

"Your daughter is seriously ill in her lungs. I do not believe it is due to a contagion. That is, it cannot be passed along. But the effects will come and go, and each attack will have a tendency to be severer than the one before. When the attacks come, you must allow her to rest. Have her lie on her

153

side. If she coughs a great deal she may vomit phlegm from the lungs; that will be a good thing. Pound on her back, that would help."

Tyrus stared at him. "But will she— She will not—"

Sodulus held up a long white hand. "I cannot say. All of us are mortal." He was not being sincere in intimating that Assia's disease was not fatal, but he had long ago learned the spiritual benefit of this. "Who knows?" he assured Tyrus, and then managed a grin at Assia. "You may defeat it. Burn *mith* leaves as an incense, if you can afford to do so. The vapors will help to clean out the lungs; throw drops of water on the coals as you do so. Are you a sailor?"

"Yes."

"It would be a good thing if you could take your daughter with you on your voyages. For some lung diseases, a dry climate is the best treatment; for others, a more humid atmosphere seems to be beneficial. I believe the sea air may do your daughter good. Are you able to do that?"

Tyrus stared at him. "I—I suppose so." He thought for a moment, then ventured, "My daughter is employed. Her income is needed."

Sodulus said nothing.

"She works as a—a servant in a rich man's house. He has threatened her. Will she be able to continue working?" Tyrus asked in an apprehensive tone.

"I doubt that," the physician counseled him. "These attacks will recur. It is best for her to rest and, as I say, burn the *mith* and take the sea air. If you can—"

Assia moaned and slumped forward a little.

Tyrus looked at her, fingered the purse at his belt. "How much?" he asked Sodulus.

"Whatever you can afford. A copper will suffice. I am here to serve; pay me what you can, according to your income."

Tyrus reached into the purse, fingered what he had. Three coppers. He took out two and handed them to Sodulus. But then he removed the third and gave him that.

Sodulus set the money aside, beside a small wooden box on the table. "Buy some *mith* leaves," he told Tyrus. "And if you can take her to sea—"

"Yes, yes. I will." He stared at Assia—weak, pale, coughing, but still a beautiful young woman, he had to admit it.

154

"Should she give birth to this child, with her condition?".
"But she wants this baby. They say it will be a girl."
"Then let her try. It is all I can do, and she may—"

It was out of the question that they should pay for a sea voyage. Tyrus knew he would not have to. He was not, however, eager to sail again; he was comfortable in Erusabad. But if he stayed in Erusabad—well, then Assia would sicken more and more and finally die.

He spoke with several masters he knew on the wharves. One took pity on Assia and agreed to give them passage on his next sailing. That would be in two days. He was carrying a load of wine and cloth goods to Elpet, within the Athadian Empire.

Assia stayed in her father's apartment for those two days. She rested, and her health began to return. Tyrus debated whether or not actually to take the voyage.

But Assia begged him; she did not wish to stay in Erusabad, which held only sad memories for her. And so the following morning they boarded the merchanter and set out for Elpet.

3.

"Oh, cynicism is in style nowadays. People have no character anymore," Mantho complained. "They've reduced themselves to personalities, and they believe that personality is all there is. They lack integrity." He drummed his fingers on the table, then moved a soldier on the *usto* board three spaces to the left. "Your turn."

Adred smiled at him and as he rolled the dice commented, "But that's true of everyone; always has been. You can't say that people today have a monopoly on those defects." The dice settled, showing Adred a three, a two, and a six. He grinned and reached for his king. "Prepare to defend yourself, my friend!"

"But it's more true today than ever before," Mantho countered. "Look at the people. They're dissatisfied and they don't know why; or if they do know why, they blame someone else. They've gotten too used to having someone take care of them. Can't take care of themselves. Who's to blame for that? Good move."

Adred removed one of Mantho's black guards and set his red king three spaces from his friend's. "Better roll a three, or you're done for."

Mantho dropped the dice: two threes and a five. Adred groaned. His host leisurely walked his king diagonally across the square and, with his advantage of five, enclosed Adred's king. "Too many people," he continued, smiling, as he moved in and knocked over Adred's king. "Usto."

Adred shook his head. "If I were twenty years older," he remarked, "I'd be like you. Smug, self-confident, wanting to hold onto everything I have."

"I've worked hard for it."

"I'll give you that. You weren't born to the silver. But you owe what you have to everyone else in the country; without them, you couldn't have prospered and what you have would be meaningless."

"Don't pull out Radulis on me!" Mantho laughed, tipped his wine cup toward Adred in a salute. "Your argument's faulty, but you played a good game."

Adred sighed. "People are upset everywhere. But the wealthy stay indoors, and their nostrils are so clogged with incense and perfume, they can't smell the stink from the streets."

"The stink from the streets is pretty strong here in Sulos," Mantho told him. "We've had these riots and protests going on for the past month. Remember the day you left for the capital?"

"I'd assumed that was just a small gathering."

Mantho shook his head. "Went on for three days. Arrested hundreds of people."

"For jobs," Adred said, anger in his voice. "For food, for jobs . . ."

"Yes." Mantho sighed, sympathizing as only the successful can with the dispossessed.

Fifty-two years old, he had had a brilliant career in finance and business, due to his combining an interest for money with a love of sport and the military. His greatest financial coup— the assumption of control of a large shipping and textile exporting firm—had been inspired by the Battle of Kadaeosh, an early glory of the Athadian Civil Wars. The successful risk had made him an extremely wealthy man at the very young age of twenty-four; and since then . . .

"If we don't see full-scale riots soon, we'll see a war. It could only help the economy, couldn't it?" Adred asked.

"I'd rather be in a war. At least there you have something solid to fight for, something to live for. It gives you ideals. Gods! Why can't we *believe* in *ourselves* anymore."

Adred stood up and stretched, fingered some of the discarded *usto* pieces. "Care for another game?"

"In a little while, perhaps. I want to go out and check up on some—" He stopped abruptly, looking at the door.

Adred turned at his stare. It was Orain, standing at the steps of the portico Her expression was grave; she was visibly trembling.

157

Adred took a step toward her. "What is it, Orain?" Now he noticed the slip of paper in one of her hands.

"A . . . letter," she answered quietly, nearly in a whisper. Stepping down into the tiled portico, she walked to Adred and handed it to him. As she did, she looked to Count Mantho. "A letter from Abgarthis," she said, "at court. A courier just br—"

"Oh, gods, *no!*" Adred exclaimed.

"Queen—Lady Yta . . . has been murdered."

Mantho's eyes went wide.

"By soldiers," Adred said numbly, looking his friend in the eye. "By imperial soldiers—under orders from Cyrodian!"

"But if—Cyrodian?" Mantho fell quiet, and the terrible truth struck him and chilled him. "Fighting Elad?" he asked rhetorically. "From exile? For the *throne*?"

"Why not?" Adred growled, crumpling the letter and furiously hurling it to the floor. "Anyone who kills nowadays has his chance at ruling the country. And with—with only the best of intentions, of course!"

"Calm down, calm down, we must—"

"Oh, why didn't Elad just ax the bastard and damn the army to hell!" Adred shot back, fire in his eyes. "We can't even feed the hungry people in our country, and these fools are killing every member of their family!"

Orain, taking the chair Adred had vacated, leaned forward, elbows on the table, and stared dully, emptily, at the gray-clothed Mantho, looking through him. Adred, glancing at her, felt his fury dissolve, bleed away, as he remembered Dursoris on the night of his death—*killing every member in their family!*—mutilated, and Orain . . .

Orain . . .

"I—" He stepped closer to her. "I'm very sorry," he apologized in a low tone.

Mantho looked on with knitted brows, but Orain shook her head silently and drew in a deep, steady breath. "You're right," she whispered. "No . . . no . . . you're right. Cyrodian should have been killed." Quietly, staring now at the floor: "But only after they'd tortured him and . . . done things to him—cruel things."

Mantho, who had found the Lady Orain charming and generous, stared at her now, utterly speechless.

*   *   *

158

"I shouldn't have said that," Orain apologized later. "I didn't mean it, I shouldn't have said it. No one should wish evil upon anyone else."

"That's true; we shouldn't. But people are only people, after all. It's trying to do our best that makes us good, not the occasional failure that hurts us."

She looked at Mantho. All was very quiet. There was but one lamp burning, and it hissed slightly with the last of its oil. Adred had gone out and taken Galvus with him—a talk between men, he'd called it. There were times when the two of them, so dissimilar in age and temperament, still seemed able to communicate in a way that was foreign to everyone else.

"Would you like to spend the night out here?" Mantho asked. They were on the enclosed balcony of a room on the second floor. "It's cooler. The breeze is cool, but it might refresh you."

"I'd like that, yes. Thank you."

"No trouble. I'll send a servant in with some things." He bowed slightly and went out, smiling a friendly, honest smile at her as he softly closed the door.

Orain lay back on the couch, closed her eyes. Time moved so quickly. There was no time to pause, relax, no time to ponder as she had when a young woman, no time to read or to discuss wonderful things with thoughtful people, no time left to laugh. . . .

Gods, was there no laughter anymore?

Or had that, too, died with Dursoris?

Soft footsteps. She opened her eyes and looked up. A manservant, middle-aged, was setting out a number of blankets and pillows on a chair. He turned to Orain as she sat up.

"My name is Euis," he announced in a low voice. "I'll be up all night; I sleep on this floor. If there's anything you need, Lady Orain, just ring the bell."

"Thank you. Thank you, Euis. I will do that."

He bowed slightly, took a step toward the door—and paused.

Orain watched him, and then she heard it, too. Distant—but nonetheless loud for the distance.

"What—" she murmured. But she knew, even as Euis explained it to her.

"The riots," he answered quickly. "Again . . . tonight . . . and close by. They fight in the streets—"

159

"It doesn't go on every night, does it?" Orain asked him.

"Almost every night. They're hungry every night. Some are killed"—his voice was almost silent, now—"and then they aren't hungry any longer." He looked down at her. "Are they?" he asked.

Orain didn't know what to say to him. What could she say? "I'm . . . sorry."

Euis smiled at her, but in the dimness Orain could not know if he was sincere. "I'm sorry, too," the servant admitted, "but not for them. For the soldiers, for the rich people, for the aristocrats . . ."

Orain was suddenly taken by a deep feeling of apprehension.

"Forgive me, lady." He bowed again. "I meant nothing by it. But it continues, every night. No one seems to have any answers, and there is no peace." He shuffled out, and Orain listened to him cross the room and leave.

She sat where she was for a very long time, thinking of what he had said.

4.

Sorcery, Guburus said, *is the ultimate awareness of Self, the profoundest realization of Nature, formed into direct action. Man is not a part of Nature; Man is Nature. When the Outer and the Inner, when the Greater and Lesser are joined, Man is a god.*

He had been impressed by the fact that Thameron was an outcast priest of Bithitu. "So you have learned," was Guburus's comment, "that religion exists only to take advantage of the spiritual hungers in men and is the enemy of the true spirit? Good. Now at least you are prepared to free your spirit and learn and grow." Too, he was impressed by the strength of the young man; for it was apparent to the sorcerer that Thameron was truly among those who burned with the inner light.

"You will be eager," Guburus warned Thameron, "to learn all things at once. You will be impatient to do mighty things without first learning to do many small things. But when did a man ever run before he learned to walk? When did anyone ever chew meat before he had sucked his mother's milk? What babe has ever handled a man's weapons without first learning to play with its toys? Therefore your progress will be slow; it will be gradual but continual as you daily, monthly, yearly toil to become a magus."

Slowly . . . gradually . . . But Thameron was, indeed, impatient with that prospect. He suspected that some children are, after all, born to a man's weapons and are special among other men; he believed himself to be one of those children.

* * *

You must first learn the secrets of colors and of light, of sounds and of echoes, and the many dimensions of illusion. For all is illusion, but we accept the illusion as a reality, for it is the channel of our strength. Your inner universe will blossom, and you will have the strength of a god. But the strength of a god is not all the strength that is. Good is not always passive, nor evil always active. Neither is sorcery a tool of evil, though a man can be: sorcery is a tool of the man, it is a thing of contemplation and resolve, it is a moment of action in a universe of awareness. Never believe that you are alone; never believe that something dead is not yet alive in some form. Know that the body is but an episode in a greater spiritual process. And know that you will battle, yes, elements that are only yourself in another guise. For you will become the All, in that moment of action.

Guburus had many homes, some in the forest, some by the sea, some in the desert. He wandered everywhere. At the moment he lived in a cave that was situated in the side of a mountain only a few leagues south of Karshesht. From the cave mouth, Thameron could look down upon rolling fields that led eastward into the heart of the Salukadian Empire. To the west, the land sloped to the sea, where small villages had not yet been absorbed by the ever-expanding port metropolises.

Thameron was bored by his first few days in the cave. Guburus left him alone, and Thameron did little but wander up and down the mountain or watch the sorcerer at his routine. Guburus spent much time sitting crouched in a chalk circle, meditating, or reading by the light of the sun; occasionally he tended to the fruit trees, berry bushes, and three goats he kept just outside the cave. For Thameron, who had had the impression that sorcerers lived ceremoniously and imperiously, it was a rude awakening to find this mage living frugally, doing little better than a poor farmer.

However: "I leave you alone," Guburus informed him, "so that you may forget your life in the city. Shall I take you from a tavern and teach you an awesome spell, so that you can damn yourself quickly? You must walk on the mountain, you must study the stars, you must feel your body beginning to move with the rhythms of the moon's cycle; you must feel your blood flowing with the pulse of growing roots; you must perceive your inner spirit, that which glows with the intensity

162

of the sun. And the first thing you must do is call yourself from yourself, look into the mirror of your spirit and awaken to yourself.''

You must follow the twenty-one paths slowly, one at a time. The first path is mu-sa-eth; *the second is* mu-oso-ith; *and so on. When you have learned the twenty-one paths of* Shod Haru *you will begin to join the paths together. Finally, you will tread the last path, the path of* Im-O Yaru. *Then you will begin your ascent into the Spheres. You will learn of the true elements: fire and air, earth and water and spirit. You will learn of the currents of your body and the spheres of your mind. Your finger is as powerful as an ax or a sword. Your mind can make flames appear or demolish a city. You have demons within you, and strong spirits. You will learn to speak with phantoms; you will learn to make the air scream; you will join life to life and terrify men with simple truths. But you will do none of these things until you confront yourself and unify yourself with the greater Nature.*

But Thameron was anxious and eager. He felt that he was indeed born to become a sorcerer—he had the strength in him; he was hungry to move upon the world and do what he would do. He envisioned himself as a powerful light, as a strong shadow. Guburus insisted that he must train patiently; Thameron felt that he had already trained patiently in things of the spirit—was he not an exiled priest of Bithitu?

Secretly one night, when Guburus had left the cave to walk below the stars and converse with images, Thameron stole into a back chamber of the many-roomed cavern and went through Guburus's things. He had not yet witnessed one of the sorcerer's rituals, but already he sensed how those things were done. For the magus had many wands and swords, many amulets and talismans, many objects and jars and oils, boxes of incense powder, scrolls of spells and ceremonies, many robes, many different-colored chalks and candles, crystals and glass spheres—all the accouterments which the learned and the initiated used to build paths into the greater spheres.

As he stood there, in the dusky light of a single oil lamp, Thameron felt a visitation come over him—a presence, almost a real voice or an impossibly strong memory. Himself speaking to himself? He felt himself to be one with that room, with those things of gramarye. He had been born to their use, and he had wasted his life in a temple of religion! He was appalled at himself. He wondered if there were not some way suddenly to absorb all that must be learned, rather than continue wasting weeks, months, even years under the tutelage of Guburus.

In a small closet Thameron discovered a cache of jewels. One in particular fascinated him, and he closed his fingers upon it. It felt warm and damp, like a living thing, although Thameron knew that it was only a gem. He opened his hands and stared at it; it glowed, seemed almost to pulse or breathe in some singular fashion—

"I suspected this."

He turned quickly at Guburus's voice. The sorcerer, returned from his walk, was at the door of the chamber; he did not appear to be angry, but rather seemed saddened.

"Guburus, please don't be cross with me. I want these things. I am a sorcerer, I am born to it! I cannot spend my days wandering and staring at the sun and listening to noises—I have already done all of that!"

The magus stepped into the room, took the stone from Thameron's grip and replaced it in his closet, closed it up, and led the young man away. "You are so eager, eager to learn, to do. I can understand this. But you wish me to teach you, and I will teach you—but you must respect your teacher."

"Guburus, I respect you profoundly! I begged you to take me. But I feel a great call in me—I feel—"

"I know what you feel. Your inner self is awakening, and it wants to have all. Your training is to control that hunger, to chain it to your command. Do not let your commands take on a life of their own; if you cannot control these impulses, they will master you and you will come to ruin."

But Thameron chafed at the promise of continued restraint. "You do not teach me fast enough, Guburus! Are you—are you afraid that I will learn more quickly than you can teach? Are you afraid that I will grow stronger than you?"

"Thameron, the teacher always hopes that the pupil will surpass him, but there are methods by which that is accomplished. Listen to me, and know this: You will surely betray the promise within you if you attempt too much too swiftly."

"I am strong—"

"You are strong, yes! You can learn. But time is a teacher, too."

"Guburus—"

"You want that gem. Thameron, you do not know what it is."

"It is power."

"It is all the steps at once, Thameron; yet it is more. It is a door which, once opened, cannot be closed. It is a challenge."

"What kind of challenge?"

"I will frighten you, Thameron; perhaps that will sober your impatience. That jewel belonged to the early gods. It must be broken in half in a certain way, to unravel its powers. If it is not done correctly, then the spirit is damned, and you surely have no comprehension of what that means. If it is done correctly, however, the highest path is attained. Now, I don't tell you this to tempt you, though I'm sure you are inspired by my story. Yet do you truly believe that you, a nothing, a boy, no sorcerer as yet, can unlock its secret, when I, who have striven through many accumulated lifetimes, still feel unprepared enough not to have dared it thus far?"

Thameron's heart beat quickly. He asked, "Guburus, do you not believe that my road met yours for a purpose?"

"Yes, for a purpose."

"And for what purpose?"

"I believe, Thameron, that I will unlock the gem, and when I have done so, my earth-spirit will be passed on to you. I am your mentor; you are my pupil."

"Could there be no other reason for our paths to have met at this time?"

Guburus read Thameron's mind and sensed what a troublous pup he must have been to his mundane masters in the city Temple. Leaning close, he lost patience and warned Thameron directly. "The jewel is mine! Do not attempt to alter the destiny that has been given to you!" His cold eyes pierced the youth's, and Guburus knew that he had won his argument. "Respect me as your teacher, and I will respect you as my pupil. That is our bargain."

Thameron stared at him, quietened. One part of him was afraid—of Guburus's powers, which were great—but another part of him wished only to attain his robe of sorcery and begin to do the things that ached in his heart. Given a destiny? True—and Thameron knew that the light which burned within him, unclear though it was, was a light beckoning him to do more than live in a cave for numberless years, slowly learning to separate fire from fog. He wanted power, and he would have it.

But he told Guburus, "I—I will do as you say."

Guburus's expression softened only slightly. "Do not attempt to steal the gem, or do anything against me in private. If you misstep once, Thameron, I will punish you; if you err a second time, I will banish you from me. But if you dare to return to me after all that, I will not speak to you; I will slay you."

Thameron nodded nervously. "But teach me," he insisted, "teach me as much as I can absorb, as quickly as you can. I want to succeed—I want all of it. Respect that in me, please."

Guburus nodded solemnly. "Then I shall do so. But if you cry out, I will not answer you. If you scream, I will be deaf."

Apprehensive, Thameron agreed to that challenge.

Guburus turned and left the cave, going out again into the cool, starry night.

And Thameron sat where he was, wondering, imagining, promising himself . . .

It is a door which, once opened, cannot be closed.

It is a door. . . .

A door . . .

5.

The day, silent as gold, drowned brilliantly at the edge of the sea, taking Assia's heart and spirit with it. From the rail of the ship she watched this gorgeous spectacle, awesome in its simplicity. All her days she had lived by the ocean and had ignored it. All her years she had felt her heart within her breast and had not known it. Was it possible that a few brief moments of pastel beauty could open doors to some sublime mystery? Or was she only sentimental? Did the poignancy of those moments lie to her? Was she searching for some mock thing, some whisper, shadow, some childhood fantasy lost, until now, in the gold of dying sun, in the wavelets of rippling ocean tide?

She was, after all, only a lonely, ill young woman, too much aware of her body and her life of poverty.

It was, after all, only a few moments in the endless rotation of sun and day, moon and night, twilight and dawn. Secrets there?

Then there must be secrets, too, in the hissing burn of oil lamps, in the sweat of grunting men, in the cool shadows and the cool coins of hot taverns, hot tongues.

And she knew that there were not. . . .

Elpet was a white city on a stretch of brown rock. As the sun died and as the merchanter was pushed on by the tide and low winds, the white became orange and the brown became purple. The city looked to be quite small; as the galley came nearer, seeming to move more quickly, Assia discerned people moving on the docks.

Her father stood beside her at the rail. His stance was

protective. Assia had not coughted for the past three days; they had been sailing for five.

Tentatively she asked him, "Have you ever been to this city before?"

Tentatively he answered her, "Yes, many times."

Daughter and father, two strangers. Was there love between them? Of a strange kind, perhaps. But love is made up of patience and habit; small concerns; incompletenesses; shared failures; unresolved, diaphanous visitations of thought. It is a conscious bond; it is intermittent difficulties despite myriad strengths. Was there love between them? Could love grow between them? Simply because one was parent, the other child?

Assia knew that other fathers loved their daughters; she knew that other fathers didn't always sell their daughters to men for money. But she did not know what it would feel like to be that kind of daughter and, in a moment's free imagination, warmed by a sunset, she wondered.

And gradually, as the sun died, as the gold was taken away, as the night became any other night, she wanted to cry. A great hatred welled up within her and, wanting to cry, she wanted to kill her father, dismiss him, or refuse in some powerful way the fact of his existence.

Then a moment of joy gripped her; she coughed slightly; she wondered who she was. She remembered Thameron and knew that she would never see him again, and she became very frightened—very frightened—of being a stranger in an unfamiliar city, and thus a new kind of stranger to her father.

Tyrus said to her, "You don't seem to be coughing as much."

"I'm feeling . . . better." She did not discern any real concern or love in his voice.

Perhaps he hoped that she could earn money in Elpet, to reimburse him for the trouble he had gone to in saving her life, in keeping her from dying.

They joined the caravan of passengers that crowded onto the docks and wended their way into the noisy city. Here and there, in the smoky, lamplit darkness, voices called out to offer payment for palanquins or carriages. Most walked, trudging up the long wooden docks, up the stone paths, into the muddy or cobbled streets. Mounted soldiers in Athadian regalia pranced their horses along the way, farther ahead in the square. Beggars cried out for coin. Thieves slipped and slid like shadows, at home. Prostitutes blatantly propositioned sailors and businessmen. Past the warehouses and the portside offices, traders offered their wares from stalls or mats: skins of wine, loaves of bread, finely honed knives, newly made boots, warm cloaks.

Tyrus carried their belongings in a sack slung over one shoulder. He guided Assia with his free hand, holding her arm and pushing her in one direction, pulling her in another, so that they could get through the press as quickly as possible. He was silent until he and his daughter were in the square and past the last of the beggars and barterers.

"We have enough to get a room for tonight."

"And after that?" she asked.

"We'll see."

There were cheap hostels just inside the square, but Tyrus walked past them. Far away from the lights and noise of the docks, the square branched off into three stony avenues, all dark and silent save for torches and occasional sounds of distant life. It was as if a curtain had suddenly dropped between this area and the one they had just left. A wind blew up, and Assia hugged herself to stay warm. It was nearly autumn, and the night was chilly.

At last Tyrus found the door of a small place around a corner. Assia wondered if he had stayed here regularly during his years as a sailor. But she didn't ask. Tyrus paid for their room—single bed and a meal in the morning—and helped Assia upstairs, never releasing his hold on her arm.

She did not like the bed. She was used to sleeping on a wooden frame cushioned with straw and cloth pillows; this one was made of strung rope, like a hammock. When she lay down beside her father, they were pulled together in the center.

Tyrus fell asleep immediately, but it took Assia a long while to relax. She listened to her father snore; she stared at the light of the torch outside her window; she listened to the dim sounds of customers in the tavern below. Her stomach growled; a heavy ache slowly formed in her chest until, forced to cough it out, she wheezed. The ache remained, dry and hot. She was chilly, and there was only one blanket, which her father, rolling around in troublous slumber, stole from her off and on during the night.

She finally fell asleep in the gray before dawn, with memories thick around her: the long voyage, Thameron, the thousand and one men she had clung to in Erusabad, her father—not cruel now. That was certainly a mystery. As she began to slumber, she had a curious dream. Thameron was in it, and he and Assia were laughing as they sat at a wooden table. There was a large fresh loaf of bread on the table, steaming hot. And they were laughing like street fools.

Assia awoke a short time later when she felt something in her hair. She murmured and realized that it was her father's hand on her head. He was stroking her hair. She wondered what it meant. But then she fell asleep again and did not dream of Thameron or of warm loaves of bread. She dreamed that she walked, on bloody feet, rags wrapped around her shins—walked on gravel, in an endless twilight, walked and walked. It was important to her, in the dream, to remain alive while she walked.

The following morning they ate breakfast in the tavern; then Tyrus told Assia to return to their room and occupy herself, take care of herself. He went into the city.

But Assia did not want to lie down. After a while she went out to explore. She did not stray far—she wanted to be in the room when her father returned—but she walked the few streets nearest the tavern. Elpet was a small city, nowhere near the immense size of Erusabad. She knew, too (because she had heard men talking on the ship), that while it was ostensibly a part of the Athadian Empire, Elpet was historically and commonly taken to be a city of the Province of Omeria.

She watched the haggling and bartering that went on, listened to the pious prayers of priests at a temple, happened to witness a swift fight between a soldier and a well-dressed young man in an alley. When she came upon a man who made puppets dance in a little curtained stall, she laughed. Actually laughed—laughed out loud, in her hoarse, girlish voice, as she watched the puppets argue and pantomime and contort. The story had something to do with a cuckolded husband and his wife's affair with a giant bear; some fairy tale. . . .

170

When she returned to the tavern, Assia found her father and another man sitting at a table, eating a meal and sharing a bottle of wine. She joined them. A dismal mood came upon her as she listened to the man and her father talk boisterously about the old days they had shared together on board ships. Occasionally her father's companion, an overweight and slovenly man, eyed Assia with barely concealed lust. A chill curled in her bowels. Feigning illness, she coughed and excused herself, went up to her room. She lay down and slept.

When she woke up a short time later, Assia saw the slovenly fat man sitting in a chair opposite the bed. He was staring at her; his teeth showed in a faint, arrogant smile. The bed creaked as Assia sat up quickly.

"Where is my father?" Her voice quaked with apprehension.

The fat man said not a word but pointed a finger toward the door. Assia turned and looked; no one was there. Jumping from the bed, she hurried out onto the landing, scurried down the stairs. She found her father sitting at a table, drinking wine.

"What are you doing?" she spat at him, fierce and angry-eyed.

"Keep your voice down!" Tyrus growled. "He's an old friend, he can help us—"

"What are you doing to me?" she asked him, anxious, almost in tears. "I didn't come here to—"

His hand slid across the table, clutched her forearm in a viselike grip. "He can help us," Tyrus snarled, eying her coldly. "I've got gold in my purse, girl. Gold! Not coppers, not breadcrumbs!"

She stared at him. What had she done to herself? Why had she ever let herself believe that there was anything else? Why had she dared look at sunsets?

"Now get up there," Tyrus ordered her. "Make him happy. He can help us, you'll see. You're not sick. Get up there! And don't let anyone know what's going on."

She rose from her seat, staring at him, thought about running to the door, never considered asking anyone else there for help . . . and finally turned slowly and walked to the stairs.

The fat man had undressed and was standing by the window. He was covered with hair; his belly gave him the

171

appearance of being a human barrel supported by doughy legs.

He smiled at Assia. "Close the door. That's it. Go ahead, take your clothes off. Yes . . . yes . . . That's it. Come on over here. That's right. Oh, you are a beautiful little thing, look at you! Come on over here. Take them off, yes . . . yes. Think you can handle this? Think you can? Come on, come on over here, that's it. Yes, you're beautiful, you're— Crying! Oh, I won't let it hurt you, I won't let it hurt you! There you go—yes, yes, see, it likes you, it wants to be your friend. . . ."

6.

After a little over a month in Sulos, Adred was beginning to feel restless. Mantho recognized his symptoms. "You want to return to the capital, don't you?"

But Adred wasn't certain he wished to do that. He knew that Orain now seemed content to remain in Sulos. The shock of Yta's death affected her greatly. As for himself, "I feel that I must do something," Adred told his friend. "The capital? No, not yet. But I know I need to travel."

"The uplands are pleasant this time of year," Mantho suggested. "It gets chilly up there—but they have pretty girls to keep you warm." He winked. "The change would do you good. You'd be listening to people complain all day about boring things like crops, the weather, who's getting married— and not a peep about the King."

It sounded splendid to Adred. He was becoming preoccupied with news that came from the capital, news that deeply disturbed him. He and Orain had been receiving letters regularly—twice a week—from Abgarthis, detailing events in Athad. Elad's purge, the elder had reported, had not proved to be the prelude to palace insurrection, as had at first been anticipated; the reshuffling of bureaucratic seats had left Elad in charge of a reorganized and substantially less obtrusive hierarchy. Abgarthis sent word that all the traitors who had plotted with the exiled Cyrodian for the death of Yta—from Lord Umothet right down to a single rider in Captain Uvars's squadron of escort—had been discovered and beheaded. The whereabouts of Prince Cyrodian, however, remained unknown. Units dispatched immediately upon the discovery of the plot had met the troop of Uvars on their return from the Bithiran border; but a thorough search of the hills and villages in the

173

wide vicinity of the borderlands had yielded not one clue of the renegade. If any of the farmers or shepherds in the region had heard or seen aught of him, they refused to admit it. Uvars and his men, with the units sent by King Elad, returned to the capital with empty manacles.

This failure had incensed Elad, but wisely he had made a political move in reaction to it, rather than one of brute force. To a gathering of army leaders invited to the palace, Elad had made an address and had discussed openly (or as openly as he dared) the situation with Cyrodian. It was never my intention, he told the imperial army, to make enemies of you; I believe that condition was artificially created by Cyrodian. Now that the matter is cleared up, I would like to acknowledge my feelings toward the army by making a gesture of good faith: a bonus for every commander, every officer, and every sword in the imperial service. You will find these bonuses in your pay allotments at the end of the month. As Cyrodian himself had said, he was beginning to learn.

Abgarthis made it clear in his letters to Adred and Orain that this spontaneous intention to buy the loyalty of the army would dangerously deplete the royal treasury. Advised of this, Elad had ordered additional coin minted. This meant the buying of surplus gold held in reserve in the mines of allied provinces and cheapening it with alloys. The expenditure must prove to be disastrous. To make certain that the treasury would not be wholly emptied by this bonus pay to the army, Elad ordered a policy of limited withdrawals from the banks throughout the empire. At the same time the government borrowed funds from several agencies and businesses friendly to the throne, at a very high rate of interest. As Abgarthis reported, this plan had caused an uproar in the Council. How could the king dare to limit available funds, simply to buy the affection of an army that mistrusted him in the first place?

But Elad had held firm. The coins were hurriedly minted from surplus stock even as additional shipments were ordered from the gold mines of northeast Galsia and southern Herulia. And the extra bonuses appeared in the pay allotments given to the army at the end of Hutt, the Month of the Horse—just in time for the soldiers to spend in celebration of the Feast of the Ascension, Athadia's most religious holiday.

*   *   *

174

On the day before the Feast of the Ascension (held to observe the rising of the Prophet into the Hall of the Gods, following his death), Adred went to a banking house in Sulos where he kept an account. The bank was crowded, as it always was on the day before a national holiday, with merchants tallying their totals and the wealthy withdrawing funds to pay for private festivities. But today the crowd in the bank was angry and volatile. Elad's verdict had come down, and there was a limit to the amount anyone could withdraw from his own banking account: no more than ten percent of what was held in one's name, per day. Adred had wanted to withdraw ten in long gold, but a quick check of his records indicated that ten in long gold amounted to twelve percent of his holdings in the bank.

"We can only give you nine in long and three in short today, Count Adred. You can withdraw more after the holiday, but for now—"

"This is ridiculous! It's my money! I shall withdraw as much as I desire!"

"I'm very sorry. If you want to complain, complain to the King . . . This is King Elad's verdict, and we must obey—at least until a new order is issued from the royal treasury."

Adred cursed with rage—as did everyone else there. But no one could do more, for the number of city guards at all banks had been doubled to prevent outbursts of violence. Jakovas, the military governor in Kendia, had been ordered to do so by Elad himself—at Athadia's expense, of course.

Adred withdrew what he could and walked all the way back to Mantho's apartment, fuming and mentally drawing up a ferocious letter of complaint against Elad. But there was another surprise awaiting him when he returned.

That same morning Orain and Galvus had left to do some shopping. Adred now found the princess and her son being tended to by Mantho's servants, and Mantho, at his most bellicose, cursing the King in three languages.

"What's happened?" Adred asked, utterly astonished.

Orain had been cut on the head and her skirt torn—a whole side ripped away from ankle to hip. Galvus's shirt was in tatters, and he had a number of bad bruises and cuts on his arms.

"A riot!" Mantho barked, tempestuous, to the aghast Adred. *"Where?"*

175

Orain winced as a servant woman applied some kind of oil to her cut forehead, but told Adred, "In the Shemtu Square. Galvus and I—ouch!—we'd gone shopping, and we were in a little glass shop when a whole squad of soldiers galloped down the street. We ran out to see what was happening. There was a large crowd—very large crowd of— All right, it's stopped bleeding now. Please! Thank you, thank you."

"A large crowd." Galvus faced Adred. "Governor Jakovas's headquarters are at the end of the square; his mansion is there. The people lined up—"

"A mob!" Mantho interjected furiously. "A mob of Osonites!"

"Osonite" was the common term to describe them; Oson had been an anarchist of the previous generation, a rebel whose hot-tempered, profoundly logical arguments on behalf of the deprived within the empire had led him to a violent end.

"The *people*," Galvus insisted, "lined up in front of the governor's mansion. Some of them started throwing bricks and rocks—so we heard, anyway. Jakovas called in the soldiers, and they drew their swords on them."

"Do them good!" Mantho growled blisteringly. "Cut them down, damned sewer rats!"

Galvus turned to him, reddening. "Can't you understand why they did it?" he asked hotly. "We have everything, they don't have a—"

"They might have killed you, boy!" Mantho retorted, leaning forward. "Don't you understand that you might have been *killed*? Your *mother* might have been *killed*?"

"All right, enough, please!" Orain cried out, reaching for Galvus's arm. "We are guests here! Galvus! We are Count Mantho's guests!"

Wounded, he shot a look at her, stood up, and crossed the room, brooding, shaking. "Will you excuse me?" he asked quietly.

Mantho looked at him for a long moment, slowly nodded, and Galvus left the room.

Breathing a heavy sigh, the businessman made a gesture to calm everyone's emotions. "Have a glass of wine," he offered Orain and Adred.

Orain helped herself, but Adred let out a low curse.

"What's wrong?" Mantho inquired. "It's over—at least

176

for now. Blood in the streets. We're almost getting used to it, here. I'm only sorry that—"

"Elad mustn't know," Adred replied desperately. "Orain and Galvus are royal blood; he'll have this city smashed to its stones if he finds out they were almost killed!" He laughed bitterly. "No—that would take money, wouldn't it? And Elad doesn't have any money right now."

Mantho and Orain stared at him.

"I went to the bank," Adred informed them. "Elad's limited the withdrawal of funds—remember?"

Orain couldn't believe it. "But Abgarthis said—"

"It wasn't to be for individual accounts. He was only interested in large businesses, merchants—people like me. This is outrageous!" Mantho fumed, becoming angry afresh. "He can't do it! He'll have the nobility crawling all over him!"

"It's only temporary. Besides, what can the nobility do? I'm sure the businesses underwritten by the throne aren't going to be affected. If anything, they'll profit by it—somehow. Elad's paying all this money to the army. You see? We don't have the good sense to use weapons, Mantho, and organize ourselves into a cavalry regiment. All we do is generate profit for the treasury. Elad's just bought himself the services of the largest palace guard in history—with our money, of course."

"Damn him!" Mantho growled, feeling personally betrayed.

"Good Feast to you," Adred replied. "We'll praise the Prophet in the Hall and the King on the earth. And if some people get too noisy—why, we'll just hire an army of cut-throats to kill them! Simple, isn't it? The Prophet had it all wrong. Ruling a country is easy—you just feed the people excuses and feed your rich friends more money. Gods! We were better off as a fishing village!"

7.

Had Ogodis's private image of himself ever become manifest as his actual appearance, the man would have been transformed overnight into a handsome giant with the intellect of a deity, the refinement of an educated squire, and the noble justice of the afterworld's weigher of souls. That he was something less than this, in fact, did not deter the Imbur of Gaegosh from seeing such a reflection in his mind's mirror. Ogodis knew himself to be superior to other men. He was the son of a long line of potentates, and he was Imbur—a title that predated, even, that of king within the borders of the Athadian Empire. An Imbur had ruled in the collected counties of Gaegosh since the beginning of time, and Ogodis would never be anything other than Imbur of his people. He had a throne—although not a throne as lofty as that of King Elad's in Athadia—and he had a court and an economy and subject peoples. It was his destiny to maintain his authority always, in the face of domestic rebels and in spite of the impolitic maneuverings of neighboring states.

On equal terms, then, with the leaders of other small nations that bordered the Athadian empire, Ogodis nevertheless saw himself as their better simply by virtue of Gaegosh's location and the interdependence it exercised with Athadia. For many long centuries trade had existed between Sugat and Athad, to the mutual benefit of both. There were no border patrols or forts strung along the banks of the River Ussal; there was no need, for neither nation had ever taken up arms against the other. Differences had historically been settled by negotiation. Even the expansionist armies of two hundred years ago had stopped their advance after crossing the river; and when the Imbur So-Mufutis, Ogodis's great-great-grandfather, had complained to the Athadian Council, the Council had decided to draw its boundary where the army had camped. As time passed, the stretch of land that had been occupied became a common territory between the two nations; the provinces there, the villages and small communities, spoke a dialect of Athadian, paid a tribute to the Imbur, and all remained well between Athad and Sugat.

This memory of a sound relationship between Athadia and Gaegosh now served Ogodis well. For as autumn fell upon the world, he observed from his capital the conflicts that besieged King Elad. Quick to offer aid to his country's perpetual ally, Ogodis, upon Elad's ascension, had forwarded his congratulations as well as a caravan of gifts. Later, learning of a plot against Elad's life, Ogodis had sent word that if he could be of any assistance in helping to punish the reprobates, King Elad should not hesitate in asking for such reinforcement. And now, as the season of the holidays approached—the Feast of the Ascension, followed in two days by the Celebration of Perpetual Grace and, six days later, by the week-long fast of the Holy Observance of the Ascension and the Deliverance—Ogodis saw an opportune time to make his presence felt more strongly within the empire. He saw an opportunity, as well, to create an actual alliance between his state and Athadia: something that had not occurred for over four hundred years.

History teaches lessons to the prescient. Time is a circle, and not a line. And where the modern seems to supersede the antiquated, those who can see realize that humanity changes only in its outward guise and never in its soul. The causes of war always remain fundamentally the same; accords of peace are ever written in the same language. Extremes are only the results of limitations, and frontiers open their doors even as one passes from one border to another. The wave of history moves from crest to crest, from trough to trough, and the prescient determine the crests and the troughs, and the deliberate can create strength where history might indicate weakness.

Ogodis, therefore, stared at the pieces on the *usto* board and noticed that all the advantages lay with him. Elad had weathered the first storms of office and remained enthroned; enemies were rife upon Athadia's borders—in Emaria, no friend to the empire, and in Salukadia, half a world away—

but Gaegosh remained as firm as ever in its commitment to amicability. Most pertinent of all, however, was the fact that Elad was young, powerful—and unmarried. A king without a wife, Ogodis supposed, is a rider without a horse, a body without a spirit. His own wife, though dead now for many years, still lived within him, in his heart. And though they had between them created only one child, that child was a daughter. And while Ogodis was remarkably unattractive as a man, his wife had been a beautiful woman, and the gods, in their wisdom and delight, had been generous with Ogodis's daughter in giving her the benefit of her mother's decisive qualities.

Ogodis, the Imbur of Gaegosh, wished to improve his power in the world, and that meant taking advantage of the instabilities in that nation which remained the most powerful in the world: the Empire of Athadia. The strongest means by which he might secure this alignment, he knew, was not by conference, was less by argument or pledge than it was by taking advantage of some very human strengths and weaknesses. Therefore Ogodis, the Imbur of Gaegosh and theoretical best friend to the throne in Athad, decided to wed his only child, his daughter Salia, to King Elad of the empire.

That Salia, overprotected since birth and catered to all her years, was regarded at large as the single most beautiful woman in the world, was—as far as Ogodis was concerned—merely the most obvious factor in his plan to approach Elad with an international policy of mutually rewarding benefit and profit.

King Elad had graciously granted the Imbur's request to visit the capital during the two-week festivities of Bithitu. On the day following his decision to augment the imperial army's pay in time for the holidays, Elad received word from Sugat that Ogodis, his daughter Salia, and an escort from their palace would arrive in Athad the day prior to the Feast of the Ascension.

Abgarthis ordered all things prepared for their arrival: generous lodgings on the second floor of the palace; an extra recruitment of guards and servants in that wing; the invitation of certain dancers, masquers, rhapsodes, and other entertainers; and an abundant supply of food and liquors.

Abgarthis thought it his duty to warn Elad that Ogodis, a

180

crafty man, had it in mind to do more than merely spend time in the company of a friendly allied monarch. Elad assured his minister that he understood that every politician—himself included—says three things when he speaks but once.

But Abgarthis insisted, "King Elad, don't you realize that Ogodis is the father of an extremely beautiful young woman, and that it would be to his advantage to see her wed to the monarch of the empire?"

Elad shrugged. "If his daughter is all that beautiful, then I'd think less of him if he didn't make such a suggestion."

"He will do just that, I'm sure of it. Our office in Sugat has reported to me that this concern seems foremost in the Imbur's mind. It would be very much to his advantage to see his family formally allied once again—as it was four centuries ago—to the lineage of Athadia."

"My friend"—Elad smiled at him—"can you see any danger in such a proposal?"

"In appearances, no."

"Then why are you concerned?"

"There may be events occurring in Sugat of which we have had no word. But even if Ogodis's action is not self-serving now—Elad, I have seen you hint at moving in any of six directions, then surprise your Council by taking the seventh."

The King laughed out loud at the accusation.

Abgarthis smiled quaintly. "You are a king, and you are a man. Squire away as many evenings as you like with the palace maids—"

Elad put on a shocked expression. "You make me sound like a stallion in a stable of fillies!"

"—as you like," Abgarthis continued, "but taking a wife is extremely serious."

"Abgarthis," Elad said to him, "try to calm yourself. I realize that your skill lies in anticipating events and in placing those events in perspective. I appreciate that; I admire it; I require you as an adviser above all others at my Council. But you don't really think that I'm going to aspire to Lady Salia's hand—and whatever else she may have—on the first afternoon I meet her, do you?"

"I'll remind you of that," Abgarthis cautioned him, "some afternoon next week."

*   *   *

181

The first snowfall of autumn, light and cool, was falling upon the capital as Ogodis's royal barge docked. The light coating of frost and ice lent, beneath the cool sunlight, a charming beauty to even the most ramshackle of the quay's warehouses and office buildings. For Ogodis, who had not visited Athadia in over three years, the brilliant beauty of the snow seemed a presentiment.

He and his daughter and their company were escorted to the palace by a contingent of Khamar palace guards: a hundred men to guide the arrival of twenty Gaegoshan nobles. Ogodis was impressed. He and his daughter were taken by carriage up the wide streets and into the main square before the palace. Trumpeters announced their appearance even as they stepped from their carriage and were led up the wide white stairs to the front portico, inside, and down the massive gold-walled and marble-pillared hall into the king's audience chamber—which had been wholly redecorated and arranged with long stone tables, sweet-burning oil lamps, purple and gold and blue rugs, brilliantly woven tapestries.

Abgarthis was there, the first to greet the Imbur, his daughter, and their company. Bowing deferentially, Abgarthis made a short speech of welcome before, with a clap of his hands, ordering Khamars to pull aside draperies hiding the throne dais and an inner portion of the chamber. Gradually, to Ogodis's and Salia's eyes, appeared a huge, sumptuous feasting hall all garlanded and lamplit, smoky with perfumes, shining with silver and gold, aromatic with the scents of cedarwood and pine, the lure of roasted meats and freshly cooked vegetables.

They entered. Ogodis, foremost, made his way to Elad's dais, where, bowing thrice, he declared his friendship unto the King of Athadia and asked that the gracious bounty of the gods be heaped upon him tenfold. Elad thanked him and stepped down from his throne, gripped his arm, looked the Imbur in the eyes. So that, in a moment, each one had the measure of the other—king and king, man and man, lion-crown and hawk-miter.

Elad turned to Salia. Peripherally he had noticed her pale pink skin, her flowing golden hair. Now Ogodis presented his daughter, and Elad felt himself tightening as, for the first time in his life, he looked fully upon her beauty.

"But you don't really think that I'm going to aspire to

182

Lady Salia's hand on the first afternoon I meet her, do you?''

The most beautiful woman in the world . . .

Surely a statue by Hovem-ovis, brought to life.

Almost intolerably young in appearance. Pale, fragile pink skin. Daring blue-gray eyes. Mouth, red-tinted . . . golden hair . . . slim hand. . . . Dressed in a sea-blue gown of silk that clung to her body as though carefully pressed upon her. Silver fillets in her hair. A ruby gem at her throat.

Her eyes smiled at him, naive but tolerant. When she spoke to him, thanking him for accepting her father's proposal to intrude upon him, her voice was charmingly quiet, enviably patrician.

Elad became aware that he was staring at her. Quickly— too quickly—he turned from her, glanced at Ogodis and noticed the Imbur's broad smile, bowed ceremoniously.

"We have set out tables," he remarked, his voice only slightly unnerved, "and there will be entertainment. If you please, my lord, seat yourselves and enjoy the evening!"

As his guests were escorted to their chairs, Elad, surprised at himself, nonetheless stared after the lithe form of Salia— the grace with which she moved, the dignity of her step, the hint of cleavage at her buttocks, the sly reminder of long legs . . .

Surely Ogodis was a crafty—

"King Elad." His adviser, standing beside him, revealed a very slight, private grin. "It is, King Elad," Abgarthis reminded him, "next week."

"Indeed it is, O adviser. Indeed it is."

8.

O Season of Hell, repugnant to the hopeful. . . .

On sees all, but waits.

O fears profound, cauterizing memories! O pain boundless, shrinking full life to a whisper of shadows! O torments—O remembrance of bloody feet, stinging heart, prayers rent, kneeling in the mud, begging for money, begging for justice, begging like some heartsick animal. . . .

O Season of Hell, to be embraced as a lover!

O sucking mouth, O wet flesh, O moving bodies, untired and damp and sobbing, angry and alone, alone, alone. . . .

Forest of shadows, mind of shadows. Speak of the ageless death. Open a crystal.

I am a god. . . .

O, beyond all hope, destruction of reason, I have lost myself unto myself, I am no more a man, I am no more a thought, I wish to scream forever, my blood burns, my lungs ache, I hate myself and I am trapped in my body, trapped in my body, trapped. . . .

O Season of Hell, O sucking mouth, O whispering tendril, O thing in my mind . . .

He was sitting in the woods, seated on the mountainside, watching the dying sun as it shattered into sheets of orange and mauve and blue, feeling his veins burn. He was afraid, because he had been inside himself, and he was like a drowning man who, sunk too many times, wishes an end to his misery as fervently as he wishes some force to lift him free of the ocean's hold.

The stranger appeared to him as he watched the dying sun. The stranger was dressed in the garb of a gentleman, and the sweat and dust of the road were upon him. Why he was this high in the mountains was a wonder. But Thameron had been a stranger himself, many times, and he knew the wary moods of strangers—not the voice of a god, perplexed, but the tenacity of suspicious desperation, wanting all to be made clear.

"I am on the road to Fortubad. Perhaps you can tell me the way."

"I am a hermit; I live in a cave and do not know where Fortubad is. But there are cities on the coast."

"On the coast, then. Fortubad is a port."

"Go back down the mountain and continue east. The coast is but a day distant."

The stranger sat down beside him, frankly studied him. "You are a priest, isolated."

"I am a sorcerer. A young sorcerer, managing my craft."

"Who is your master? I may know him."

"Indeed?"

"Indeed, it is true. I myself, when a youth, studied the arts to a limited extent. I attained the path of *Shiol* before my fortune changed and I was put out into the world."

"My master is Guburus, feared and respected."

"His name is known. You must be an able young student to have won such a master for yourself."

"He tolerates me, and I drink wisdom at his feet. He is a stern *mu-apath,* but wise in the paths."

The stranger remained silent for a time before asking, "Has Guburus halved the stone, as of yet?"

Thameron went cold. "You know of the stone? The gem?"

A smile in the twilight. "The Brotherhood is far-ranging, but we know of one another. All know of the stone. Some were jealous that it came to Guburus, but all support his right to learn from it and to gain his chance at halving it."

Thameron, still astonished, made some unwise comment.

"I halved it once," pronounced the stranger.

Thameron called him a liar to his face.

The stranger sighed. "It is true. It was in another lifetime, long and long ago. But I attained the right to attempt it, and I succeeded. I gained the highest of Spheres. But even there, I erred, and was cast back down to earth to learn again. Do you not believe me?"

"Such a thing is . . . possible," Thameron allowed.

"Do you not wish to halve the stone?"

185

Thameron trembled. "In time," was his answer. "I am young yet, a neophyte, nothing. I have no right."

"Your soul is ancient. You have been alive for many lives. Do you not know this?"

"I—suspected it," Thameron whispered, moving now from his *tofi* position and relaxing.

"I can feel it in you. You have as much right to attempt it as Guburus."

Thameron was quaking with tension. "I have approached him about this, but he refuses me. He claims I am too young, unlearned."

"You are a boy in this life, but your soul is at least as ancient as Guburus's. I know these things. Look you, place your hand upon your forehead. Thus." He showed Thameron how he meant.

Thameron did as instructed; Guburus had never shown him this gesture.

The stranger asked him, *"O-tomu ra, se sedi ke niu?"*

Thameron did not know the words, but before he had a chance to stop himself he answered the stranger in the same tongue: *"Es sedi no-bu uru, uf suffa omu art."*

"You see?" the stranger said to him, pulling Thameron's hand from his face.

The young sorcerer was shivering and sweating. He didn't know what he had done, nor how he had done it. But he felt as though a tidal wave were pounding inside him, immense and elemental, cosmic, surging for release.

"The stone," the stranger told him, "is easily halved. If you believe a thing to be complex, it is complex. If you believe it to be simple, its essence speaks to you."

"Tell me," Thameron whispered, staring at the last of the sun.

The stranger looked at him.

Thameron faced him, eyes burning, flesh hot, body shaking. *"Tell me."*

The stranger smiled, held up his hands. . . .

The morning of sorrow will never arrive. The dark night of endless suffering will not be released. I am no longer my name.

O Season of Hell, you are a bosom to me, you are a pliant

186

lover, I am divorced from the world, memories lie, what else can I love but that without love, being what I am become?

O deep, deep, deep as the endless reaches of a gulfed infinity, my fallen heart. There is no weight to shadows, no light in Hell, no light, no light. . . .

I am my own prisoner, reduced astronomically within myself, and unable to escape.

Guburus was crouched before a small table, reading a book by the light of an oil lamp and eating roasted seeds. He looked up, perplexed, as Thameron rushed in, glanced at his master, and, without a word, hurried on into the farther rooms of the cavern.

"Thameron!"

Too late. Guburus rose to his feet and crossed the room, moved toward the tunnel corridor—and was knocked to his knees by a fiercely cold wind that burst into the cavern without warning. Guburus groaned and managed to stand upright; he turned, looked out the open-front of the cave.

No one. Nothing. Only the scintillant white stars, distant, in a chill black sky.

"Thameron! Do not, *do not*!"

He moved again toward the tunnel, and again the wind blew down on him, forcing him to his knees. Furious, Guburus pivoted on his boots and threw out a hand, aimed his bony fingers at the night.

"In the Name of the Seven *Tosirim*, stand you back, guard against my anger, unknown *essusus!*"

The wind held back, but Guburus could not be certain that it was due to his warning. Again he stood up and faced the tunnel.

"Thameron, do not—!"

And a scream answered him—hollow, piercing, damned.

"*Thameron!*"

The wind came again. Guburus howled in rage, directed a fist at his oil lamp, and demanded of it, "Take the form of my enemy! Fire him to ashes! *Isbosutu me teh oro!*"

Immediately the small flame of the lamp leapt into the air, a line of white-red blazing inside the cavern. It formed itself into a circle and spun in the center of the chamber like a spokeless wheel, sent out geysers of smoke. It expanded and, more gaseous, elongated toward floor and ceiling.

"Show yourself, emissary of Hell!"

The flame did exactly that—but only for a moment. Guburus, wide-eyed, stared at the form of a virulent *ashomin*. Then it was gone, the flame dispersed from the smoke, the smoke pulling back in a gray wind toward the cave mouth. Gone to the night.

Shaking, Guburus turned at the sound of footsteps behind him.

Thameron.

At the mouth of the tunnel.

Facing him, with the stone in his bleeding hands.

Look of horror and surprise in his eyes.

"You . . . have . . . not—!" Guburus gasped.

In each red palm, one half of the stone.

Guburus sucked in a slow breath. *"Damned be you!"* he screamed at Thameron. *"You could not have—!"*

But Thameron, all stunned, seemed little more than a corpse. His skin was white and shiny with perspiration, his cheeks gaunt, his eyes blazing with yellow terror. Tears began to roll down his face.

"I—" His voice was a croak.

"Fool!" Guburus shrieked at him. "Fool! *Fool! Damned be you!* That creature has sold your soul to Hell!"

"He—" Thameron gasped, shook his head; the halved stone fell from his hands, dropped to the floor. Immediately the two portions melted away, sending up plumes of yellow steam.

"Fool! Fool! Foo—"

"I am . . . ancient!" Thameron whispered to him.

"He has *damned* you!" Guburus yelled. "It was an *ashomin!* Ancient as the gods! They feast on us! They rise from *Gehem* on cold nights to answer the prayers of the soulless! Fool! You are trapped, you are damned! A thousand lifetimes will not release you!"

Thameron's eyes glowed brightly; he stumbled forward a step, and the tears dropped from his face. But he did not seem to express agony at the prospect of annihilation.

"You lie," he whispered to the sorcerer.

"You called him forth!" Guburus charged him. "You called him forth! You summoned him from the Spheres! Is your ambition limitless, that you would sell yourself on the moment for an eternity of—"

188

"I am a power now, Guburus!"

"It is not the power of the *paths*, Thameron!" his master screamed at him, quaking now with fear for the youth. "Gods of the gods, you are undone!"

"I am immortal."

"You are foul! He has stolen your dream; he has clothed you in shadows and flame!"

"I scream inside, Guburus, with wisdom, with strength. . . ."

"It was an *ashomin*, Thameron! It was foulness, foul! You called it forth!"

Still Thameron stood, like some corpse reanimated. Shivering, awakening, pulling himself into Thameron once more—awakening from a trance, or fighting to keep his spirit enclosed within his body.

"Fool!" Guburus screamed, voice rising again in shame and anger. "Thameron! Thameron, let me kill you now!"

Thameron's eyes lit up.

"Gods, gods, let me kill you now, free yourself from this hold!"

"He does not hold me, Guburus. I am ancienter than he."

"He feeds your lust! Do you not know what you have done?"

"Guburus, I am a sorcerer, now. The door is opened."

"Close the door! Name of Aeiham, *kill yourself now!*"

Thameron hissed at him.

Quickly Guburus moved to do what was needed. Crouching, he swiveled on his feet and hurriedly traced a circle around him in the dust of the cave floor.

"*No*, Guburus!" Thameron threw out a hand. Flames licked at the sorcerer's finger where it touched the earth, and Guburus pulled his hand back, hurt.

"What has he done to you, Thameron?"

"I am what always was in me, sorcerer. I am your equal—no, I am beyond you. You saw the strength in me; you knew what I was."

"It could not be released at once," Guburus argued with him. "The power of the gods does not reside in the vessel of youth."

"*I am as old as the sea*, Guburus! I walked the earth when the mountains were groaning and rising up from the plains."

"You cannot do that now. You must control it! Your quest

is not for power, but for enlightenment. Bithitu!'' he screamed. ''Do you not believe in your—

Thameron snarled at him. Moment by moment he was becoming himself again—young, proud, but with a shadow upon him, and a darkness in his eyes. ''The greater that was in me—''

''All men have it!'' Guburus screamed at him. *''It is as ancient as the race! Chain it, or it will destroy you!''*

''I . . . am . . . *Thameron*!'' he howled back, as if announcing himself in the Hall of the Gods.

''Chain it! Name of Omro, chain it, *chain it*, or you will destroy your—''

Thameron moved toward him.

Guburus fell back. ''Thameron,'' he whispered, ''stand before me.''

Wary, the young man approached his mentor.

''The first path, Thameron. Visualize it. The color—the scent. Lift yourself—''

Thameron's eyes glowed brightly. ''You seek to trap me!''

''Thameron, you cannot—''

''You want to kill me?''

''Free yourself from this evil!'' Guburus shouted at him. And then, swiftly, he raised his hands and gestured, drawing power into himself.

Thameron jumped away and moved his arms, drawing up his own defense. ''I have all the paths now!'' he hissed at his master. ''I am more than you, Guburus! Do not embattle me!''

''Slay yourself,'' the elder demanded of him, coldly, succinctly.

''Remove your aura, Guburus, or I will destroy you.''

''I am well learned, Thameron. My strength is old, it is—''

''Die,'' Thameron said then, and clenched his left hand into a fist, pointed it at Guburus, and spread his fingers.

Guburus screamed, *''Nefusith ala alam!''*

Thameron grunted.

Guburus's eyes went wide. A sphere of pink mist surrounded him. He dropped to his knees, and the light of terror filled his eyes. Once more he gestured—but he was unable even to complete the movements. Deep sweat broke out on him and ran in rivers down the seams of his face; he gasped for breath;

190

his body shook as violently as if he were caught in a furious tempest.

"*What are you?*" he screamed at Thameron, although his voice, within the pink shell, sounded distant and muffled. "What have you become? *What are you?*"

Thameron spoke a word at him, whispering it; and it was done. Guburus howled, and his dwindling howl, the echo of it, hung in the air even as his body was swallowed by a sheen of brilliant light. Then the light vanished, the pink sphere evaporated as a mist, and where the sorcerer had knelt there remained only the smoking black bones, half eaten, and the grainy dust of his body, still glowing.

Slowly, slowly, Thameron's arm fell to his side as he stared at the corpse.

What have I done?

Breath returned to him, and strength, his own spirit. He came awake and knew what he had done, but only dimly perceived himself as the creator of it.

What have I done?

A cold wind blew upon him, and he looked up.

Brilliant light at the mouth of the cave. Thameron gasped, turned away.

You are become your destiny, O man. You are chosen, the vessel, the being, the embodiment of the last days. Demand that shadows bow before you and mountains bend in praise, for you are become your destiny, O man beyond men, O Prince of Darkness, Master of the Hell of Men!

Thameron stared at the brilliant light, even as it faded.

Tremendous fear suffused him. Trembling, terrified and alone, he cried out into the night, "What have you done? What have you done to me?"

But the light was gone, the voice—the voice was but an echo.

. . . O Prince of Darkness, Master of the Hell of Men!

"*Tell me!*" Thameron screamed as he began to sob. Groaning, he stared at the remains of Guburus, blasted dust, and, crying wildly, he dropped to the floor of the cave, fell forward on his hands—and yelled in pain.

He pulled his hands up. The palms, where they had struck the floor, were burned.

Burned.

Thameron stared at his palms.

191

"No-oho-ooo . . ."

Burned. Branded—the right hand with two intertwined crescent moons, the left with the inverted seven-pointed star.

". . . oho-ooo!"

Master of the Hell of Men. Ancient evil, vessel of evil, Prince of Darkness.

Ancient—promised—and now returned . . .

PART V

The West Is Dying

1.

Alone, he had wandered south through the fieldlands for two days, stopping once at an isolated farm house to buy food and water his horse. "Do you speak Athadian?" They had shaken their heads; but the elder son, who had traveled a bit, was able to fabricate with Cyrodian a mutually comprehensible jargon. *Ebu*—food. Water for my horse. I can pay you in Athadian gold. . . . When he left them, at twilight, he made sure that one essential message was quite clear to them: If others come after me, others who speak Athadian, tell them I rode north.

He had been concerned all during the ride that Captain Uvars might kill him. Cyrodian couldn't believe that Elad hadn't given the commander such an order. When he had been freed and no threat to his life made, the import was clear: Assassins would come later, or riders had been sent ahead to wait for him. So he journeyed cautiously.

Two days south; another day brought him to border posts, obelisks, which marked the beginnings of the kingdom of Emaria. At a point which he had earlier indicated on a map, Cyrodian found shelter in a small huddle of rocks. He waited. There was a lake, and so he fished—doing as well as he could, devising a makeshift rod and string without the use of any weapons. But he had flint and steel, and so he was able to keep himself warm with a fire. The days were cool and, here on the open plainfields, chilly with wide breezes. At night the air turned cold, and Cyrodian was surprised that it didn't snow.

He waited, day after day after day. No sign of riders coming to assassinate him. And no sign of Umothet or Umothet's hirelings, bringing him weapons and decent food.

194

A week passed. He was becoming ill, surviving only on small fish. He couldn't understand what delayed Umothet. It occurred to him that their plot might have been uncovered, but Cyrodian dismissed that; they had planned too well, and every man was trustworthy. Yet his allies did not appear. Had Yta been murdered? Had Umothet been discovered somehow?

Cyrodian began to wonder if he was a fool for having trusted anyone other than himself.

Finally, disgusted and hungry, weaponless and ready to kill to salvage himself, he mounted his horse and continued south. Into Emaria. He did not have a map with him, but he had led enough campaigns and had surveyed enough maps of the continent to know that Lasura, the capital, should be but a week distant.

That evening, as the cold wrapped around him and as his horse staggered, he sighted an Emarian fort. It was situated on a low rise, and the land around it had been denuded. Cyrodian approached and watched, amused, as soldiers lined up on the wall to observe him. Coming within speaking distance, he hailed them and called, *"Iro supeke Athadaki?* Anyone here speak Athadian?"

The soldiers looked at one another, surprised, and finally one yelled back, "I speak Athadian! Who are you? Where are you from?"

Leaning forward on his horse, giant frame a shadow in the dusk, voice booming like the rumble of coming thunder: "I am Cyrodian! Sent into exile by my brother Elad, King of Athadia! I need food and rest and weapons!"

There was furious confusion on the wall; the speaker slapped one man on the shoulder, and that soldier hurried down from the battlements.

"Let me in, damn you!" Cyrodian yelled. "My horse is ready to drop!"

The soldier returned to the wall, his commander beside him. The commander stared down for a space, then went down again.

Suspicious bastards, Cyrodian thought. It came to him that perhaps Elad had entered into an agreement with them, with their king. Were they the assassins?

Slowly the great doors of the fort were pulled open. A voice called, "Enter, Prince Cyrodian!" so he nudged his horse forward. Through the gate, beneath keen eyes in the guard towers. Into the open court. A soldier in Emarian armor took his mount's reins, held them while Cyrodian dismounted; then the horse was led to a nearby stable.

He stood, erect and proud, regarding the gathering before him. Their commander, a tall, slim man with the rangy physique of a hillsman, stepped ahead, lifting his arm in an openhanded Emarian salute.

"You are welcome here, Prince Cyrodian. I am Commander Laguro. Are you in need of food?"

"I'm famished." He returned the salute with his own: a seriously executed Athadian fist over the heart.

In the dining hall, where he sat opposite Commander Laguro while many retainers and officers crowded around, Cyrodian asked, "You have heard nothing from Athadia, have you?"

"Only that Elad had taken the throne, that Queen Yta stepped down following King Evarris's death. Other than that—nothing. Our forces here were doubled, of course."

Cyrodian smiled. The relationship between Athadia and Emaria had ever been a cautious one. As he chewed on his beef and drank deeply of his wine, he explained to Laguro and the others exactly what had precipitated his appearance at the fort. Elad, eager for the throne, had forced his mother to step down; he had ordered the assassination of Dursoris, the youngest prince, and placed the blame on Cyrodian. But the army would not let one of their own go to the ax, and so—under pressure—Elad had ordered Cyrodian into exile. "I am still," he informed Laguro warily, "in fear of my life. Elad may have sent killers." He said this defiantly, staring the commander in the eyes.

Laguro was not a man to be intimidated. "We knew nothing of this," was his reply. "Are there men upon your trail?"

"I saw none as I came here."

Every man in the room began muttering, and Laguro ordered them to silence.

"I would like," Cyrodian said to him, "weapons for myself, and a night's rest. With your permission, I intend to ride on to Lasura and approach King Nutatharis."

"For asylum?" Laguro interpreted. "That may be agreeable to him." The commander knew that his monarch was ever ready to take advantage of political strife.

"Can you loan me an escort?" Cyrodian asked him. "Even a dozen men?"

"I intend to do exactly that," Laguro agreed. "Do not fear for your life here, Prince Cyrodian. I certainly don't care to have an incident take place under my command. Your safe passage to Lasura is assured."

Cyrodian grinned savagely at that and wiped wine drops from his beard.

He slept that night in the fort, after first choosing for himself large, heavy weapons from Laguro's armory. And as Cyrodian slept, a rider from the fort departed under the clouds of night to warn Nutatharis in Lasura that an international incident was in the making—a weary horse, an exiled royal rider, and a tremendous advantage.

2.

Two day's north, the *Padai's Wave* docked at its first port, the small city of Mirukad. Adred disembarked and spent the morning leisurely strolling through the streets. The day was chilly; in fact, Adred was glad that he'd remembered to bring along his heavy coat, because just this slight distance north made all the difference in climate. Street vendors that morning were predicting snow overnight.

But there was more than a difference in climate apparent in the northern provinces and in Mirukad. Adred had recognized it before, and it had never failed to awaken in him a better estimation of himself and the world, when he experienced it: the difference between clean, cool fresh air and the stagnant, clogged, perfumed incense of a palace. The same good air of the open sea.

There was very little in Mirukad, or in the north, of that which made the great ports and metropolises of the empire so attractive to some and such traps to others. Descended from local tribes that had farmed and sailed here for thousands of years, the northern populaces had, to a large extent, maintained independence. The Athadians had never come this far north. Officially, it had been felt that little could be gained from the territory; the richer farmlands and more productive ports had already been assimilated. Unofficially, however, the opinion had been that the far north was better left to itself. United only by a common heritage, the smaller cities of the northern provinces had nevertheless passed laws among themselves restricting the quota of immigrants they would allow from the southern climes.

As Adred walked the streets of Mirukad, he reflected on this. That policy—immigration restrictions—in itself indicated the intelligence and foresight peculiar to the region. How many times had he sat in taverns up here and listened to the arguments, the squabbling, the debates? If we take money from the empire, the northern territories said, then we are bound to it as surely as though we had sworn an oath. If we allow them to house soldiers here—even a regiment, even a single troop, for even a limited time—then their violent expansionism has its wedge placed in us. We take nothing from them, we give nothing back. We do business with them; we visit with them; but we will not trade tomorrow's wheat for this year's promises and gold.

Radulis, the philosopher, the author of *Reflections on Injustice* and *Man's Hope Is Man*, had been a northerner, a Salutite.

Adred had never considered himself to be a conservative, yet in admiring the qualities of the northern cities he knew that within the empire he would have been considered a conservative—when, in fact, he was simply being practical and fair and judicious. Such qualities as those had come to be liberal—threateningly so—while the conservatives within the empire had become little more than reactionary, snapping guard dogs of a system in its protracted death throes.

As he shopped in Mirukad, Adred bought bolts of cloth for Orain and had them sent to his rented room. And as he stood in the bookshops and sat in the taverns, listening to the many knots of debate and argument, he felt at first depressed, but then again hopeful. Depressed because Mirukad symbolized everything that the Athadian empire should be; but hopeful because Mirukad, and the northern territories all, symbolized what Athadia could become.

That evening, however, Adred's hope began to wane again. He had taken a meal at a tavern, relaxed and listened to the lutist and the singer that had entertained. He had felt comfortable and oddly at home. With his beard filling in nicely, he judged that he didn't stand out as an obvious stranger, and he had taken care to dress informally, even adopting the loose woolen Dilusian breeches that everyone wore north of Sulos.

But as he left the tavern and returned along the street to his room, he passed one of these enclaves—*sirots*—that were so common in northern cities. No more than short, dead-end alleys, they provided stalls for street merchants during winter or bad weather, served as shelters, often homed the irregular groups of jobless or poor that roamed freely, and—as well—were used by speakers addressing street crowds. Tonight, in this *sirot*, a rather large assembly had collected before an *ikbusa*—one of those odd provincial wandering priests who were unknown in urbanized Athadia but were still commonplace in the north and in the provinces of the east. *Ikbusa'i* were ordained priests of one sect or another who, in deference to their faith or in answer to personal belief, disdained serving in a church or temple but instead traveled alone, from village to city to farm, preaching. They were greatly respected, and while most were simply fundamentalist in their beliefs, some were mystics and were regarded by ordinary persons as akin to fortune-tellers or diviners.

Adred paused to listen to this particular *ikbusa*. The night was quite cold, but his room was not far, so he lingered. These priests were colorful and diverting. And this one, tonight, was speaking of things very close to Adred's own mind.

"You have seen cattle dying, have you not?" the priest asked of the crowd. Many nodded and grumbled; the *ikbusa* pulled on his long white beard, pointed his staff at faces before him. "And have you not heard how ill has befallen the empire to the south? Their Queen is dead, their King is dead, murder has taken place in their family. I will tell you why this has happened. I will tell you why animals are dying and why the gods are angry with the kings and queens. Listen to me, I know how I speak! One is coming! Yes! He is near, he is close by. He is *ro kil-su*, he is the Evil One, he is born and he rises up even now, far away from us, but he will shatter the world. And listen—listen to me!—for even as he grows strong, as demons did in the old days, there is another who will come. Yes! I will tell you! He is the messenger of On. Yes! He is *lo abu-sabith*. He is the One with the Word, the Light. He is the gift of On. He is the Word in the Flesh. He is no one. You will think he is your neighbor, you will think he is your father or your brother or your uncle, but he has been touched by the Light. Yes! This is happening now! Do you think I lie? Animals are dying, and kings are dying. The old gods are dying, dying. On watches, On guides us. But the world is foul. He sees that the world is foul, and so he will cleanse it. Yes! He is going to send upon us evil, such evil as

200

you have not known! And then he will send upon us good, such good as you cannot conceive. And the world will be reborn. There are signs. I have been shown them in a dream."

Disturbed, Adred listened. The man was not a rabble-rouser; it did not seem to be his intention to cause civil disturbance. He was only a priest; priests had said many similar things, tirelessly and endlessly and profusely, in their many sermons and speeches in temple and church. But this—this was different.

Someone in the crowd called out, "*Ikbusa!* Are you *lo abu-sabith?*"

The priest laughed with a hearty peasant laugh. "I? No, never! I am only a man. Only a man! But my eyes have been opened. I have been shown many things, and I tell you of them. Animals die. Kings die. Men die. Evil comes, evil is coming even now. Evil is a boy, a young man, I can tell you this. You will think him wise and priestly. And good is—"

Adred turned away.

He did not believe the man, not literally.

But he was far too familiar with many of the things this old priest was preaching: events distilled through the devout but misguided mind of a crank fundamentalist.

Perhaps . . .

The Evil One? From children's storybooks. Another priest of On? Well, they would continue coming, every generation, as long as there were men.

But animals, sickening . . .

Birds suiciding in the ocean, and Evarris . . . Yta . . . Cyrodian . . . Elad . . .

Adred did not ascribe any supernatural reason to these things, but deep in the core of him he felt that something terrible was upon the horizon—man-made, and man-willed. And he suspected that somehow—had Yta guessed it when she had spoken to him?—somehow, ridiculously, it had something to do with him. . . .

3.

Cyrodian arrived in Lasura without fanfare; he was escorted to the palace, where he was expected, with efficiency and discipline that impressed him. Just as the capital of Emaria itself impressed him.

Lasura was a city of Spartan elegance. The buildings were of stone and brick, unadorned with the golden and bronze facades and decorations so common in Athad. The streets were clean and well paved with brick or cobblestone. The palace, like the city, was simple. Made of well-fitted, massive blocks of granite, it rose from its central square to a height of six stories. Columns, porticoes, balconies lent an impression of sheer strength. Cyrodian knew intuitively, although he had never met King Nutatharis, that the monarch of Emaria was a self-controlled, unimpressionable military man. And that this city, at least, was the better for it.

His horse was taken from him when he and his escort reached the outer stairs of the palace. He was greeted by one of Nutatharis's court seneschals and guided, without his escort, through the main foyer and hall, up stairs, and into a small chamber. This mildly surprised him. Again—without fanfare.

The seneschal led the way past the guards in an outer room and ordered the doors of the inner chamber opened. He led Cyrodian inside, bowed, and backed out.

A large stone room, decorated sparely with hanging arras, oil lamps, wooden furniture. Seated behind a long table was a short man, bearded and mustached, with keen, intelligent eyes. He rose as Cyrodian was admitted, betraying a lithe quickness that more than offset his moderate physique.

Beside him, to left and right, sat older men: advisers or

counselors. And standing behind, against a window, a slim, almost sinister individual with burning eyes and the stance of a mistrustful Khamar.

Cyrodian strode forward, slapped his heart with his fist. "Lord King Nutatharis?"

Nutatharis, the small dark man, extended his hand, palm out, then took Cyrodian's arm in a grip and shook it. "Prince Cyrodian. Word came to me yesterday of your plight. Please sit down. Are you hungry? I can have food brought in."

Cyrodian pulled up a chair to sit across from him. "The food can wait. Perhaps some wine?"

"Please. Here is a cup."

Cyrodian tipped a jug and began to slake his thirst as the four pairs of eyes in the room centered on him.

"I am disturbed by your brother's betrayal," Nutatharis told him. "Know that I keep a keen eye on events surrounding my country; your brother's reign so far has not been an overly prosperous or calm one."

"My brother—" Cyrodian began, then paused. "I am in exile, King Nutatharis. Let's set certain things straight. Am I correct in thinking that you have granted me official refuge in Emaria?"

"You are correct. You are welcome to stay here for as long as events in your country dictate, for as long as you please. But I hope you understand that I appreciate a man of your gifts and—discipline, shall we call it? I think you and I can accomplish much that will be mutually beneficial."

"I am of the same mind, Nutatharis."

The monarch smiled. "That is good. That is very good." He tapped his fingers on the tabletop; his hands rested on a map of the continent. Cyrodian glanced at it. "Before I go further, however"—Nutatharis nodded to the men around him—"I would like you to know my advisers. These are men I respect and have trusted long. To my left is General Kustos, the commander of my army." General Kustos nodded. "To my right, Sir Jors, long a friend of my father's." Sir Jors appeared to be an amiable sort of man, good-humored, over-weight. He smiled at Cyrodian, teeth showing beneath a bristling red mustache; if he was a strong man, his appearance belied it. "And behind me"—Nutatharis indicated the tall slim man, who now advanced—"this is Eromedeus. He has only recently joined me; he came here a little more than half a year ago. He is not a soldier but a world traveller, knowledgeable and an asset to me.''

Eromedeus stepped forward and bowed his head slightly.

Cyrodian nodded and looked the man in the eyes. Something chill settled within him for that moment—something sinister or untrustworthy, deep, in this strange fellow, this Eromedeus. But Cyrodian could not place it, so he dismissed the feeling.

''Now,'' Nutatharis said, ''as to the mutual benefit you and I are destined . . .''

In the course of that afternoon, Prince Cyrodian came to realize that King Nutatharis was indeed a man he could understand and accomplish things with. To a large degree their feelings toward the world were similar, and their temperaments complementary. Practical, straightforward, appreciative of intellect in the service of action, Nutatharis, while still a relatively young man, was the inheritor of a nation defiantly begun by his great-great-grandfather, which had been held together, generation after generation, in the face of almost insuperable odds. Emaria was not a large country, and it was landlocked; its economy rested to a great degree upon exports of produce, ores, and metals. Sprawling to the west was Athadia, for which Nutatharis had no love, and which in even the best of times was a cold neighbor and inactive ally. To the south lay those loose confederations of sea-bordering regions, all nominally under the direction of Athadia's lion, to which they paid tribute. To his east, Nutatharis looked upon the Low Provinces: ostensibly existing unto themselves, small backward provinces of farms and countryside with no centralized authority or common unity other than a historical tradition of poverty, low productivity, and economic stasis. But the Low Provinces bordered upon the Salukadian Empire, and the Salukadian Empire was immense—and hegemonic.

All around him Nutatharis saw many locked rooms under a single roof, and it had been his policy, as it had been his father's and grandfather's, to keep the doors of those rooms securely locked and barred. Yet it had also been the policy of Emaria to maintain its sovereignty and independence at the expense of any distemper or confusion in surrounding lands. The dissimilation of the Low Provinces had up to now provided a suitable buffer between Emaria and Salukadia. Even so, the present disunity in Athadia might create an opportunity for a monarch who could take advantage of it to strengthen his own position.

Nutatharis spoke frankly of these things to Cyrodian, and he found that the exile—no true lover of an Athadia ruled by his "weak pup of a sibling"—was amenable to suggestions of fostering disorder and coalescing strengths for the furtherance of Emarian expansion. Victory, Nutatharis claimed, goes to the man who moves first. Thought is a stronger weapon than steel, strategy a surer device than muscle. An enemy divided is an enemy conquered.

"This city," Nutatharis told Cyrodian, "used to be nothing but a field. In my grandfather's youth you still saw furrowed fields just beyond that temple. In my father's day half the buildings in this capital did not exist. We are a small nation, but we have the strengths of the small—resilience, intelligence, diversity—and none of the weaknesses. And we will grow, Cyrodian. I intend to grow. I intend that the nations around me, as they die, will fall to me. It is my frequent dream that one day a son of mine shall own the lands all along the River Hiso, and that his son shall own Gaegosh, and his son—all of Athadia."

Cyrodian laughed pleasantly at the prospect. "And what of the Lowlands?" he inquired. For they had been discussing those backwaters all afternoon.

"The Lowlands," replied Nutatharis, "shall fall to me. Within the coming year. I have relied upon them as a buffer up till now, but now I have men and money to turn that buffer into a wall."

He meant it literally, which surprised Cyrodian; but it was a measure of the difference between the two men, both of them leaders, yet the one strong in his authority over men, the other profound in his ambitions to own, control, and never yield.

"A wall," repeated Nutatharis, showing Cyrodian the map on the table.

The afternoon had grown late; the other three in the room, still in attendance, had quite obviously grown weary and hungry. (Although Eromedeus, still as the wall against which he leaned, seemed as grim and silent as some guardian sentinel.) Yet Nutatharis, as he expounded his idea to Cyrodian, glowed with fresh vigor. It was apparent that the plan had

205

long fascinated him, and that he was wholly committed to seeing it accomplished.

He traced on the map with a finger, following a bold line in red ink, a line that stretched, sometimes straight and sometimes curving, from the Emarian border just north of Omeria east to the roughly indicated boundary of Salukadia, northeast to enclose Tsalvia, then west again, to embrace all of Emaria as well as the provinces of Bithira north of it.

Cyrodian smiled grimly, undecided whether or not to offend his host with a frank appraisal of the plan or to admit simply that the design was ambitious. He sipped wine and allowed as to its ambitiousness.

"True!" Nutatharis agreed, "but the building of a nation from swampland was ambitious, was it not? And my forebears did it. Now I extend that empire. And I do not mean to waste my own men in doing it. I do not intend to make my plan obvious, even. Winter comes down soon, but in the Low Provinces the winter is damp and chill, the land is seldom frozen deep. But it's marshy, and floods can pour down from the mountains with the force of a god's vengeance. So we build breaker walls. It's as simple as that. We enter the territory as a friendly force, asking only food for our men, to construct breakers, dams, and canals, or to repair any that were once built there, simply to help the farmers realize greater farm productivity; in return, we'll expect them to favor us with their exports." Nutatharis smiled. "That, of course, may very well happen, too. And within a year, what do we have? Half the Lowlands enclosed and fortified. And in another year?"

Cyrodian made some comment on dispensing with the fabrication of helping the farmers.

"But we will turn their swamps into a breadbasket," Nutatharis assured the exile. "To feed soldiers and women, and to feed a new generation of soldiers. And with the soldiers"—he traced along the route of the Fasu River, which emptied into the Ursalion Sea—"we begin to erect fortifications upon the river, and we take control."

"You risk intrusion into the empire," Cyrodian reminded him.

"By that time, my friend, Athadia will be in no shape to respond to any provocation. Nor will Omeria or any of its surrounding regions. By that time we will have begun to

206

economically deprive those areas with our own increased trade and harvests.''

It was a bold plan, and apparent behind it were Nutatharis's many years of training at his father's knee—not only in matters military, but in matters of politics, economic life, geography, transportation, human nature. . . . Foresight.

"What do you think of my plan?" Nutatharis asked Cyrodian. "Tell me—frankly."

Cyrodian smiled foully. "When you began to talk of a wall," he confessed, "I thought you stupid, but now that I see the larger shape—"

Nutatharis openly laughed. "Yes?" he insisted.

"It is the destiny of the continent that you propose. The empire of the future."

"Yes," Nutatharis replied, warming to the phrase. "You're right, Cyrodian. I am indeed building the empire of the future. . . ."

4.

The Celebration of Perpetual Grace was observed throughout the Athadian empire two days after the Feast of the Ascension. To commemorate the Light which had been given to humanity upon the Prophet's rise into the afterworld, the holiday was ostensibly a solemn affair in which devotions were to be shared, candles lit, prayers whispered, and the day spent in restorative silence. Thoughts were to be given over to the contemplation of the Prophet's words and the signal gift which he had given to mankind through his courageous sermons and life-delivering death.

In practice, the Celebration of Perpetual Grace—like the Feast—had become something less than a soul-deep spiritual challenge. Few nowadays (save for priests in the temples) passed the day in silence; merchants often did a very brisk trade on the afternoon of the Celebration, while the morning was usually given over by most households to sleep or temple visits.

Still, while the original meaning of the Celebration had been lost or degraded, it was a day when, habitually, people at least tried to act with dignity or restraint (feeling that the prophet might be looking down over their shoulders) and to remind themselves that they were, after all, civilized persons living in a civilized world. It was a day to drop a little extra into the temple donation box; a day to trade pleasantries with neighbors and speak politely with strangers.

To have done otherwise on the one day of the year commemorating the Prophet's love for an imperfect world would have been a gross rejection of accepted behavior, and for even the most spiritually dank such deliberate spitefulness would have been unusual on the Day of Grace.

Shortly after lunch, Orain was sitting on the balcony of her chamber in Mantho's apartment. The afternoon was chill, yet because the stuffy air of her room was giving her a headache, she had drawn back the doors and stepped outside for a fresh breeze. As she relaxed, she leaned on the railing and looked out upon the city. Before her stretched an avenue and, bisecting it, one of Sulo's major boulevards. Just down the avenue she could glimpse the outermost partitions of the Abu Square, a merchandising center. There were only a few people on the streets, no crowds. The early afternoon seemed almost strangely quiet.

When she heard the first of the disturbances, then, Orain was surprised. The commotion sounded very near; she wondered if it had to do with the holiday.

Looking to see what was happening, she leaned over the rail. Without a doubt, she heard the sounds of screams—loud screams, and many-throated. As she watched, a wave of people erupted suddenly from the direction of the square and raced down the avenue. Orain stared, shocked, as hundreds of people, ragged and armed with sticks, bricks, tools, and knives mobbed the street, screaming at the top of their lungs, "Death to businesses! Death to all merchants! Death to the King! Death to money!" They carried placards and banners with pictures painted on them, showing working people being stepped on by boots filled with gold coins, and throats being strangled by the fists of political and business interests.

Rocks and bricks began to fly through the air. As the crowd passed beneath her, Orain drew back. A brick, hurled by a strong hand, jumped toward her and clattered against the outside wall, nearly striking her. A stone followed the brick, shattering into powder as it hit Mantho's apartment house.

Orain hurried into her room even as the cries of the mob carried on down the avenue. Heart racing, she returned to the balcony, aghast and wholly disbelieving. She knew that the rioting had never before reached this end of town.

The mob had hurried on down the avenue, but now another followed it, again from the direction of the square. Screaming as loudly as the first, brandishing weapons and tools and rocks, hundreds and hundreds of ragged, howling people—men and women, even children—pushed and shoved their way beneath Orain's balcony, filling the avenue from side to side. Into the air exploded the sounds of shattered glass, the crashes of thrown rocks and bricks, fists pounding on doors to alarm those inside.

Orain stepped back again from the balcony. As this second crowd hurried on—"Death to the merchants! Death to the King! We want all or nothing!"—she heard the distant clatter of a thousand horses' hoofs and the blaring trumpets of imperial troops. Staring down the boulevard, she saw the first of the mounted soldiers gallop down the cobblestones, armor shining dully, pennants slapping on the wind. They broke, four abreast, into the avenue as the last stragglers of the crowd pushed on, still screaming and throwing rocks. In perfect formation the mounted troops galloped into the avenue and took the sharp turn to their right, beginning to run the crowd down. Horses neighed and shrilled. Human voices lifted in agonized screams. The cracking of weapons striking against stone, brick, flesh, metal, filled the hollow avenue with an incredible din.

Orain, drawn back to the balcony, continued to stare, heart slow, a witness. . . .

Now half the troops wheeled about and headed down the avenue in the opposite direction, hastening toward the Abu Square. Screams broke from that end of the street. Orain, watching, saw a loose band of knife- and tool-wielding rebels burst suddenly into the center of the avenue, appearing from around the corner of Mantho's house. Horses approached them, the guards in their saddles brandishing longswords and spiked poles. Shrieks cut the air.

Orain began to whisper a prayer.

Behind her, a door burst open with a crash. She screamed and turned, fell forward, and nearly dropped to her knees.

"They've broken in!" Galvus yelled to her. "Mother! They're inside the house! Mantho's trying to bolt the doors!"

"What?" she yelled at him, wholly disoriented. *"What?"*

"They're *inside!"* Galvus hurried to one wall of the room, where weapons had been hung as decorations.

Orain, terrified, stared at him, unable to think.

"I don't know what it is," Galvus told her. "A rebellion of some kind. I don't know. But they're doing damage out there. Mother, people are being killed." He looked at the wall, surveyed the assortment of weapons.

Loud screams, directly beneath the balcony. Horses' hoofs.

Howling voices. The sounds of steel. Bodies, pushing and shoving. Children crying. . . .

Galvus took down a knife; it was something totally foreign to his hand. "I—I can't kill anyone," he assured his mother, voice apologetic. "But we've got to get out of here. I don't know where we can go, but . . ."

Orain couldn't think; she didn't know what to think. She glanced down, unable to comprehend the fact that the street— she had just walked in it this morning, she and Mantho—had been turned into . . .

The screams. And three horses, just below the balcony, were prancing on the ripped, contorted body of a baby. At the sound of a wailing cry a woman's head—only her head— rolled beneath the dancing hoofs and bumped into the smashed baby. The eyes of the head were wide; the mouth was filled with blood, pulsing, dripping.

Orain tried to turn away, just as one of the mounted soldiers was thrown from his horse. Immediately someone dressed in rags jumped on top of him, cried, "Die! Die!" and stabbed him in the face with a knife. The soldier tried to fight back; he rolled and kicked, but the man in rags continued to plunge the knife into his throat, cheeks, eyes. Blood shot out in long jets.

Orain dropped back. She felt herself slipping; her stomach rolled; she fell back and back . . .

Galvus caught her. "Mother!"

"Oh . . . Hea . . ." She groaned, coughing terribly, half bent.

"Mother, *please!*"

Through the open door of the chamber came the crashing noises of many feet stampeding up the stairs.

The rebellion took the city completely by surprise. Governor Jakovas had consistently turned a deaf ear toward the protesters. Incidents that occurred were trivialized in reports submitted to the King. The ranks of the indigent seemed only to be composed of the ragtag, the impoverished, the chronically unemployed and unemployable. That the numbers of the dispossessed were large would have astonished the well-to-do and propertied of Sulos.

In fact, the demonstrations in Sulos were but the most obvious and visible sign of a growing underground of resentment against the governorship specifically and the government's mismanagement generally. The imbalance between wealth and poverty, the advantaged and the disadvantaged, had been allowed to grow into an abyss that seemed impossible to bridge by any constructive means. Spurred on by dozens of intelligent voices—intellectuals, students, educated men, small businessmen whose businesses had been foreclosed, schoolmasters, and even some dissident priests—the ranks of the dissatisfied swelled to enormous proportions. Shopkeepers, taxed to the brink of poverty, listened to the speakers in the streets; young men and women who saw their older brothers and sisters educated but without jobs listened to the excoriations of a system that mocked the ambitions of the ordinary person; servants and householders, long held in their debilitating stations, now listened to the words that promised them their human rights in a world of prejudice and duplicity.

To the wealthy and the successful, their ears clogged with money, these words sounded like the trumpet-blast of anarchy. That the society which had allowed them to prosper was essentially unfair, they could not believe; that the economic bias which had handsomely rewarded their rapacious greed was at its core rotting away, these people would not accept. That the bureaucracy which protected them from misfortune and calamity was a monster of gluttony, they denied.

That a disease, virulent and unstoppable, was growing within their body economic, these plutocrats dismissed as a wild impossibility. They had treated the first signs of the fever as they would have placated a simple head cold; and now, when the disease broke out with a rush of pain, injury, and destruction, they were astonished that so malignant a thing had given so little sign of its coming.

The general revolt, planned for the afternoon of the Celebration of Perpetual Grace, burned like a wildfire. The first, apparently spontaneous protests at the docks had drawn quick response from Governor Jakovas: he had sent two units of imperial guards to the waterfront to put down the demonstrations quickly and efficiently. With attention thus diverted to that end of town, other pockets of rebellion sprang up all over in a preplanned consolidation designed to bring Sulos to its knees.

A huge mob attacked the Governor's mansion in Shemtu Square. Jakovas, protected for the holiday only by a limited number of guards, was taken utterly unawares. He was slain by the mob. The confrontation that followed left thirty-two protesters dead within the mansion; corpses of men and women lay in the boot-deep blood that covered the tiles of the portico and entranceway. Seven of the guards, too, were slain.

A second wave of rebels then attacked the Governor's mansion. The remainder of the guards were slain, sixteen more protesters were killed, but the swollen crowd of rebels took control of the mansion and barred its doors from inside. One hundred and twenty-four, housed within the dead man's home, taking it as their own headquarters for the command of the new political and economic order they had devised.

Galvus and Orain moved toward the bed, away from direct view from the door. The small army of footsteps thundered past.

Galvus had a glimpse. "The servants," he whispered grimly. "Are they part of this too?"

There was no answer for him. Bravely he moved toward the door, peeked out, glanced up and down the corridor. He motioned for his mother to cross the room.

"If we can get down this hall"—he pointed to the end of the corridor, in the opposite direction from that which the servants had taken—"we have a chance to get downstairs."

"And then?" Orain whispered.

"I don't know, Mother. We hide in a cellar, if we can get to one. At least we'll have . . ."

He said no more; he was wasting time. Gripping one of Orain's hands, he pulled her behind him and moved into the corridor.

They made their way quickly down the stairs, and at the bottom passed through an antechamber that led into the kitchen. The door at the opposite end of the kitchen was open. Galvus and Orain were familiar with it: the door led outside into an alley, and the alley opened upon a small street.

They heard no sounds from beyond the door. Possibly they might be safer outside.

Yet Galvus did not move. Indecisive, he paused where he stood, knife up, listening, trembling.

Orain felt his trembling. She reached up, touched his shoulder. "My son," she whispered, "we will be safe h—"

A grunting voice came from the doorway that led into the

213

dining hall. A man stumbled there; he fell forward with outstretched arms, supported himself for one moment within the opening, stared at them, shocked. . . .

Mantho.

His bearded gray face was awash with blood, his chest ripped and running with gore, his breeches in tatters.

Orain screamed, and Galvus stepped in front of her to block the view.

Mantho gurgled to them; red spittle drooled down his neck, and he slammed forward, not throwing his arms out. He smashed full upon the tiles and sprawled, unmoving.

A heart-pause of silence, before a second figure lurched into the doorway, throwing a shadow that swept upon Mantho's corpse like the bleak promise of a hawk over a cornfield. In its hand was an ornamental sword, dripping with purple blood.

Orain gasped; her fingers tightened on Galvus's arm.

It was Euis, the servant. He stared at Orain, darkness in his eyes, a scowl on his lips.

Galvus, trembling, shook his small knife before him. "Come at me," he threatened, voice barely audible but thick with emotion, "and I'll use this on you—I will."

But Euis did not move; he made no threatening advance, and he entirely ignored the body of the man he'd murdered. He continued to stare into Lady Orain's eyes—staring deeply, watching her. . . .

No one seems to have any answers, and there is no peace.

Galvus swallowed, reached up with his free hand to wipe his nose. He did not—

A grunt came from Euis as he stared at Orain. And then, words. "I am a *man!*" he yelled at her.

Orain nearly buckled to her knees, held onto Galvus for support. "Oh, *Hea!*"

"I am a *man!*" he yelled again. "Not a dog! Not a slave!"

She could not look at him. But Galvus, tense and anxious, ready to explode with movement, stared unflinchingly at the man, daring him, daring him. . . .

Abruptly a line of blood drooled from a corner of Euis's mouth; he coughed, and a spray of dark red vomited from him. Tilting forward, he threw an arm out to support himself in the doorway. Orain, looking, saw a wet run of blood pour from his right leg and collect on the floor beneath his boots.

"I—" He gasped. "I would not—" Then he sank to his knees, coughing foamy blood. "I . . . am a . . . man."

And he sprawled, face down, twitching, the blood streaming down his boots. Buried in his back was the broken half of Count Mantho's gold-topped walking stick.

Galvus moved. With his first step he dizzied. Orain clung to him. As he hurried across the floor his dizziness passed, and he became so excited that he wanted to burst through the wall, swing his knife, leap into the air. Accelerated, he raced into the alley, making sure that Orain stayed by him. Down the alley, into the street . . .

Another mob, another crowd.

Astonished, Galvus and Orain stared upon the street full of aristocrats: huddled, some clutching a few belongings, all crouched in the middle of the avenue and surrounded by mounted imperial guards, protectors. Trumpets blasted intermittently; soldiers were calling back and forth to one another— and in the distance, still, came the confused noises of battle, the screams and the crashes.

Someone in the crowd spotted them. "Hurry!" she screamed. "Hurry, please! Come with us!"

They ran. Joined the crowd as, at the urging of the mounted troops, the whole collection of them began to move on down the avenue, protected by their escort.

The wails. The moans. The sobs and cries. My family . . . my baby . . . my father . . . my son . . . my daughter, they raped her . . . blood . . . I saw my little girl, my little girl was . . .

Protected, the fractured and the bruised, moving down the avenue, closed and clogged, cursing and crying, even as the cloudy afternoon began to drizzle cold rain on them and as the darkening sky began to fill with a strange orange glow, far behind buildings two or three blocks away. Fire.

They'd begun to set fire to Sulos.

They'd begun to reduce the city of injustice to ashes.

And as they were moved on, protected and escorted, one well-manicured hand reached to the stones to pick up a gold piece which someone else, in fleeing or dying, had dropped.

5.

Snow was falling in Mirukad, the first true snow of late autumn. Fat, wet flakes piled up alongside the streets and settled heavily on the rooftops. In the bright blue of the early morning they lent a picturesque beauty to the port city which Adred found himself enjoying—despite the chilliness.

He watched the falling snow through the window of his second-floor hostel room, as he stoked his fireplace, whistled a tune, and packed his belongings. It was two days after the Celebration of Perpetual Grace, and Adred felt that he'd stayed long enough in Mirukad. He was in much better spirits than he had been when he had left his friends in Sulos. He had seen the sights; he had talked with friendly strangers in taverns and in the sellers' stalls. He had bought himself a new pair of boots and for the first time in his life had trimmed his beard and mustache—both now full enough to require daily attention. He had bought Orain more material than she could possibly use, and, for Galvus, two books. He'd even bought a gift for Mantho: an exquisitely carved figurine that he knew his friend would add proudly to a collection that contained some of the finest—and rarest—miniature sculptures in the world.

When his things were packed, Adred finished dressing and took his breakfast downstairs in the hostel's serving room. He was in a light mood, so he joked with the woman who brought his meal, the hosteler's wife, a portly woman, friendly and talkative. He settled his bill with the house master and asked if one of the man's sons could porter his belongings down to the dock later in the morning; the hosteler assured him that one of the lazy good-for-nothings could be hired for the purpose.

216

After finishing his breakfast, Adred walked down to the docks. He might have taken a carriage, but he preferred the stroll. The day was cool, but there was only a slight wind. He noticed few others on the street, however, and many who passed him had indeed hired carriages. Adred wondered idly if civilization had brought with it a distaste for the cold.

When he came to the docks he entered one of the port authority offices and inquired about buying passage on the next sail out to Sulos. To his surprise, the clerk behind the counter seemed astonished at the request.

"To Sulos?" he repeated.

"Yes," Adred told him, imagining that he'd been out in the cold too long. "You know—south of here? In Kendia? Rather a large town—lots of ships, quite a few tall buildings—"

"But, sir—excuse me—we can't release any passage or—or shipments to Sulos until we hear word of what's happened about the revolt there, sir."

Adred missed a breath; he felt his insides suddenly coil. "The *revolt?*"

"Don't tell me you haven't heard?"

Fear gripped him. The room blurred. "*What* revolt? Tell me. What's happened, what—"

Now the clerk seemed to become as frightened as Adred. "They had a revolt break out there two days ago—on Celebration. You didn't hear? Half the city's burned; they killed all the aristocrats—"

"*What?*"

There was a second clerk in the office, an elderly bureaucrat, who, overhearing, now moved from his desk and approached the counter. "Careful, now," he cautioned the younger man. "We don't have all the facts yet."

"Tell me what's happened!" Adred implored him. "Please—please!" He was shaking and trembling terribly, sweating, panicking. "I have—"

"We don't have all the facts yet, as I say. But we received word two days ago. They've had a bad fight down there; people without work just decided to start some trouble. We don't know how bad it was."

"Was anyone *killed?*"

"Apparently so. We don't know how many."

"This—this can't— I have *friends* there, those people are

217

like family to me, I . . ." He stopped suddenly, feeling self-conscious. "When will the ships sail out again?"

"We don't know, sir. We can sell you passage on—"

"Is there a way overland?"

"Sir—calm down, please, sir."

He stood there. Why hadn't he heard before now? All those people in the taverns, in the streets, yesterday, the day before— had they been discussing it? When had they learned of it? Why hadn't he overheard?

He looked up again. "Can't you at least—"

The door to the office opened, a cold wind blew in, and the clerks looked up. An old sailor entered, stamping snow from his boots. He slammed the door behind him and tramped up to the counter, shaking his feet. He reached beneath his long overcoat to produce thick envelopes of paper, slapped them on the counter, and began to untie them.

"In from Port Aru," he announced dully. "My mate's unloading now. You'll want to check with the—"

Adred was staring impatiently at him; he knew that Aru was a small city farther north, but perhaps the captain had heard . . .

The older clerk noticed; he interrupted the ship's master with a curt "News from Sulos?"

"None." He shook his head quickly, noticed Adred. "You don't want to be going there, do you?" he asked.

"If I can board a ship, yes. Yes, I do."

"It's a dead city, lad. They've killed themselves off. All of them—went crazy, set fire to the place. I been to Sulos a thousand times. Had some land there, was going to retire there after a few more boatloads. It's toasted now."

Adred left. Wandered up the street. Numb. The wind had come up; it blew in off the sea, attacked him, bit into him, sent hard flakes of snow and hail into his hair, the back of his neck, his legs. He began to shiver uncontrollably; tears burned hotly in his eyes, and he fought to hold them back. Name of the gods, but he had to get back there, he had to!

"Oh, there's a sea to the north
And a sea to the west,
But the see I love best
Is to see her . . . un—dressed!"

218

He cackled with laughter. Drunk. Old dog. Glanced over at Galvus and nudged the youth with his elbow.

"Understand?" he chuckled. " 'Sea'—'see'? Understand?"

Galvus looked toward Orain, who was sitting across from him, huddled by the fire and stirring the soup pot. Trying to keep warm. Not that it was much of a fire. The wind might have whipped it to life but instead had reduced the flames to only hot coals.

The old aristocrat, pulling at his wine jug (where he had gotten hold of it, Galvus had no idea), laughed and laughed at himself and at the lad beside him. Galvus glanced from his mother to their tent; it was ragged and would need to be redraped and tied down again before they could spend another night in it.

Another night . . . .

That tent was as damp as the field. It kept the wind from them, or the worst of the wind, but that mattered little. Galvus was already soaked through, and had been for three days.

Beyond the tent, the field. Dusk was settling down, and the huge crowd of outcasts, homeless, frightened—reduced to senselessness by their lack of plush cushions and servants, their warmth, their fine clothes—was becoming an indistinguishable blot of shadow, lumpy against the high darkness of the purple sky and the gray of the wind-combed field.

Orain glanced at her son. "We might as well eat it now," she whispered to him. Her voice was hoarse. "Are you hungry?"

He shrugged.

"Galvus?"

"No," he said tiredly. "Not very hungry." But he pulled his arms out from under the blanket he had wrapped around him, extended an army-issue ration cup he'd been given. Orain dipped it into the warm pot of soup and returned it. Steam lifted into Galvus's face and made him blink; he sipped, but the broth was hotter than he'd expected. It faintly burned his tongue.

Next to him, the aristocrat began another verse. Galvus tightened.

"Don't," Orain cautioned him, nodding quickly to the man. "He's not as strong as we are. He needs to do it this way."

219

Galvus shook his head at her but continued to sip.

At the sound of an approaching horse, he looked up. A soldier, surveying them. "Everything all right?"

Galvus nodded but jerked his head toward the drunk next to him.

The soldier smiled. "We'll get you back into the city tomorrow," he promised. "Or the day after. Soon, now."

"What about the rebels?" Galvus asked him. "The Governor's house?"

By this time everyone knew what had happened—everyone knew. . . .

The soldier's expression turned grim. "We've sealed off the Square," he answered Galvus somewhat curtly. "But the rest of the city's safe."

In order to invite no more unwanted questions then, he cantered off, asking the next clot of huddled exiles, "Everything all right? Anyone sick? Anyone need an extra blanket?"

Galvus continued to sip.

Orain sneezed.

All around them sounded the low din, the whining; the complaints.

While inside the city, Galvus thought, the corpses were piled as high as monuments, out here these purebloods and gentry (now that the shock had passed, of course) complained about small injustices, or leaks in their tents, or lack of an extra jug of wine.

Complained—because they were still alive.

It disgusted him. Disgusted him to the core of his being.

He turned to the drunk and growled angrily, "Shut up!"

But the man laughed at him, invited him to sing along, and, after another long swallow of the Silesian ale, continued with:

"Oh, she gives me a wink
As she passes. I think
With what pleasure I'd sink . . ."

Orain patiently reminded Galvus again, with a smile, to remain temperate.

But Galvus now was concerned with more than the stupid, drunken aristocrat. Other thoughts had taken hold of him.

220

That he was nephew to the King, that his mother was sister-in-law to the crown, neither of them had mentioned. They preferred it thus. There was too much danger in their identities, and they had no reason to flaunt their royalty.

Galvus looked upon the walls of Sulos and, in that moment, by the dark light of the night and his reflective, embittered soul, saw them as enclosures of a trap, saw them as the fortifications of an enigmatic maze, an illusion, and a lie.

And he had no reason to think of himself as a liar, and he had never been a friend of illusions or deliberate injustices, or traps. . . .

Evening had fallen, and King Elad was at supper with the Imbur Ogodis, Lady Salia, and members of the Athadian Council, when Consul Captain Lutouk's messenger arrived at the steps of the palace. A Khamar, appalled by the man's ashy face and exhausted gasp of dire news, conducted him inside and interrupted Elad's meal with a whispered, "My lord, we have grave news from Sulos."

Elad excused himself with much formality and, as he had been in the midst of telling the Lady Salia a particularly humorous story, he warned the Khamar underbreath (as they exited) that this grave word from Sulos had better be such that it required his immediate attention.

Yet one look at Lutouk's messenger swept away any doubts. Elad met with him privately in an antechamber to the audience hall.

"Lord King, I have been sent by my commander. Governor Jakovas has been murdered, and Sulos taken by rebels."

Elad sat still and silent for a terribly long moment, listening to the pounding of his heart. Then, in a quavering voice, he asked several precise questions of the rider; as the man told what he knew, Elad insisted upon specifics so as to get as entire a picture as possible of what had occurred. The man answered as well as he was able.

Finally King Elad told him to get himself to the kitchen for some food. The rider thanked his monarch, saluted, and went out. Elad coldly and purposefully took a sheet of parchment and a pen from the desk where he sat, opened an ink horn, and scrawled a brief message to Consul Captain First Class Lutouk. Heating a bar of wax at an oil lamp, Elad affixed his royal seal to the document, rolled the parchment, tied it with a golden ribbon, and placed it in a wooden holder.

Standing up, he moved to the door and opened it. Two Khamars, ever-present and at all times within the sound of their King's voice, saluted him.

Elad faced one of them with "Rouse my men of Council. Immediately. We hold session as soon as all are present."

The man slapped his chest and hurried away.

To the second Khamar, Elad entrusted the parchment scroll. "Find a man to ride this north, to Sulos. It is to be delivered into the hands of Consul Lutouk and none other. If Lutouk is dead, it is to be delivered to the acting consul. Mind this well: The man is to proceed with all haste; he is to stop only to change horses. There is gold for him when he returns, but if he fails he will be banished. Am I understood?"

"You are, my lord." The soldier saluted. "I go."

Elad made his way into his Council chamber and seated himself upon his throne dais; he had not even bothered to return to the dining hall, assuming that Abgarthis would manage such civilities as an official excuse to the Imbur and his daughter. Sitting motionless with one fist raised to his chin, Elad did not greet his advisers as, one by one, they filed in, uncertain and doubtful. Not even Abgarthis received a nod or a glance from his lord.

The Councilors seated themselves behind their tables, facing Elad. His voice was crisp, almost sinister in its detachment, as he announced to them, "Upon the dawn I am ordering the Twenty-third and the Twenty-fourth Legions to Sulos. They will be sailed north with all speed under command to seize and restrain any rebel forces found within the city and to execute anyone—man, woman or child—who resists questioning or arrest, and to quarter themselves in that city, under the jurisdiction of Acting Governor Consul Captain Lutouk, until further word from myself. In the morning I will reconvene this Council and read into the record my precise orders to Consul Lutouk and my reasons for taking this military action of extreme emergency.

"I have already sent a rider to Sulos with specific orders for Consul Captain Lutouk to proceed as he sees fit until the arrival of our legions. Gentlemen, rebels have taken over the city; they have slaughtered at the very least several hundred citizens there; they have assassinated Governor Jakovas and occupied the Governor's mansion. My orders to Lutouk, and for the legions, are to take those revolutionaries in the mansion prisoner and execute them.''

Abgarthis sat frozen; he knew, as did Elad, that Orain and Galvus were vacationing in Sulos. Uncertainly, nervously, he rose to his feet and in a hoarse voice asked his King, "My lord, is there any word of the royal family?''

Elad replied gravely, ''No word of them. But we know that the rebellion was directed against the aristocracy of Sulos. I know nothing more. But I think, Lord Abgarthis, under the circumstances, that we may assume the worst.''

Word of the rebellion in Sulos spread rapidly. Rumors sped from city to city, giving the impression that a general revolution had come at last. Spontaneous demonstrations broke out in every major city of Athadia, from Bessara to Sugat on the coast as well as in Isita, Himosis, Irkad, and other inland cities. These demonstrations in themselves, although quickly and forcefully put down, brought home to Elad what neither he nor any of his Council had ever suspected: that the discontent which had occasionally surfaced was but the hint of a widespread, deep-seated anger with the throne and the throne's economic mismanagement.

In Sulos, Lutouk received King Elad's orders a week after the revolt, on the day of the Holy Observance of the Ascension and the Deliverance. He had, over the past several days, entered into a dialogue with the rebels. He had listened to their grievances and accepted from revolutionary spokesmen lists of demands to be presented to the King. Lutouk took these grievances seriously; he did not seek to punish violence with more violence. Long years in the imperial army had taught him much, had made of him a resourceful, understanding leader. Men in the mass seldom act irrationally when a rational issue is at stake—Lutouk believed that, although he knew that the irrational always waited to be unleashed. For Elad to presume that this rebellion was simply an anomaly or a fabrication (as he seemed to feel, from the tone of his orders) was, for Lutouk, a glaring misapprehension of the facts.

Still, he knew, on the afternoon he received his orders from Elad's rider, that the legions on their way north would be arriving quickly. It had taken the messenger three and a half days overland, and a ship could make the sailing faster than that. Immediately, therefore, Lutouk met with spokesmen from the mansion and, after his assurance that he would do all he could to protect their lives, he informed them of Elad's decision and argued for the rebels to give themselves up to the mercy of the throne.

They scoffed at his proposal, but common sense told them that, even if their leaders were executed, they could go to their deaths nobly. And surely some, the least of them, would be spared. Even after serving prison terms, these survivors would still be alive to carry on the essence of the revolt, the education, the demands for reforms and justice.

Late that afternoon they gave themselves up peacefully, leaving the mansion one at a time and handing their makeshift weapons over to Lutouk's soldiers.

The legions arrived that evening and presented to Lutouk his current orders.

The Consul Captain faced a dilemma.

He read King Elad's orders, reread them, read them again. Held the parchment open in the wind until the falling snow, striking the ink, wetted the paper so that the monarch's words blurred and smeared and ran down the page in black rivulets, like tears.

To the embarrassment of his soldiers, then, Consul Lutouk crossed the Shemtu Square and, beneath the eyes of two legions sent directly from the capital, spoke on familiar terms with the leaders of the revolt.

"I swear to you that, before the eyes of On and his Prophet Bithitu, I am ashamed this day to be an Athadian. Despite the violence you have done, and despite the long years of injustice done to you, I truly believed that debate could be managed. I see that our King does not wish this. The deaths of you men and women will only fan more fires of rebellion. But I am sworn to my badge of command as a captain first class of the imperial army, and I am bound to honor the edict of my King as acting governor of this province. King Elad has ordered you to be executed immediately. All of you."

The wind blew; the snow fell; the icy cold wrapped around them. Not one voice of pain or anguish, sorrow or regret came from that crowd. And the only answer Lutouk received

224

came from one of the revolutionary leaders, who told him proudly, "Tell Elad that sooner or later he will have to kill everyone in his country."

That was all.

Captain Lutouk turned from them and recrossed the square.

To the commanders of the Twenty-third and Twenty-fourth Legions: "I will not raise my sword against these people, nor will I command my men to do so. Your orders from King Elad are precise. Execute them, then."

They sneered at him. "Traitor. This will be reported!" And they chose soldiers to cross the square and fulfill the throne's demand.

Lutouk did not watch. He retired to the shop he had occupied since his entrance into the city, and he sat in the shadows. But the sounds came to him. Not only the sounds of the murderous work, but the cheers of those aristocrats still within Sulos, who had gathered to watch, and the rising grunts of bloodlust that roared from the throats of his own men.

For despite the optimism of Lutouk and a handful of others, men in the mass seldom act rationally, whether or not the issue at stake is a rational one itself.

When it was done, Captain Lutouk went out and handed his sword, his badges, and his rings to Captain First Class Sildum of the Twenty-fourth Legion. "Return these to Elad. I hereby renounce my rank in the army and retire from my post. Any money due me, tell the King to distribute to the families of Athad's ghettos."

Perilously close to treachery with those words, Lutouk turned on his heel and, in the bitter cold of night, mounted his horse and left the city, returning to his villa.

In the morning the soldiers of the legions and the soldiers of Sulos, now under the command of Captain Sildum, fulfilled the last of King Elad's commands: they gathered up the severed heads of one hundred and twenty-four rebels executed on the square, disinterred four hundred and fifty-one additional rebel corpses previously buried in a common grave outside the city, decapitated those bodies, then carted their gory trophies to one of the ships that had been sent from the capital.

By midmorning the top deck of the war galley was filled to its sides with bloody severed heads, by Elad's command. A mooring line was stretched from its bow to the stern of the first galley. As a wind blew up, the flagship steered out into the ocean. Crowded because of its double crew, it began the slow, gruesome task of towing King Elad's cargo southward, down the coast, to the capital.

6.

When Galvus and Orain returned to Mantho's apartment, they found it still standing. The bodies of Mantho himself, Euis the servant, and who knew how many others, had been carted away; all that remained as evidence of the night of hell were torn furnishings, blood-spattered walls and floors, ransacked stores, looted closets. . . .

"We can't stay here," Galvus said to his mother.

It wasn't even their home. It wasn't even their city. They took themselves to one of the common buildings run by the army and were given two beds. Here they listened day and night to the continual whinings and complainings of the lost and the bored and the depressed—the alive. My mother was killed . . . I had all sorts of fine jewelry, now it's gone . . . you should see what they did to my uncle's portrait . . . it's just all madness, what happened to the carpets and the draperies I had in the rear room. . . .

They couldn't stay there, either. They were aristocrats, but they had nothing in common with these people. They were related by blood to the throne, and a simple mention of that fact would have brought them anything they wanted.

But Galvus couldn't do it.

He had only one thing with him, besides the clothes on his back: the volume of Radulis which Adred had bought him months earlier. He had not abandoned it; he had carried it under his tunic, and though Galvus nearly had it memorized, he could not set aside the book. The words in it, and the words and arguments that burned in his brain, made far more sense to him than the whinings of the displaced wealthy, the military law of the occupation army, the blood in the streets.

"We could take a ship," Orain said to her son. "Return to Athad—"

"No."

"Elad will be worried about us. He probably thinks we're dead."

Galvus told her then, "As far as I'm concerned, Mother, I am dead, and I want to stay dead. I want nothing more to do with Elad; I want to forget who my father was; I want to forget all of it. All of it. I hate it. Mother, if you want to return to Athad, then do so. Go there. You'll be safe there. I'm a man, not an aristocrat, not a prince. I'm going to stay here in Sulos. For the rest of my life. I'm going to live on docks and learn to sail. I'm going to spend the rest of my life working at a trade, laughing at the government, complaining and paying my taxes—and I'm going to keep my secret, Mother. No one other than you or I will ever know that. Can you understand?"

There were tears in her eyes as she nodded her head. "Yes, I understand."

"Mother, you and I never belonged there. You weren't born to the gold and the scarlet. But you have a right to it."

She smirked and touched his hand. "Return to the capital? My son, the only comfort I ever found in the capital was with Queen Yta and with Dursoris. Both are gone now. We shall stay here and stay as we are."

That was what Galvus wanted to hear, and he thanked her.

Yet he couldn't guess what she was thinking but did not say: that they would not spend the rest of their lives living as ordinary people. She did not believe that Galvus could do that; Orain did not believe her son's destiny would allow that.

She had come to believe, had the Lady Orain, through the nights of horror and pain, through the loneliness and the terror, through her reflections and memories, that Elad would not forever be King of Athadia. She had come to believe that her private suffering, her own character, her own destiny, had been decided by the gods—*we are the gods, Orain*—for one purpose. She was who she was, Lady Orain and the mother of Prince Galvus, for one predestined meaning: her son would one day be the king of the empire.

"Thank you, mother. Thank you."

King of Athadia.

What else could all the turmoil be for, all the crises of her

228

life, all the questions that seemed otherwise to have no answers? There was an answer. And when she looked upon her son—less with a mother's prideful hope than with a woman's intuitive judgment—she knew the answer.

She was the mother of the man fated to become the greatest king the Athadian Empire had ever known.

"There are the remains of the revolt against the empire!"

Elad's voice carried on the wind and echoed through the avenues and alleys. Horses nickered, chill breezes blew, thousands and thousands of faces stared up at him; and, when he pointed, thousands and thousands of eyes turned to look upon the two war galleys moored just beyond the docks.

"They sought by rebellion to overthrow your empire!" Elad screamed.

Beside him, Ogodis—and beside Ogodis, the Lady Salia. Frozen in the morning cold, disgusted by the spectacle. Abgarthis, frowning, stood tall beside Elad.

"Set fire," Elad called, "to the death ship!"

A thousand horns picked up his command, and Khamars stationed on the docks aimed flaming arrows into the sky. They sped up and arced down, like clouds of fiery locusts, and landed upon the decks and masts and sails of the gore-filled galley. A tornado of flames rushed up, the ship having already been heavily doused with oils, tar, and naphtha. And as the thousands watched, hanging from windows and standing atop buildings, crowding the streets from dockside all the way back to the Effu Square, the death galley with its rotting piles of heads shook and trembled on the cold gray waters, and sent up columns of thick black and orange flames like tall towers in the air.

And Abgarthis was furious.

He watched as the galley, aflame, was towed out into the ocean and cut free. He watched, with Elad and the others, as it rocked awkwardly, pulled by the waves, and slowly sank as it burned.

He turned to King Elad to whisper, "Are you doing this to impress the Imbur of Gaegosh?"

Elad faced him quickly with a wrathful expression. "I do it to prove that I am King, and that *I* rule my nation—not a band of criminals."

"Criminals?" Abgarthis returned in a shocked, low voice. "Those people were the taxpayers of Sulos! They were businessmen, students, people with minds, my King! For you to—"

Elad noticed the Imbur Ogodis smiling at the show with cruel approval. "The only way to be a strong master and remain a strong master"—he spoke loudly and quite frankly to Elad—"is to show that one is without question a strong master. I do such things often in my own land."

Elad thanked him, nodding affably, and glanced smiling at the Lady Salia, who did not seem overly impressed either by her father's comment or the violent display.

Abgarthis, however, meant to have his say. "This is wrong, Elad," he pursued, whispering.

"Nonsense." Elad continued to smile at the Lady Salia until, unencouraged, he turned once more toward his elder adviser. "I will not have revolts within my nation. I am the King. I will guide my empire, and I will not allow it to fall into the hands of cowards."

"You have martyred them," Abgarthis insisted in a grim tone. "You have given those who live a standard to bear. You acted too hastily—"

"This is neither the time nor the place, Abgarthis."

"It is precisely the time and the place, King Elad. Look at that! Your father would never have acted this way."

Elad growled, "My father never had to deal with radicals and rebels."

"But he did," Abgarthis replied. "He did, Elad. Only he met them halfway, in private, and tried to be king to all, not just to those close by the throne."

Elad was appalled. "You cannot speak to me in such a way."

"What would you have me do, then? Not speak at all? Will you dismiss me? Do I speak treachery? I am in this position to inform you of—"

"*Enough!*" the King yelled at him, losing all patience and forgetting where he was. Faces turned, drawn to his outcry, but Elad did not notice. "That is *enough*, Abgarthis! Hold your tongue! I *won't* have *treachery* spoken in my face!"

Infuriated and embarrassed, feeling as if Abgarthis had made a fool of him before his Council and his guests, Elad warned his minister, "Begone from here." Trying to control himself and save face: "It grows colder. Perhaps it is time all of us returned to the palace."

He led the way from the rooftop, moved to where Khamars guarded the portal in the roof and the inner stairwell.

Abgarthis followed, not intimidated by Elad's outburst, but thinking to himself with mighty regret that Elad was not the monarch his father had been and might never become so. Pathetic—and a dangerous situation, indeed.

Out on the sea, the last of the blackened galley sank under the gray, cold waves, sending up a tall, steaming column of black smoke, which spread and veiled the shoreline like a cloud of atrocious incense.

At last Adred had been able to buy passage on a ship to Sulos—the first ship out since the official ban had been lifted. With his gifts, and with very little money left in his pockets, he paced restlessly along the rails all afternoon, finding no comfort in the swell and rush of the cold gray sea. He spent a restless night working himself into a near-panic. When his ship finally docked early the following evening, it was only with the greatest restraint that Adred held back from throwing himself onto the dock without first waiting for his belongings to be carted ashore.

He hired a carriage and urged the driver to hurry to Count Mantho's address. But when he arrived there, he found that the apartment building was no more than an empty shell. No lights burned, and the doors at the top of the entrance stairs had been locked with a chain. A wooden placard with the city seal on it hung on the chain.

"Where is Count Mantho?" Adred asked his carriage driver. "Was he killed in the revolt? Tell me!"

But the man knew nothing. Adred ordered the driver to take him to the local military office. There he learned that his friend's name appeared on the official roll of those killed or missing during the rebellion. But neither Orain's nor Galvus's name was on any list.

"Are you certain?"

And when the officer in charge began to lose patience with this son of money, Adred at last revealed, "They are royal blood! Don't you have any record of them at all?"

"Royal blood? Sir, our records indicate that no one attached to the throne is—"

It was ludicrous. Surely Galvus and Orain, if they hadn't been killed, would have left some hint of their location.

Adred, already exhausted by his journey on the ship, ordered his carriage to take him to a hostel. There he advanced money for a night's stay and put his things in his room; then he began a methodical search for the refugees.

He searched and questioned, without success, until the middle of the night, when at last, cold, hungry, and utterly fatigued, he returned to his room and fell asleep.

Awakening late in the morning, he breakfasted hurriedly and resumed his search. By midafternoon Adred had questioned the officers of the final temporary shelter in the city. And none had any record or recall of Lord Prince Galvus or Lady Orain. The authorities did not seem particularly alarmed by this; as royalty, the mother and son had probably done all they could to keep their identities a secret and then, as soon as the port was cleared, returned to the capital.

Adred, depressed and anxious, had to admit that this was most likely. Yet there was only one way to make certain, short of sending a letter to King Elad on the next boat out: take that boat himself. He went down to the port authority to buy passage. Told that a merchanter was set to leave at dusk, he had little to do but hire a porter to trundle his belongings to the shipping office, then loiter the rest of the day by the docks.

It was a cool afternoon. There was a light snow on the ground; the air was chill enough to send Adred indoors after a while. Into a shop he went and ordered himself some food; he sat at a table by a window and stared gloomily out the frosted window, ate his broiled fish, sipped his hot tea.

He was watching the thin crowds in the street when he noticed Galvus outside, walking in the company of a large man who appeared to be a sailor.

Adred was stunned. He stared, a bite of fish half-lifted to his mouth. He rose from his chair, staring out the window, watching the young man and the sailor as they casually passed by.

"Galvus?"

In a flurry of movement that left his chair knocked to the floor and his teacup dripping on the table, Adred hurled himself outside and raced down the icy street, waving his arms like a maniac.

"Galvus! *Galvus!* Gods, *Galvus,* it's me, it's—"

The youth and the large man turned around, looked.

Adred slowed down in his run. Was he wrong? Was this Galvus? Had he—?

"Adred."

Galvus! He caught the young man's hand, then threw his arms around him and hugged him madly. "Gods, gods, I thought you'd been killed! I didn't know where you were. Mantho's house was chained and bolted, I had no idea that you'd—"

He babbled on and on, excited, gripping Galvus by the shoulders—until he realized that the youth didn't seem very excited to see him.

Adred was perplexed. "What's wrong? Galvus—gods, aren't you glad to see me?"

Galvus seemed more confused and upset than joyous. "Yes—yes, of course I am." He turned to his comrade. "Sars, excuse me, please."

"Surely." The sailor nodded agreeably. "Good day to you, sir." He turned and walked off.

Adred was astonished. "Galvus! What's going on? Where's Orain?" He panicked. "She's not—"

"No, no, she's all right. Mother's alive."

"But—" He didn't understand this at all. "Are you staying *here?* On the docks? What's happened? Why aren't you—?"

"We want to live here now," Galvus told him. He grinned slightly at Adred's expression. "Come. We have a place only a little way down. Come on."

Adred followed him. They had a room on the second floor of an apartment building, where they lived in conditions no better than those of ordinary dockworkers. Orain greeted him with a hug and a smile and said, "Rather cozy, don't you think?"

Galvus moved to a chair by the window, took a piece of fruit from a bowl on a table, began to munch on it.

It was so strange! Adred looked at both of them, drew a hand through his hair. "But when are you going back?" he asked Orain.

"We don't want to go back."

"You're going to *live* here?" he asked in disbelief. "But—why?"

"Because, Galvus replied, "most people live this way. What's wrong with it?" To Adred's silent stare, he patted

233

the copy of Radulis, which was on the table beside the fruit bowl. "These words live for me, Adred. Remember?"

His answer was an outburst of laughter from his friend. Adred roared with delight at the irony of it, the madness of it—the perfection of it.

"Don't," Galvus warned him in a cold tone. "Don't mock us."

"Mock you?" Adred returned. "Gods on high! *Mock* you? You've totally shamed me! All *I've* ever done my whole life was walk around feeling guilty—and buying *you* books to make you feel guilty too—then worrying my head off because I was afraid that the prince-inheritor to the throne had been killed in a bloody damned—"

"Shhh!" Orain cautioned him, raising a hand. "No one's to know who we are!"

"No one knows?"

"We're aristocrats, yes. Homeless because of the rebellion. And weary of it all, sympathetic to the people. That's all anyone knows of us. Adred, we've begun to make friends, we live here because we're happy here." She stopped, thoughtful; she reached for her heavy coat and pulled it on. "Let's go for a walk, Adred."

"All right."

Galvus didn't seem to mind; he sat where he was, finished his apple.

They went out into the bracing cold, walked until they came to some benches alongside a building. There they sat, adjusting themselves on the cold stone, and Orain told Adred, "Galvus wants this. Do you understand? Adred." She reached for his hands and held them, and he was taken back to a cool evening in the palace gardens. "Adred, he is my son. He is Cyrodian's son. Sooner or later he must inherit the throne. But he—he has things in him. Not much of his father in him, thank Hea, but much of people like you and me and Yta. He believes in things, Adred. The things his philosopher has written about and the things he's seen—his own father a murderer, his uncle a criminal but king of the world, the people here treated like animals. He's sensitive to all of that, and he knows it's all wrong. If this had been any other time, any other place—if Elad had taken the throne honestly, if there had been no rebellion—I'm sure Galvus wouldn't be acting this way. But we live in dangerous times, and he's part

234

of these times. Galvus is sensitive; he wants justice. He's trying to find himself, Adred—and, after all, he's a young man."

"You're indulging him, then."

"Don't say it like that. He and I have only one another. I'm his mother—I'm the mother of the man who will one day be the lord of the empire."

"If the empire lasts that long," Adred commented.

"Yes," Orain replied, unafraid of the implications of that. She looked away from him. "I don't know, Adred. Yta had strange visions before she—before she left. We talked the night before she went away. But"—she faced him again—"I don't think we'll be here very long, I really don't. But can you blame Galvus for wanting this, for wanting to be with these people—our people!—and work honestly, speak freely, when all he's ever seen is treachery and blood and evil?"

"I don't blame him," Adred said. "I'm astonished at his strength."

"He is strong—terribly strong. And he's wise, too. In another year he'll be a grown man. By that time I'm sure we'll be back in the palace. And then Elad will have to listen to us—listen to Galvus. He's living, Adred. He's living life, he's facing it, in ways that Elad knows nothing about. He'll be a *man*. Can you imagine the kind of king he'll make?"

"You want that for him, don't you, Orain?"

She told him, "He's all I have. And I don't want him to become another Elad or—or Cyrodian." She sounded ashamed.

"I'm surprised," Adred told her. "But Galvus is right in what he's doing."

"He is, isn't he?" She smiled, pleased that Adred understood.

"He's doing the right thing. Elad doesn't want him now. But Athadia *will* need him." He chuckled. "I guess it's not so different from those stories about kings in the old days dressing up like beggars and going into the streets in disguise."

They sat silent for a few moments and stared at the wharves, at the great ships, at the people and the sailors. The empire . . .

Adred turned grim. "Mantho was killed, wasn't he?"

"Yes," Orain told him. "We saw him die. One of his own servants murdered him. Euis. You remember him."

She told him what she'd heard about the revolutionaries—the ones who'd taken over the Governor's mansion on Shemtu Square—how they had died almost nobly, and how the army

235

commander, Lutouk, had wanted to treat them fairly. They'd given him a list of grievances to present to Elad. But Elad had sent in two legions of troops, and the people had been massacred.

"They slaughtered those men and women," Orain said. "Like cattle. I don't care how much violence they caused. I heard that, and I thought about it. I look around the docks now—look at how these people live. Adred, what's happened to us? What's happened to our country? We used to stand for everything strong and good. People were proud to be called Athadians; everyone worked hard; we had a good king; we were a good nation."

He didn't have an answer for her. There were too many different answers, too many different reasons. Thinking about it: "What went wrong with us was—well, we made too many promises, Orain. The people believed us. We failed them. We lied to them."

She reached into an inner pocket of her coat and pulled out a piece of cheap paper; on it a crude printing device had printed a message.

"They pass these out down here constantly," she told Adred. "This is what the rebellion is about. These are the people we betrayed. It breaks my heart to read words like this. I saw people killed, but—I've been reading Radulis, too. Do you know where I got this? A merchant who sells fish. He's barely able to make a living, but the rich people in Sulos are complaining now because there was an open rebellion and some $\frac{1}{8}$ of the windows in their homes were broken. Oh, Adred . . ."

He took the paper from her, read it.

Te so keth ellulu k. se kofuti. . . .
    It is the privilege and the duty of men and women in a civilized society to create a cooperative community of common good for all. Where that commitment weakens or is lost, or where that ideal is reduced to intolerance, injustice, or much for the few and little for the many, all the aspirations which civilization claims for itself become a mockery. Men are born free to realize all that they may become, and where any economy or religion or military places one man above another without that man's consent . . .

Trembling, Adred stopped reading. "This isn't just philosophy, is it?"

"No, Adred, it is not."

"They want to overthrow the government, don't they?" he asked Orain.

"Yes." It frightened her, almost, to admit the obvious. "I think they do, Adred. If you stop and look at what's happened . . ." She swallowed thickly. "Dursoris . . . saw the corruption in the palace and he tried to fight it. So Cyrodian and Elad killed him. Now the people on the street are trying to fight it, and Elad's killing them too. Adred, I'm not a rebel. Galvus isn't a rebel. Neither are you. But we're decent people, we were raised with certain values, and how can we pretend that things aren't the way they are? This society has changed so much, and people like Elad—he was raised with the same values, yet he manipulates them. And the Councilors, the businesses—but I don't want to see anyone hurt. I don't want to see babies trampled in the street." She began to sob.

Adred moved closer to her. He held her tightly.

"We're just going to end up killing one another!" Orain cried out then. "Don't you see what's happening? Evarris should never have died! The gods are doing something terrible to us!"

"Orain, please, please," he comforted her. "Not the gods, not the gods—just us, Orain." As she controlled herself: "Do you have more?" He meant the revolutionary paper.

"Yes. In our room."

"Give them to me," he told her. "Please."

She didn't understand. "But why, Adred? You're not going to—"

"I'm going to Athad, Orain. I want to talk with Elad."

He had seen injustice daily and tried to correct it wherever he could. But one man alone could hardly correct the imbalance of an entire society. Athadia was an empire; it had always been ruled by a king, and it had always paid homage to its aristrocracy. Ideals of true freedom, the concept that men, that society could correct injustices, could actually rule itself, had always been an ideal. Fantasy. But now?

It is the privilege and the duty of men and women in a civilized society to create a cooperative community of common good for all.

The enormity of it, the affront of it—the promise of those

237

words overthrowing two thousand years of accumulated history and custom, belief and inertia . . .

While some deep core of him knew that it was true, knew that it must be true. Knew that the march of history must inevitably, sooner or later, deliver such freedoms into the hands and hearts of the invisible crowds of history. Knew that the throne itself, king by king, generation by generation, had moved closer and closer to it.

Could the empire still be an empire, and the nation remain solvent and strong itself, without a king, with every man, high and low, from dock to throne hall, an equal partner in managing a nation that was half the world?

It frightened Adred.

And it emboldened him.

For deep in him, he believed it, he knew it must come, and he wanted it to come.

PART VI

Far Paths, Other Shadows

1.

She was a young, slightly built girl, little more than a child, and that was what Nutatharis appreciated in her. She never spoke. She had the look of a young doe, which brought out in King Nutatharis emotions of both protectiveness and mastery. Whenever he glanced at the girl, a rapt expression of gratitude seemed to fill her face. She had found favor with the king; that must be her only defense in the world. Nutatharis relished the thought. Of the hundreds of women, most of them peasants, who served in various capacities through his male-dominated palace, only this one roused in Nutatharis interest that was something more than animal lust or desire for domination.

The king of Emaria knew that if he brutalized this young woman she would enjoy even that, accept the brutality with gratitude, as favorable attention from her master. And that suited Nutatharis, who loved power.

So he was staring at this young woman with something bordering on affection, as she cleared away trays from a table in his dinner chamber, as she hurried on her small deerlike feet. Appreciatively he watched her, and when the other woman servant present (an older matron who took charge of the kitchens) turned her callous eyes upon her lord just before departing for the evening, Nutatharis raised a finger to her. And the young woman nodded, jerking her head the slightest bit in understanding. When the young woman left, arms filled with empty trays and dishes, the matron followed after, prim and stiff.

While Nutatharis smiled to himself, lifted a wine cup to his lips, and imagined the wine to be the young girl's wine. Already he could taste the sweet buds of her dark brown nipples; already he could feel the light pressure of her slim young legs.

Eromedeus, sitting nearby, said to Lord Nutatharis, "Give me that one."

Nutatharis started. "The blonde-haired girl?"

"Auburn-haired," his minister corrected him, as though this trivial perception was quite important. "I would make use of her."

Nutatharis's brow creased. None else in the room had overheard—not Sir Jors, still seated at his table and pouncing on the final half of a roast duck; nor General Kustos, sitting alone by a window, staring at the snow and meditating over his wine cup; nor Prince Cyrodian, who was avidly availing himself of two large women seated beside him. Prince Cyrodian, in fact, was in no condition to overhear anything that passed between the two men, whether significant or ephemeral: the second son of the Athadian empire, becoming well acclimated to his life of exile, was busy pouring small amounts of wine into the cleavage of one of the young women, pushing her breasts together so that the wine rolled in the long crease like water in a trough, and then nuzzling his hairy face into the sticky bosom to lick up the flesh-warmed spirits.

Nutatharis watched these antics out the corner of one eye and after a moment replied to his minister, "Correct me if I am in error, Eromedeus, but whenever I give you young women to . . . make use of, they never seem to be returned to me. Or if they are, they are so mindless that they are no good to anyone. I assume there to be some important reason for this. Just as I assume that the gradually dwindling population of sheepherders' and fielders' daughters around here has something in common with my loss of servant girls." Half-facing Eromedeus, he raised one brow and awaited an answer.

"There are," Eromedeus told him, "mystic avenues, Lord Nutatharis, that certain strong men attempt by their wills to travel."

"Oh, yes. That. Your sorcery." Nutatharis smiled. His servants had told him months earlier of Eromedeus's peculiar nighttime habits, his use of some of the cellars, his creation of odd incenses, and his orders for the metalsmiths to create for him a variety of strange implements.

"Not sorcery," his minister corrected him. "Sorcery is crude and foul. I speak of greater things."

"Ah. Greater things."

"Do you make mock of me, Lord Nutatharis?" Eromedeus asked almost scornfully.

The Lord of Emaria could be diplomatic. "I seldom make mock of other men's ambitions," was his answer, "when such men do not mock my own. Each of us has his calling in this world, and strong men must respect one another, in their faults and in their achievements. I presume that, since I have given you shelter for the past half a year, and many comforts, and even a place at my table—not to mention the dozen or so young women—that these 'dabblings' of yours are in some way connected with my own ambitions?"

"That which I hope to accomplish is very vague and very personal—personal in the manner in which it will affect my own destiny. I seek in no way to confound or interfere with any of your plans."

"Were that the case, Minister, I would have known of it long before now and put an end to it."

"Then—as to the young woman?"

Nutatharis turned his head on his hand, glanced about the room. "Singular, isn't she?" he commented. "Sometime you'll have to . . . compare techniques with me, Eromedeus." Looking at him once more: "I have heard your young women shrieking. They shriek when I bugger them myself." He chortled. "If you can gain great insights from that, then, by the gods! you are welcome to them!" And he laughed aloud.

Eromedeus was deeply wounded and disgusted by this coarse remark, but rather than pursue the matter further, he felt it best to let Nutatharis think what he would think. "I cannot have the young woman, then?"

"I lust after her myself, and she is only just beginning to understand me, Eromedeus. Do you know how rare that is—to have a simple young child like that, as slim as a twig and as pale as sunlight, anticipating every urge, delaying and conniving with her fingers and her mouth?" He stopped suddenly; Eromedeus was not one of his soldiers, not a confidant. "I am becoming too drunk. No, you cannot have her. But she has a sister—"

"I have seen her. She is common to many of the men here."

"Take her. Use her. Her obvious charms are ample, and you may do with her as you will. Or take someone else for

242

your . . . mystical buggerings." He set down his wine cup, placed it insecurely on a table close by. True, he was becoming very drunk; the cup tilted, and Nutatharis reached again to straighten it lest it fall to the floor.

Then he got to his feet. Turned, looked down upon his minister, and smiled wantonly. "Mystical paths . . ." he murmured and belched slightly. "Yes, there are cults raised to those things. I've wondered . . . I admire you, Eromedeus. Even in your lusts, you are more high-minded or star-guided than I, eh? I am merely gross beside you, aren't I? You grasp for the stars."

He laughed shortly and went out, removing to his sleeping-chamber and to the doe-eyed young thing that anticipated his every urge.

While Eromedeus, wondering if it was becoming dangerous for him in Lasura, wondering if he should perhaps move on, sat back and looked upon the tableau of human excess in the dinner hall, and sneered with a mighty contempt that mirrored the revulsion of ages.

Late toward morning, Cyrodian awoke. It had been his custom to do this, so far during his stay at Nutatharis's palace: rising just before dawn, urinate into his chamber pot, then leave his room to wander for an hour or so, poking his head into this room and into that room. Spying. Learning on his own some things Nutatharis had not yet had the opportunity to tell him—or never intended to tell him. And if anyone, guard or early riser like himself, might chance to encounter him thus and inquire, Cyrodian had a simple answer prepared to disclaim suspicion: "I could not sleep."

He had been engaging in these early-morning excursions in a methodical manner. His chamber was on the second floor of the west wing, so he had begun by exploring that floor of the palace, then had moved on to the east wing, and the north and south. And from there, to the lower floor. And from there, into the subterranean rooms of the palace. Eventually, he intended to move on to the upper levels.

This morning Cyrodian explored the farther end of the lowest level of the west wing; he had only partially explored the central corridor and some adjacent halls previously, and now he meant to make sure that he'd covered the territory thoroughly before moving on.

243

The main corridor was a very wide gallery with a few doors opening upon it—unlike the halls upstairs, which let into rooms and chambers every few steps. There were sconces with torches on the walls, but these were lit only intermittently. Further, there were no guards or soldiers down here, although Cyrodian knew that they patrolled (or were supposed to patrol) all the major passageways of the palace. This struck him as being very curious.

Even more curious were the dull, faintly echoing sounds of voices which he heard down here this morning. Very odd in so isolated an underground—he had not heard voices on earlier visits. He wondered if Nutatharis kept his torture instruments and chambers and jailing rooms down here, as was usually the custom.

As Cyrodian walked on, the voices sounded somewhat louder. They were muffled, however, by the heavy stone walls of the palace.

He moved toward the sounds, trying to pick out tones or inflections which might identify the speakers. One certainly belonged to a woman; the other, perhaps, to Nutatharis, or perhaps General Kustos.

Far down at the end of the corridor a wavering pattern of light showed on the wall opposite a large door: torchlight or lamplight streaming through the barred window of the door. Very cautiously Cyrodian approached, easing his feet down carefully so as to make no noise.

Now the voices were distinguishable. The woman's voice was very distinct. She was pleading for release, pleading for mercy.

Cyrodian came to the door. Stepping up to it carefully, he pressed close and peered through the open bars, wanting to see what was happening within.

He looked upon a very large room, lighted in its center with torches and hanging lamps. Chains hung upon the walls, and instruments of torture. In the center of the chamber, seated in a tall wooden chair, hands folded upon his chin, sat Eromedeus. He was facing a dark-haired young woman who had been tied, naked, to a large stone block; she was whimpering and pleading with Eromedeus to free her, whimpering and pleading that she did not understand what he meant.

Cyrodian noticed that her arms had been strapped straight down her sides, roped tightly; and one arm—at least the one he could see—had a long incision in it from wrist to elbow. Blood dropped down this incision and was dribbling into a bronze bowl just beneath her hand.

"There would be no need to continue this," Eromedeus was telling the girl in a calm, reasonable voice, "if you would simply agree to—"

"I—I don't understand," she sobbed. She rolled her head from side to side; her face glistened with wet tears.

"—simply agree to give your life to me."

"I—I don't—" She broke into a series of heaving groans.

"Simply say it. Simply will your life to me, and I won't injure you anymore, I won't bleed you anymore."

Collecting her blood? Why?

Cyrodian did not understand.

Surely for some foul purpose, but—

A distant bell tolled, far outside. Cyrodian started when he heard it. At its sound, Eromedeus sighed heavily and stood up, walked to the girl. He produced some bandages and began to wrap a length of them around her arm. "This will stop the bleeding. I will bring you food."

Weak, helpless, she slumped and moaned.

Cyrodian, not wanting to be discovered, silently eased himself from the door and hastened back down the corridor and upstairs toward his chamber.

Late that morning General Kustos departed the capital to make an inspection of border outposts along the north. He expected to be gone for three or four days. At King Nutatharis's request, General Cyrodian accompanied him on this excursion, so that Cyrodian might better acquaint himself with the rank and file of soldiers he would be commanding when the time came to move into the Low Provinces.

The opportunity presented itself, late in the afternoon as they were approaching the first of the far outposts, for Cyrodian to broach the subject to Kustos. He drew his horse near the old soldier's and said, "There is a man at court who bothers me."

"And who is that?" inquired Kustos, guessing already.

"This one, Eromedeus. I'll tell you frankly, General, I could not sleep last night, just before dawn, so I went looking for wine and began to explore the size of the palace. No one bothered me, so I helped myself. Down in your cellars, I saw

245

Eromedeus torturing a young woman. He was bleeding her.''

"Does that appall you?''

"I'm a soldier; I am appalled by nothing. But I would like to know if—''

Kustos chose his words carefully and spoke them frankly but earnestly. "General Cyrodian, you and I have nothing to do with Eromedeus, and he has no effect upon our work. Therefore, it might be better if you didn't ask too many questions concerning him. He has been in that palace for over half a year's time. What passes between him and Nutatharis, I do not know. The King admires the man's intellect. That Eromedeus has Nutatharis in his grip, I do not believe for one moment; but no one speaks against him to the King. That Eromedeus from time to time passes his evenings torturing young women is a known fact, and why he does it I do not know. Nor do I wish to know. He may be a sorcerer; he may be a madman. I do not know, and I do not wish to know.''

Many words, each chosen to emphasize Kustos's refusal to pull aside the drape. Cyrodian was abashed; he hardly expected to encounter such an attitude in the general of Lord Nutatharis's army. "Then," he ventured, "there is something you do know, General, which you aren't telling me." He grumbled, "If Nutatharis doesn't yet trust me enough to—''

"It isn't a question of trust," Kustos told him, facing him in the cold wind. "It is simply a matter of I, myself, not wanting to know. That is what I'm not telling you, Cyrodian—things *I* don't want to know." And, as he urged his horse ahead through a low snowbank: "The man has tortured babies, by all the gods. Taken babies and tortured them until they died, shrieking. What foulness is it that would make a man torture babies?''

2.

Lamentoso doloroso on the eve of the fall of the first world.

Patterns of Man, late during the night or with the heavy tread of years: echoes and foreshadowings, the Fate held clasped tightly to the bosom like some old vow or promise resuscitated:

An old man's eyes in the face of a newborn baby.

Life, your renewal is a path of decay and blemished wonder, fear without answers.

Time, your tread is unerring as the loud roll of soil down the hillside, the slow breathing of moist growing roots, the fleet shadows of clouds; relentless as dripping frost in the new-old sun.

Trapped on earth, trapped by hopes and memories, where is our answer if not within ourselves? Where is our cause, if not within ourselves? O many-faced, all-voiced humanity, your enemy is astride your shoulder, it is fast held in your mirror, it breathes with your breath, quickens with your life, dreams with your dreams.

O Time, your face is human.

O Death, your name is Man.

O humanity, reducing strong elements to dust, your name is blown on a tempest, you frighten the stars, you are ever young, but old, and ignorant as some force of nature.

O Man, your names are legion. And misery and defeat, anguish and rot, curl invisibly in the crib of the newborn beside the newborn, baby or hope or ambition.

Strive, strive to be wise, many-faced and all-tongued one, intolerant one, killer of dreams, conniver and eater; destroy yourself, humanity, in justice's name, and let nature rest awhile, spinning silently new carpets of unsoiled colors.

These things that come, they come with cause. . . .

Ilbukar the golden-shored, the early-skied, where the road ends.

The Athadian Empire had embarked on its centuries-long course of expansion for reasons purely economic and political. Not so the east. The peoples of the east had not intentionally entered into a hegemonic policy, but this had grown as they had grown. At a time when the Athadian High Council was moving toward a bold new economy and a drastic encroachment upon its surrounding territories, the peoples of the east found themselves faced with an ever-increasing population that at last burst the bonds of millennia-old tradition and set its clans on the march. Like a tidal force the eastern peoples, consolidating and uniting, moving and gathering, spread westward across the vacant steppes and plains of their central continent and created a nomadic way of life suiting their barbaric, splendid, and colorful ways. With cattle in their wake and families in wagons, their small-ponied riders swept ever toward the sunfall place, capturing cities, absorbing the conquered, slaughtering the reluctant, intermarrying, breeding, building, moving and ever moving on. The loose clans necessarily gave rise to tribes, and then to far-flung tribes; and the tribes gave birth to nations, and then to an empire. An empire consolidated by Guragu, master of Salukadia, which reached from the sea-where-the-sun-rises to the mountains-of-purple-eyes: the Kalussian Range.

When he died peacefully in the twenty-third winter of his *chevauchade* in the fortress-city he had built which bore his name—Gurakad—the Blue Wolf of the Tribes observed a vision of world conquest: the extension of his empire unto the western-sea-that-reaches, the Ursalion (which he knew of only from crude maps). His eldest son, Hamurlin, was charged with continuing the conquests of the Salukadian clan; but Hamurlin the Limp died two years later of a fever, and his weak brother Huabrul—"Wind-destined"—inherited the iron sword, the jade scepter, and the brand of the wolf-mark.

Disregarded as a boy by ambitious *hetmuks* and belligerent *aihmans* within his rule, Huabrul gathered to him the strongest, fiercest, and most loyal of his generals and put all dissenters to the sword; and in a life of twelve years' conquests—seven of which were spent besieging the city of

Surulman in the icy passes of the Iltaran Mountains—Huabrul at last moved his armies as far west as the Sidesian Pass. Here he died, peacefully like his father; for it had been predestined that the *ghens* of Salukadia would die three generations in peace and three in terror. Huabrul, before expiring, ordered the execution of all his sons save the eldest, and he passed on to the Wide Plain of Clouds with the skulls of fourteen children piled beside his bed. The rule of the empire passed on to Huagrim *ko-Ghen*, Master of Masters and son of the son of the Master of Masters.

In the third year of his reign Huagrim the Great took the city of Ilbukar, which sat upon the Owal Sea, and which controlled the busy trade passing through the narrow Strait of Owal. From his palace, built in Ilbukar, Huagrim could nightly look upon the purple waters of the endless Ursalion Sea and visit the memory of his father and his father's father in the temple of the Endowui, the pantheon of animal totems and nature gods revered by the Salukadians. It was with the taking of Ilbukar that Huagrim settled, with his wife and his two sons: Attarea the Dove; and Agors, the elder; Nihim, the younger. He hung up the iron sword and the wolf-brand, and with the jade scepter administered justice across all the reaches of his far-swept empire.

Ilbukar was his western capital; Kilhum, far back across the steppes, his eastern. Huagrim *ko-Ghen*, like his father, had never seen that city which had marked the beginning of his grandfather's war-marches. And so, in the fifth year of his reign, with his wife and two sons Huagrim set out upon a wide and long journey to visit the stretches of his empire, visit with his chiefs, and administer his justice personally.

The odyssey took nearly eight years to complete. Huagrim and his vast train and his army spent their winters in Surulmankad, Gurakad, Boshan, Hiusu, and other major cities of the conquests. But on the return journey Attarea fell ill, and she died one warm spring morning en route to Gurakad. She was buried there, in the city of the Blue Wolf, first of the masters of men. Huagrim ordered a great temple erected in her honor, and he and his sons and his train and his army spent a year in Gurakad while the mausoleum was built. Then he dedicated it with the ashes of a thousand slain cattle and a hundred slain horses and seventy aromas of incense; and Huagrim the Great, supplicant before the watching Endowui,

249

ordered those gods and spirits to guard his wife's ghost, the meaning of his heart, until such a day should come that he must reside with her in the Wide Plain of Clouds.

He returned to Ilbukar in the thirteenth year of his reign, to find the city under his appointed ministers and *aihman-sas* more prosperous than ever. Yet Huagrim brooded. Not an old man, he entered his middle years with all the stoppered anger and frustrated-temperament of an elderly desexed priest. He began to spend more and more time within doors, in the temple or in the vast rooms of his hundred-chambered palace.

And, as will happen sometimes with a man, great or small, in his grief, Huagrim looked otherwhere than fate for the blame of Attarea's early demise, and it came to him one day in a temple ceremony, amidst the crashing of gongs and the smoking of incenses, the chantings of the priests and the shadows of the pillared Endowui, that the blame for his wife's passing lay at the feet of the western nations. The cause for this was perplexing, but Huagrim knew that it was so. And the more he brooded upon it, the clearer it became to him; the more he considered it, the more apparent it was (in the circumventive, veiled way of destiny) that he had to do more than meet the western nations at their borders: he had somehow to answer his wife's death.

True, the Holy City meant little to him. It had long ago divided itself into east and west, and the imposing of Salukadian law upon its eastern sections had not bothered the citizens there at all (used as they were to the vicissitudes of such things); nor had it angered the Athadian government, nominal ruler over the western section of the city, to speak now with Salukadian officials rather than spokesmen from some other tribe or culture. And yet, Erusabad was important as the last jewel in the crown. (Like Attarea, a jewel?) It was a symbol, just because of the importance both east and west placed upon it. Perhaps Huagrim should erect a temple to the Endowui there and consecrate it to Attarea's memory.

Or, if the city were entirely under the control of the Salukadian empire, then Guragu *ko-Ghen*'s ghost, watching from afar, might laugh pleasantly with thunder to see his empire stretch from the mightiest city of the east to the greatest city of the west.

Huagrim thought long upon it. He spoke with his sons. Agors, the elder, hot-tempered and with the blood of his father and his father's fathers in him, wished to take the Holy City immediately; Nihim, the younger, no warrior but learned in the skills of negotiation and book-wisdom, declared that it would stir up a hornet's nest. Why, he asked his father, should we do such a thing to Erusabad when already we have the benefit of it without doing more?

To which Agors replied, typically, "Little brother, had you lived in our grandfather's day, you might well have asked why he should conquer the world, seeing that the world was there already without his having to take it."

Huagrim laughed mightily at this logic and took himself to the temple to pray to his wife's ghost and the ghosts of his father and grandfather, and to be guided by them. He ordered readers and speakers to him, old men of the steppes who still spoke only the language of the steppes and who burned animals and spilled blood to divine the future. These men assured the conqueror that the gods and spirits favored such a thing. Huagrim met with his generals and administrators, and they told him that the nations of the west were in uneasy alliance with the Athadian Empire, that the provinces sometimes chafed under its yoke, that its King was a young man unlearned in statecraft and ill-solaced with life (as were all in the west), and that Dusar, the Athadian military governor in Erusabad, had spent long years there and was corrupt.

"Therefore, wise son of conquerors, *khilhat, domu ghen sa ko-ghen,* make war in the cities of the west the way the men of the west make war: so, with money, and not as you and your father and his father, Guragu *ko-Ghen,* made war in the plains, with sword and torch. Buy Dusar. Buy Nutatharis, King of Emaria, who is an enemy of Athadia, and bid him hurt Athadia however he can, as our ally; for he hates Athadia but loves power, and we are the power of the world. The west is weak and tearing; let us rip it as we would rip an old robe—not with the sword, as we would cut the corpses of cattle for food, but more precisely with our fingers, with fingers full of gold and mouths full of promises. The west is dying, O *Khilhat,* O *ghen sa ko-ghen,* and we are born now, new like a sun, strong and mighty, to rule the world."

Huagrim considered all this. He prayed mightily in the temple of the Endowui. He spoke at length with his ministers concerning Nutatharis the Emarian and the man's apparent interest in the Low Provinces over across from Ilbukar.

251

And at last, praying and thinking and deciding, Huagrim scorned his son Nihim's advice and nodded in agreement with Agors's; and in the fourteenth year of his reign he took down from his wall the iron sword and the wolf-brand and plotted to make Erusabad, the Holy City, a Salukadian city.

3.

When Adred reached the capital, he took a room in a lodging house near the central square and sent word via messenger to Lord Abgarthis that he would like to meet with the man at the earliest opportunity. A short time later he was very surprised to answer his door and admit, not his returned messenger, but Lord Abgarthis himself.

The old man entered without formality. Adred, taken aback, closed his door and bowed politely, stammered something, then gestured to a chair. Without a word Abgarthis settled himself upon it and rested his ivory walking stick against the wall behind him. For the first time Adred noticed that Lord Abgarthis was dressed, not in his robes of state (which, by custom, he always appeared in), but in a fine robe more suited to a nobleman than to a high-ranking member of the palace elite.

"You are astonished to see me?" Abgarthis asked rhetorically, fixing Adred keenly with his eyes.

Adred smiled, slightly embarrassed, as he took a chair opposite him. "Yes. Very much so. I was certain that you were much too occupied to see me before this evening at the earliest."

"Count Adred, much has changed since you left here. I no longer serve on the Council."

"*What?*"

"King Elad has removed me."

Adred's amazement was complete. "But you've served the throne for over forty years!"

"Nevertheless . . ." He gestured. "I'm afraid I overstepped my bounds and insulted Elad in public."

"What? Abgarthis, what has happened?"

The elder grinned mirthlessly. "The revolt in Sulos? The ship cargoed with human heads? Yes—exactly. When it arrived in port, King Elad made a grand spectacle of it. Turned out the army and everyone at the palace, made it a public show. Ordered the thing burned—right out there." Abgarthis nodded. "We were watching from a rooftop. I was appalled and told Elad so. Even went further—rebuked him and suggested that he was only creating more harm by this, that he was accelerating mistrust toward him rather than discouraging further protests. He took offense. The next morning he served me with notice of my dismissal."

Adred was silent for a long, terrible moment. Then: "Yet you still serve in the palace."

"Oh, certainly. I am still High Adviser. He simply has removed me from Council, where even my lowest whisper carried like thunder. Henceforth anything I say is not officially noted; without record of my sentiments or arguments, I can be gracefully ignored during sessions or debates. But no; I am too much respected and too . . . powerful, in my way, for Elad to do away with me completely."

Adred said nothing to this.

Abgarthis asked, "Does Elad know you have returned?"

"No. I contacted you only."

"He is anxious to know what's become of Orain and Galvus."

Adred sighed heavily. "He won't like to hear it."

"Killed? Ah, I was—"

"No, not killed. They survived the revolt. But both of them are living in a tenement apartment down on the docks. Living the life of sailors, common rabble."

The old man's response to this was loose, hearty laughter, joyous and savage. "Ah, that lad will be the only hope of us, I know it, I am sure of it! Thank the gods for him! Damn his father, but thank the gods for Prince Galvus!"

Adred asked him if there were any word (by the way) of the treacherous Cyrodian. Abgarthis answered that they had heard nothing; the dog might very well have died already in exile, although he himself did not believe that.

And then Adred told him why he had returned. "Abgarthis, you know what I mean when I tell you that there is a revolution in the air."

"A general uprising? From the people?"

"From anyone not aristocratic—but much of the gentry, as well, are sympathetic."

"I'm far from surprised. We have made too many mistakes for too long. We rub their faces in dung and expect them to love us for it."

"Is Elad aware of how pronounced the problem is?"

Abgarthis frowned. "King Elad is aware, these days, only of the fair face and form of Lady Salia of Gaegosh. Oh, yes—you had gone by that time. Ogodis of Gaegosh is a crafty fox; his daughter is an extremely beautiful young woman, and it is Ogodis's intention to trade her on the market for as high a price as he can manage. Elad is quite taken by her."

"A marriage?" Adred sounded doubtful of it.

"Within the month, or I'm no judge of events. Surely. It is just what Ogodis wants, and the last thing Elad needs. The man is a coward, Adred. I swear by the high ones, there was hope for him once. He was dutiful. There were a few weeks when I know he intended to give his best and his all—he was reading his brother's law books! But"—Abgarthis shook his head—"he is too weak. He admires too much, in others, traits he does not possess himself. Ogodis is a puffbag and an ass; he puts on a show, he is all pretense. Elad is impressed. True! Though he sees the foolishness, knows it for what it is, he enjoys it. Ogodis has honeyed the trap, and our lord steps into it, grinning. Oh, she'll warm his bed at night, and her father will be right there in the next room, goading her on. She's like a puppet in his hands. Foul, foul."

"Elad can't possibly be this stupid."

"Actually, he's not. I've tried to warn him that anything he says or does is like dropping a pebble in a pool—but he cannot grasp it, not practically. No matter what he attempts, it becomes sour for him; and now is not the moment for Elad to learn by failures. He's turned the bureaucracy upside down, bribed the army with shortened gold—he's devalued our money even more—and, to cap it, he's marrying this wisp of a woman-child while he's still dizzy from ordering the execution of hundreds of his subjects." Abgarthis sniffed. "Things move more rapidly for Elad than they do in a burlesque by Sivon-otis. Only what Elad's doing isn't humorous."

Adred insisted, "I must speak to him, Abgarthis, about this discontent in the empire. And I mean speak to him frankly."

"Certainly you must—if you can get his attention."

"Go to him for me. He'll listen to you. Tell him I bring a message from Orain and Galvus. Tell him—anything. Just get me alone with him for an hour or two. He's got to understand how crucial this is."

Abgarthis smiled sadly but said nothing. He rose, reached for his stick, and crossed the room to the door. Hand on the latch, he turned; Adred stood and faced him.

"You look well," the old man told him graciously, "despite all of it. The beard suits you. All of this," he said, "does it fire your blood?"

"I don't understand."

"Haven't you joined the revolution yet, Adred?"

He thought for a long moment, looking into the deep eyes of this wise old man, this long-serving and prescient, quiet and dignified man of the imperial halls. "Yes," Adred replied quietly. "In my heart, I have."

Abgarthis nodded, understanding. "I sometimes wish I had again the impatience of youth—if only for an hour, a day. If I were younger, you know, I suppose I would join it too, this revolution. For justice's sake. But one man alone . . ." He smiled pathetically. "But I am too practical, you see. And I am too trapped by—convention? Trapped by my years, perhaps. Weary . . ."

Adred stared at him, and an immense shadow of sorrow gripped him.

"I will tell King Elad," Abgarthis promised him, "that you have word of his sister-in-law and nephew. Be prepared to be received tonight."

"Of course."

Then Abgarthis went out, and Adred listened to the quiet tread of his feet and the hollow tapping of his cane, dull and dimming, like the muffled beat of an ancient heart, weary and hurrying to cease. . . .

4.

Odossos: a small volcanic island in the Ursalion Sea, perhaps thirty leagues west of Ugalu. Sparsely populated with farmers and goat-tenders. Thirty ships made port here a year, trading artifacts from the cities of the east in return for cheeses, cloth goods, barley, pottery. The inhabitants were poor. Odossos had no cities, only villages. Lush fields grew alongside dead land, arid, rocky soil. A few small mountains, spotted with deep caves, toward the center of the island.

It was to this place that Thameron came, demolished in spirit, weary of body, terrified of soul, to confront himself.

"I will tell you why animals are dying and why the gods are angry with the kings and queens! Listen to me, I know how I speak! One is coming! Yes! He is near, he is close-by! He is *ro kil-su*, he is the Evil One, he is born and he rises up even now, far away from us, but he will shatter the world!"

In his cavern home, rocky and barren and unlighted, unwarmed—wholly different from Guburus's cavern home— Thameron, foodless and drinkless, weaponless, dressed only in a sackcloth robe, ponders and ruminates, tries to will himself to die, and remembers all that he has been, all that he has done. He seems to be a ghost to himself. He has chased himself since his escape from Guburus's cave.

Now, with the chill of winter in the air, with nights cold-black and dawns bitter with frost, Thameron, shivering, feverish, sits crouched in the darkness high above the small villages of the isle of Odossos—wishing to know.

Wishing to know.

Wishing to be whatever he has become, wishing to do whatever he has done to himself.

You are become your destiny, O man. You are chosen, the vessel, the being, the embodiment of the last days. Demand that shadows bow before you and mountains bend in praise, for you are become your destiny, O man beyond men, O Prince of Darkness, Master of the Hell of Men!

He stared at his hands. Stared at the marks burned on his palms, the intertwined crescent moons and the seven-pointed star.

. . . *the embodiment of the last days* . . .
. . . the house of evil . . .
. . . the sower of discord . . .
. . . *ro kil-su* . . .

He turned his hands over. Stared at the ring he still wore on a finger of his right hand.

Hapad's ring.

"Know that there was good here. Please. The world is wide. I am afraid for you. Wherever you may travel, my friend, please, keep this with you, to remind you . . ."

Stared at the ring . . .

Until his mind was dissolved by memories, and he was brought back to Guburus's cave and faced the flames again, and the explosion of the gem.

He traced a design on the floor of his cavern, a design—a symbol—never taught him by Guburus or any other, but which he knew, being now who and what he was.

The symbol came to life as Thameron stared at it. Lips of dust, eyes of sand, wrinkles of dirt. Alive.

"Was it pride lured me?" Thameron asked the lips of dust.

O man, your day has come, and it has come for the world. Look beyond yourself, for that which comes, comes with cause. The air trembles at your breath.

"Am I damned?" Thameron asked of the eyes of sand.

That is an old question. Your nature has joined the world's; events come and, coming, create a new world.

"Am I the Master of Evil?" Thameron asked of the wrinkles of dirt.

You have been chosen, O *ro kil-su*. Time will cease, only

258

to begin again. You sought, you have been answered. Your destiny is everywhere. You have been chosen.

"What am I?" Thameron asked of himself.

You are Evil.

He removed Hapad's ring, dropped it in the dirt.
It struck the symbol, and
Thameron screamed
screamed as he was
p u l l e d
into a darkness
to become his mother, giving birth to himself

EVIL
As the ring died and was eaten
All the paths at once
And he saw himself in a misted flame, and he was a woman with laughing jaws, he was screaming and laughing
He worshiped the moon like an animal, he
danced like a savage, he
was a river and a current, and he
was all that all was

EVIL
A l l . . .
The cold wind
Take me!
All the paths at once
What am I?

EVIL
Not m e e e—h e e e eeeee!
As he was twisted and pulled born torn stretched—
ro kil-su

EVIL
O man beyond men, O Prince of Darkness, Master of the Hell of Men!
The chosen one.
Thameron
I am eating my own flesh and I am drinking my own blood small things are crawling there they look at me with my own eyes
Thameron
I am the Lamp in a Storm
The Lamp

259

    dies in darkness
EVIL
    Thameron
      see
      know
      know
    the sky is screaming at you, angered with your flesh
EVIL
    Thameron
    His name is night-starred, surely this was decided at the
    beginning of Time
    I want to go back
    go back
    go back
    go
EVIL
    surely this was decided
    Thameron

He awakens, half dead, to the cold sunlight of dawn filling his mountain cavern.

He stares at his hands.

Stares at the symbol in the dirt—vanished, the symbol—and sees that the ring has been destroyed, twisted and bent by some force into a simple piece of slag, a twisted lump of gold.

Half dead, from the concussions of his journey, his many paths, his awakenings and deaths and reawakenings.

Brought back or reborn, or awakened at last from the throne of the dawn, for his awareness in this time of times.

Nameless, truly. But aware, yes. And now in this Thameron, this boy, this once-a-priest, this confused walking thing of clay and fear, this wet and membraned human which had sought and, seeking, had discovered the web of existence, and was chosen—in the same way that a path of water, one with a rushing current, is chosen to move around a rock while other paths of water splash against the rock.

Thameron: alive, but aware.

Evil.

Knowing himself to be the house of evil, the sower of discord, the future of the world.

Time, housed in humanity.

The challenge . . .

He rose up, walked to the mouth of his cave, and looked up at the sky. Far down below, beneath the mountain, beneath the gray, clouded sky, lay one of the villages.

He looked toward the village.

He made his sign in the air and returned inside the cave to make his sign in the dirt.

Very soon a storm came from the sky, to rain and snow upon the village.

Thameron, from the mouth of the cave, watched it. Watched as the village was attacked by the sudden storm, and its people cried out, as its huts were demolished, as its peasants swirled and smashed in the flow of snow and ice that trapped them, as the fields turned gray with death.

He returned to his circle, muttered, and brought a halt to the storm.

He is beyond knowledge, beyond the paths, beyond all. He is the vessel, and he is all that the vessel contains.

Thameron, Master of the Hell of Men.

When he went down from the mountain later that morning, he passed through the village. Death was everywhere. Dull sunlight glinted off the smashed huts coated with icy rain. Women were screaming and crying; men were pulling broken red bodies from the wreckage; animals killed; children bent in bizarre death poses; trees brought down and twisted in the ruinous upheaval of icy-blue gardens.

Perhaps half of them remained alive, ignorant, shrieking, terrified, sobbing.

Blood everywhere, frozen in phosphorescence.

Animals barked and lowed.

The breeze pushed helplessly at the numb, frozen locks of corpses' hair.

One small baby, frozen in a womblike posture, its mother curled up beside it protectively, lay dead.

He looked and felt nothing, and knew that it was necessary.

Knew that he was necessary.

Someone—a face, a young girl's face, still alive—looked up at him beseechingly. Stranger, please, help us, please, there was an ice storm. . . .

He said nothing but lifted out his arms, showed her his hands. The signs of old.

She became terrified and screamed and screamed.

Men looked at him.

Thameron turned his back on them and went away.

What am I?

You are Evil.

And it was necessary. . . .

He made his way back to the shore and the tide; eventually a boat would come, and he would return to the world to do what he had been chosen to do.

Remembering what he was, and knowing what he had become, he loathed himself.

Was it pride lured me?

Am I damned?

Am I the Master of Evil?

What am I?

He had discovered the web of existence and was chosen.

Thameron.

The Prince of Hell, the Sower of Discord, the House of Evil . . .

ro kil-su . . .

the necessary one . . .

5.

They met in private, in a chamber of the state palace. Elad was quite informal; he paced while Adred sat at a table and picked nervously at his fingernails.

Elad's first question concerned Lady Orain and Prince Galvus.

"They are safe," Adred assured him, and told him where they were living and what decision they had come to.

Elad was upset by this bit of foolishness. "This is absurd. Their lives are in danger there, don't they know that?"

"No one knows who they are. They seem intent upon staying—"

"It's ridiculous," Elad pronounced again. "I'll order them back to the capital immediately. They don't know what they're doing."

"With all due respect, Lord Elad, I think they do. They are members of the nobility, yes. But their sympathies, Elad, lie with the people."

"Nonsense."

"My lord, may I speak frankly?" Adred was nervous. "I came here to do more than tell you of Orain and Galvus. I came here, King Elad, to warn you—to forewarn you—that the riot in Sulos was not an isolated incident. The threat of revolution hangs heavily in the air. The streets are rife with talk—and plans."

"Do you expect me to take them seriously?"

"There were demonstrations in every city following what happened in Sulos."

"We have taken measures," Elad replied crisply, "to make certain that those sorts of things won't occur again."

"My King, no matter what you do, they *will* occur again

263

unless you take some very specific measures to answer the grievances of the working people." Elad stopped his pacing, but Adred held up a hand. "No, please, let me have my say. Orain and Galvus are not acting foolishly. They are doing what they think is right. They've become aware, my lord, that the economy is tremendously unstable, that it favors few over the many, that the mass of our people are quite well educated but out of work, and that the people are being victimized both by the economy and the people who control it."

"You speak," Elad snapped at him, "as though you were a revolutionary yourself."

"In a way, I am," Adred temporized. "Just as Orain and Galvus are." When Elad did not answer that: "There is a great deal of injustice, my King. The people feel that the time for justice, even equality, has come."

Elad walked to a table and sat down opposite him. He stared directly into Count Adred's eyes. "The people?" he asked gruffly. "Have you any idea how many *innocent* people were butchered in Sulos by these—rabble?"

Adred answered him defiantly, "You mean innocent aristocrats, or innocent victims of the economy?"

"You walk very close to treason, Count. And—if the reports I received are correct—your good friend Count Mantho was among those brutally slain. I find it hard to believe that you're actually defending his murderers."

"Yes, Mantho was slain, but he would have been the first to have me fight for what I believe in, whether it be for an empire or for what may be a revolution." He sighed heavily, wiped a nervous hand through his hair. "King Elad, if you— if your Council—insist on seeing riots and demonstrations as isolated incidents, if you insist on ignoring the fact that the great mass of your citizens are hungry and out of work, if you remain blind to what is happening just outside your window— gods! You will fall victim to it, the rulers of the empire will fall victim to it, and nothing will have been accomplished except blood, and more blood, and even more blood! The *people* are in such despair that they're beginning to organize. This is the truth! They're organizing, they're circulating broadsheets, they're gathering in groups to decide on what actions to take, what reforms to demand. My King, I've visited some of these gatherings. I've listened to these people.

264

Listen to me, please! They are not the outcasts of our cities! I've heard *aristocrats* speak passionately on these issues and challenge the throne. I've read the petitions that are being circulated."

"They want to overthrow their government; they want to depose their King."

"They do *not*!" Adred lied. "They want *reforms*. And they want them now, Elad. There is too much bureaucracy—"

Elad held up a hand, and Adred fell silent. "If you have knowledge of who is plotting these riots, then it is your duty to the throne to report these criminals to the authorities."

"I have no names," Adred told him, "unless you wish to arrest Lady Orain and Prince Galvus."

"You don't expect me to believe that?"

"My lord King, these people are not attacking you. They are attacking an inefficient system of government, an unfair economy, a deadly bureaucracy which has held them down for generations. They speak of freedoms. It is not those who have nothing who are rebelling, King Elad. They've never known otherwise; why would they rebel? It's the people who *have* had some, and were working to get more—and now we're taking it all from them faster than they can earn it. I don't mean just property or money, but ideals, opportunities, even principles. The smaller mercantilists and shopkeepers, the students, the young aristocrats—they want whatever there is—money, property, justice, laws—to be distributed fairly. They were taught this as children—to act fairly and impartially— and now they see men succeeding who are no more than criminals, and liars, and murderers. Do you see why they're revolting? My lord, have you ever read the treatises of Radulis?"

Elad's expression was suspicious. "I have tried to read him with an open mind."

"He, too, was an aristocrat who saw the flaws inherent in what has become of our culture, and he wrote of ways to correct them. Are you familiar with his Three Ages of Society? His words are the mainstay of the revolution."

"Yes," replied Elad bluntly.

When a house has grown so racked and weathered that it no longer serves the purpose for which it was constructed, that house is torn down, and a new one, of better material and workmanship, is erected in its place.

"He calls for the overthrow of the monarchy, in his *Philosophy*."

"He calls for an end to unjust rule—unjust simply because it places the few over the many—but it does not need to take place violently, or even illegally."

Elad growled and reached for a cup of wine.

Adred withdrew from his pocket some of the broadsheets he had brought with him from Sulos. "King Elad, if you can, for a moment, put yourself in the place of the lowest man in this empire, try to understand what words like this mean to him." And he read a number of paragraphs: "Men who gain at the expense of others tend toward conservatism, and it is these men, more than any others, who are the enemies of the society which has permitted them to become its enemies. . . . A society which presumes that mercantile competitiveness creates an ongoing good is a society of vermin feasting on the corpses left by competitive struggle. . . . Competition is essentially self-destructive, for it destroys those qualities which, in a cooperative atmosphere, are meant to be enhanced—"

"Are you quite finished?" Elad interrupted.

Adred looked at him.

"This is all well and good as an exercise," the King told him. "But I must answer to more than wish-fulfillment, to those in this society who want to gain more than they are willing to give."

Adred reddened with subdued anger. "And what do the aristocrats give, my King? What do the lords of commerce and merchandising give? The competition is *over*, King Elad! It has been over for a long time! There *is* no more competition! There is only a landscape full of very large businesses, dominating the people they are supposed to service, and entrenched and immovable because they are protected by the throne and the businessmen on your Council. These people cannot compete. Don't you realize that half the men involved in that riot in Sulos were *businessmen*?"

"Please, be seated." Elad gestured for Adred to take the chair across from him, as he himself moved to assume a relaxed pose. His attitude was that of a man suffocating beneath intolerable pressures but doing all he could to be practical with his opponent's good will. "You and I, Count Adred," Elad began amicably, "are men of the world, are we not? The romantic aspects of all this aside, let's be realistic

266

about it. You seem to be arguing for a moral, generous society—and a very naive and impractical one, as well. Shall I institute legislation changing man's basic nature? Do you think to astonish me by revealing that most of my administrators in the cities are corrupt? That illegal gambling goes on in the closets of public administration buildings? That there are men in government who have planned the murders of opponents? That the trade guilds have criminals ruling them? That taxes are often paid with prostitution, or with bribes, or stolen money? Do you think any of this surprises me? Furthermore, do you think that these faults can be laid wholly on the shoulders of a mercantilist, capitalist economic system? If you do, then you are surely naive—and I don't believe that you are naive, only idealistic. Believe me, if the gods recreated humanity tomorrow, corruption would begin the day after tomorrow. If all of us were wiped out tonight, save for only two survivors, by tomorrow afternoon one of those survivors would begin telling the other what to do, and you may be sure that the man taking charge would do so for some sort of profit. I can't help it if most men are dishonest at least some of the time in their lives; I can't help it, and I cannot legislate against it. All I can do is institute a system of economy and rule a government which seems to me to work best for most of the people over a long period of time. Our system is doing this. Have you any idea where we were as a nation two hundred years ago? A hundred years ago? We *were* a nation then, Count Adred—but today we are an empire!''

Adred was fidgeting, eager to respond to these slanders, but Elad had more to say. ''Do you actually believe that those people out there want to take responsibility for their own lives? That they're interested in anything bigger than themselves? You can't mean it. Experience has taught me otherwise, Adred. Next week or next month, when they've sobered up—when they have full bellies again—they'll forget all about it. You flatter them, my friend—with the best of intentions, I'm sure, but you flatter them. You foist your own personality onto them, your own grievances. These people are not educated—they know how to read; there's quite a difference there. They are not thinkers; they let others do their thinking for them and are entertained by the endless debates. Count Adred, realistically, we have some hungry, bored people in our society, due to a temporary business setback. These things happen; but rabble-rousers are agitating them. And the rabble-rousers are only in it for themselves, be sure of it. They don't really want a revolution; they don't want a new system of business enterprise or fair economic distribution. The rabble-rousers simply want *this* system, but with themselves on top rather than on the bottom—and the hungry people want food in their bellies. Your exaggeration of this condition into a 'revolution' is an appealing fantasy—like the Prophet saving souls in the afterworld. It appeals to the common man you raise so loftily by my side, but it is very dangerous if it gets out of control and spills onto the streets. If it spills onto the streets, however''—and here King Elad's voice became very dire—''then we always have an alternative method for curing hunger.''

Adred collected himself and answered in as calm a tone as he could muster, "King Elad, despite the worst that is in men, we pride ourselves today on being a civilized society, do we not? We owe it to ourselves to make life as fair as it can be, opportunities as widespread as possible, and justice as even-handed as is practicable. King Elad, any society can pass laws to insure that the wealthy retain their wealth. That's easy—but it's also unfair, and it frustrates any opportunity to improve ourselves. It's no secret that most people, at least some of the time, act injudiciously; true—that's human nature. We will always have human beings, in the gutters and in the throne halls, who are no better than caged beasts; but unless we do everything we can, as a civilized society, to show them that there *are* opportunities for them to better themselves, then we will *never* have human beings who *are* any better than caged beasts! And if you argue now to keep things as they are, then you merely block up a dam which, sooner or later, must burst before the tide rising behind it."

Elad was becoming irritated; both men had voiced their beliefs. Adred was as impolite—and as canny—as any solicitor in an assize. Now Elad offered to take the complaints under consideration, but stated he was becoming weary of all the talk and wished Count Adred a good evening.

Stunned, Adred rose to his feet. Angrily, losing control, he pointed a finger at his monarch to unleash a noble denunciation that was as powerful as the explosive tide he had promised.

"Damn you!" he yelled in a charged tone. "Do you think I came here to argue philosophy? Don't you see what is

268

happening? My lord, these events in the streets . . . My King! We have no money any more! Athadian gold and silver have been minted with tin since the thirteenth year of your father's reign, and you continue to stamp too much gold and silver, and you're ruining us! You can't increase the value of money by making more money.

"And it is *money* that is the root of this condition, my King—because our society has taught people that *money* is the only thing of value, and it is a *lie*! The common people of this nation are screaming for dignity and respect. Are the people stupid, King Elad? Are they uneducated? I've seen men and women starving, men and women who would gladly work for a pittance, if they could find a job. Do you know why they can't? Because what money there is circulates among those who need it least, while the crowds can only sit and watch that money being traded back and forth, out of their reach! Is that money somehow supposed to be applied to businesses to give those people jobs? Then where are the jobs? Those men and women can't get work because the work governors in every town and province take bribes first, then set quotas, then hire friends and relatives to serve on public programs!

"Our system of government has created lords and aristocrats with money, businesses and wealth to appeal to the basest of natures, a system of currying favors, influence peddling, rights bargaining, and lease thievery—and it was never designed to employ people, only to create profits. It has put more and more money into the grasp of fewer and fewer people, and now the iron hand of those people is strangling the very process which allowed them to take advantage of it!

"King Elad, if you do not take measures to help them—if you do not assure the people of this empire that you are their King, as well as the King of the wealthy and the aristocratic—then they *will* turn against you! They want their lives! They want the future! *Give* them their lives! *Give* them the future!"

Adred, trembling and sweating, suddenly afraid that he had gone too far, stared at his monarch with wide eyes and burning throat.

Elad was not looking at him but was watching the tabletop, hands fisted upon his chin. Slowly he looked up. "I am a good man, Count Adred."

"I know you are," Adred answered him, still breathless,

uncertain what that had to do with the issue at hand. "I'm not questioning that. But you must understand—I have been in the streets—you are caught in events none of us ever expected, no one ever anticipated. They are events which cry out for justice, for redress, for reform—"

"For abdication, Adred?"

"If you gave up your throne, you would still be a man—a good man, a powerful man. Your voice would be heard in the *sirots*, the collective assemblies which the people want to institute with represen—"

Elad shook his head firmly. "I am their King, Count Adred. I am *King*."

Dursoris, live! Oh, gods, I do not want this! I do not want this throne!

"Try, *try*, for the sake of the empire—*try* to be *more* than their King! Elad, you had your opportunity to reorganize everything when you altered the seats in your bureaucracy. You can actually make room for the people in that bureaucracy, or do away with it entirely, serve the people in more direct ways. But if you continue to be what they see you as—a plutocrat and a general, a thief and a killer of innocent, hungry people—then there will be a revolution. Give them their society, or fight them in the streets. I'm afraid they give you only those options. And they are not going to allow you much time to decide between them."

Adred returned to his room, furious with himself. What had he done?

He sulked in his room, not lighting any of his lamps, staring out the partially open windows. Fool! He'd ruined everything—everything. He sat, immensely depressed and over-wrought, unable to sleep, waiting for Elad's guards to come to take him away. For surely Elad would not let him go far. Surely the King would not let a seditious aristocrat wander freely to spread his inflammatory treachery.

Musing thus, Count Adred was not in the least surprised when a knock sounded on his door just before eleven calls of the bell; and when he opened it, he was not surprised to see a palace guard on his threshold.

"From the palace," the man announced. "I'm to escort you."

"From King Elad?"

"From Lord Abgarthis, sir."

Adred was puzzled, but he pulled on his heavy coat. As he and his escort made their way down the quiet stairs of the hostel: "I'm under arrest, then?"

The soldier regarded him quizzically. "Not that I know of, sir."

Adred didn't know what to make of that. He said nothing more as he and the soldier crossed the few blocks of snowy streets to the brightly lighted palace. Inside he was ushered upstairs to Lord Abgarthis's sitting room.

Abgarthis smiled at Adred's perplexity. Handing him a glass of wine: "You should be very pleased with yourself."

"What for? Thank you. For getting myself arrested?"

The old man laughed. "You're not under arrest! No, no. For that episode with Elad, you mean? Oh, precisely. No, Adred, no. He's not going to have you arrested. He and I talked tonight, after you left. He doesn't want me on his Council, you understand, because I'm too honest. That only means I'm the sole person he can trust late at night, at times like this. Adred, your . . . outburst seems to have made an effect."

"I'm sure it—"

"It's done you some good."

"You must be joking!"

"As I say, you should be very pleased with yourself. No one else has spoken that frankly to him, ever. Now, he's hardly going to step down from the throne, but tomorrow he intends to lose his temper with his Councilors, and he's going to institute a committee to investigate the people's demands. He spoke of reforms."

Adred set aside his wine, not heartened. "Abgarthis, he's only stalling for time, isn't he?"

"Of course. But the moment he proclaims his intention of even considering any sort of reform, the bulk of the people will sit back to listen, and to wait. The demonstrations will drop off, the riots will stop; a calmer attitude will prevail."

"But—no, no, listen. If he begins a committee, if he opens the doors to rebel spokesmen—Abgarthis, it could be a plot to simply draw them out, to find out who they are. Later on there'll be arrests, there will be more—"

Abgarthis laughed heartily. "You certainly *think* like a revolutionary!" he proclaimed. "Or at least a champion *usto* player. I don't think that's his intention, Adred. Elad can't allow himself to alienate any one large sector of his empire. He's already treading marshland with the business sector and the army; you made him realize that the working people, if they're consolidated, far outmatch either business or the army—in numbers, if not in political acumen or military strength. No, I believe he is sincere. You must understand that Elad plays very hard at being King, but in his soul he is a decent man. I truly believe that—a decent man in an immoral world. He is young, he is inexperienced, and the one tool he needs to insure his growth is time—time the gods have not allowed him.''

"You're a monarchist," Adred told him. "You're no revolutionary." He didn't sound embittered, only aware. "So—how long must we wait for these reforms? A month? Two months? Will it drag on for years?''

"Please, don't you see how crucial this is? You've won a hearing for the people of the empire, and you did it without threatening an army revolt or economic confusion. You've done well."

Adred smiled at him. "Do you think he'll ask me to serve on this committee to examine reforms?''

"No, I doubt it. You're a trifle too radical for him, Adred. As I say, don't expect a great deal all at once. Give it time. A few months, at least. We've lasted this long; you can't overturn in a day what it's taken decades to accomplish.''

"Well, everything finally reaches its point of diminishing returns. I suppose that's as true of being king as it is of manufacturing shipping tar." He looked at Abgarthis, shrugged. "If I'm free, then, I might as well go north again.''

"Stay in the capital," Abgarthis urged him. "Why must you always travel? You're never in one place. You're like those heroes in stories, always wandering, always searching for a treasure or a princess.''

The young aristocrat shrugged again, feeling moody. "Maybe I *am* searching for treasures and princesses, Abgarthis. I've never found any. Never found any in books. Haven't found any yet, in fact. But if I travel long enough, I might surprise you.''

Abgarthis grinned. "You surprise me constantly as it is. I wish we had ten of you in this palace.''

"But we wouldn't stay," Adred replied, grinning with tired mischief as he turned to cross the room. "We wouldn't

272

stay. We'd just leave to wander, wouldn't we?'' He shook his head. ''Good night, Abgarthis. Thank you very much, my friend. Thank you.''

''Not at all.''

Adred glanced out the window; the shutters, partly open, showed a black night with whirling snow. ''Look at it out there,'' he commented. ''Terrible weather. Well''—half smiling—''when the revolution comes, we'll fix the weather up right, too.''

Abgarthis laughed loudly at the self-deprecation. ''By the gods, I like you!''

''I like myself, too, Abgarthis. Most of the time.'' Adred yawned again, waved lightly, and went out, closing the door quietly.

And Abgarthis stood for a long time, staring after him, staring at the closed door. Wondering about this provocative, intelligent, lonely young man. . . .

6.

The sword of war, the march of conquest, the yoke and the flames and the moving horses of slow, rumbling thunder. Blood on the horizon. Evil against many to elevate the pride of one.

Nutatharis had received in his court ten envoys from Ilbukar, sent with an address from Huagrim *ko-Ghen*, war chief of the Salukads. The envoys presented to Nutatharis this plan: that as Huagrim *ko-Ghen* wished to take for himself the entire city of Erusabad in an act which might be deemed an overt gesture of war, and as Nutatharis (it was well known) was no friend of the Athadians and had his own designs upon the Low Provinces of the east, let there herenow and hereinafter be a state of martial truce and even of alliance between the empire of Salukadia and the nation of Emaria.

Nutatharis asked Huagrim's envoys if he understood this correctly: did it mean that the two governments were allied, insofar as it was deemed advantageous by their monarchs, against the Athadian Empire? Did it mean that, should Nutatharis's advance into the lowlands bring against him Athadian forces, he might expect military aid from Ilbukar? Did it mean that, should Athadia engage Salukadia in war, the Emarian forces might be called in to buttress the troops of Salukadia? Did it mean that, should any such confrontation between the Athadians, the Emarians, and the Salukadians result in the despoilage of the Athadian Empire, then Nutatharis and Huagrim would between them decide which territories would be apportioned to each ruler?

The ambassadors from Ilbukar replied affirmatively to each of these questions.

That evening Nutatharis met in Council with his retainers

274

and announced to them that within the week Emarian cavalry would begin an invasion of the Low Provinces.

"And—the wall?" Cyrodian asked him.

Nutatharis smiled grimly. "For the time being, should we need such a wall, then let the Salukadian empire be our wall. Should we need to rely on them, they will augment our own forces."

"And if they request soldiers from us?" Cyrodian pursued.

"From us?" Nutatharis shook his head slowly. "Huagrim is an old man. He wishes only to possess the city of Erusabad, so that he may die in peace. Will your brother complain much, Cyrodian, if the east plucks that hair from his beard? As for us, we will *begin* by marching into the lowlands. By winter's end, I think, the border of Emaria will stretch as far as the mountains this side of Ilbukar!"

As ever, King Nutatharis was eager to place himself in guarded jeopardy. He signed his name and affixed his seal to the documents presented him by the Salukadian ambassadors, and ordered bilingual copies to be made by court scriveners. And within a week following the departure of the envoys, Nutatharis ordered two regiments—twenty thousand men— under the leadership of Generals Kustos and Cyrodian to begin their advance into the Low Provinces.

In Abustad, Governor Şulen reacted quickly to the encroachment on his northern border. Immediately as word reached him of Emarian forces crossing into his provincial territory, he sent a letter of alarm to King Elad in Athadia and dispatched seven legions to augment his border outposts and confront the intruders.

On the ninth day of the Month of Gara the Bear, the provincial forces from Abustad met the first of the Emarian legions in the frozen marches just ten leagues south of the Emarian border. In the engagement which followed, several hundred men lost their lives over the course of three days, and the provincial commander of the First Gold and Third Green Abustadian legions ordered a withdrawal. His troops retreated and set up barricades in a forest just south of the marches, and word was relayed to Governor Sulen of the battle and losses incurred. Riders were regularly dispatched, twice a day, to keep the governor informed of the Emarian movements; but the Emarians did not pursue the provincials into what was properly territory under the jurisdiction of the Athadian throne.

Eleven days after the ordering of his troops into the north, Governor Sulen received word from King Elad: he was commanded to engage the Emarians in open hostilities only if they proved to be a direct and immediate threat to Athadian-controlled lands. Otherwise, it was pointless for the throne to risk military action.

Sulen was outraged. A direct breach of international policy by King Nutatharis should have been met, he felt, immediately and insistently with equal force by the empire. Elad's decision to acquiesce to the Emarian affront smacked to him of cowardice; worse, he feared it might lead to a series of appeasements rather than confrontations.

Nevertheless, he dispatched a second rider to the capital, informing his King of the engagement in the marches and the severe loss of life resulting from it, noting in his conclusion that it was this battle which had prevented the Emarians from encroaching further upon Athadian territory. He informed the throne that no further military action was being taken by the city of Abustad, save in response to additional movements by the Emarians; but Sulen also informed King Elad that he was requesting reserve units from the city of Elpet. He wished five legions of men from that city, ruled by Governor Ovalus, sent to be quartered in Abustad as a necessity against possible further intrusions in the marches. In the meantime, the legions from Abustad were holding a defensive line and awaiting any further provocation by the enemy.

While Governor Sulen awaited a reply to this from King Elad, word came to him by rider that a very small patrol of Emarians had been on the provincial side of the Burul-Gos stream, a tiny waterway in the marches. Appropriate action had been taken; of the seventeen men in the patrol, twelve had been killed, one wounded so severely that he had been butchered where he lay, and the remaining four taken as prisoners by the commander of the Third Green legion. Questioning was taking place even as the rider was sent on his way to Abustad.

Sulen was intrigued by this. He ordered his first retainer to assume temporary control of the city government, as he had it in mind to leave in the morning and himself visit the battlefield to pursue this questioning of the war prisoners. Howev-

276

er, Sulen's visit would not prove necessary; he was awakened in the middle of the night by the arrival of Lieutenant First Class Mutus, sent from the line to inform the governor precisely what had been learned from the captives.

Sulen saw the messenger in his bedchamber, where Mutus informed him, "Two of the dogs managed to kill themselves, my lord, before we had a chance to question them. The third died under torture. But we did learn a few things from the fourth man."

"He still lives?"

"He was alive at the time I left, early last evening."

"What did he reveal, Lieutenant?"

Mutus gave what details he could. The Emarians had no intention of taking any overt action against the Athadian Empire—at least not at the present time. Nutatharis had apparently entered into some kind of agreement with Huagrim of the Salukadian empire. And the exiled Prince Cyrodian, it was discovered, was in some capacity acting as a commander or an adviser to the Emarian troops.

Sulen was astounded. He dismissed Lieutenant Mutus, telling him to get his night's rest before returning to the lines in the morning. Then the governor lit an oil lamp at his desk, took out parchment and pen, and proceeded to write his King.

. . . Furthermore, we have it on the information of this captive that your brother . . .

Done with it, he reread it, then stamped the letter with his seal, placed it in a wooden tube, and addressed it to King Elad's attention. The ring of a bell brought a guard to his door, and Sulen ordered him to find a man of the army still quartered in the city—the best horseman they had—to report to him immediately. Shortly, a young sergeant was ushered in. Governor Sulen was still dressed in his nightclothes.

"To the capital. Immediately. Deliver this into the hands of King Elad and none other." He slapped the tube into the soldier's hands.

The sergeant saluted and exited.

And Sulen, unable to sleep the remainder of the night, sat heavy-eyed in his chamber, sipped wine, and stared at a map of the empire which hung upon his wall.

What, he wondered, would Cyrodian be staring at, were he looking at this map?

* * *

It was not until the twenty-eighth day of Gara that Governor Sulen at last received word from King Elad. The monarch had contacted Governor Ovalus in Elpet and had recommended the assignment of four legions to be quartered in Abustad as a reserve against further military actions by the Emarians. These troops were forthcoming. Furthermore, Governor Sulen was to maintain order in his territory, and his men were not to anticipate or invite any action by the Emarians, or engage them in any hostile maneuver unless directly provoked. Sulen was further enjoined to deploy scouting parties into the Lowland marches and forests just west of the Salukadian border in Tsalvia, to ascertain to what extent Salukadian advisers or soldiers were involved with the Emarians. The Lowlands being properly independent and not allied either with Emaria or Athadia, any direct confrontation with western troops by Emarian forces in this region must be regarded as a grave sign of belligerence.

Politicians' words. There was no mention of the King's reaction to the intelligence that his exiled brother was in partnership with the Emarian King. But Elad had made the comment that he did not feel it to be politically or militarily expedient at this time to engage the Emarians in any direct assault, if such could be avoided.

Governor Sulen read this missive from King Elad and turned red with anger. "Fool! Can't he see what they're up to?"

His outburst drew the attention of his assistant governor, who was sitting across from him at their supper table, where Sulen had been delivered the letter.

"What is it?" the man asked, concerned.

"King Elad," the governor replied snidely, "will be marrying very shortly, and he seems to consider a political alliance with Gaegosh's daughter somewhat more important than a direct Emarian provocation to war!"

7.

Elpet.

The tavern was crowded. The usual dockhands and sailors and irregular customers came in from the streets, and now soldiers on their way to Abustad. Hundreds of them crowded the place, bawling out orders for beer and beef and wine and bread, whistling at her, trying to grab her hips or slap her on the buttocks. And she hurried here and there, almost spilled her plates of food, nearly tripped over the many legs, the boots, the long, dangling swords. So busy, almost disoriented, and fighting the cough that was building in her chest, fighting the fever that tried to swell in her brain.

She didn't notice, at first, the two of them sitting at the crowded table against a far wall. She was just setting down a plate of food at another table when someone drunkenly grabbed at her vest, wanting to peek inside; she jerked away, moving awkwardly, and as her eyes swept the room, she saw them.

There, at that table.

Just as they were standing up and pushing their way forward to get to her.

Gods, no, no! I've stayed here too long, they've found me!

She tried to run. Hands reached for her, voices grunted, the other serving women in the place yelled at her. Hurrying, she tried to get into the back rooms, into the kitchen, maybe she could hide there or run out into the alley, somehow get—

"*Assia!*"

"Gods, *no!*" She screamed it out loud, her voice lifting above the raucous din.

Faces turned toward her—soldiers, sailors, rough men. Some amused, others scornful, vaguely interested.

"*Damn* you, girl!"

Tyrus grabbed her. She fought him, tried to break from his hold, but he was too strong for her. He slammed her against a wall in the short hallway that led from the tavern's serving room into the back rooms. Assia coughed, writhed—but Tyrus pinned her.

She stared into his fierce eyes, glanced beyond him, and saw the fat man coming up behind him. His face was greasy, and his bloated jowels bounced as he showed his brown teeth.

"We've been hunting for you for *weeks*!" her father hissed at her. "Why did—"

Eyes full of fear, stomach aching, she kicked at him, bent her head in an attempt to bite his arm savagely. Tyrus slapped her for that. She whimpered and pushed herself flat up against the wall. Stared at her father, stared at the fat man, quickly scanned the serving room. No one cared; this sort of thing went on all the time.

"Now you're coming back with us!"

"No, you can't make me," she moaned, voice choking. "You—"

He shook her roughly. "I told you you're—"

"Leave that girl alone!"

Tyrus, holding his daughter thickly by her shoulders, stared over at one of the tables. A young soldier, swarthy and dark-haired, handsome, was sitting in a relaxed pose, watching it all. His eyes burned contemptuously.

"Stay out of this," Tyrus warned him in a low, threatening voice. A quick glance at the other men around the table indicated that they were wholly unconcerned.

Assia whimpered. She recognized this soldier. He'd been in here every night, pestering her, attracted to her.

Tyrus's grip tightened, hurting. "Now come along with—"

"I thought I told you to leave her alone!"

A few nearby faces turned toward them now, interested. Entertainment. But the fat man, standing behind Tyrus, sneered at the young soldier. "We told you to shut up, so just shut up. It's none of your affair."

"It is if you're hurting that girl," the soldier answered proudly.

Tyrus glanced at the fat man; at the same time he dropped one hand from Assia's shoulder, moved to pull her along with the other. But just then the alert master of the house stepped over to investigate.

"What the hell's going on here?"

The fat man placed a careful hand on him. "Don't be concerned. We're only—"

"Get your hand off me, you pig."

Tyrus, dragging Assia, tried to step between them.

"Hold on! She's one of my—"

"I told you to leave her *alone*!"

The fat man looked in the direction of the cry, started to say something to Tyrus. There was a scuffle of squeaking chairs and tables, loud cries from many men, and the sudden blur of the young soldier throwing himself forward. The fat man pushed Tyrus in the chest to get him out of the way. Assia screamed. Tyrus lost his grip on her and, as he stumbled, caught a glimpse of silver flashing between him and his fat friend.

"Thought I *told* you—"

It was lost in the grunts and the sounds of boots scraping on the wooden floor. Assia screamed again as Tyrus, backing up, bumped into her and sent her crashing once more against the wall. Jarred, she jumped away from him and lurched down the hallway that led into the kitchen.

The fat man bellowed hoarsely. The silver knife dented his swollen belly, swept out on a hanging trail of wet blood, shimmering. Tyrus, enraged, pounced forward, arms out to grab the soldier. But the young man was quick.

"Arrest him!" the tavern-keeper yelled, running out of the way, as his patrons whooped and pushed to give the fighters room.

Whipping his arms furiously, Tyrus caught the soldier on the side of the head. Now he reached behind him for his own knife. But the soldier, reacting as he fell, sliced upward. His blade caught Tyrus's neck, ran up the side of his face.

Assia, half-waiting in the hallway, threw a hand to her mouth as she saw her father crumple to the floor, fingers clawing at his jetting throat.

A chair, lifted high, knocked a hanging lamp—

"Arrest him, *arrest him*!"

—and smashed down, splintering heavily as it struck the flailing, unbalanced soldier. He dropped instantly, stained knife flying from his hands.

Assia, sobbing, ran forward, then backed away. From behind her hurried the cooks and several other serving girls, attracted by the sounds. They pushed past as she turned and ran down the hall, hurried into the kitchen and across it, threw open the back door, and hastened down the alley outside.

On the floor, the fat man groaned and rolled back and forth, holding his hands to his seeping belly; a length of his intestines, like a pulsing gray worm, tried to slosh from his torn coat, dripping wet. Yet he was alive; Tyrus, sprawled on his chest on the floor, hands at his throat, was dying quickly, the blood pouring from him like thick wine and pooling on the grooved boards.

The grunting, half-awake soldier was dragged clear of them, and, while his companions swore and yelled, others in the room tied his hands together behind his back and waited for the city patrol to arrive.

She changed that night as she ran away, escaped into the night. Intending to return to the tavern to learn if her father had actually died, intending to wait and think before going back, but nevertheless . . .

Wasn't he dead to her already?

She changed that night, as she wandered the streets, as she huddled in the alleys and the dark doorways to escape the cold, and to think.

As she walked beside tall, dark stone-faced buildings, someone came by with a cart and horse; he paused and yelled at her—some farmer from the outlands—invited her: "Little sweet! Come on up here and get warm! I've got a nice surprise for you! Big surprise!" Giggling like a fool.

And she, dressed in her thin tavern-wear, her torn vest, her damp shoes, plagued by demons and haunted, angry, turned and faced the man in the cart, threw her arms out, curled her hands into claws, and screamed at him, "Touch me and I'll stab you, you dog, you piece of vomit!"

He laughed at her, laughed boldly at her.

And Assia, trembling from the cold and from her anger, screamed so loudly that her voice carried down the misted caverns of the city streets. "Come on! Come down here, you want me so bad! I'll yank it off for you, you stink, I'll show you what it's good for, you son of a whore, you son of a rutting pig, you piece of vomit!"

Startled. The girl was crazy. Crazy girls in this city . . .

"Come *on! Come on, you son of a vomiting pig!"*

Bewildered, almost a little frightened, the farmer had begun to move on.

"Come *on! Come on, you vomit, you puking—whore! You— come onnnnn!"*

Screaming. Screaming at him, losing her mind, even after he'd disappeared.

"Come onnnnn!"

Screaming.

Until she'd finally dizzied and broken down, sobbed, gasped, and run to hide in another alley.

Moaning . . .

"I want to die. . . ."

She crouched there, listening to the dripping silence. Then, moving spasmodically, Assia tore open her vest and her shift and took up some half-frozen mud from the alley floor. She was going to smear it all over her breasts, make herself so cold that she would become ill, so she would die.

Die.

But as she sat there, mud in hand, numb and half frozen, she paused in what she was doing, like some mechanism that had suddenly burst a pulley-line. She stared into the darkness. And slowly, half willfully and half regretfully, she let the cold mud slide from her hand.

No . . . I don't want to die yet.

What am I?

A whore?

Groaning: "Oh, Thameron, as long as I believe in myself . . ."

I believe I'm a whore.

Men should piss on me, men should vomit on me, women should beat me and shove sticks in me, oh, Thameron, what am I, why am I here, I can't believe in the truth anymore, I can't believe anymore, I can't believe, it was all a lie, I'm nothing but a lie.

I shouldn't be me, but I am, I am, I am!

She sat in the alley and lost that half-innocent, half-noble, somehow wise but insubstantial, confident declaration of herself. Lost it, and disowned herself, readied to accept whatever life gave her without fighting back with belief, belief, self-belief. . . .

* * *

If she slept that night she did not know it. As dawn began and as the sounds of early morning activity carried to her, Assia made her way out of the alley and into the street. There were crowds, though it was hardly daylight, and shortly she understood why: the troops were gathering to board ship for their journey to Abustad. Assia followed the people moving toward Elpet's dockside mall.

There, mounted officers were keeping the throngs under control, as the legions filed together in the frosty air. Already the first of them were marching down to the wharves; above the heads in the crowd Assia could see, far away, the blue pennants and golden flags of Athadian warships waiting to receive them.

She made her way through the press, attracted to the warmth of the fires. For stone troughs had been set around the wide mall, filled with tinder and firewood, and set aflame. At one end of the wide mall, away from the formations of troops and the collecting passersby, Assia spotted the loose congregation of camp followers. She paused, and a knot grew in her belly.

For here was her chance of escape from the city, a chance for food and warmth, even under humiliating conditions. Armies on the march meant that a cadre of escorted followers marched with them—prostitutes, most of them, and young homosexuals (those not already taken into the tents of the commanders), and the whole odd assortment of young men who would do errands, tend to the horses and the armor and the weapons, hangers-on who might help (unpaid) with the food, and all the motley others who would act as nurses one day, wine-getters the next, eventually to become (perhaps) human grease for war machines or fodder for catapults.

But it meant warmth and a chance for food. And an opportunity to get away from this city and the memories here.

Assia approached. Hardened in her heart, fearful yet portraying fearlessness, she boldly moved forward and joined the prostitutes crowded around one of the firetroughs. There were spits over the fire, and meat was sizzling.

"What's this?" crowed one old hag. "Out of the way, you little bitch!"

"Oh, but she's a darling little thing," cooed another, next to her, wrapping an arm around Assia's shoulder. An older woman, hardly younger than the hag, yet well painted, with bright red cheeks and lips. "And look at the size of them, look at the size of them!'' she exclaimed, pressing a bony hand against Assia's vest. "She's coming along with me, I'll take care of her!"

Assia stared at her, resentment in her gaze. An old trick—assault by one, effusive friendliness by her partner, and both out to dupe the unsuspecting. Assia had done it herself at Ibro's.

"You'll come with me, won't you, darling little thing?" Pushing her face close, poking her beak of a nose into Assia's.

Assia started to back away, bumped into someone else. She turned, looked up into the features of a tall, gaunt woman-man—skeletal, blond, with rouged cheeks and painted eyes. He smiled at Assia, bent close to give her a kiss; Assia, caught between him and the cooing woman, couldn't escape. He pressed his painted mouth hard upon Assia's, forced her lips open with his tongue, and slobbered something warm and wet—drool? wine? semen?—down her throat. Then he moved on, cackling like a hen, laughing and laughing.

Assia sneered and wiped her sticky lips with the back of one hand.

Trumpets blared across the mall.

"Oh, don't mind him!" fussed the cooing woman. "What's your name, little darling?"

There was nothing else to do. She might not get aboard the ship, otherwise. "Assia," she answered softly.

If this company of women and followers were well known by the commanders, she was guaranteed passage.

"Well, little Assia, you stay with me and you'll be all right, you understand? We'll take care of you, you just stay with me. I know all the right people, and you'll be treated with some respect, you'll be treated very nicely. . . ."

Half the women and other assorted hangers-on were left on shore when the last of the ships set sail, toward midmorning. But Assia was aboard; in the company of fifty other prostitutes, quartered below decks, fed nothing, but assured her transport to Abustad, and assured a meager existence in the train following the Athadian march toward the Lowlands.

PART VII

New Chains

1.

The march of aggression into the neutral Lowlands, caught between the hegemonic Emarians and the colossal, unyielding Salukads.

In the frosty breath of a midwinter morning they thundered down out of the hills to astonish and attack yet another village of Lowlanders: two full legions of Emarian cavalry under the command of General Kustos, who had ordered his men to take and hold every village fronting the wide Tuveski Forest. Three weeks of the campaign—three weeks of lightning-quick strikes and battles that, in their one-sidedness, did not deserve the name of combat—had brought Kustos seventy leagues into the provinces.

But resistance was mounting. The Lowlander villages, normally fiercely jealous of each other and proud in their isolation, had united as one against the Emarians. Kustos and Cyrodian had witnessed their advance gradually slowing down, the deeper they entered into the provinces. And they had met their greatest resistance in the Tuveski region, populated as it was by hardy men and strong women.

Outposts stretching behind, to the Emarian border, had secured the westernmost of the conquered territory. The most recent word from Cyrodian, two days to the south, had guaranteed General Kustos that control had been managed from the border of Omeria to the great forests that marked the beginning of the Tsalvian Lowlands.

But here, this morning, in the Tuveski, Kustos was meeting resistance that would have made even Cyrodian doubt the sense of continuing the advance.

Midwinter. With snow-covered fields, icy rivers, hail descending in frozen bolts; the forests, black and shadowed, deep with maddening cold, became a trap for the Emarians. Kustos soon found that it was impossible for his lines to advance in customary fashion. He ordered his legions broken up into smaller units, until he had hundreds of compact troops—little more than reconnaissance teams—forcing their way through the crusted snow, cantering slowly over icy streams, climbing up the hazardous hillsides that at any moment might unleash a small avalanche of ice, mud, and rock.

And in the frosty breath of a midwinter morning, in those frustrating forests and foreign hills, Kustos listened to the death screams of his men, his small units of soldiers, as they failed. Some by falling through the ice and drowning in the swift current of freezing water. Others engulfed by loosened hillsides of snow and mud. But most of them—by far, most of them—slain by the invisible craftiness of the resourceful Lowlanders.

A tree limb, hidden in the snow, would suddenly jump to life and impale a man with the edge of a rusted field scythe hidden in its branches. The ground, ice-covered, would abruptly give way, and a dozen Emarians would drop howling into a deep pit, its bottom studded with sharpened poles. Boulders dropped from nets in trees. Razor-sharp farm implements, cut and heated and honed into weapons, shot through the brittle air to rip out throats, savage bellies, destroy arms and legs. Iron poles and steel balls, suspended by cords in the treetops, would swing down in deadly arcs, to stab or brain slow-moving soldiers.

Screams. And more screams. And men only a short distance away remained unseen, so thick was the forest, so heavy the snow and ice, so rocky and steep the hills and outcroppings.

By midafternoon, Kustos called a halt to the advance. After conferring with his retainers, the general decided to withdraw from the forest and set up barricades in the fields through which they had come. The horns sounded retreat. Not one enemy had been sighted.

But traps not triggered during the advance sprang to life as the troops moved out. More screams; more deaths; more drops of blood, frozen as they struck the air, dappling the hoary white ground of the Tuveski Forest.

General Kustos, only a short distance from safety, within sight of the open fieldland and sloping hills beyond, was struck suddenly by a sharpened knife. It had been attached to a pole and fixed by a taut rope to a tree; Kustos's horse had tripped the line of it, a boulder wrapped in chain fell free behind a bush, and the pole jerked, the rope snapped, the knife struck. Kustos cried out as the razor edge caught him just below the throat and ripped across his shoulder. Deeply. Warm blood poured down the inside of his cold armor, sticky and uncomfortable.

Not realizing how badly he had been wounded, Kustos waved away helpful retainers and continued his retreat into the fieldland. As dusk came down and the men built fires, a count was taken, and it was reported to General Kustos that the day's advance—a debacle—had cost him fully one-fifth of his men. Hundreds upon hundreds of corpses hidden deep in the snow-silent, ice-secret forest of the Tuveski.

And not one enemy had been sighted.

When General Cyrodian arrived at Kustos's encampment two days later, he was surprised and confounded to find that the Emarians had gained no ground whatsoever against the Tuveski; and he was more irritated than concerned with General Kustos's injury—even though Kustos, as a result of it, had become quite ill. The wound had swollen, and it still seeped blood. Compresses and ointments applied by the army physicians had done nothing to alleviate the general's pain or begin a healing process. He suffered from a continuous low-grade fever, and as a result Kustos drank steadily: warm wine sweetened with roots, which variously invigorated him or subdued the pain to an extent where it was manageable.

Cyrodian immediately saw his opportunity to take charge of Kustos's outfit and do with the Tuveski what he had done in the southern stretches. "Can you do anything more for him?" he asked of Kustos's physicians; and when those leeches replied that the severity of the wound and the intense cold thwarted any progress they had hoped to make, Cyrodian suggested that General Kustos might be better off back in the capital. The physicians reluctantly but, under the circumstances, sensibly agreed.

That very evening, the night of Cyrodian's arrival, a protesting General Kustos was placed within a makeshift litter and, escorted by a hundred soldiers, began the long westward trek back to Lasura.

That same evening Cyrodian met in Kustos's tent with those retainers and unit commanders who had stayed behind, and in talking with them he learned what had occurred to the first invasion force. He developed a counter-strategy.

"We burn the forest," he told Kustos's retainers. Furthermore, to those men's shocked responses: "We work day and night. Break the men into four shifts. Use your swords and your hatchets. Begin felling every tree you find. In a day or two we'll have everything a quarter-league deep leveled. Then we'll set fire to it. The winds will do the rest; we just follow behind in the ashes and count the heads. Am I understood?"

He was understood. The insight of it, the sheer common sense of the strategy, impressed the Emarians, but the enormity of the plan somewhat unnerved them. He was setting fire to the oldest forestland in the world.

To their doubts Cyrodian replied, "Then what the gods have done, let men undo! We want these bastards to know who's here, don't we? We want them to know who we are. We want them to feel the pressure of our boots, don't we? We want them to feel the strength of our fists!" He clenched a furry hand and showed it all around, smiling cruelly.

In the morning, the legions began felling trees.

However, before the plan for firing the Tuveski could be carried out, Cyrodian received a summons to report back to the capital and present himself to Nutatharis. The message was brought into camp by a lone rider coming from the south; the man had intercepted Cyrodian's forces there and, told by them that the general had moved north, he had come in a roundabout way.

The letter from Nutatharis predated the wounding of General Kustos; nevertheless, its instructions were not obviated by that man's condition. Report to me at once, King Nutatharis ordered Cyrodian; winter has set in, and we cannot hope to gain more territory now without severe damage and loss of life. He had, apparently, gained all that he had desired this far into the campaign: a very substantial region of the Lowlands. The lands already taken could be held without his two chief generals remaining in the field; it would be better for Cyrodian and Kustos to retire to the capital and plan strategy with

Nutatharis, rather than waste two or three months in the frozen fields.

Unspoken in the order was the intimation that the king did not want these men waxing independent away from the collar of the throne.

Grumbling, Cyrodian decided to answer Natatharis's request by doing as instructed. He told Kustos's retainers to refrain from firing the Tuveski until they received word to do so from either Nutatharis or himself; then he set off, on horseback, westward.

It took him five days to reach Lasura, and even though he had traveled quickly, he had not overtaken Kustos's litter before arriving in the capital. General Cyrodian found King Nutatharis very disturbed over Kustos's severe injury.

"He should have returned here at once!" the monarch fumed, distressed that the man was so ill and so near to death. "The fool! Do I value his life more than he does?"

They were sitting at table with wine; it was late in the evening.

"The wound is not so severe," Cyrodian reminded Nutatharis. "Kustos is a soldier. If a soldier can't—"

"The wound has had more than a week to fester and go bad," the king replied grimly. "General Kustos is gravely ill." More quietly, then, and almost to himself: "I fear he will die."

Cyrodian's eyes sparkled at that subdued comment, although he continued to act as though the possibility of Kustos's death was not of paramount importance. "Even if he is incapacitated for the winter," he offered Nutatharis, "surely there are many other men of ability in the army who would relish the chance to show their generalship, to take greater command of men in the field."

Nutatharis eyed him quickly, aware that when Prince Cyrodian spoke he spoke with two voices, one apparent and one silent. "Do *you* wish to take greater command over my army, Cyrodian?" he asked.

"You could make a worse choice than elevating me to Chief General of Emaria."

"Deciding who, if any besides myself, should have supreme command over my army is but one of my current concerns, Cyrodian. A second reason for holding our line of attack where we are, in the provinces, is the simple tactical decision of anticipating developments in Erusabad.''

"The Salukadians have moved into the city?"

"They are about to do so, in a day or two. I've received word from Huagrim."

Cyrodian frowned agreeably. "That could only be to our advantage; we've agreed upon that already."

"But something like this"—Nutatharis reached inside his tunic and withdrew a parchment letter—"could prove to be to our *dis*advantage." He opened the folded letter, showed it to Cyrodian, but did not pass it to him.

The exiled prince's eyes went wide. "This is from my brother!"

"It is indeed."

"What does he want?" Cyrodian growled, half-rising to his feet.

Nutatharis held the *capias* still as he answered, "He wishes you returned to Athad. He knows you have taken refuge in my court, and he wishes you returned at once on criminal charges."

"Criminal charges?"

"For plotting the death of your mother—for murdering her by proxy."

Nutatharis had stated the charge very calmly; now he watched, hawklike, to discern Cyrodian's reaction. The huge man did not deny it; he gradually replaced himself in his chair, rested his large forearms on the table, flexed his fists. The veins of his arms rippled like cables.

"What," he finally asked in a dry tone, "do you intend to do about this request?" There was an urgent, disquieting edge to his growl.

"What do I intend to do about it?" Nutatharis answered, still in control. "Only this." With a flick of his wrist he twisted the parchment around in his hand, so that one corner of it caught the flame of an oil lamp resting on the tabletop. Very soon the flame crawled upon the paper; Nutatharis released it, and the parchment burned to a few shards of crumbled black on the polished marble.

Cyrodian's sigh of relief was audible.

"As far as I am concerned, Prince Cyrodian, this letter was never sent, never received."

Cyrodian nodded and grunted.

293

"And what has passed here between us never occurred."

"Agreed."

"But I ask you to reconcile yourself to one condition, and this condition above all others."

"What is that?"

"I have done you a service, Prince Cyrodian. One day you must repay me. Will you swear to me that you will respect this condition? From one soldier to another?"

Cyrodian stared at him long and hard.

"This allegiance, Cyrodian, this oath between one soldier and another—it goes beyond any national or political ties. You do understand this, don't you?"

"I do." Cyrodian spoke calmly.

Nutatharis spoke the truth. A bond sworn between two soldiers was regarded in the west as an oath older than any law code, and it was respected in the courts even more than was the testimony of a dying man or the sworn disposition of a temple priest. It was an oath that predated civilization, and profound it was.

"Do you swear this, Prince Cyrodian?"

Cyrodian swallowed a deep breath, stared keenly into Nutatharis's eyes, and it seemed to him in that severest of moments that they were two equals. "I swear it."

He had never before done such a thing in his life.

Later that evening, Cyrodian visited General Kustos's chamber. A court physician was just leaving the room as the prince reached the door.

"He still lives?" Cyrodian asked the leech. "How does he fare?"

The physician showed him gray eyes full of regret. "He will not last the night, unless I am mistaken. The wound was poorly tended to; it developed a poison and spread quickly. Kustos is in a bad fever and he is sinking quickly. I go to alert King Nutatharis."

Cyrodian placed a heavy paw of a hand on the doctor's arm. "Nutatharis has gone to his rest, I think; do not disturb him. I will look in on Kustos and inform the king myself."

The physician eyed him warily, but there was still something akin to gratefulness in his expression.

"Go ahead," Cyrodian insisted. "You're exhausted. You can make a full report to Nutatharis in the morning."

"Yes. I will do that." The physician thanked Cyrodian, warned him not to trouble the general with a prolonged visit, then walked on down the hall.

Cyrodian watched him go, then entered the chamber. It was dark, save for a circle of lamps lit around Kustos's bed, and the ever-present incense braziers which burned mint and *gola* leaves, supposedly to aid respiration. Cyrodian quietly approached the general's bed and stood above the supine man, eying him carefully. Kustos's old face was seamed with exertion, and sweat pooled in the wrinkles like water in gullies. The moist eyes opened, stared up.

Cyrodian lifted a hand, held one of Kustos's in a false gesture of heartfulness. "My friend," he whispered, "you are doing well. You will live."

"No, I will not." Kustos's voice was a croak. "I am dying. I . . . know it; I . . . feel it. . . ."

Cyrodian showed no expression.

"I have many regrets," Kustos whispered thickly. His tongue swiped at the sweaty corners of his mouth. "Cyrodian, please . . . call me a priest. Find one. There are temples in the city."

"A priest?"

"Please. In my youth . . . I was devout."

Cyrodian swallowed hard but nodded. "I will find you a priest," he promised, thinking such a request odd from so seasoned a soldier. "Rest." He turned from the bed and crossed the room to the door, determining to find some palace servant to fetch a prelate for the general. But as he reached the door, Cyrodian turned to look again upon Kustos, and he heard a whispering voice, saw the movement of some shadow just beyond the smokey lamps.

Someone else in the room?

Wincing, studying the far end of the chamber with half-shut eyes, Cyrodian opened the door as he stood by it, then closed it again without exiting.

In a moment a figure appeared from the shadows at a far corner of the room and approached Kustos's bed.

"Swear it to me!" its voice hissed. "Make the proclamation! All you need do is swear it to me, and all will be transformed. Don't you understand?"

Kustos moaned and writhed.

"Swear it to me!" hissed the shadowy figure. "Give me your life, Kustos! *Give me your life*, and all will be—"

Cyrodian jumped across the flags, grunting an obscenity. Immediately, at the sound of his bootsteps, the shadow lurched upward and dropped back; the light of the oil lamps swept across him, revealing him.

Eromedeus.

"What the hell are you doing?" Cyrodian growled angrily.

Kustos, from the bed, whined, "The priest! The priest!"

"Because of *him*?" Cyrodian asked the dying man. "You want a priest because of *him*?"

"Please!"

Cyrodian stared into Eromedeus's dark, shadowed eyes. "Answer me, damn you! What are you doing here, sorcerer?"

"I am no sorcerer," was the languorous, arrogant reply.

"What are you doing to him, Eromedeus?"

"It is no affair of yours, barbarian."

"Damn you, you'll answer me or . . ." He dropped his hand to his sword pommel.

But Kustos still pleaded frightenedly, "The priest! The priest! Only a priest can help me!"

"What did he mean," Cyrodian grunted to Kustos, losing his patience, "about you giving him your life?"

Eromedeus whispered, "Fool."

"Please . . ."

"Get from here," Eromedeus ordered Cyrodian. "Leave here and do not—"

"*Dog*!" Cyrodian's temper snapped at last; with a quick movement he pulled free his sword and, in a warning, whipped it across Kustos's bed.

The steel shimmered with patterned colors in the lamplight; the tip of it flicked toward Eromedeus like an orange tongue. The man reacted, falling back and throwing up a defensive arm. Cyrodian had not intended for his blade to cut Eromedeus; nevertheless, the sword caught the man's right hand and sliced it neatly from knuckles to wrist.

"Foul dog!" he growled again.

Eromedeus sneered; he swiftly covered the wounded right hand with his left. Cyrodian stared at him, sword still stretched out above the bed; the giant glanced at the hurt hand.

He saw no blood.

296

Yet he had felt the slight resistance on the edge of his steel and knew that he had made a cut.

Eromedeus grinned a sinister grin.

"Oh, gods!" moaned Kustos.

Cyrodian whispered, "You're not bleeding."

Eromedeus moved his left hand, baring the right. Where a wound should have been, deep and dripping, there was no mark at all.

"I struck you!" Cyrodian yelled.

"You did not," Eromedeus replied frostily.

Cyrodian lost all sense. Ignoring Kustos's pallid protests, he stepped hurriedly around the bed and lifted his sword to confront Eromedeus directly. The man made no effort to move away. Without warning, Cyrodian thrust his sword forward, plunged the steel directly into Eromedeus's belly.

The long blade disappeared halfway into Eromedeus's body. Cyrodian felt the mild resistance of organs against the steel; yet as he withdrew it, there was no sign of any blood upon the shining metal, and upon Eromedeus's person was only clothing sliced and torn.

No blood.

Eromedeus laughed cruelly, the wind of his mockery moving the flames of the oil lamps.

Cyrodian's face dropped. He looked from his sword to Eromedeus, back to his steel.

No blood.

"He cannot die!" Kustos whispered from the bed, beginning to sob powerfully. "Cyrodian! *He cannot die!* He can die only if . . . another gives up his life!"

Again, the low, cruel laughter.

"Name of the gods!" Prince Cyrodian swore, staring at the man. Orange-painted face; dark black eyes; mocking, evil smile.

"He cannot die!" Kustos sobbed once more, writhing in his bed. "Please, please, find me a priest, to save my spirit from him!"

297

2.

The conquest of Erusabad by the Salukadians was accomplished in less than one day. Two ships set sail from Ugalu and, under orders from Huagrim the Great, made port early one morning in Erusabad. The soldiers disembarked routinely from their ships and entered the city in four neatly arranged units, after the Western style. Because changeovers of army personnel in Erusabad took place occasionally, no one paid any particular attention to them.

In a prearranged schedule provided by Governor Dusar, each of the Salukadian commanders led his troop to one of the four bridges crossing the Usub, the river which divided Erusabad into halves and, logically and traditionally, marked the demarcation between the Athadian northern and the Salukadian southern sides of the Holy City. The crossing of the Ibar, Bisht, Avarra, and Nasub Bridges by armed Salukadian hosts was in itself an act of military occupation and an outright declaration of belligerency. But Erusabad had lived so long divided yet at peace that those Athadian citizens who stood in the squares this morning, or leaned from their windowsills, or peered from their shops to witness the advance of the forces, did not presume to consider that the intrusion meant a military takeover. Not daring to entertain the worst, the Athadians in the northern half of Erusabad assumed the least: that for some unknown but wholly legal reason, King Elad had sanctioned this entrance of the Salukadians.

When the first of the four units reached the Kinesh Square, they were approached by twenty of the Athadian mounted city patrol and asked to identify themselves and state their business. Calling a halt to their advance, the Salukadians stood at rest while their commander presented a written notice, signed by Governor Dusar, allowing the soldiers entrance into the northern section. The city guards were uncertain what to make of this. Dusar, while the reigning Athadian authority in the city, did not have the privilege of granting foreign troops access to government soil.

The city patrol politely but firmly requested that the Salukadians remain as they were until the issuance of the order could be verified. The Salukadians, far more aware than the guards of what was occurring, complied, and maintained their pose of rest while a number of the city patrol made their way to army headquarters to inquire about Dusar's order.

By this time the remaining three Salukadian units had moved, uninterrupted, through the city to station themselves at positions arranged by Dusar: one at the Vilusian Gardens, the second at the Temple of Bithitu, the third at the Himu Square.

One hour after the arrival of the eastern troops into Port Erusabad, the city commander of the army furiously burst into Governor Dusar's central authority office, just off Himu Square, and insolently demanded to know the meaning of an armed Salukadian entrance onto Athadian soil. He was not immediately granted access to Governor Dusar's office, but was told to wait until the governor could see him. Captain Thytagoras, the army commander of troops in Athadian Erusabad, was a man of short temper and long experience. He was a reactionary; he saw only two sides to any question—his own opinion, and the wrong one—and the presence of an armed Salukadian host on his country's soil meant but one thing to him: a provocation to war.

As well, Captain Thytagoras was not a man used to waiting when the moment demanded action. He stalled in the outer offices of the central authority for just over a minute, barking and ranting and fuming. Then, crying out that the damned eastern sewer-dogs had broken the peace, he shoved his way past the desks in the front hall, threatened to kill any bureaucrat who tried to stop him from entering the place, and moved like a stalking animal up the first stairwell he came to, until he reached the second floor, where he knew Dusar's office was located.

He burst into the Governor's chamber to find Dusar in a compromising position counting his gold that Huagrim delivered as his payment for sanctioning the entrance of the foreign occupation force. Dusar, a man of practical tastes, had demanded for his treachery four thousand in long Athadian gold, secret passage south on a Salukadian merchant vessel, and two Salukadian servant girls—one a dancer (a long-limbed, high-bosomed beauty with whom Dusar was already familiar), the other the creamy-complexioned daughter of an inner-city merchant.

Captain Thytagoras drew his sword.

The women shrieked. Dusar, going white at the intrusion of his army commander, dropped a basket of coins and ran across the floor of his office, away from the bared steel.

"Stay back, Thytagoras!"

"Dog! *Dog!*"

"This can be explained!"

"You are a *traitor*, son of a—"

"I warn you, stay back! I have soldiers within call!"

"*Salukadian* soldiers, son of a slut?" shrieked Thytagoras. "Scum! *Traitor!*" Unleashing an oath, the captain jumped forward, sword aimed for Dusar.

The screaming women ran to escape—out a rear door and down a stairwell. Dusar picked up a chair and heaved it at Thytagoras, who easily ducked out of the way. Very frightened, unused to thinking in crises, Dusar at first considered running out by the way the women had taken; then he decided to throw himself out the window. He was a stout man, however, and his moment of indecision cost him precious time, while the effort it took him to haul himself up onto the stone sill gave Thytagoras all the time the captain needed.

His heavy sword, notched from many combats, carved Governor Dusar open from shoulders to buttocks, all the way down his back.

"Traitor!"

Blood erupted, and Dusar screamed insanely. Falling away from the window ledge, he smashed into a desk, crumpled upon the floor, and writhed. His knotted hands and squirming legs, numbed and awkward, jumped with lives of their own, due to the damage the steel had done to his spine.

"Son of a—*Traitor!*"

Dusar attempted to speak, but only a runnel of blood poured from his mouth. Thytagoras, disgusted, brought his sword down once more, this time driving it point-first through the Governor's chest. The man coughed another stream of blood, shivered, and went limp.

"*Godsssss*!" Thytagoras howled, throwing back his head and yelling it to the empty chamber.

The door of the office burst open and three dozen clerks from downstairs rushed in. At the sight of the murdered Governor they cried out in rage and shock and threatened Thytagoras with legal action.

But Thytagoras waved his bloodied sword at them and grunted obscenities, then kicked open the window shutters where Dusar had tried to escape and cried out into the square below, "Traitor! Dusar is a *traitor*! The Salukadians are in our streets! It is *war*!"

War.

But the war did not last a day.

Captain Thytagoras, despite his headstrong intentions to the contrary, did not have the opportunity of assuming control of Erusabad upon Governor Dusar's death; that office fell to one of the bureaucrats of the authority, an old man named Sirom. And it was Sirom who, in the absence of any order from King Elad, thought it best to make a gesture of peace with the Salukadians until he was notified by Athad to do otherwise.

This decision did not sit well with Captain Thytagoras, who ordered out his legions and made combat with the Salukadians in the Himu Square. But the engagement was little more than a skirmish that lasted only a few minutes. When Thytagoras, seeing what losses his men were taking, ordered a retreat to the walled cisterns and the overturned carts in the street, Sirom angrily presented himself at an upper balcony of the authority and—upon a blast of trumpets from city troops who had moved to guard the authority—called for an end to the conflict. He ordered Captain Thytagoras's soldiers to set down their arms and called for the leader of the Salukadians to enter the authority for a conference.

Thytagoras, utterly outraged, retired with his soldiers to the barracks houses, and the commander in charge of the Salukadians, with his retinue of retainers, met in private with Sirom. Sirom spoke to the easterners calmly, announcing that their entrance into Athadian-held Erusabad was an outright invitation to war, but that he—because of the legal ramifications of the late Dusar's contract with Lord Huagrim—would

301

refrain from ordering his city troops against them. Rather, he would communicate with King Elad in the Athadian capital, and if King Elad ordered war to be declared between the empires, then the streets of the Holy City would become the first battlefield of that conflict. If, however, King Elad (for whatever reasons) decided to accept the occupation and the terms which Dusar had illegally entered into with Emperor Huagrim, then Sirom and the city of Erusabad would have no choice but to capitulate as well.

This de facto resignation to the current conditions was fully agreed to by the Salukadians, who quite naturally regarded Sirom and his government as little more than a collection of weak fools.

Lord Sirom then spoke with Captain Thytagoras in private. "I am not stupid," he declared to the commander, "and neither are you. It will avail us nothing to react immediately to this occupation; no doubt the Salukadians are prepared for it, and no doubt Dusar warned them of such an eventuality. Have you considered that? Do you want to have these bastards hiding in the sewers? Do you want to go into the sewers and fight them there? Use your head, Captain. I am sending my message to King Elad today; we can let him decide what to do about all this. It's his city; it's his empire."

"And we merely sit here while these pieces of animal dung in armor proceed to do as they like?"

"No, we do not. We, Captain, keep the peace. Do you understand? The political and legal ramifications of this are immense, and since we no longer live in a barbaric time, those ramifications will drag on forever, in courts of law, royal courts, between emissaries and judges and kings and advisers. That is not your concern, nor is it mine. Our concern is with four Salukadian legions which have now housed themselves in Athadian Erusabad. There will be protests against them; there will be attacks by the citizens; there will be violence. You are to triple—quadruple—your street patrols, and in the event of any dispute or show of violence, you and your men are to keep the peace. Do you understand me?"

"Keep our own people from defen—"

"Keep the peace, Captain Thytagoras. I don't presume to tell you that the life of one Salukadian soldier is worth as much to me as the lowest Athadian beggar. I'm sure the Salukadian commanders feel likewise. Their troops are expendable; Athadian citizens are not. If there is a demonstration of violence in our streets, and if one single Salukadian raises a fist at one Athadian citizen—well, keep the peace, Captain Thytagoras. Keep the peace, until we learn more from King Elad. Now, am I understood?''

Thytagoras nodded; Sirom was understood.

Three days before the official announcement of his marriage to the Lady Salia of the province of Gaegosh, King Elad learned of the Salukadian occupation of Athadian-held Erusabad. His Council, of course, argued for a turning out of the entire army in an immediate military response to this deliberate provocation. Their hastiness had less to do with patriotism than it did with the advantages to be gained from war-profiteering. But Lord Abgarthis, in private counsel with his King, warned Elad against overreacting to the emergency—as he had done with the demonstrations in Sulos.

"Look at your maps," declared Abgarthis. "See what the Salukadians are doing. What difference is it to us if all Erusabad is held by the easterners, or if we allow them to control the entire city? Let them have Erusabad—but let them pay a price for having it. Let them leave our people free to worship in the Temple, let them pay us an annual tribute, let them pay the revenues to have the sewers cleaned and the docks manned and the administration run. Huagrim is not a fool, and neither are we. Do not let him force you into making of this a military matter; turn it, my King, into a legal and a judicial one. We cannot afford to let it become a military matter—not with our troops scattered in the Lowlands.''

"Do you sense here," suggested Elad, "some collusion between the Emarian advance and the Salukadian occupation?"

"Certainly," replied his adviser. "And again I say: Our advantage does not lie in military maneuvering."

Elad debated the matter longer with Abgarthis, but he was prone to agree. With dissension at home and his alliance with Gaegosh but days away, he didn't care to take up arms against the eastern empire over something as trivial as Salukadia controlling all, rather than part, of Erusabad. As Abgarthis pointed out, all that was actually occurring was the culmination of an inevitable shift in cultural partisanship; Athadian supremacy in the east had been dwindling progressively over the course of generations, even as the ports of the empire's southern seaboard had blossomed and grown. Now, so long as the current trade agreements and pilgrimage rights of Athadian citizens in Erusabad were retained, Elad was not much concerned about political rule of the city.

And this was the essence of the message he relayed to Lord Sirom, and it was the crux of the official documents he entrusted to Lord General Thomo, his emissary to Huagrim. Thomo, on the day before the announcement of King Elad's betrothal, left Port Athad in the company of several hundred noblemen, advisers, lawyers, and mercantile specialists, to meet with Lord Emperor Huagrim and his sons in the now Salukadian held Holy City of the east.

So that when, some days later, Lord Sirom advised Captain Thytagoras of this turn of events, it was with the comment "We placate them. That is what King Elad intends to do."

To which a wrathful, disbelieving Thytagoras retorted, "They are buying us for money. You understand that, don't you? What kind of King do we have? What kind of empire do we have? What has happened to us? Name of the gods," he thundered, "what has happened to us?"

"What has happened to us," Sirom replied, a rueful grin on his face, "is that we have become like the merchants we respect so highly. We have sold ourselves to the buyer who has offered us the largest purse. That is all we have done. Everything, captain, is today a commodity. Wines, furs, ships, sovereignties."

"Are we no longer a people?" exclaimed Thytagoras. "Are we only a bank? We have given poison to a serpent! We have given poison to a serpent already fat with poison!"

"Perhaps . . . perhaps," sighed Lord Sirom. "But whenever did the businessmen of our nation stop selling poison for a profit, even when that poison might be used against them?"

3.

Bessara.

When Count Adred returned there in the middle of the winter, it was with every intention of remaining in the port city for some time. With money drawn from his bank in the capital, he took up residence in one of the less expensive hostels in Bessara, and he began to attend the meetings of the revolutionaries.

He was remembered by them and by Lord Solok, the nobleman in whose house the revolutionary meetings were held. And as he took part in their meetings and became their supportive ally, Adred was aware of a changed atmosphere at Solok's. There was a stronger sense of desperation, but also of purpose, unity. Too, Adred found that he was not regarded suspiciously by his new acquaintances, and this was because of certain precautions taken by Solok.

"You are Count Diran's son," that nobleman said to Adred privately, following the dispersal of the first meeting he attended since returning to Bessara. "Don't be upset with me, please. But we are on our guard constantly for infiltrators; they are eager to identify and arrest us. Before Sulos, they only harassed us; but now we are considered true criminals, and our lives are in danger. So I had to check up on you and be certain of your sincerity. And I'm proud to have you with us."

Taking Solok into his confidence, Adred told him that he had journeyed to Athad after witnessing the rebellion in Sulos, and had made a point of stressing to King Elad that the demonstrations which had taken place there, and which were bound to continue across the empire, were not spontaneous resentments but were the first signs of a very real revolution

305

rising up within Athadia. Solok was intrigued; he asked Adred if Elad had taken this warning seriously.

"He did," Adred replied. "And he promised to look into methods of reform."

Solok was dubious about that, as Adred had been. "Methods of reform. That means only that nothing will be accomplished. Or that government agents will attempt to join us to unmask us."

The revolution, gaining strength and numbers, had become a widespread underground organization. The nominal head in Bessara was Lord Solok, but other sympathetic aristocrats throughout the city had made their homes centers for meetings and discussions. More, the revolutionaries now had a name, an identity. Evolving from a disunited group of divergent, angry people without direction, they had rallied as one behind the brutal massacre of the demonstrators in Sulos. In honor of that first great battle of the revolution, the insurgents had named themselves Suloskai, after the city; and for their banner they devised a red cloth square—to symbolize the blood shed—with a simple black "S" on its face—proclaiming their name, their unity, and the beginning of their struggle and separate history.

And many were now arguing that real violence ought to be used in the struggle. They will not listen to reason, was the rationale; they use violence against us, let us return that violence to them. This, despite the knowledge that violence only begets itself, and the violent acts in Sulos had brought down upon the rebels the iron fist of the throne.

When informed that King Elad was looking into methods of reform that might answer some of their grievances, the collective response of the fifty or so seditionists who gathered at Lord Solok's was this: "It is too late for reforms! We want no reforms—we want change!"

Solok and Adred and some of the others there knew, certainly, that violence was not an answer to the problem; yet neither was the political charade of a "reform." And week by week, as the insurrectionist fever mounted, as the dispossessed of Bessara threw themselves into the widespread organization of their blossoming Suloskai brotherhood, the calmer voices of reason were persistently drowned out, and the frustrated voices wanting to match fire with flame grew louder.

Adred, sitting in, listening, knew that resorting to such methods had become almost inevitable. . . .

On the tenth day following Adred's arrival in Bessara, the next scheduled demonstration by the Suloskai took place on the docks, in the loose open area shouldered by warehouses, emporia, and seamen's inns. Adred did not join in this demonstration, for so far sympathetic aristocrats had not been pressured to assert their feelings publicly, out of concern that reprisals against them might strangle the birthing revolt in its crib. But he did watch from the roof of his hostel, as did all the other guests. The amusements at the arcades and theaters had been indefinitely suspended (due to fears of demonstrations in the streets), and so the demonstrations themselves had come to be regarded as substitute amusements.

This protest, as all had been so far in Bessara, was a peaceful affair. But Lord Uthis of the city, breaking beneath the pressure of the demonstrations he had witnessed so far, and privately fearful that Bessara would suffer a reenactment of the bloodshed that had occurred in Sulos, took extraordinary precautions this morning by ordering out his city guard in triple force and commanding them to "keep the peace."

The effect was similar to Bithitu the Prophet asking that no church be raised in his name, the same as warning a child to stop crying lest he be punished—the same as ordering Athadian soldiers in a Holy City to keep a peaceful watch over Salukadian invaders. The city guard promptly began inciting trouble on the docks, then attacked those demonstrators who defended themselves. Blood flowed; heads fell beneath steel blades; bodies were trampled under boot and hoof. The docks erupted with the screams of many voices, the thunder of many feet, and the wild prancing of horses, the mad trumpeting of horns. Those who did not escape or who had not been killed were arrested and dressed in chains, to be taken away for interment— and thus kept peaceful.

And when the docks were cleared, only a short time after the demonstration had begun, the city guards piled forty-seven corpses against the front wall of an emporium and announced a proclamation, effected by Lord Uthis, that henceforward any persons banding together in groups of four or more would immediately be arrested on charges of sedition.

* * *

Adred, agonized over this recurrence of what had happened in Sulos, nonetheless forced himself to remain within his hostel rooms. He would only draw attention to himself if he were to rush to the aid of his fellow insurgents immediately upon their public spectacle of violence and arrest. He paced furiously, began a letter to Orain and Galvus (only to tear it up), and at last, in midafternoon, went out to get a meal and learn what he could. He ate in a small tavern across the street from his hostel, and there gathered from what he overheard that Lord Uthis absolutely forbade any further civil disobedience and intended to crush the dissidents as they had been crushed in Sulos.

Following his meal, he strolled as calmly as possible through the streets, always apprehensive that others regarded him suspiciously, although he knew that that was not the case. Yet whenever he passed by a city guard or a mounted patrol, he seemed to tighten; and when they greeted him with a friendly good day, Adred found himself answering politely but nervously, afraid that they could read his mind. He made a circuitous path to Lord Solok's, half anticipating city troops standing guard around it.

Yet if Lord Solok's home from the outside seemed ordinary and beyond the flow of events, its appearance belied its interior. For within, as Adred discovered when he was allowed cautious entrance, the place was a veritable hospital ward.

There were at least twenty wounded revolutionaries, with nine or ten others, unharmed, tending to them. Men and women, young and middle-aged, some dressed in fine clothes, others in garments obviously long-worn and ragged. The wounded were stretched on floors and divans, leaning in chairs, propped up with pillows or cushions, and covered with blankets. Trails of blood drops crisscrossed on the carpets. Adred could hear the muffled moans issuing from rooms on the first floor and on the second. And in every direction, bumping into him or stepping around him, hurried the helpful, arms loaded with rags and cloths, bowls of warm water, jugs of wine. . . .

"Here." Someone—a young man with a thin beard—thrust a bowl of steaming water into his hands. "Hurry, please!"

Adred followed him into a small room off the main entrance hall. It was little more than a closet, but there was a

308

bed to one side and, set against the wall opposite it, a low cot. In the bed lay a feverish, stout man, his right hand resting nervously on his bloodstained chest; on the cot slept a woman, her head bandaged but with no sign otherwise of any wounds. In the tight aisle between bed and cot a red-haired woman sat in a chair and tended to the stout man.

"Rhia, here." The young fellow handed her some clean towels. "We have hot water. Is there anything else?"

"She's all right; just got her insides bruised when they kicked her, but she's sleeping now. I'm not so sure about this one. But get upstairs, see if they need anything."

The young man grunted and pressed past Adred as he went out. The red-haired woman glanced briefly at Adred. "Bring the water here, please."

He carried it to her, stood there holding the pan beside her head while she pulled back the bedclothes to bare the stout man's wounds. Adred swallowed thickly. The poor devil had caught two sword strokes, one across the right shoulder, the other—deeper and more severe—across most of his chest. Perilously close to his heart, Adred guessed. The wounds had not stopped bleeding, and the man's breathing was shallow and labored.

The woman reached up to rinse one of the towels in the pan of water; as soon as she did so, she cursed.

"Damn it! *Cold* water! I told him I wanted *cold* water, not hot water!"

Adred tried to calm her. "That's all right. It'll catch the blood. We can get more."

"Yes, yes, yes." She wrung the towel, leaned over the stout man and wiped his cuts clean, pressed the cloth upon his chest and held it there with her hands.

"Damn it," she muttered in a whisper. "I wanted cold water."

Adred smiled faintly. He bent to set down the pan, then thought better of it; excusing himself, he stepped out and walked down the entrance hall, following it until he came to the kitchen. An older woman in there was heating a kettle. Adred told her he needed some cold water.

"Check that jug on the table; there's some in there."

He emptied his pan into the kettle, refilled it with cold water, and returned to the small room.

"Cold," he announced.

The red-haired woman thanked him, soaked a clean towel in it, and applied it.

"We're going to have to sew him. Could you—"

He returned to the kitchen and inquired after a thin metal needle and some gut or cotton thread; the woman at the kettle directed him to a box in a cupboard and told him to take a lamp with him. "It works better if you heat the needle first."

"Does it? Why?"

"I don't know, but it does. My husband was a soldier; they always heated their needles first when they sewed them up on the fields."

Adred returned with the needle, thread, and oil lamp, watched as the red-haired woman sewed up the long gash on the man's chest—just as though she were repairing a vest or a pair of leggings. When she'd finished, she washed her hands, dried them, then sat back with a heavy sigh.

Adred complimented her.

She made a grimace. "He's the last bad one, I think. So you don't"—she faced him—"so you don't faint at the sight of blood, eh?"

"I suppose not."

"Rare breed of tough men, these aristocrats." She wiped her face, then apologized. "Sorry. But you should see the ones with their insides hanging out."

They were silent for a few moments. Adred wondered aloud if there were a bottle handy; the woman said she didn't care for any right now. She leaned forward and felt the stout man's forehead.

Adred told her, "I know you."

"Do you?" She didn't seem much impressed by the fact.

"Well, I've seen you before. Thought you looked familiar, and now I remember." She was the slim red-haired woman dressed in rags who, during his stopover in Bessara on the way to King Evarris's funeral, had harangued street crowds for money for the poor.

"Rhia—isn't that your name?"

She was intrigued now, and studied Adred more carefully; absent-mindedly, she reached a hand to her chin, fingering her cheeks as though she had a beard. "You're the one who gave me all the gold."

"Right."

She smiled sadly. "I remember you. Not often someone gives me a handful of gold for telling them to go to hell."

He chuckled at that, and when she asked him his name he told her.

"Adred—sounds familiar. Have you been in the revolution very long?"

"Not long. I was here once before, at one of the meetings. But I was in Sulos."

"Oh, you're the one who talked to King Elad. Solok mentioned you."

"Yes, I'm the one."

They lapsed into silence again, Rhia watching the wounded man, Adred watching her.

They both looked up at the sounds of footsteps then, in the hallway outside. Lord Solok, accompanied by the young man of earlier, entered the room and asked if everything was under control.

"This one's cut pretty badly," Rhia informed him. "But she's sleeping soundly. All she'll have are bruises."

Solok, politely excusing himself, moved past Adred and leaned over the bed, examined the stout man's cuts and Rhia's stitching of them. "If he makes it through tonight, he should live. We've lost one already; we'll have to move him out of here tonight. There's another one, still uncertain." But then, in a gesture of supreme patience, he touched Rhia's hair and bent forward, kissed her briefly on the face. "We will win," he told her, pulling himself erect. "We will win."

Solok went out, followed by the young man.

"You know Lord Solok well, do you?"

She eyed him directly. "We were married once. Does that surprise you? We separated a few years ago, and I joined the street people; Solok traveled, we still met occasionally. He has aided the revolution immensely. If he were found out . . ."

She let it go. The result of such a disclosure was obvious.

As night came, Rhia moved from the chair to the floor, stretching out and resting her head on a bunched towel. Adred turned up the wick of the oil lamp and placed the light on the chair, the better to illumine the stout fellow's suffering. He crouched in a corner, and he and Rhia talked from time to time, until her words became mumbled and at last she fell asleep. Adred periodically checked on the stout fellow, rinsing out the sweat-dampened towel in the basin of water and

311

reapplying it to his forehead. At last, lying down beside Rhia in the cramped space of the room, he too fell asleep.

He was awakened in the middle of the night by the scuffle of boots in the hallway. Drowsy, he watched the boots, decided they must belong to Solok, and closed his eyes again. As he did, he heard the boots walk off and for the first time became aware of Rhia's arms wrapped around him.

A natural enough reaction, Adred mused; it was chilly in the room.

And he fell back to sleep.

When he awoke again it was dawn, and he was startled to overhear loud voices coming from the front of the apartment house. Cautiously Adred sat up, easing Rhia from him. He heard the voices stop, heard the front doors close. Adred stood up and went out into the entrance hallway.

Solok sent him a severe glance.

"The city patrol?" Adred asked him, wiping sleep from his eyes.

Solok nodded grimly. "I'm not sure if they suspect anything or not. They warned me that insurgents had been spotted in the area last night, and that I should be on guard for my life. But I'm afraid they may know something."

Adred muttered an obscenity.

"We can't do anything about it for the moment," Solok told him. Throwing an arm on Adred's shoulder: "Go on, there's food in the kitchen. I'll look in on our wounded friend."

He turned into the small room as Adred made his way down the hall.

The conversation that morning turned upon one issue only: what sort of retaliation should be done against yesterday's attack by the city guards? The consensus, to Lord Solok's displeasure but not to his surprise, was a call to answer in kind. Let us settle upon a victim, declared those gathered there, and murder him. Let that be our warning to Lord Uthis and to King Elad. They may flush some of us out and kill us, but there are more revolutionaries than there are aristocrats, and we can kill all of them before they can kill all of us.

Solok, and Adred as well, protested this decision. The ultimate aim of the Suloskai was not to kill those who dis-

312

agreed with them, but to gain access to the halls of government and redirect the course of the economy.

But when a show of hands was called for, all but four present voted for the assassination of some bureaucrat or aristocrat in Bessara. Not that this would become a pattern of behavior, or that the intention was to include such tactics in the future; but many had been killed in Sulos, now many had been killed in Bessara, and if those in power came to regard the revolutionaries as unable to defend their principles by sword as well as word, then the revolution would surely be crushed before really building a strong opposition against the plutocrats.

Before Solok would give his consent to such a thing, however, and before any person could be settled upon as a likely victim, he wanted certain things attended to in the city. Carefully and secretly, four or five of them must go out and try to discover the whereabouts of others dispersed during the clash, and additional supplies must be bought. Because Count Adred was unknown in Bessara, Solok asked that he shop for foodstuffs, wine, and some extra clothes and medicine—being sure to buy the supplies in different quantities at different stalls and shops in different sections of the city. Adred was agreeable to this. Rhia left by a back door to begin searching for other Suloskai in the city; a few minutes later, Adred prepared to begin his shopping.

He had suggested to Rhia that she meet him in his room at the hostel—simply as a precaution, later, before heading back. She was agreeable to this and told Adred that she would come in by a back way and knock on the door in a code.

He spent the morning wandering around the city, buying a few things but mainly wasting an hour here and an hour there in various taverns, picking up bits and pieces of gossip and news. Adred took his lunch in the tavern across from his hostel, deposited in his room what he had bought so far, then went out again to finish purchasing supplies. By late afternoon he had enough of everything Solok had requested, but he was surprised that Rhia had still not come to his room. He wondered if something had happened to her. It worried him.

Concerned, and eager to make sure of her safety, Adred placed half the supplies he had bought in a satchel and left his hostel, going out by the rear door. Snow was falling as he hurried down the alley; the lamps along the streets had already been lit. Patrols had obviously been increased, too: the city was vacant except for groups of soldiers making their way up and down the avenues and squares.

He was not far from Solok's apartment when he saw a figure running toward him down the dark, white-dusted street. Rhia. A pang of fear shot through him.

Rhia, breathless, panting hard in little white clouds, pushed Adred into the shadows of an old doorway. "I was just on my way over to your room. I decided to come past the apartment. Adred, soldiers are there."

His heart dropped. "They know?"

She bobbed her head fiercely.

"Did they see you?"

"No. Or if they did, they didn't recognize me. But they were lined up all along the street and down a side alley. Surrounded it. They know, Adred!"

"Gods!" He threw his head back, ground his teeth together. "How many were in there? How many still?"

"I don't know. Almost all, if not everyone except you and me."

"Gods!" he swore. "*Gods!*"

"They'll arrest them," Rhia told him.

"We've got to—"

"Adred!" She gripped his arm and shook it, warning him still. Horses' hoofs clattering on the stones, very close—just around the corner.

"Walk on," she whispered. "They don't know who you are. I'll wait here until they've gone past; then I'll come to your room. Go on, Adred!"

He stared quickly into her eyes—gray eyes, hard and brittle as the frost—and turned from her, hefted his satchel, and began walking down the street in the direction of his hostel. He fought an urge to turn around and see if Rhia was safe.

The clatter of the horses' hoofs turned the corner behind him and began to follow him. Adred ignored the sound, pretending that he was preoccupied with the slippery street. A husky voice called out, "Excuse me, sir!"

He turned.

One city guard on his horse. He cantered up to Adred, patted his mount still. "Did you know there's a curfew in effect, sir?"

Adred stared up at him. Couldn't see his face beneath his

helmet; couldn't tell much from the official tone of his voice. "I—I'm sorry. No, I didn't know."

"Curfew in effect for everyone; takes effect at nightfall."

"Well, I'm sorry. I didn't know. I just arrived in Bessara yesterday afternoon."

Oddly, the guard said to him, "Yesterday, hey? Just in time for all hell to break loose."

"I'm afraid it did," Adred agreed.

"Where do you come from?"

"The capital. I'm an adviser to Councilor Abgarthis." It was a lie, concocted on the spur of the moment; and suddenly Adred chided himself for his stupidity. It sounded reasonable enough and could even be proved—except that Abgarthis was no longer a Councilor. If by some chance this man knew that . . .

"The capital, you say?" He didn't sound suspicious, only doubtful.

But Adred, jostling his satchel, lifted his right hand so that the guard could see the signet ring on his middle finger. And, daring to take a somewhat superior tone: "I can understand if you're suspicious, officer, but I hope you don't think I'm lying to you."

"No, no, that's not it at all."

"Do you mind if—"

"If it's all right with you, sir—"

"Count Adred. My name is Count Adred."

"Count Adred, I'll escort you to your lodgings. Wouldn't do my conscience any good to leave you out here alone after curfew. Can't let you take the chance of something happening."

"If you insist," Adred answered him. "I assure you I know how to defend myself."

"I'm sure you do, Count. But there's no telling what might happen. Are you far from here?"

"Only a few blocks. I'm staying at the Sign of the Crest."

The guard kneed his horse into a slow walk. "That should be fairly safe. I know the proprietor; he's an honest rogue."

The walk was a nervous ordeal for Adred. Not entirely trusting this guard, he fought down the impression that the soldier was gaming with him, recognizing in him a sympathetic liberal. But when they reached the hostel, the guard merely reminded Adred again to respect the curfew and watch out for himself during his stay in the city.

Breathing his first full breath since the encounter, he hurried up the stairs and dumped his supplies onto a chair, then fell upon his bed and forced himself to relax, put things in perspective—and listen for Rhia.

When she arrived, she was not the strong-willed, defiant Rhia whom Adred had admired in Solok's apartment. Exhausted, bitter, torn emotionally, she collapsed onto the bed while Adred poured her a cup of wine.

"They'll kill them," she said, repeating it in disbelief. "They'll kill them. I never thought this would happen, I never did. I stood in the streets for years and yelled at them every day. No one threatened me. But now—just because of the riot in Sulos, because people got desperate and because King Elad called out the—" She stopped, sat up, looked squarely at Adred. "How well do you know the King?" she asked.

Adred didn't understand. "I know him to speak to him informally," he replied. "I consider him my political opposite, but I respect him; I respect his struggle."

"Solok was the leader of the revolution in Bessara, Adred. He's a brilliant man; he organized everything. People listened to him; they respected and trusted him. If there was ever any chance for the revolution to meet with the throne, to honestly decide on anything, Solok was that chance. Now, with him under arrest—he'll be executed, we both know that—with Solok gone, any opportunity to act reasonably is gone as well. Without his direction in Bessara, the revolution will split into a thousand fragments, and nothing will be accomplished. You'll see violence now, Adred—you'll see volcanoes of violence. They wanted to assassinate Lord Uthis. You didn't hear that, did you?"

"No."

"But they're not going to stop with Lord Uthis. Adred, they want to kill the King."

He was stunned. "They'll never accomplish it! There's no possible—"

"Whether or not they accomplish it, they'll attempt it. And not just once. No matter what they call themselves now, they're determined to draw attention to themselves, to take over the throne or topple it. They'll fight the army; they'll fight the aristocracy and everyone who stands in their way."

316

So it was true. The darkest fears he had imagined—barely imagined, and dismissed as madness. True. How could they even pretend that the words they had printed and distributed on broadsheets meant anything any longer?

Rhia, silent, stared at him or beyond him, sipped her wine. . . .

And Adred, in Bessara, alone with this woman, a revolutionary, in the midst of the swelling storm of revolution, began to wonder who he was and what he was, why he was—and remembered, as abruptly and unmistakably as though she had returned to him as a phantom to speak them, the words Queen Yta had told him just before going to her death.

We enter a dark age, friend of Dursoris. I have seen the future, and it is dark. . . .

The death of Dursoris—the death of law.

The death of Yta—the death of the last bond, womanly and true, fragile but sensitive, brave, to the order that had reigned before.

The deaths of hundreds in Sulos, and now in Bessara—and hundreds, thousands more deaths to come . . .

We enter a dark age. . . . I have seen the future, and it is dark . . . .

4.

When he returned to Erusabad, he found it greatly changed. As the merchanter slowly made its way up the Usub, he stood at the rail and watched the docks and streets slide by, the crowds and the soldiers. Troops of soldiers everywhere—Salukadian soldiers—on both sides of the river. And Salukadian emblems on the rooftops of every dockside building and warehouse. A greatly changed city . . .

As he disembarked, he noticed lines of Salukadian officials making cursory searches of all packages his fellow passengers had brought with them. He joined a line, and when he reached the head of it he was questioned by a dark man with a well-trimmed beard and a coat marked with emblems and badges.

"You have no personal belongings?"

"No. None."

"What is your business in Erusabad? Are you visiting relatives?"

"I have no relatives."

The official eyed him warily. "State your business in the city, please."

"I am returning after a long absence. Erusabad is my home."

Trained Salukadian eyes observed him. Long-grown hair and beard—dressed in a worn cotton robe and a leather vest, horsehide boots, weaponless, no jewelry or ornaments.

"Are you a priest?"

"I am."

"With what school are you affiliated?"

"I once served in the Temple of Bithitu, but I was dismissed. I am a wandering priest, now—*siamu.*"

318

"*Siamu*, eh?" The official pursed his lips, studied him frankly, then lifted a hand and snapped his fingers. In response a young soldier, looking very bored, moved ahead. "Would you mind stepping into that office over there?" the official asked him.

"Am I under arrest?"

"No, you are not under arrest. Would you mind stepping into that office?"

He shrugged and did as requested, accompanying the bored young soldier across the way and into the office. It was a compact hole—little more than a closet with a door and a board partitioning it into receiving area and office. A grossly fat Salukadian official, smelling of perfumed oils and cheap wine, stepped up to the board and motioned for him to approach.

"What is your business in Erusabad?"

"I am returning after a long absence."

"Are you a priest?"

"I am *siamu*."

"Have you anything to do with the Temple of Bithitu in this city?"

"I served in it once, but left it."

"Have you ever been employed by the Athadian government or been retained by it or by any of its offices, legal or military?"

He almost laughed out loud. "No, never. Would you mind telling me what the—"

"If you intend to stay in Erusabad for more than three days, you must report back to this office and get a badge of residence. What is your name?" The official produced a long scroll and unwound it, reached for his pen.

"I am called Thameron."

"Tha—meronnn," he wrote, with some difficulty. "Athadian by birth."

"That is correct."

"And where will you be staying while you are in Erusabad?"

"I have no idea."

The official regarded him seriously. "You must give us a place of residence."

Thameron smiled blandly. "The Temple, then. I still have friends there. I will stay at the Temple, or in one of the streets nearby."

319

"I'll mark you down for Lekusa Street."

"As you wish. Am I free to go now?"

"Yes, yes, hurry along. Remember to report back in three days if you're going to stay. Longer than three days, that is."

A light smile played on Thameron's lips. Glancing past the official, he looked through an open door and saw into a back room. There were piles of wooden crates in the shadows, sacks and amphorae; and on the floor he glimpsed the ample legs and hips of a very large woman. Suppressing a chuckle, he bowed his head and assured the Salukadian that he would do as requested. Then he left.

So they had finally done the inevitable—taken complete control of the city. It did not surprise him, but surely the empire would not allow this occupation to go unchallenged. Yet life in Erusabad, as he saw it, seemed to flow along as normally as it ever had. No signs of warfare or combat.

He stopped in a small tavern off Kurad Square, ordered a plate of fish and a cup of wine. He was amazed, as he finished his meal, to have the owner of the place—a Salukadian—approach him for payment.

"I have no money," Thameron told him.

Anger reddened the taverner's face. "What? You come in here and order food and you have no money to pay for it? You want to be arrested? Where is your money?"

Thameron replied, "Where is your respect?"

"My—what?"

He reminded the taverner that he was a priest—a wandering priest—and it had always been the policy in this city to provide free meals to priests, out of respect for their station.

This explanation calmed the owner to a degree, but: "I respect you: you're a priest. But you still have to pay me for the fish. I can't afford to—"

Thameron became impatient with him. He stood up, pushing back his chair, and momentarily adjusted his vest and belt; as he did so, the sleeve of his robe dropped back and the irate taverner had just a glimpse of the scar burned into the palm of Thameron's left hand. "I have no intention of deceiving you or of—"

Certain symbols were universal; everyone knew what the circle meant, and the sign of the lamp, and the different kinds of stars. The taverner, whitening, stepped back a pace. "I—I've decided that it's all right now. I don't want to—"

Thameron stopped talking, wondering what could have so changed the taverner's attitude in the space of a breath. But as he dropped his hand again to his side, he suddenly realized.

A businessman seated at the next table stood up and walked over. He asked Thameron gruffly, "You Athadian?"

"That is correct."

The businessman reached into his purse, pulled out a few coppers, offered them to the taverner. "Here you go, dark meat. Take it and leave him alone. He's a priest."

"Yes, yes." The owner, still shaken enough not to react to the racial slur, automatically accepted the coppers, bowed awkwardly toward Thameron, and moved away.

"Dog," growled the businessman.

Thameron thanked him for his intervention. "I only arrived here a few hours ago. I had no idea that this had happened to Erusabad."

The businessman's temper was slanderous. "The bastards moved in three weeks ago. Just marched right in and took us. Dusar sold out to them; the troops murdered him for it, and there was a little bit of fighting—but Elad gave them the city. Can you imagine it? The King just told them to go ahead and take the city. So now anybody Athadian is treated like dung." He looked around and added, "My brother used to run this shop. Did a fair business. But the dark meat came in and told him his taxes were tripled; he couldn't pay, of course, so that son of a sow took it over. I come in here every day. I'm going to knife the ugly suck when I get the chance." He paused, aware that he was somewhat drunk and that he was admitting such feelings to a robe. "Sorry," he apologized. "But you can't blame me for feeling this way, brother."

Thameron looked him in the eyes. "No," he replied in a quiet voice. "I hardly blame you. Thank you again for paying for my meal."

"No trouble at all, brother."

He watched as Thameron left the tavern, astonished that so odd a man actually was a priest. He was, wasn't he? Even though he talked so strangely, and had the damnedest eyes the businessman had ever seen. . . .

As he moved down the street in the direction of the Temple, Thameron could hear, over the noises of the crowds, the very distinct sounds of construction work; and the closer he

321

approached the Temple, the more certain he became that the sounds came from precisely that region of the city. Walking past the tall authority building—which now had Salukadian emblems flying from it—he noticed that the huge golden dome which had capped the Temple was missing.

Astonished, Thameron hurried through the crowds, crossed over two streets, and hastened down the wide boulevard that led to the huge white gates of the Temple. But the boulevard had been blocked off with wooden railings; before the facing sat a loose group of Salukadian soldiers. And behind them, on scaffolds raised halfway up the sides of the Temple, hundreds of workmen were chiseling away the stonework facades and the ornamental sculptures, plastering support columns in new designs, erecting new door gates. . . .

Utterly destroying the Temple of Bithitu, which had stood, a monument, unchanged, and supposedly immortal, for nearly two thousand years.

Thameron felt a grin of absolute astonishment spread over his face. He stared for a long while, watching the reconstruction work, witnessing the curses thrown at the Salukadian soldiers by occasional passersby. Yet there were no large crowds demonstrating against the sacrilege, and—wholly amazing—no priests whatsoever within the vicinity.

Thameron glanced down nearby streets and alleys. Lekusa Street, the official had said? Obviously for a reason. He crossed to where Lekusa Street opened upon the square, and walked down it.

A long, narrow street—one of the oldest in the city—giving the impression of being little more than an extended alley, not wide, and overshadowed by tall stone buildings, some of which even predated the temple. From windows leaned tired, haggard faces, all of them Athadian. Farther down the street, Thameron saw a newly carved wooden sign hanging over a littered doorwell; it was crudely done, with a lamp depicted inside a circle, and these words upon it:

OMUDU d. BITHITU
Urebe imdai d. ∅. allumu

TEMPLE OF BITHITU. Welcome, Faithful of the Light.
He went in.

The entrance hall was not long, and the far end of it let onto a stair, while in rooms off either side Thameron noticed, as he proceeded, makeshift altars and rude benches. The Temple had fallen to this? He saw no one in any of the rooms; the building might have been entirely vacant, for all the indication of life that he saw. He moved to the stairs and made his way to the second floor, and as he ascended he heard sounds of persons above.

The stairs continued upward, but Thameron turned onto the second floor landing. Looking into the first of the rooms he passed, he glimpsed rows of beds and low cots, saw two or three young priests gathered in discussion in a corner. Continuing on, toward louder voices that emanated from an open doorway halfway down the landing, Thameron drew back as a tall, bald young man moved quickly from an open door and almost knocked into him.

The bald young man looked up quickly, a thousand emotions in his eyes, and asked Thameron impatiently, "What do you want here?"

"I am . . . looking for someone."

"Who?"

"Hapad."

"He's very sick. It might not be well to disturb him."

"Just let me speak with him. Where is he?"

"Down there. In that room." The man pointed.

Thameron bowed his head. "Thank you." But the bald man had already hurried on.

He made his way to the door of the room, knocked lightly upon it, then opened it. The room was dark—the window shutters closed and no oil lamps lit. What light there was came from the daylight that seeped through oilskin-covered openings higher on the wall. Thameron noticed a number of beds and cots lying around; his eyes searched the gloom for sign of Hapad. Closing the door, he walked in, his boots kicking up gusts of dust.

Someone grunted from one of the cots.

Thameron turned. A pale-faced man on a cot underneath one of the oilskin windows. He approached, intending to ask where Hapad might be found; but as soon as he looked into the white, sweat-dappled features of the man, Thameron recognized his old friend.

"Hapad?"—almost in a whisper.

323

"Please . . . get me a cup of water."

"Hapad, open your eyes. This is Thameron."

The eyes opened; the weak arms struggled to push. Hapad, drowsy or feverish, quite ill, managed to prop himself up. His stare was white and wide in the dimness.

"Th—*Thameron*?"

"Yes, my friend."

"Name of the Prophet!" He coughed. "Name of—*Thameron*! Where have you been? What has happened?" He was tremendously excited, but too ill to do more than fluster and cough and hold himself uncertainly upright.

"Hapad." Thameron reached to touch his old friend's cheek, feel his flushed brow. The man was on fire. "My friend, what has happened *here*, Hapad?"

Hapad grinned mirthlessly. "The Salukadians came into the city. Took it. They . . . took the Temple. Thameron, they're—they're destroying it, rebuilding it. They have their own gods."

"I saw them doing it. Did you not fight? Where are Andoparas and Muthulis, the Temple leaders, all the—"

"Dead, Thameron."

"Dead?"

"They . . . killed themselves." Hapad admitted it in a despairingly quiet voice. "They called upon the Prophet to destroy the infidels, begged for some sign from On. But the soldiers just marched in and ordered everyone out. Insanity! They cordoned the street, blocked up the windows and doors. All of us took refuge within the Temple. Some of us fought, but not many. The soldiers killed them. Finally Muthulis and Andoparas drank poison. It all happened in—in one night. So quickly, Thameron! The rest of us—we left. What could we do? These buildings—the people in them had left, to get out of the city. We moved in to them, most of us."

"You are ill, Hapad."

"The fever. I know it will kill me. I don't—I don't care. I want to die now. I'm sorry I ever lived to see this sacrilege!"

Thameron leaned forward, urging his old friend to lie back on the damp cot; he pressed his hands gently on Hapad's chest. Hapad noticed that Thameron's fingers were naked of any ornaments.

"Thameron, where is the ring I gave you?"

The sorcerer sucked in a heavy breath.

"My friend, you have not lost it, have you? I wanted you to keep it with you."

"It was not lost, Hapad." Thameron stood up, tall in the shadows, and in a dark-toned voice admitted, "Not lost. I destroyed it, Hapad."

"Destroyed it? Thameron, why? Why would you—"

"Because"—his voice quaked—"I am fallen, my friend. Because I have changed. And it was a reminder to me of things that could never be again—ever again."

"What—what do you mean?" Struggling, Hapad lurched forward on the cot, stared into Thameron's gloomy features.

"I journeyed, Hapad. I learned more of this life in a month than I ever had in my years at the Temple. I despaired of men and despaired of myself. I wandered aimlessly until, one night in a tavern, I met a man—Guburus. A sorcerer."

You are become your destiny, O man.

"Hapad, my friend, I was so weak and disillusioned. I knew truth must exist somewhere, but all I saw were lies and the underbelly of all life. How could this be? Guburus showed me a way to attain greatness: sorcery. But . . ."

You are the chosen, the vessel, the being, the embodiment of the last days.

". . . I was weak, Hapad. I wanted everything, I strove to know all, become all—and I was visited by a demon—I was challenged and I answered. I answered."

Demand that shadows bow before you and mountains bend in praise.

"I answered, Hapad. And I have become a house of darkness and immense power. All that I have ever desired can be mine now. But . . . do you know the weight of good, Hapad?"

For you are become your destiny, O man beyond men.

"Do you know how, only young men, we struggled with the burden of good? Never certain that we knew the way, saw the Lamp, embraced the good?"

O Prince of Darkness.

"I know now what good is, Hapad. I know, because I will never touch it again. Never. Never will I struggle beneath the profound weight of good, because, my friend . . ."

Master of the Hell of Men!

"Hapad, I struggle beneath an even greater burden—an awareness of the All, and the burden of evil. Evil . . .

All-powerful and immense, human, endless, dark, with no lamps."

Evil.

"My friend? Hapad? Please, answer me, Hapad."

From the cot, from the shadows, coughing with his fever, and frightened now . . .

"Hapad? My friend?"

"Do *not* call me friend."

"Hapad, I have struggled, I have journeyed, I have fought!"

"Liar! *Liar*! When have you struggled, when have you fought, *what* have you fought? What? Yourself? You damn your soul, you have never struggled! And you damn *me* by returning to the House of the Prophet! Why? What do you want of m—"

"Hapad! Please"—a whisper, agonized. "I have immense power, my friend. You are ill; I know I can cure you of this illness. I am able to, I am powerful. Hapad, please, if you do not allow me to help you—if you turn me away—I will surely be damned. Only you—"

"Go," came the voice from the darkened cot. Coughing: "Go, then. Do not call me friend. Do not cure me. I wish to die. Go, then, and be damned. I wish you to be damned, and damned forever."

"Hapad—"

O Prince of Darkness.

"Be . . . damned. . . ."

5.

Lady Salia and her father the Imbur had returned to Sugat to make preparations for the marriage. As furious activity for the wedding took place within the palace in Athad, under the direction of dozens of seneschals and masters and hired officials and servants, Elad fell to brooding. He consented several times to speak with Abgarthis; but even that elder statesman, who knew his young King well, could not dispel the shadows and the doubts that hugged the man's heart.

No word from King Nutatharis in Emaria. Elad had deliberately but politely requested that the King reply to his query regarding the presence of Prince Cyrodian in the Emarian court. That Cyrodian was behind the troubling events in the Lowlands seemed quite apparent to Elad. (He had even feared, earlier, that Cyrodian might somehow have been behind the seditious outbreaks in Sulos, until reports appeared that substantiated the falseness of that concern.) But while Elad in his communication had addressed Nutatharis as an equal, that man had not deigned even to answer the Athadian inquiry. Elad was worried that Cyrodian had become a member of Nutatharis's court.

And Erusabad? Daily—hourly—his advisers and Councilors railed against Elad's decision to allow the Salukadians access to and control of the northern quarters of the Holy City. What possible purpose could this serve the west? To show the eastern empire how foolish we are? Shall we allow them to tread upon us at their leisure? Shall we answer the clamor of their arms with a meek request for increased revenue? Has the crown of the sun and lion truly fallen this low?

And again they reminded him: "If we want funds, my king," said more than one Councilor to Elad's face, "if it is

327

increase in revenue and capital that we require, then there is one sure way to get that, and get it quickly, and at the same time solve many of the dilemmas which confound us now: Let us go to war with the Salukadians.''

And more voices than Elad could count had raised that chorus.

War.

Let us go to war with the east, and we will cure our ills, said the Council.

And Elad, moody-browed, staring at them with his shadowed dark eyes, answered them only with his thoughts, and there critically, as he recalled an evil morning in a cavern in Mount Teplis, and the words of an Oracle, and the foreseeing of a strange new world—long and long ago, when the palace seemed still innocent and the ambitious dreams of his heart no more than idealistic fiction.

You will take the throne, and none other after you, and you will rule to see everything precious destroyed, every hope ruined, every man and woman wailing in torment. You will rule Athadia and see the world die in anguish.

That remembrance was answer enough for Elad, and decision enough for him, when his men of state called for him to throw his nation into a war. Should he move forward into a conflict that promised to bring about the end of the world?

So, then. Elad would not see the world die in anguish, and while literally such a thing was impossible, he would not allow himself to be drawn toward any escalating conflict, nor would he allow any other of influence or power to make one move, speak one word, do anything which might push Athadia close to that. He did not believe, actually, in what the Oracle had said; but she had conferred upon him a warning, and he took that warning literally.

Surely a time of ''everything precious destroyed'' would not begin with himself, or with those he knew.

Surely it would begin in some far corner of the world and—just as surely—if Elad did not act to fan the flames of it, then certainly everything precious might remain unharmed, intact, and inviolate.

He did not believe, actually, in what the Oracle had said; and yet . . .

He was King. King—yes—of insurgents and rebels, madmen and seditionists. But he was also King of everything precious and every hope, and every man and woman's torments.

Whether or not he was truly good, or endangered, or owned, or frightened, he was King.

Sugat.

"Are you not proud, my daughter? Are you not happy?" Ogodis asked her, admiring her, touching her cheek gently, touching her as if she were some other-worldly creature, some gift or thing, a gift for him, and not quite issue of his flesh.

The ships already full-laden with clothes, jewelry, cages of her animals, casks of wine, foodstuffs, ornamented chairs and cloths, tapestries, pillows, plants, and birds.

"Are you not proud, my daughter?"

"I—I am proud, my father, if you are proud."

"Oh, Salia, my daughter. I am proud! You will be queen of the Athadians! You—gods!—but a thousand poets have written of your beauty, called your beauty down from the sun and the stars and—you are my daughter!"

For the gods, yes, had been generous with Lady Salia and had exacted their price: uncommonly beautiful in form and face, yet she was cursed with submissive emotions and an inquiring mind that had no outlet. Growing, she had been like some toy ape or pet animal, prettied and pampered, its growth, its thinking, its desiring all unrecognized by those around it. Every man who had ever looked upon her, save for some few anonymous lyricists, had seen only her outward beauty, full and astonishing, yet had not guessed at the beauty that raged and stormed deep within her. The beauty of a moon overpowered by a sun . . .

"Oh, Salia!" Ogodis smiled at her, himself excited at this wedding, this marriage with empire, a union of such dimensions. "Why do you not laugh at life? Daughter, here is a secret I have learned. I share it with you, so that as queen of Athadia you will know one small secret of being a great leader: laugh. If you can laugh at a thing you can control it, Salia."

She should laugh at him, then? Laugh at Elad? Where was the difference between these two men, after all? Was she not trading one sort of father for another? Ogodis did not know her; neither did Elad; nor did anyone. No one knew her, and she did not know herself. Did flowers and pet animals which had kept her company all her life know her? Did her servants?

329

Ogodis was her father, yet he did not know her; he was only like other men, more sincere in his earnest blindness than they, but still—staring upon her outward beauty, dazzled by it, impressed by it, wanting to accomplish something with it for his own purposes. Her own father, prostituting her for his own gain. Is a man guilty of a crime if he is ignorant of the fact that what he does is a crime? Her marriage was a charade; it was a political act and an economic act; and even if most marriages high or low were political or economic acts, still—she was the daughter of the Imbur; she yearned for freedom; her body and her spirit ached for release; she wished poetry, passions, feelings.

Her duty, perhaps . . . but did she not have a duty to herself, as well as to her parent and to her state?

"I am . . . ready now, my father, to begin the journey." She admitted this to him in a sad voice, her face pale, unexcited, untransported—uncertain and frightened. It was as though she reckoned on some doom awaiting her.

Ogodis, naturally, thought it only her concern for her eventual separation from him—that, and some hesitation or doubts about the wedding night.

But he could not know that his daughter, the Lady Salia, had for many years suffered a recurring dream, a wishful dream, which was this: imagining herself in some place vague, in which she was alone. Alone. With no father, no servants, no palace, no animals. Alone. Nude and innocent as a young child, no one around to comment on the milky softness and blonde paleness of her skin, no poets to yearn wistfully for her breasts or her lips—content and happy, without a care, wholly alone, expecting nothing from herself, suffering no pressures from others who expected from her.

Alone.

"My daughter, this is the answer to a long dream of mine," Ogodis confided to her. "From this unity between our nation and Athadia, great things will result. You were born to glory, Salia. Is this not the answer to a dream of yours as well? Ah!" He smiled, embracing her, then stepping back to examine her. "I know it is—I know it is!"

She looked into his dark, smiling face, stared into his eyes. . . .

*   *   *

And often, late at night, Elad would suffer from more than brooding indecisiveness, from more than cynicism, or apprehension. Sometimes, late at night, he would awaken trembling and sweating, ready to vomit, desperate with the image of some phantom, some nightmare visitation.

Himself in a cavern of smoke, killing a bronze-masked goddess of war and revolution. Her blood jumping along the length of his iron sword. Her blood hanging in the air and forming words in the air; her blood in the air bursting into flames, like many small frozen comets, words . . .

As each human being has three selves, so do you have three enemies. Your first is a mirror, your second a blade, your third a foreign countenance. Mirrors betray depth while having no depth. Blades have two sides, two edges and one point. Countenances are masks for the minds beneath.

And as the flaming words fall away, the masked goddess comes to life again, head joined to body, the robe thrown off. Elad sees her step forth from the endless recesses of a smoking mirror; it is Salia, nude and gorgeous, blonde-haired, gray-eyed, her ripe body thrust out before him in an amorous pose, arms reaching for him, brown-nippled breasts swaying before him, white wine-colored thighs pulsing for him, hips hunching like those of some sleek forest doe's, animal in a spasm of rutting heat . . .

Furious, knowing she is false, he rips free his sword once more, jumps at this Salia, and strikes her head again from her shoulders. Her screams break free in waves of flame as blood spurts from her neck, as her breasts explode, as blood courses in steaming rivers down her trembling golden legs, as each of her fingers puffs up like a fat worm in rivers of endless blood.

While the head, on the ground, shrieks with laughter . . .

And when this dream came to him late at night, Elad would awaken, trembling and sweaty, ready to vomit, and sit crouched in his bed, stare at the mirrors hung around his room, stare at the swords crossed decorously on the walls, look at his shivering hands as though they were a stranger's, and wonder what personality lay in those shivering hands—wonder what personality lay in those mirrors hung around his room. Mirrors that did not smoke or scream or explode with blood . . .

On the twenty-third day of the month of Avru the Sky, in a celebration the grandness of which Athad and the empire had not witnessed in over twenty years, King Elad in the first year of his reign was wedded to Lady Salia of Gaegosh, daughter of the Imbur of those lands, in the name of the grace of Bithitu the Prophet and the high god On, for the glory evermore of the empire.

The ceremony required hours for its completion, accompanied as it was by choirs of singers from the Temple, announcements, blessings and benedictions, raised praises, supplications, and devotions. When at last King Elad and Queen Salia spoke their final promises to one another and turned upon the dais and faced the gathered crowd of witnesses—aristocrats and ministers, priests and Councilors—it was to face a sea-storm of applause and cheers, well-wishing and outbursts of joy. For Elad, whatever else he was, was King; and Salia, innocent and pure, the most beautiful woman in the world, was surely destined to become all that she could become at the side of her King and husband. Both of them young, a joining of man and woman as the gods had always intended—and a union between a great empire and its peoples.

It promised something great, this marriage.

It symbolized a balance, it heralded a completion of a circle, a new beginning.

And it was necessary, in the minds of its witnesses, that it promise these things.

Elad and Salia, leading a train of nobles and court retainers, left the festooned and decorated Temple. Stepping out into the front portico, they waved at the collected crowds of citizens in the square below. A ring of Khamars held back the surging throngs of excited Athadians, while other guards ordered the royal palanquin brought to the front of the stairs so that the King and Queen might be escorted to it and begin their journey to Elad's villa outside the capital.

It was a chilly day. Despite the fact that thousands of eyes were upon them, Elad nevertheless held Salia closer to him than public decorum might permit, and looked into her misty gray eyes, whispered to her, "We will come to love one another. . . ."

Then they started down the stairs to their palanquin. One of the Khamars stationed below broke from formation and started moving quickly up the stairs toward Elad. Elad saw him, then glanced beyond him; his first thought was that something untoward was occurring in the crowd. The Khamar was hurrying up to protect him or warn him. Instinctively, Elad stepped ahead of Salia and, glancing at the approaching Khamar, said to him, "What is it? What's happening down—"

The three of them—King, Queen, and guard—were still in that moment isolated on a small area in the middle of the wide stairs. Around them on all sides stood the formation of Khamars, and, just below, at the foot of the stairs, the palanquin.

Elad glanced again at the crowd, once more at the Khamar.

The Khamar's right hand shifted to his short sword, which was scabbarded; he nodded his head succinctly, indicating something behind his King.

"What is it, what—" Elad turned to look.

The Khamar, stepping up to Elad, quickly drew his short sword and lunged. *"Die in the name of the people, traitor!"*

Salia screamed.

Elad, falling backward in an automatic attempt to escape the thrust, bumped into her and knocked her sprawling upon the stone stairs. The steel blade, catching him in the side, sliced through his robes and underclothes, ripped free on a wide arc of bloody spray. Salia screamed again. Elad, flailing for balance, dropped to one knee. The false Khamar, aware that his initial thrust had not killed the King, jerked awkwardly on the stairs, steadied himself, and pulled back for his second thrust.

Howling with one voice, a dozen Khamars swooped in from both sides of the stairs. The crowd below surged forward, the guards there unable to hold them back. Ogodis, standing off to one side, screamed something incomprehensible and ran for his daughter. And as a leaking river of red unfolded liquidly down the stone stairs, between the stamping boots of the palace Khamars:

"My King, are you all right?"

"Queen Salia, are you—"

"He's dead! We killed the—"

"Where the hell did he come from? Where did he—"

"King Elad, don't try to speak, don't—"

"Who is he? Can you recognize him? Do you have any idea—"

"Hold back there! Hold back! Keep those people away!"

". . . can't seem to tell what—"

333

"Gods! The blood, he's slipping in the—"

"Salia!"

"It's her father, it's the Im—"

Die in the name of the people, traitor!

"Elad! My King! We must get him—"

"Clear that square down there! Clear those people out of the way!"

"Get back, now! Come on, get back!"

"Oh, gods, is he dead, is he—"

"Elad! Elad!"

"Salia, come—"

"Clear them out of the way! Now! Now!"

"Revolutionaries! Gods, what can we—"

"What are they trying to do? What do they—"

"Revolutionaries! Revolutionaries! That's all we hear, revo—"

The Fall of the First World

The End of Book I:

The Master of Evil

BLADE

by Jeffrey Lord

More bestselling heroic fantasy from Pinnacle, America's #1 series publisher.
Over 3.5 million copies of Blade in print!

HELP YOURSELF
To Bestsellers from Pinnacle